# It began in Florence

Gordon L. Thomas

Published by SellMy Books

Copyright © Gordon L. Thomas 2021

The right of Gordon L. Thomas to be identified as author of this work has been asserted in accordance with sections 77 and 78 of the Copyright, Designs and Patents Act 1988.

A CIP catalogue record for this title is available from the British Library

ISBN 978-0-9956778-5-2

Cover design by Rohan Renard (www.RenardDesign.com)

Cover picture: Group with Parasols (Siesta) 1904 by John Singer Sargent

First published 2021

Printed in the UK

SellMy Books
(contact: www.gordonlthomas.com)

## About The Author

Gordon L. Thomas is retired and lives with his wife in London, England. He began his career lecturing in physics at King's College, London. He then worked in the UK Home Office as a scientist and also as an administrator. Latterly, his responsibilities were in police science and physical security. Since retiring he has become a keen writer and this is his fifth novel. For more information please visit his website www.gordonlthomas.com which you may use to contact him.

# Acknowledgements

There are a number of people I must thank for helping me with the writing of this novel. First, my darling wife, Janet, to whom the book is dedicated and who gave me constant support. During my researching and writing she selflessly encouraged me to share my life with her and that other woman, Ethel Smyth. Janet also proofread one of the later manuscripts and pointed out a number of errors.

A number of others read the first draft and commented. I am therefore also grateful to fellow authors, Loretta Proctor and John Chamberlain, my friends Chris Forkan and Peter Holden as well as my sister-in-law, Karen Teuber, all of whom gave me helpful feedback.

I am also grateful to our daughter Mel Hartley, her husband Guy, and Greg and his wife, Sue, for their constant encouragement and for pressing me to complete this novel.

# Foreword

It Began in Florence is a novel based on the extraordinary life of the once universally famous but now less well known English composer, Ethel Smyth. She was born on 22 April 1858 and from an early age harboured the ambition of becoming a composer. She eventually overcame her father's constant objections and began to study at the Conservatoire in Leipzig in 1877 at the age of 19. This energetic and outgoing woman soon made many friends in this city of music. She met many famous composers there including Brahms, Grieg, Tchaikovsky and some less famous, such as George Henschel and Heinrich von Herzogenberg who became her main teacher.

Ethel enjoyed a number of relationships with women she met at home and abroad. At an early age, she made a list of 'passions', who were women and girls she would willingly marry, if she were a man. Some of her relationships with woman were doubtless physical, almost certainly the one with Herzogenberg's wife, Elizabeth, with whom she fell deeply in love. The most enduring and important of the many relationships she formed was with the American writer, Henry ('Harry') Brewster. She found it difficult to understand how she could love him so intensely when her other loves were of women.

She encountered endless difficulties in achieving the public performance of her works. Few in the conducting profession were prepared to accept any work written by a woman. Brahms refused to believe she had written a brilliant set of songs which George Henschel showed him. Others were equally dismissive of her work. So, not only did she expend much effort in composing music, an enormous amount of her energy was spent in putting them forward for performance. Her success as a composer began with a performance of her Serenade at The Crystal Palace in January 1890.

This novel is based on the period of Smyth's life from a few years before she went to Leipzig up to and including her lengthy relationship with Brewster. It covers her development as a composer of stature and how she and Brewster collaborated over the writing of her first three operas. It shows how, with determination, energy and with a refusal to accept defeat, this remarkable woman, discarding convention, achieved her success and fame.

The aim of the novel is to heighten the profile of Ethel Smyth both as a composer and an outstanding woman of her era. The hope is that it will lead to more performances of her compositions and their acceptance in the regular concert hall repertoire.

To Janet

# IT BEGAN IN FLORENCE

## CHAPTER 1

### The Smyths

There is nothing any of us can do about the family we are born into, whether rich or poor, aristocratic or humble, sane or deranged, righteous or criminal, healthy or sick, happy or unhappy. We simply arrive in the midst of it. Neither is there anything we can do about the era we are to be born into, whether in peace or in war, famine or plenty, chaos or order. Our heroine's good fortune was that she was born into a wealthy, upper class Victorian, military family which lived in a substantial house in Frimley, near to Farnborough. The Smyths had moved there six years before when her father, General Smyth, was transferred from Woolwich to take command of the Royal Artillery Depot at Aldershot.

In terms of appearances, the family had everything the prosperous could wish for: a battery of servants and housekeepers, governesses, horses and carriages and a good few acres of land. They could tirelessly indulge in parties, hunting and other leisure pursuits. Because of her father's eminent rank, and her mother's wit and French education, the local gentry fully accepted and embraced them and their eight offspring.

Strains, tension and a dark blanket of unhappiness lurked within, the source of which could often be her mother, her father or any of her older siblings, or Ethel herself, but not the three youngest who were frequently the victims. Alice was the firstborn, followed by Johnny, then Mary, then two years later by Ethel. Nina followed Ethel, then their mother gave birth to Violet and Nelly. Bobby, the only one born at their house, called Frimhurst, was the youngest.

Although Ethel loved her mother, she did not feel close to her, not in the emotional sense. She badly wanted her to love her intensely and with loyalty, but her mother seemed to lack that capability, and made things worse by her unpredictable mood swings. She could charm anybody, the local clergy, the butcher's delivery boy or anyone in her upper class circle of friends. However, she could descend into the deepest of depressions which would bring out violent, unprovoked outbursts. Then she would apologise, usually through a veil of tears.

General Smyth had a pathological loathing of anything connected with art. Once he caught Johnny, poised with brush in hand, painting a watercolour of a scene in their garden. Johnny was portraying a robin, feeding on their bird table. He went up to his son, snatched the paintbrush from him and threw it into the fire. To the General, the works of art which Mrs Smyth had hung on the walls, were nothing but poor imitations of flocked wallpaper. He regarded music as a noisy aberration, meant only to waste the time of those lazy enough to listen to it.

A wedding always lifts the spirits of a family, doubly so in 1875, as Alice and Mary were about to be married in a joint ceremony. Mary was to marry a Charlie Hunter, the brother of a school friend of hers. Alice was to marry a Harry Davidson to whom she had been engaged for some time. The family needed a lift as Johnny, three years older than Ethel, was confined to a wheelchair, having suffered badly in a riding accident two and a half years before. A few weeks prior to the planned joint wedding, and after a series of violent headaches, he was sitting at the dinner table with the rest of the family.

'Do you know?' he said. 'Something queer is happening to me. I can't read the letters on this biscuit.' He then fell out of his chair onto the floor.

'Help me lift him into his room,' said the General. The family rallied to Johnny's aid and, although he was barely conscious, he could still put one foot in front of the other but not to bear his own weight. His mother and a maidservant rushed down the hall ahead of Johnny and his helpers, went into his bedroom, which was the study before he became disabled, and made the bed ready for him.

'Don't let this illness of mine stop the girls' weddings,' he said with difficulty, but with his usual fortitude and selflessness.

Ethel and Mary sat by his bed, right through the night.

'I don't like this,' said Mary to Ethel. 'Although he is breathing, he looks so contorted.'

'I am afraid for his life,' said Ethel. 'It seems he is going to pass away.' She stifled her sobs with her handkerchief so as not to wake him.

By the time dawn was breaking, both girls were completely exhausted. 'We can't do this every night,' said Mary.

'I agree,' said Ethel, sitting on the end of Johnny's bed. 'I could fall asleep right here.'

'We need to work out a rota,' said Mary. 'We should take it in turns to keep watch on Johnny, day and night until he improves or…'

At breakfast that morning, the General presided over a family meeting at which they agreed a rota. Having spent a full night with Johnny, Ethel and Mary didn't start again until a full day later so that, according to their mother, 'they could catch up with their sleep.'

Alice and Mary's wedding was only a week away. At the same breakfast meeting, they decided to write and cancel the invitations. The wedding would go ahead, but they would scale it down and make it an immediate family occasion.

While the family were still sitting at the breakfast table, Ethel said she wanted to say something. 'If you are not aware already, despite your previous objections, I remain determined to go to Leipzig to learn to compose music. I am absolutely adamant.'

The General's face reddened, and his eyebrows rose to their maximum. He stood up. 'You really choose your moments, don't you, Ethel? Your brother is dying not ten paces away and you remind us of your nonsensical ambition. No! You are not going to Leipzig. Forget the idea. Now!'

'I simply won't forget it, Papa. You have known for years that I want to go there and I will. I intend to go, whatever the price! With your blessing or despite you!'

'Blast you, woman. Don't you dare talk to me like that! If you were one of my men, of whatever rank, I'd have had you Court Marshalled for such effrontery! Just clear off out and go to your room!'

Ethel stood up and left the room.

Wasting no time, the General's rota took immediate effect. The two youngest, Bobby and Nelly led off. They stayed with Johnny for six hours. Then the two next youngest, Nina and Violet, took over. This meant they did not deny the youngest of Ethel's brothers and sisters their sleep. The night shift began with Mrs Smyth and Alice who stayed with Johnny all night, so Ethel and Mary were fresh to begin their shift just after breakfast.

'I wonder how long Johnny can last,' whispered Ethel to Mary.

Mary just lifted a finger to quieten Ethel and got up from her chair. She leant over the apparently sleeping Johnny and held his hand. She squeezed it, hoping that Johnny would react. But he didn't move. It was as if Johnny was in a deep coma from which he might not awaken. She crept back to her chair, next to Ethel's.

'I don't know. It could be days, months, or even years. But we are doing our best for him. We mustn't let him die alone.' She then sobbed quietly.

Ethel put an arm around her shoulder. 'Let's hope for the best,' Ethel said, thinking that Johnny was unlikely to survive much longer. By then, he had stopped eating and could hardly swallow water.

The joint wedding took place in Frimley Church on the following Saturday. It was limited to being only the church ceremony. Ethel was the only other member of the family present. She never understood why, but both bridegrooms left the church immediately afterwards and went back by train to London. The two brides - there were no bridesmaids - returned home.

For the afternoon, some two days later, Bobby, Nelly and Violet went to a kind neighbour's house, to give them a short break from the sad atmosphere in the Smyths'. After playing in the garden and enjoying scones and cream for tea, they romped back home feeling jolly and refreshed. Their joy soon evaporated.

'Johnny is dead,' said Mrs Smyth, as she opened the front door. Tears streamed down her face. Johnny was Mrs Smyth's favourite by far. She never really recovered from his death. Her mood swings became even more extreme and her health suffered. She showed signs of arthritis and deafness. Because she could not hear well, she would complain at the dinner table that her family members were talking about her and plotting against her. All this was, of course, completely untrue.

A few days after Johnny's funeral, the General spoke at the dinner table. 'With your two older sisters married and dear Johnny having passed away, you Ethel, are now the oldest of your siblings left at home and I and your mother expect you to act accordingly. This naturally means you can completely forget about your inflated ambitions to go to Leipzig. We need you here, at least until some worthy gentleman takes your hand in marriage. And he's not likely to pack you off to Leipzig.' He then let out a guffaw of laughter. None of the others responded.

For once, Ethel stayed seated at the table. She glowered at her father but said nothing. In her thoughts she became even more determined to go to the Conservatoire in Leipzig and study there. She had no intention to marry, however attractive the suitor.

*** 

At the time Johnny died, Ethel was seventeen and was becoming an attractive woman from several points of view. Others noticed she possessed an exceptionally good figure, a pretty face, a powerful intelligence and the ability to sing and play the piano. However, she was aware she differed from other young women. In contrast to the great majority, she was sporty and mannish. She found women, especially those older than herself, far more attractive than men. These feelings felt perfectly natural to her. Over the years, she had kept a list of 'passions', the women she would gladly marry, if she had been a man. She would soon add a new and prominent name.

A musically gifted family had moved to Aldershot and lived about five miles from the Smyths. These were the Ewings. Alexander Ewing was a captain in the Army Service Corps where he was in charge of pay. He was the famous composer of the popular hymn, 'Jerusalem the Golden' and had composed other hymns and songs. His wife was an author of children's stories who wrote under the name of

5

'Aunty Judy'. Their arrival prompted much excitement in the Smyth family. Even the General showed mild interest. The one form of art that he liked was the hymn and was well aware of Ewing's famous contribution to the *oeuvre*. Mrs Smyth decided she would visit Mrs Ewing. She discovered where they lived and, unannounced, stood on the threshold of their quarters in the camp and knocked on the door.

'Good afternoon,' said Mrs Ewing. 'To whom do I owe the pleasure?'

'I am Mrs Smyth. I am General Smyth's wife and I thought I'd pay you a social call to welcome you into the area.'

'That's uncommonly kind of you, Mrs Smyth. Do come in.'

Mrs Ewing ushered Mrs Smyth into her modest lounge. 'Take a seat. May I make you some tea?'

'Oh, most grateful.'

Mrs Ewing soon came back into the room with a tray upon which balanced two cups of tea on pretty flower-patterned saucers. She proffered Mrs Smyth a cup.

'So where were you stationed before you came to Aldershot?'

'We were in Greenwich for a few years… but before that and just after we married we were in Fredericton in New Brunswick. Alex was in the Army Commissariat. We loved New Brunswick and had many friends there. We still write to some of them. Alex did much for the cathedral. He played the organ and wrote several hymns, especially for the congregation. It was a shame they posted us back. What about you, Mrs Smyth?'

Mrs Smyth told her about her own family, the children, and named them. She shed several tears in talking about Johnny. She said a little about each, including Alice and Mary and their new spouses. When she reached the subject of Ethel, she said what a talented writer she was and talked about her ability and ambitions as a composer. Mrs Ewing's eyes opened wider.

'She must meet Alex. He could launch her into composing as a profession. He learnt his skills in Heidelberg and would love to equip her to study at a higher level in Leipzig.'

'Please don't let my husband know I mentioned her wish to go to Leipzig. He totally opposes the idea. All he can think of is her marrying some local worthy, in his view an army officer.'

'I promise not to mention it. I simply won't, I can assure you! But Emma must meet Alex.'

'Ethel, actually.'

'Sorry. Ethel.'

'We'll arrange something. Why don't you come around for dinner, perhaps on Saturday?'

'I'll let you know if we are both free.'

Ethel found a staunch ally in Alex Ewing. Over dinner, he asked her if she would play some of her compositions for him. The General said nothing but glowered and almost snarled at him. As a much lower rank officer, the General regarded Ewing as an inferior being, despite his fame as the composer of the hymn. Straight after the meal, Ewing and Ethel adjourned to the drawing-room, and Ethel retrieved some sheets of her music from the cupboard near the piano.

'I'd like to start by playing you the first movement of a piano sonata I am working on. Please sit on the sofa, Mr Ewing.'

Ethel placed a sheaf of music sheets on the piano stand. She shuffled herself into a comfortable position on the stool. 'It's in C major,' she said, 'and it starts off *allegro vivace.*'

Ethel hammered the keys as if she was playing a hefty percussion instrument, rather than the little family piano. Occasionally, she would shout out. 'There, a couple of chords in the tonic!'

Ewing sat there quietly, listening intently with one hand on his chin and the other resting on the arm of the settee. Ethel finished the movement with a flourish and both arms in the air. Ewing broke into applause.

'Ethel, you are a phenomenon, a real composer…'

'Let me play you this,' said Ethel, with enthusiasm. She had found an admirer and was going to capitalise on it. 'It's a poem I wrote in homage to Lady Sitwell and which I've put to music. I'll sing it to you.' As loud as ever and thumping away at the piano, Ethel put her full, thrusting energy into the performance.

Again, Ewing applauded after Ethel concluded. 'Really, Ethel, you are a true musician. Is anyone helping you with your composing? Do you have a teacher?'

'No, but when I was at school, I had an excellent music teacher, I've actually taught myself. I'm good, aren't I?'

'I have to agree,' said Ewing, grinning at the vanity of this young woman. 'I can help you, if you'd like me to give you some lessons.'

'I'm not sure what my father would think. He constantly disagrees with my wishes to become a famous composer.'

'I'll start you off with some lessons in harmony, but I don't relish a breakdown with your father who outranks me by miles!'

The General seethed when Ethel's mother put the idea to him. His moustache twitched and his brow furled. She had volunteered to speak to him rather than let Ethel take the risk.

'Famous hymn composer he may be, but he's becoming a blasted and interfering nuisance! I don't want him flattering her. She's vain enough and arrogant enough already. Some besotted amateur telling her she's a genius is what she doesn't need. She isn't going to Leipzig whatever she… or he… says. He's a cad. An artist. They are all depraved. He looks a mess. His hair is too long. His clothes are dingy and, dare I say, he doesn't smell too nice either!'

Several days later and exhausted at confronting the continuous onslaught of Ethel and her mother, usually vacillating, but for those few days at least

8

constantly siding with Ethel, the General succumbed. He had lost the battle to keep Ewing at bay. But had he lost the war? With great foreboding he agreed that, twice a week, Ethel should take the pony and trap to the Ewings' quarters for lessons.

Ethel regarded this as a major triumph and thrived on the attentions of Ewing and his wife. Ewing introduced her to the works of Wagner.

'Today I'm going to play you an opera. It's called Lohengrin. Wagner finished it seventeen years ago, in the year you were born! Did you say you can sight-read?'

'No, I didn't but I can, better than my mother can!'

'In which case you can sing the women's parts and I'll sing the men's. We'll both sing in the choir!'

'Let's perform then,' said Ethel.

'I'll start with a condensed version of the overture,' Ewing played the piano with consummate skill. He was more sensitive than the boisterous Ethel and determined that he, at some point, would teach her to play with greater feeling.

It took most of the day to perform the opera. Ethel leaned on the piano, exhausted. Ewing put his arm around her.

'Well done, Ethel. You are a skilled performer and a composer.'

'Who wrote the libretto, Wagner or someone else?'

'Wagner wrote it, and all of that music. He is a genius!'

'I've decided. I'm going to compose operas and what's more, I'm going to have them performed in Germany!' Ethel voiced aloud her ambitions.

Mrs Ewing came rushing into the music room. 'What is all the shouting about? What's going on?'

'Nothing, my dear. Ethel is determined to become a composer. She said it so loudly she must have wanted the universe to know!'

True to his word, Ewing taught Ethel the art of harmony. He also taught her orchestration and about the techniques for writing choral works. Not one to conceal her delight with her new relationship with the Ewings, the General became even more suspicious of the man. He liked Mrs Ewing to whom he expressed much gratitude for befriending his wife, giving her a new interest and someone to discuss her various literary interests. Every time Ethel mentioned the man's name, he seethed beneath his military moustache. Ewing confirmed the General's view that all artists were undesirable reprobates who one should avoid at all costs.

'It's all very well to teach you the art of composing,' said Ewing at one of their bi-weekly encounters, 'but Aunt Judy and I have to take you to some concerts in London.'

So they took Ethel to a Wagner concert, which the composer himself conducted. Herr Wagner, almost unknown in England, had contracted to perform a series of concerts in London which turned out to be a financial disaster, mainly because of the length and general unpopularity of his work. Nor was he much of a showman. From where Ethel and the Ewings sat, right at the back of the auditorium, they could just see this large headed, short, stocky individual waving his arms about as if he were in some uncontrollable rage, rather than conducting a performance of one of his own operas. Ethel thrived on the music and the drama. She would have to come to London again to more concerts, even if on her own. The Ewings loved Ethel for her energy, boisterousness and wit. Mrs Ewing even helped Ethel with her writing, correcting her mistakes and showing her how to write in a style that flowed naturally, rather than in the uneven style with which she was more familiar. Naturally, Mrs Ewing became one of Ethel's passions.

Ewing owned many scores by Schumann, Brahms, Schubert, and Beethoven among others, and delighted in talking about these composers to Ethel and guiding her through the scores, often playing excerpts on his piano. He spoke about Brahms who people could often see walking the streets of Leipzig.

'When you go there, you might even bump into him yourself! He is the best composer in late nineteenth-century Germany, by far.'

'That would be a genuine miracle!' said Ethel. 'But I've yet to defeat my father on that one!'

'Hmm. We must work something out which will change his mind. He can't keep you at home forever.'

Ewing admired the works of Berlioz and annotated several of his scores for her. He especially admired the Symphonie Fantastique and The Grande Symphonie Funèbre et Triomphale, which Ethel equally fell in love with when she realised it was a work of such massive scale. They played it together with Ethel singing the choral lines and each sharing the band parts.

# CHAPTER 2

## Father's decision

Given any opportunity, the Ewings would tell the General and his wife that Ethel's talent as a composer fully justified sending her to Leipzig to complete her musical education. The General loathed the man and every utterance he made.

While Ethel had the unfortunate habit of leaving her room in a state of profound untidiness, the General had the habit of nosing around his children's rooms when they were out. He was appalled to discover in Ethel's room an intimate letter from Ewing which expressed his great love for Ethel and delight in their newfound relationship. The General read far more into the letter than was the truth. He imagined that Ewing and his daughter were being physically intimate to the extent of adultery. While they had become good friends, they never indulged in any such activity. The letter caused an almighty row between Ethel and her father, which led to him engineering the posting of Captain Ewing to Manchester. Poor Ethel cried herself to sleep for several nights, having discovered her father's reaction to this innocent missive.

Once he realised how distraught Ethel had become, and with the encouragement of his wife, the General sent Ethel to stay with an army friend of his in Ireland. There she met William Wilde, brother of Oscar who immediately fell in love with her. She didn't know how to react. They had so much in common. Like his famous brother, he loved literature and was an accomplished writer himself. Between playing lawn tennis and croquet on her father's friend's lawn, they discussed the finer points of French and German literature. Their mutual exploration in the nearby bushes was the closest that they approached to anything physical. She ensured that actual intercourse, the prospect of which Ethel dreaded anyway, did not take place.

Once they returned to London, the new friend who doubtless had lifted Ethel's spirits had a proposal for her.

'My dearest Ethel,' he said on his bended knee, 'I want to marry you!'

Ethel was in shock. 'I don't know what to say, William. I don't know if I want to marry you!'

'Please, Ethel. I beg of you. I shall die if you desert me!'

Nothing remotely like this had happened to her before. She had never felt so wanted. 'I accept then!' she said, with just a semi-quaver of doubt.

'We'll now go to buy a ring,' he said. They visited a jeweller in The Strand and he gave her a choice. He put it on her finger, right in front of an embarrassed shop assistant.

'The one thing I ask is that we keep our engagement a secret, just for the time being,' he said.

'Why's that?' she said. 'I'm a very open person. I'll have tremendous problems denying my parents from knowing how happy I am.'

'Please respect my wish, Ethel. Over the next couple of weeks, I will write to you and we can plan an announcement.'

Ethel agreed. They kissed and went their separate ways. William sent Ethel a stream of love letters, each professing his deep love for her. Her heart was torn. She couldn't imagine him letting her disappear to Leipzig for a year or two, however much he loved her. The more she thought about it, the less she loved him. In fact, she felt nothing for him at all. So she wrote to him to break it off. She made several attempts at writing the letter but eventually wrote what she regarded as a sensitive but conclusive text. His brief reply expressed the minimum of regrets. She was relieved as she didn't want to upset him. She kept the ring but didn't show it to her parents.

Ethel's love of classical music grew and grew. Occasionally, she would go to London to attend a concert at St James Hall, Piccadilly. She had no money so would go to the local grocer and ask him if she could borrow five shillings he could put on the General's account. The poor man could hardly refuse. She would take a train from Farnborough to Waterloo and often meet Mrs Anita Schwabe, a petite, generous friend of Ethel's mother, who would escort her to the concert hall. One concert left her in raptures and more than a few tears.

13

'My dear Ethel,' said Mrs Schwabe, after the concert. 'There is someone I would like you to meet!'

'Really?' said Ethel.

'Yes. We will have to go out of a side door to the platform and then go to one of the dressing rooms.'

'I'll follow you,' said Ethel.

The two of them walked down the central aisle and turned off to the right. 'Here we are,' said Mrs Schwabe. She knocked on door number 7. It opened.

'There you are, Anita,' said a voice with a German accent. 'Do come in. Bring your friend with you!'

They entered. The room smelt of rose water and lemon.

'Please allow me to introduce you to Frau Clara Schumann,' said Anita Schwabe.

Ethel was in shock. She didn't expect to meet the wife of the eminent composer, also a composer in her own right.

'And these are my daughters, Marie and Elise. I understand you are an aspiring composer, too!'

Ethel shook hands with all three and when able to speak simply said, 'I'm pleased to meet you.'

Once she settled, she said how much she had enjoyed Clara Schumann's recital and that her friend Alexander Ewing had introduced her to some of her other music, including her early piano concerto.

'I hadn't realised that my friend Anita was a friend of yours,' said Ethel.

'There is no reason you should,' said Frau Schumann. 'We have known each other for some years. We met when Anita lived in Germany. I've also met your Mr Ewing. He wrote to me to say he much admired your ability as a composer. I hope I can listen to some of your music!'

14

This famous woman totally entranced Ethel. Once again, she vowed to study at the Leipzig Conservatoire.

And another concert in London, this time at the expense of the postman from whom she borrowed 7/6d, on her father's account. She went to one of the Saturday Popular Concert series, once again at St James Hall. She wanted to listen to some Brahms. The Liebenslieder Walzer were to be performed by four artists, three of whom were German: Fräuleins Friedländer and Redeker, George Henschel; and a Mr Shakespeare. These pieces hypnotized her. They sent her mind to another world. The fire they lit in her heart became an unquenchable blaze, a conflagration.

At home, she said again she intended to go to Leipzig, come what may. She would go there, even if she needed to run away and starve. She knew what reaction to expect but said it regardless. It enraged her father. His fury overcame him.

'I'd rather you became a whore and worked on the streets,' he said.

'Don't be so disgusting,' her mother said. 'No daughter of mine will ever walk the streets, not while I'm alive.'

'I don't really care,' said the General. 'Put it this way. I'd rather see her under the sod.'

'You can say some evil things,' said her mother.

Ethel had no choice. She would begin a campaign of attrition. Whatever the price, she had to win this war. The General would have to give in, as she would make life at home intolerable. She would shut herself in her bedroom and come out only for meals, which she would put on a tray and, sulking, take to her bedroom. She would vanish from Frimley and catch a train to Waterloo to attend more concerts at St James Hall. To buy her ticket, she queued for hours to see and listen to Joachim in Schubert's A minor Quartet. A true revelation.

Then, one day, she forced her way into the Artists' Room at St James and introduced herself to Fräuleins Friedländer and Redeker.

'I trust you don't mind me expressing my great admiration for your wonderful performances. It was only last week I had the pleasure of listening to your exceptional performance of Brahms' Liebeslieder Walzer. They were stunning. I adored them! I am a composer myself, in fact!'

'My goodness,' said Redeker. 'We've never had such a compliment from an English woman. You flatter us!'

'Flattery was not my intention, merely admiration. You are two extraordinary performers!'

Fräulein Redeker had the most seductive blue eyes, and Ethel immediately fell in love with her.

'I'm grateful also for that beautiful performance of Wie bist du meine Königin,' she said, looking straight into those eyes. 'It touched me so much it almost broke my heart.'

'It was a pleasure,' said Redeker. 'It was far from perfect but I'm glad you enjoyed it. I hope your English press gives it a good account tomorrow!'

'I have an idea,' said Friedländer. 'Let's invite our new admirer to our apartment. Could you be free on Wednesday? We have a rehearsal in the afternoon but would love to see you in the morning.'

'What a wonderful idea,' said Redeker.

Ethel could not believe her luck. 'I'd love to meet you there! I'm certain I am free then. I don't even need to consult my diary!' Whatever her commitments, she could not miss even a few minutes with these wonderful performers.

Fräulein Redeker gave Ethel their address. It was on the other side of Regent's Street, at 22a Sherwood Street.

'May we see you at say half-past ten? You can have breakfast with us, but only if you wish! Bring some of your compositions. We have a piano and can play some with you!'

Both women kissed Ethel, and Redeker took her to the Artists' Exit. She hailed a cabriolet, gave the driver 3d and instructed him to take Ethel to Waterloo Station.

'We usually expect a tip, madam,' said the driver.

'All right, here's another tuppence!'

On the way to the station, Ethel could not stop thinking about these two enthralling women. She simply loved Redeker who was gorgeous. She was slim but full-breasted; her hair was fair and piled onto the top of her head. But those blue eyes… Friedländer possessed a different type of beauty. Her figure was altogether fuller. Her eyes were quite dark for a German and her hair was brown. She could have been Russian or even Italian. Ethel was dying to meet them again. Who knew where all this could lead?

With uncharacteristic discretion, Ethel said nothing to her family about the forthcoming meeting with the two singers. It was only two days away and she could see nothing to be gained from mentioning it. She continued with her programme of resistance and spent most of her time in her room, composing or reading Proust. Nor would she announce her departure on the Wednesday morning. She would simply vanish at about 8 a.m., walk to the station and catch a train. For once, she had sufficient change for the journey, even enough to pay for the cabriolet to Piccadilly and back to Waterloo.

To make the most of her limited funds, she bought a third class ticket. There were many people on the crowded train, but she managed to sit next to a chimney sweep who had his boy sitting on his lap. 'Good morning,' she said to the sweep, a man of about thirty, clean-shaven and wearing a cap. He had no teeth that Ethel could see. The dejected looking lad had a frown on his face and looked at the floor.

'Morning, Miss. You sound high class to be sitting with the likes of us! Where you off to? Somewhere posh, I'll be bound.'

'I'm meeting some friends. They are singers and have an apartment near Regent Street.'

17

'Well, I'm damned! We are heading that way. The lad's going up a chimney in Piccadilly, not far from there.'

'I'm catching a cab from Waterloo, if you and your boy would like to join me?'

'Grateful for the offer, Miss. But can't do that. You're too classy for us. We'll make our own way there. Thanks, anyway.'

Ethel arrived at 22 Sherwood Street about five minutes early so instead of knocking at the door, she walked further up the road for a few minutes and back again. She knocked. There was no reply. After a few minutes, she tried it again. Still no reply. She looked again at the number. Clear enough, it was 22. Then she realised that Fräulein Redeker said it was 22a. She pushed at the door, which opened in front of her. She quickly gained her balance as she almost fell in. Just inside was a door to apartment 22c. She walked up the stairs and to her relief found 22a, right at the top of the building. She banged on the door.

'Do come in,' said Fräulein Friedländer, showing only her head.

Ethel stepped in. What she saw stunned her into silence. The two Fräuleins were completely undressed. Fräulein Redeker was standing, facing Ethel, in the middle of the room. It looked as if she had just got up from sitting on a settee.

'You look shocked, Ethel. Please relax. We are often naked at this time of the day. It is a matter of appreciating nature. Clothes are an encumbrance!' said Redeker.

'You can take yours off, but only if you wish!' said Friedländer, and then took a sip of something from an eggcup. 'Would you like an early morning drink? It's a very nice port.'

Ethel didn't know how to react. Perhaps her father was right after all about the unacceptable behaviour of artists! She could not help gazing at the beautiful bodies of these women. She felt a *frisson* of excitement pass through her body, which made her shake a little. What an unexpected sight.

'I hope you don't mind, but I'll keep mine on,' said Ethel, still standing by the door.

18

'In which case we will put on our bathrobes. Could you please fetch them, Augusta,' said Friedländer.

The unclothed Redeker strolled to the bathroom and returned carrying two gleaming white robes. She helped Friedländer into one before putting hers on.

'There... we are all equal now,' said Friedländer.

They asked Ethel to come further into their palatial lounge. She noticed a white upright piano, against the wall opposite the window. Thekla Friedländer invited Ethel to sit on the sofa. Within a few moments, Ethel had recovered from her initial shock and the three of them were chatting together like old friends.

'I hope you have brought some of your music, Ethel,' said Augusta Redeker.

'Yes, I've brought some of my best, a movement from a piano sonata in C Major, a string quartet and some songs for which I have written the words and the music.'

'We must play them,' said Thekla. 'Let's start with a song. You choose one, Ethel, and we'll all sing it together!'

Ethel placed the music of one of her songs on the piano music stand, and the three of them gazed at the first page. 'At the count of three then, one two three...,' said Augusta.

The three of them burst into song and played the work as if they had already rehearsed it. They played another of her songs and then another. 'These are lovely, Ethel,' said Augusta. 'You are a natural songwriter and composer. I detect a hint of Schubert in the second one!'

'Let me see your piano sonata,' said Thekla. 'I'd love to play it!'

Ethel shuffled through her papers. 'Here it is!'

Thekla showed outstanding talent as a pianist and played the piece exactly to Ethel's expectations.

Augusta and Ethel applauded when she finished.

'There is no escape from the fact that you are very talented, Ethel,' said Augusta. 'What are your ambitions as a composer? Maybe, we can help you achieve them.'

Ethel explained her burning desire to go to Leipzig to study composing at the Conservatoire. She told them about her father's unbreakable wish to stop her.

'How unkind,' said Thekla. 'I'm sure we can help. Tell your father we live in Leipzig and that I have an aunt who will want to have you lodging with her. She is Professor Frau Heimbach. I can write to her to tell her to expect you. She is a lovely woman and will take you in until my mother has a room free. Let us know how your father reacts and we can complete the arrangements.'

'I am so grateful,' said Ethel, almost in tears. 'I will tell my father as soon as I arrive home. You are so kind and I've only just met you!'

After a half-hour more of talking about each other, their music and Thekla and Augusta's forthcoming performances, Ethel left the singers but not without promising to keep in touch, especially over the coming few weeks.

\*\*\*

'I don't care whether she keeps you in cotton wool and escorts you everywhere you wish to go. You are simply not going to Leipzig. We can't afford it anyway. We'd have to sell your mother's diamonds,' glared the General. Almost in the same breath, he condemned Ethel for abusing his accounts at the grocers and his credit with the postman. Her response was simply, 'You won't let me go to Leipzig, so I went to London to listen to music.'

The mention of selling something, albeit these treasured family gems, gave Ethel the impression that perhaps her father was showing signs of relenting. All she needed now were friends to talk to her father and persuade him to surrender. Not all of them agreed, but two mutual friends of Ethel and her mother were convinced that the General was softening his view. Mrs Schwabe, and Mrs Napier, wife of General William Napier, the commandant at Sandhurst, became strong supporters of Ethel's cause. One evening at a modest dinner party, to which her mother had carefully ensured she could attend, Mrs Napier squared up to the General and made her case for 'dear little Ethel' to go to Leipzig. Ethel had become even more intolerable: she refused to go to church; wouldn't sing at family gatherings; didn't even attend them; and regularly locked herself in her bedroom. During one day of unusual outrage, the General was so furious with 'dear little Ethel' that he almost put his foot through her door. That very act made him look silly, so stupid, he felt compelled to capitulate. He had lost the war he himself had declared.

They had to discuss various important considerations before she could go. Ethel's mother wanted assurances she would be safe with Thekla Friedländer's relative, Frau Professor Heimbach, so Fräulein Friedländer herself provided testimonials. The General worked out a budget and provided the necessary funds. Ethel was on her way to Leipzig. Nothing could prevent her now.

# CHAPTER 3

## Beginnings in Leipzig

'I wish I knew this city,' said Ethel, as they trudged the Leipzig streets on a bright summer morning in July 1877.

'I thought you said you knew where it is,' said Harry Davidson. He had married Alice and, not quite at the instruction of the General, agreed to escort Ethel to the city of her dreams. He knew Germany well and spoke the language fluently. So he played the temporary role of guide, interpreter and mentor. Although he looked younger, he was in his late twenties and a bright young man whose intelligence easily matched Ethel's, despite her doubts.

Ethel took a crumpled piece of paper from her jacket pocket, straightened it and read out what she had written on it. 'Place de Repos, Treppe G.'

'There's something wrong there, Ethel. It sounds more French to me. But treppe is German. It means stairway. Stairway to heaven by the sound of it!'

Ethel did not think that was funny so didn't react, except to the actual address. 'It must be right. It's exactly what Thekla Friedländer told me. I showed her what I'd written, and she said it was correct.'

'Did she say where it was in relation to the station?'

'Yes, to the south-east and just about half a mile from the centre of the city.'

They felt sure they were heading in vaguely the right direction. They continued and turned from right to left, down backstreets and up side-alleys.

'I don't understand it,' said Ethel. 'It has to be here somewhere!'

'Here it is!' said Harry. 'Right along there.' Harry was right.

'Place de Repos' must have been the ugliest apartment block in Saxony. Two equally ghastly, similar-looking blocks enclosed it. So what, thought Ethel. Her dream was rapidly coming true, a stairway to heaven or not. They reached Stairway G by passing under a dark, ivy enshrouded archway and crossing an equally dingy courtyard. They then clambered up three flights of rickety old wooden stairs. Harry constantly sniffed the air as he climbed. It was an odd odour which probably emanated from the dribbling River Pleisse which, as Ethel later discovered, flowed quite close to the apartment.

Frau Professor Heimbach greeted them with what seemed a reluctant smile. The plump Frau, dressed in a colourful gown, spoke to them with a strong Leipzig accent which defeated Ethel's German but hardly challenged Harry's. She exuded the kindly qualities of a motherly person, if she seemed a little shy with these odd-sounding foreigners. As she showed them in and took them to Ethel's room, she became more trusting and relaxed. Small though the room was, it had the deepest feather mattress Ethel had ever seen.

'Could you please tell the Frau Professor that I'm sure I shall be happy here? Shall we leave and explore the city?'

Harry did as Ethel requested. The Frau Professor responded at length. Then Harry and Ethel found their way back into the street outside.

'What did she say?' said Ethel. 'It seemed an excess of words to answer my compliment and request.'

'Yes, besides saying she would make you feel at home and very comfortable, as if you were still in England, she mentioned another lodger. Apparently, a charming young Englishman who works in publishing and who is a pupil of Frau Schumann. And she wants us to join her, the other lodger and her niece in a garden she owns... in an area near where the city wall used to stand.'

'A garden?' said Ethel. 'What's wrong with her garden at the apartment?'

'There are hundreds of these peculiar gardens there, and she owns one of them. She gave me directions so we should find it easily enough.'

'That's all very interesting,' said Ethel, knowing full well she would not be developing an interest in the other lodger, however close to the Schumanns he might be.

The two of them spent hours walking around the streets of Leipzig. Harry had been there on business several times before so could give Ethel a well-informed conducted tour. First, they called at the Thomas Kirche where J. S. Bach was the Organmeister. The dismal architecture of this world-renowned structure saddened Ethel. It hardly fitted the genius of the great man, and this quite affected her. Close to the Thomas Kirche stood the impressive Pleissenburg, with its squat tower and outbuildings, no longer surrounded by the city walls and moat which had been filled in many years before.

'You will enjoy living here,' said Harry. 'It is an amazing city. Leipzigers are proud people. They defeated Napoleon in 1813 in a famous battle. Mind you, an army of Austrians, Russians, Prussians and Swedes seriously outnumbered him. Our man, the Duke of Wellington, played his part by weakening Napoleon's army from the west. More blood flowed than at the battle of Borodino. There were over two hundred thousand casualties, mainly in Napoleon's troops. His occupation of the city led to some French street names, including the Place de Repos, I suppose. I admire their sense of irony in keeping some!'

'That's amazing,' said Ethel, 'but I'm more interested in the musical side of the city's heritage.'

'Let's visit the house where Bach lived then.'

A short walk from the Pleissenburg, Bach's house nestled in the Thomaskirchof.

'Here it is,' said Harry. 'What an incredible building.'

'That's better,' said Ethel. 'Seeing his place at the Thomas Kirche really upset me. It's simply not fit for a genius! This is so elegant. I love those French looking balconies!'

'A wealthy gold and silver merchant, Georg Heinrich Bose, owned the house and consequently named it after himself! Bose and Bach became friends and he let Bach live there. Quite a privilege, eh?'

'Bose is the privileged one, having a brilliant composer living in his house! I hope to become a modern composer of Bach's stature but it will take time.'

Having also visited the school where Bach taught, Harry took Ethel for a meal in one of the best restaurants in the central area.

'Have what you like from the menu, Ethel. This is my treat. At least the Pound goes a long way over here. I can help you with the translation if you don't understand some items!'

'You know my German is good, Harry. Maybe not as good as yours. However, I can understand everything on it!'

They hoped they had given themselves plenty of time after their lunch to arrive at the Frau Professor's garden by 4 p.m. But by 3.55 they hadn't found it among a sea of tiny plots separated by tall hedges, obviously designed to give the owners privacy.

'There's the Frau Professor,' said Ethel. 'I can just see her over that wooden fence. And the English lodger is with her. Oh, no!'

'The next question is how we reach it?' said Harry.

'I'm sure I can see a way. Follow me!'

Ethel led them through a maze of crisscrossing paths and avenues and eventually opened a wooden gate into the Frau Professor's garden. She came to the gate to greet them.

'Welcome to my little plot and our little party,' she smiled. 'I hope you enjoyed your tour of our great city!'

'It is truly wonderful,' said Ethel, as she and Harry walked into the garden towards a small summer house on the opposite side. Outside and leaning over a table of tasty looking snacks, Thekla Friedländer was pouring some black coffee into an array of cups.

'Here's Ethel!' said the Frau Professor, looking towards Friedländer.

Thekla put the coffeepot on the table and rushed over to Ethel, only to kiss her fully on the lips. She wore a formal-looking emerald green dress which hardly fitted the occasion.

'It is truly wonderful to see you in our great city, Ethel. Welcome! I'm glad your father agreed to you coming here. In fact, I'm thrilled! We will make you into a brilliant composer. That is a certainty from what I've seen and, of course, heard of your work already.'

For once, Ethel didn't know quite what to say. 'Well... hmm... that is kind of you, Thekla... I will do my best, I can assure you!'

'This is my lodger, Joseph Brock,' said the Frau Professor. 'Everyone calls him Joe... except me because I don't like to shorten names.'

'Delighted to meet you,' said Ethel, as she shook hands with the lad, unsure whether or not she was. This scruffy, long-haired, unkempt youth fitted exactly with the General's prejudices on artists. The mere presence of this unshaven youngster would have appalled and affronted him.

Much to Ethel's surprise, half a dozen croquet hoops punctuated the lawn. After a cup of coffee and a slice of German gateau, the Frau Professor organised the other four into two teams. Harry and Thekla against Ethel and Joe. Joe hit the ball with uninhibited bravado. Ethel had her own style. She tucked her skirt into her knickers and swung the mallet between her legs, high up her back, and hit the ball with equal vigour. Afraid that they would smash the crockery, the Frau Professor moved it to behind the summerhouse. They totally discarded the rules of the game. If any tree put itself in the way of a shot, the competitor simply moved the hoop and placed it in the direct line for the stroke. Laughter abounded and balls flew across the garden, into bushes and adjacent gardens, while the Frau Professor sat and knitted, with her cat on her lap, presiding over the furious game. None of them knew who won, if indeed a victor emerged.

After the croquet, they all returned to the Frau Professor's flat for supper. She vanished into the kitchen to cook and left the others sitting in her lounge chatting awkwardly.

'Where is your next concert, Thekla?' said Ethel, after a minute of silence and attempting to start a conversation.

'Augusta and I are performing in Schubert's Rosamunde with the Dresden Staatskapelle at the Gewandhaus. We are playing there on Saturday night. Why don't you and Harry come... and you, Joe, if you wish? I'll give you some complimentary tickets.'

'I leave for England tomorrow, Thekla, so bless you for inviting me, but I simply won't be in Germany on Saturday.'

'I am pleased to accept, Thekla. I can escort Ethel.'

'I shall be deeply honoured. So yes please!' said Ethel, thinking that she'd rather he didn't go.

'Where in England do you live, Harry?' said Joe.

'In London. The best city in the world!'

'I would doubt that,' said Thekla. 'You are now in the proudest and best city in the world!'

'I can understand your views,' said Harry. 'After all you've been through with the French.'

'Some of us can remember seeing Napoleon,' said Thekla. 'Not me, of course. I'm too young! But Frau Professor Heimbach knows an old lady who saw Napoleon ride out of the city gates, to fight in the battle of Leipzig. She says he looked angry and insignificant.'

Just as Thekla mentioned Napoleon, the Frau Professor appeared to ask them into the dining room. 'That's right, isn't it, Aunt, you know that lady who saw Napoleon?'

'Yes, I do. He was going to the battle. Many of the men urinated on the street behind him! Some more common women did, too!' Harry translated for Ethel.

'Sort of a mark of respect,' said Harry. They all exploded into laughter.

'I've put the dinner on the table. Do come through. You sit next to Joe, Ethel, and Augusta can sit on the other side of the table next to Harry. I'll sit at the head.'

The Frau Professor had prepared a typically Saxon meal of partridges stuffed with sauerkraut and uttered the words '*fein und begannt*' - fine and piquant, as Ethel later discovered - as she lifted them out of a large pot and placed them on the plates.

Harry stayed the night at the Place de Repos and Ethel saw him off early the next day from the station. She acknowledged him for bringing her to the city, kissed him on both cheeks and left him there, sitting in his carriage. Her heart leapt as she began her life in Leipzig with uncontrollable enthusiasm. Everything there seemed like heaven, even the little bread rolls seemed like manna and the miserably weak coffee, the Leipzigers all consumed with joy, tasted like fine wine.

The Saturday concert was a sell-out. It seemed as if the whole of Leipzig wanted to be there. Ethel had never heard Rosamunde performed. As its rhythms and melodies flowed, it entranced and delighted her. Thekla and Augusta sang with such sensitivity and brilliance.

'What did you think of the Schubert, Joe?' said Ethel to her escort.

'Not much. All of Schubert sounds the same to me.'

Ethel couldn't stop herself. 'You just don't appreciate the genius in music. And you are studying under Frau Schumann? You've got much to learn.' Looking shamefaced, he didn't respond.

Ethel found her way to the Artists Rooms after the concert and eventually discovered Thekla and Augusta. She had told Joe what her intentions were, and he went back to the flat alone.

'We are so glad you came and took the trouble to find us here,' said Augusta.

'Yes, we have an idea for you. In a few days, we are going on a fortnight's break to the Thuringia Forest. Our friend George Henschel is coming, too.' said Thekla.

'Please tell us you'll come,' said Augusta. 'Term doesn't start at the Conservatorium for another three weeks yet so do come with us!'

Ethel glowed with inexpressible joy. She had already fallen in love with the beautiful Augusta, so an opportunity to spend two weeks with them would be a beggar's delight. 'Yes, I'll come,' said Ethel. 'I'm enormously grateful to you for inviting me. It will be wonderful to stay with such accomplished musicians!'

'We will all be musicians together,' said Thekla.

'Where is Joe?' said Augusta. 'I'm surprised he's not with you... your escort!'

Ethel explained that he'd gone back to the apartment.

'Not especially gallant,' said Augusta. 'We'll arrange for someone to take you back. Not just to shame him!'

***

Ethel spent the whole of Sunday in a state of ambiguity about the holiday to come. Was she wise to agree to this? What was there to do in the Thuringian Forest, other than to walk among the trees? How would the four of them spend the time together? How would they all interact with each other? What sort of character was George Henschel? Would Ethel's music impress him, or would he dismiss it as the scratchings of a poor amateur? I must pack my scores, thought Ethel. Not even Thekla and Augusta have seen or heard all of what I've written.

The three women met at the Leipzig Central Station foyer at 9 o'clock on the Monday morning and greeted each other with kisses on both cheeks.

'Where is Herr Henschel?' asked Ethel.

'He'll join us later,' said Thekla. 'He's performing in Munich until Wednesday. Then he will come to meet us. You will love him. He is a truly superb musician.'

'I've brought plenty of money,' said Ethel. 'Which station are we travelling to?'

'You are the student among us so we are paying your fare,' said Augusta. 'You can buy the beers when we arrive there.'

Ethel saw no point in arguing the point. 'You are incredibly generous and I don't really deserve it! But I'm much obliged.'

'Our tickets are for a little town called Eisenach, which is right at the northern end of the forest. The train will take about two hours to reach it and then we take a carriage to our little hideaway, near a beautiful lake where we can swim if we like? Do you swim, Ethel?'

'Yes, not too badly.'

'The lake is quite shallow, so you will be in no danger.'

'You obviously know the area well,' said Ethel.

'Yes, we've been going there for years,' said Thekla, smiling at Augusta. 'It is a true haven, an escape from the world.'

They soon settled into the opulent, first-class carriage for which Thekla had bought the tickets. A few minutes later, a high-pitched whistle sounded. The train slowly gathered speed, and they were on their way.

The scenery they encountered on the journey took Ethel's breath away. Trees completely covered the steep hills, which looked almost as tall as mountains. Some of the deciduous variety, many hundreds of years old, stood like ancient guards over the gorges. Rivers glistened in the rich morning sunlight. The train puffed its way westwards up a gentle incline, through the deep valleys of the Thuringia towards their destination. The range of colours staggered young Ethel, who wondered how she might pay homage in music to these stunning vistas.

'Are you in a dream, Ethel?' said Augusta, as the train slowed to its first stop.

Ethel shook herself. 'No. I'm wide awake but utterly intoxicated by this lovely scenery. Scotland must be like this, from pictures I've seen. I am so enjoying this journey!'

'We knew you'd like it,' said Thekla.

# CHAPTER 4

## Thuringia

Within another hour of wondrous views, the train eased its way to a halt in the station at Eisenach, which glowed in fresh green and blue paint and seemed to welcome them. Ethel had packed far fewer items than the other two, who called for a porter and trolley. They were soon sitting in a horse-drawn carriage on their way out of the town to the 'hideaway' by the lake. What she saw surprised Ethel. A large wooden cabin, tucked between clumps of conifers, greeted the three women. The roof sloped gently towards each side of the structure with the door placed firmly in the centre of the side facing the track they had ridden up. From the number of widows which Ethel could see, there could be a good number of rooms.

'Welcome to our little holiday home,' said Thekla. 'You will love it here. It's a little basic. We rely on candles for the lighting, and the only source of water is a well at the back of the cabin. It's the best water you'll ever taste!'

'I love it here already,' smiled Ethel, her doubts of the day before dispelled. 'I'm going to enjoy my stay, I'm certain!'

The carriage driver helped them take their luggage into the cabin. He touched his forelock as Augusta paid him for the ride. He then mounted the carriage, bid them farewell, and went.

'Before we do anything else, we must sort out the sleeping arrangements. We only have three bedrooms and there will be four of us.' said Augusta, as they all stood in the hallway.

Ethel's heart shook. She couldn't quite see where this was leading. She took an inspired risk. 'I don't mind sharing with one of you! Would you wish to share with me, Augusta?' She hoped her latest 'passion' would agree.

The two singers looked at each other with eyebrows slightly raised. After a momentary pause, Thekla spoke. 'Um… as you are our guest, Ethel, you must have a room to yourself. What do you think, Augusta?'

'I have to agree. The only option is for us two to share. Would you be happy with that, Ethel?'

'Of course!'

Augusta and Thekla gave Ethel a choice of two rooms. 'George can have the one you don't use!' said Augusta, smiling.

'Seems a bit of a nerve,' said Ethel. 'I'm just a beginner as a composer and he is on the verge of fame!'

'He won't know!' said Thekla. 'Why don't you unpack your things, change into something to relax in and we can show you around the house and the outside?'

Ethel chose the room that let in more light, one at the side of the door they entered by. It was large with a plain wardrobe to the side of a wide single bed. A chest of drawers, also in unpainted wood, stood against the opposite wall and a mahogany desk overlooked the window ledge. Wonderful, thought Ethel. I can sit at the desk, composing or writing, and have a view of the outdoors in front of me.

Thekla and Augusta showed her the rest of the house. The drawing-room looked like a tiny concert hall. Five armchairs faced a piano which stood against the wall opposite the window. Ethel could imagine many musical events were played out in this room. They took Ethel into the dining room, at the centre of which stood a large circular table and eight chairs, all in polished mahogany.

'Now we'll show you the outside,' said Augusta.

A few hundred yards of walking through the woods brought them to a small, tranquil lake, on the opposite side of which rose a wide, steep, tree-covered hill that must have reached at least a thousand feet into the blue sky. 'I simply can't believe this,' said Ethel, almost in tears at the wonder of what she was seeing. 'I can't express my gratitude to you both for bringing me here. It's like heaven on Earth!'

'It is to us, too,' said Augusta. 'It may seem that it takes only a slight effort for us to perform, but it is really exhausting. We come here to refresh our bodies and our minds. We are so glad you like it so much.'

By then it was past one o'clock in the afternoon and time for something to eat.

'Fortunately, we have a man who looks after the cabin while we are away. He also fills the larder with food, just before we arrive so we are well stocked with victuals,' said Thekla. 'Would you like some German white bread and some sausage? You can also have a beer, if you wish.'

The three of them sat for lunch in the kitchen in which there was a stove fully primed with wood from the forest and ready to be lit. Ethel was not used to alcohol and felt quite muzzy after drinking only about half a pint. But she enjoyed the bread and sausage.

'I feel quite tired,' said Ethel. 'Do you mind if I go for a snooze, now we have finished our lunch?'

'Not at all,' said Augusta. 'We will probably go down to the lake, if not for a swim, just to relax by the water's edge. Do come down to join us when you wake up. Only if you want to, of course!'

The unfamiliar effect of the alcohol meant that Ethel fell asleep, almost at the moment she lay on her bed. She slept for at least an hour, probably more, and woke with a start. For a few seconds, she couldn't work out where she was. She suddenly realised and climbed off the high bed, still fully dressed. Not wanting to appear unsociable, she went down to the lake. She remembered her way through the woods and walked the two hundred or more yards. Sure enough, there were Thekla and Augusta, next to each other, sunning themselves, sitting at the edge of the lake with their feet dabbling in the water, their backs to Ethel. They were both naked.

Ethel took a sharp intake of breath. She wasn't as shocked as she might have been, not after the welcome they gave her at 22a Sherwood Street. Wondering how to handle this, she walked towards them.

'What a lovely afternoon. No wonder you want to make the most of the sun!' The two singers moved their hands towards their dressing gowns, which were on the grass next to them, as if to want to cover themselves.

33

'You made us jump, Ethel,' said Augusta. 'We didn't expect to see you yet!'

'Please don't cover up because of me. In fact, I'll join you, if I may!' Ethel undressed. The two singers turned towards her, their mouths wide open and eyebrows raised.

'You surprise us, Ethel, but you are welcomed to join us in our natural state,' said Thekla. 'Let's make the most of this glorious weather.'

Ethel stepped towards a large round rock and lowered her bare bottom onto it. 'Oh, it's cold,' she said, as she was half facing the singers whose shoulders were close to touching. 'So, what do you know about the Leipzig Conservatoire? I begin studying there in three weeks!'

'I studied there myself, as did Augusta,' said Thekla. 'I studied under Franz Götze. He used to be a tenor, and I learnt a great deal from him. An odd character, though. I never really liked him. But that was twelve years ago and things may have changed since.'

'I am two years younger than Thekla, so missed Herr Götze, who was more of an administrator by then. Amalie Joachim taught me, although she was only two years my senior! I loved her. She has the voice of an angel!'

Ethel couldn't help noticing that Augusta and Thekla had an even, all-over tan which betrayed their frequent indulgence in sunbathing. Ethel felt just a little self-conscious, having only her arms tanned and her face. This didn't inhibit her from actively taking part in the conversation.

'So what was it like, performing for the first time in public?'

'Not as difficult as you might think,' said Thekla. 'Herr Götze forced us to perform with the student orchestras in the Conservatoire concert hall, mainly for other students. So I was used to seeing a sea of faces, when the time came for a real, paying audience. This was seven years ago in Bruch's wonderful cantata, The Flight into Egypt. That was at a famous singing club, the Ossian, in Leipzig.'

'I broadly agree with Thekla,' said Augusta, as she shook her foot in the water. 'Amalie Joachim taught us how to control our emotions in public. She didn't force public performances on us but showed us how to exploit an audience.'

'How did she do that?'

'She taught us to engage with them from the moment we stepped on the stage. Look them in the eye! So as not to be afraid. She was a brilliant teacher!'

So the conversation continued, well into the afternoon. By the time the three women had finished, they knew much more about each other, their upbringing, education and their general approaches to life. Ethel put her clothes back on and the singers helped each other into their respective dressing gowns before walking back to the cabin.

'Who's cooking tonight?' said Thekla.

'I can cook,' said Ethel. 'But I don't yet know many German recipes!'

'I'll cook,' said Augusta. 'Our man has brought some fresh trout, caught in the local river.'

'You can't beat river trout!' said Thekla. 'I love that earthy, natural flavour.'

Thekla's utterance of the word 'natural' made Ethel wonder if they would eat their dinner in the nude. She had seen enough unclothed bodies for one day.

'I don't know about you, Ethel, but while Augusta is cooking, I'll change into something a little more formal for dinner.'

Much to her relief, Ethel replied. 'I will, too. We'll leave the cook to her preparations.'

'Then we'll have a pre-prandial drink,' said Thekla.

Within half an hour, Ethel and Thekla appeared in the dining room, Ethel in her tweeds and Thekla in a long, pink dress, down to her ankles. Probably one she had performed in.

'I do like your dress,' said Ethel.

Thekla looked briefly at Ethel's tweeds and turned her nose up, if only slightly. 'Many thanks,' she said. 'Shall I pour you a drink?'

Ethel was unsure how to react. The lunchtime beer had all but made her pass out. She wondered about the effect of a beer again or an alternative beverage.

'You'll enjoy this, Ethel. It's a sherry from Jeréz. An Oloroso, ideal for a pre-dinner, palate sharpener!'

Thekla was already pouring it into a small glass so she could hardly refuse. She took the glass and placed it on the dining table, not sure she wanted to try it just then.

Augusta then appeared from the kitchen. 'I hope you intend to pour me one as well!'

'Of course! That's why I have brought out three glasses and I know you like an Oloroso, especially when I've sweetened it with a splash of Ximenez!'

Ethel picked up hers and all three touched glasses with a gentle clinking sound. 'Here's to our holiday together,' said Augusta. 'The fish will be about ready by now.' She turned to go back to the kitchen and took her glass with her.

Ethel took a small sip, swirled it around her mouth and swallowed it. 'This is gorgeous, one of the nicest drinks I've tasted,' she said, knowing that it was the only alcohol she had ever consumed, other than the beer they had with their lunch.

'I'm bringing in the meal,' Augusta shouted from the kitchen. 'You can sit at the table now!'

Already served up on large, hot earthenware plates, the fish looked appetising and betrayed Augusta's enthusiasm as a chef with its little garnishes and a golden sauce, a combination of lime juice, herbs and honey, all served with a variety of vegetables.

'There! Please enjoy it!'

'Let me pour you some more sherry, Ethel,' said Thekla.

Ethel couldn't remember enjoying a meal so much. The trout was so tasty and the sweetened sherry complimented it beautifully. It wasn't long before they'd finished one bottle and Thekla stood up to go for another. The conversation became louder and more uninhibited. 'Have you sunbathed naked before, Ethel?' asked Augusta.

'I can honestly say never… but I enjoyed it. Partly because of you two being so relaxed and in the same state! What about you two? That's twice I've caught you *au natural*!'

'All the time! We've even had snow fights here stark naked in the depths of winter and rushed in afterwards to warm ourselves by the stove and dry off. Isn't that so, Thekla?'

'Yes, it's lovely. Gives you such a sense of freedom. We've even stood by the lake rehearsing, completely undressed!'

'It's a wonder no one's seen you,' said Ethel.

'We are lucky that it is so secluded here!' said Augusta.

'Someone caught us out! Do you remember, Augusta? We did a rehearsal a few years ago, right at the edge of the lake, and as we were walking back, arm-in-arm, our man who looks after the place, was walking towards us!'

'What did you do?'

'Absolutely nothing! You should have seen his face as we continued walking towards him. He didn't know what to say or do!'

'What happened?' said Ethel, laughing with her entire face.

'He said, smiling, "You two look rather delightful today" and carried on walking to the lake, straight past us. We didn't know why he was going there. We just said, "Thank you" and carried on walking up to the cabin. When we got inside we just burst out laughing, didn't we, Thekla?'

'Yes, it was funny. He was in total shock. We gave him a real treat! We didn't care!'

37

Once they'd finished the fish course, Augusta disappeared back into the kitchen and returned with a cake of some sort, which their man had brought them. 'This is special. It's a Thuringian Forest Gateau. You'll love it, Ethel. Pour her another sherry, Thekla.'

The drink was by then having its effect, so Ethel was feeling more than a little tipsy. 'Not too much,' said Ethel, her speech slurring. 'You can have too much of a good thing.'

Those were her last remembered words for that night. She woke up the following morning with a horrendous headache. She lifted the bedclothes to step out. Then she realised she had been sleeping nude. She thought for a moment. She didn't remember taking her clothes off. Did Augusta and Thekla undress her? Surely not. Or did they? How could she know? She'd ask them. She realised she'd had an enjoyable day the day before, but wondered if she could cope with all this nudity and drinking. It really wasn't her style. She adored Augusta. Even the thought of her made her shudder. She felt she could hug and kiss her at any opportunity.

'You look distinctly fragile,' said Augusta, as Ethel stepped into the kitchen.

'I have a terrible headache,' she said. 'Something to do with the sherry, maybe?'

'For sure,' said Thekla. 'We probably all feel groggy this morning. I meant to serve you with beer during the meal but we all seemed to enjoy the sherry so much…'

Augusta stepped towards Ethel and placed a kiss on her lips. Ethel shuddered slightly. Then Thekla kissed her. 'We are already very fond of you, Ethel, and hope we can stay friends after our holiday together,' she said.

'I hope so, too,' said Ethel. 'I'm becoming very fond of you two. By the way, did one of you undress me last night, before I went to bed?'

'Yes, I did,' said Augusta. 'It didn't seem right that you should fall asleep fully clothed. I hope you don't mind!'

The thought of Augusta undressing her sent shivers down her spine. 'No, not at all. Very considerate, if I may say!'

They sat down to a breakfast of cold meat, cheeses, coffee and fruit. 'This will help your headache,' said Thekla, who had prepared it. 'Eat as much as you like, but don't overdo it. You don't want to be ill.'

'We'll be going for a swim this morning, Ethel, if you'd like to join us?'

'I have a swimming costume!'

'We have, too, but we won't use them! We just cover ourselves with towels to walk to the lake and then ...'

'I'll do the same,' said Ethel, not at all surprised. She wondered whether they would be more modest in the company of George Henschel. Or would he parade around undressed too? She dreaded to think. She wondered if all artists behaved like this. Surely not. She would have heard by now. This had to be unusual if not... She hesitated at the word 'abnormal'. She thought about how her parents would react. Her father in particular. She dared not tell them. The General would be simultaneously delighted and disgusted to have his prejudices confirmed. She had promised to write to them soon after she arrived there, but she would have to omit some details.

Ethel had swum before but never enjoyed it much. Those heavy woollen swimsuits made it so difficult, but swimming without a costume was simply bliss. The water glided over her like a sheet of silk.

'You are a natural swimmer, and composer,' shouted Augusta, knowing Ethel would hear her as she performed the breast stroke with her head out of the water. 'I thought you said you weren't a good swimmer! You are enjoying it!'

'I am in fact!' replied Ethel. 'Just being modest! I'm good at sport, so swimming comes quite naturally to me.'

'Let's race each other to the other side of the lake!' shouted Augusta. 'You must come back here so we can all start together!'

Ethel set off at a raging pace and was soon three or four lengths ahead of the other two. Then Augusta put on a spurt, caught her up and overtook her. Not to be outdone and not a good loser, Ethel then changed her stroke to the crawl and caught up with Augusta, who flicked her head to one side and also changed stroke to stay ahead. They left Thekla, the eldest and not the fittest, about twenty lengths behind. Augusta climbed triumphantly out of the water on the far bank. 'You really put up a fight,' she said, crouching over and covering her exposed body with her arms.

'That was terrific,' said Ethel, also showing some modesty. 'We must do that again!'

'We've plenty of time, young lady.'

Minutes later, Thekla scrambled up from the water. 'I'm exhausted. Well done, you two. You were so quick.'

'We'll walk back along the water's edge. I don't think anyone will see us. We can always use our hands to cover up!' said Augusta.

That afternoon, clothed but dressed for the heat, they took Ethel on a long walk in the woods. Ethel had no idea where they were taking her as on and on they walked, climbing up the hills at one moment then descending the steep slopes into the valleys the next. Suddenly, they reached a clearing. 'Here it is,' said Thekla.

Sure enough, there stood a small building with about a dozen people scattered on benches outside. It was some sort of tavern. 'I'm thirsty. Are you both?' said Thekla.

'Could do with a drink,' said Augusta. 'A beer for you, too, Ethel?'

'I'd love a small one,' said Ethel, and in the three of them went.

As they entered the inn, a bearded man came out from behind the bar and ran across towards them. Ethel turned as if to run out.

'Don't go, please!' he blurted. Ethel stopped.

He went up to Thekla and kissed her on both cheeks, then to Augusta to give her the same welcome. 'It's lovely to see you again, Thekla and Augusta. Have a beer on the house. You can pay for the next one! Who is your new friend?' he said. 'The one I nearly scared away?'

Thekla explained who Ethel was and introduced him. He shook her hand. 'You don't see many English people in these parts, let alone a pretty woman, like yourself, and a composer too!'

Ethel smiled with embarrassment. Few had called her pretty, not up to then. She could feel the colour rising from her neck.

'She is truly pretty,' said Augusta. She delighted in the compliment, especially as Augusta had made it. It made her feel as if Augusta might have the same feelings towards her as she had for Augusta.

Greetings over, they sat and enjoyed the local beer. 'My turn to buy you two a drink. Don't you remember, I promised on Leipzig station I would?'

'Oh, go on then,' said Thekla. 'Then we must head back before dark. It becomes pitch black up here.'

# CHAPTER 5

## George Henschel

That night, having taken less of the sherry, and only a small glass of beer, Ethel lay in bed, wondering where this holiday might lead. It had cost her virtually nothing up to then and, if only to that extent, her family would be proud of her. She wanted to keep control of her limited budget. She was still sceptical about these women. This nakedness was quite alien to her. She enjoyed the freedom of not being encumbered with clothes, but wouldn't make a habit of it. Then her mind turned to Henschel. She was dreading his presence. There was something that made her quite apprehensive about meeting and holidaying with him, and she wasn't sure what. Could it be the sheer ability of the man, his exuberant skills as a singer, his ability as a composer or simply his outstanding ability as a musician? And how would he behave with Thekla and Augusta? As far as she knew, he was unattached. Could he…? She drifted into sleep.

Ethel admitted she felt relaxed with the singers, whatever their state of dress, made easier for her by restricting their nakedness to the lake-side or the path up to the cabin. They surprised her by something they said on the fourth day of their collective break. Thekla came out with it. 'Ethel, so far, we have all spent our daytimes together. Please don't feel obliged to being constantly with us. You can do anything you like while you are here. Do you want to do some exploring, some reading, composing or writing? It's entirely up to you.'

Ethel thought for a moment. Surely, they weren't regretting her presence there and were hinting that she should depart. No. Were they genuinely feeling that they were restricting her and wanting to give her more freedom to come and go as she wanted? She would assume the latter.

'You are immensely kind, Thekla. That's very considerate of you. I have brought some work with me and would in fact like to do some composing. Maybe, I could start after breakfast tomorrow.'

'Of course, Ethel. Start whenever you like,' said Augusta. 'But on one condition.' She paused.

Ethel wondered whatever that could be.

'That you play us anything you decide to write!'

'I'd love to,' she smiled. 'In fact, I have started on my second piano sonata and I'll play you some of that, once I'm happy with what I've written!'

For much of the following three days, Ethel sat at the desk in front of her window writing and re-writing her piano sonata. At irregular and unpredictable intervals, she would interrupt her writing and go into the drawing-room to try out what she had composed. She hesitated to play it with full force for fear of attracting the attention of Thekla or Augusta. She would guard the work from them until, as she said, she was happy with it. Occasionally, she would be distracted by the sight of one or both of the singers running up to the cabin laughing or one chasing the other, just like a couple of schoolgirls. Despite spending much of the day without Ethel, all three met up for meals. Ethel even prepared or helped with preparing quite a number. 'I feel almost obliged to share with the domestics' she would say to the welcoming singers.

At about three o'clock on the Saturday afternoon, while Ethel was concentrating deeply on her composing, she heard a gentle knock at her bedroom door.

'Ethel, may we come in? We have someone to introduce you to.' It was the voice of Augusta, presaging a moment Ethel had been dreading for days. 'We want to introduce you to George Henschel! Are you decent?' Ethel hoped they were.

'Just a moment!' Ethel placed her pen into the inkwell and took a sheet of blotting paper from a file. She carefully spread it over the few bars she had just completed and smoothed it over them. It was as if to delay meeting the man, but realised the time was approaching. There was no escaping the fact. She ambled over to the door and opened it, straight-faced.

All three of them stood there smiling. 'What kept you, Ethel?'

'I felt compelled to write the last bar of a tune I had in my head,' she lied.

Ethel didn't remember what a handsome man Henschel was, even through his transparent beard. He looked so young, especially with this attractive smile, but appeared to be at least in his mid-twenties. His gleaming brown eyes captivated her, so her fears vanished in an instant. She suddenly wanted to know more about this famous baritone and even make him a friend.

'Ethel, this is our lovely friend and co-performer, George Henschel,' said Augusta.

Ethel and he shook hands and, at Ethel's instigation, with excessive vigour.

'I've been dying to meet you, Ethel,' said Henschel. 'I gather you are a composer, too. You must play me some of your works.'

'I'd love to!' she gleamed.

Ethel's music had made a good impression with Mr Ewing but, despite his fame through 'Jerusalem the Golden', he was but an amateur. Here stood a consummate professional so, if he could see talent in her work, that would give her even more motivation to pursue her chosen career.

Then Thekla took over the agenda. 'George needs to relax for a time. He's had a very trying journey here from Munich, after giving a number of concert recitals.'

'I'll listen to some of your music tomorrow, Ethel,' said George. 'I'm seriously looking forward to it!'

'You must, George. We've heard some of her music. She is truly a budding composer!' said Augusta.

'Come and join us for a drink, Ethel,' said Augusta.

'Yes, please.' Ethel decided that she'd have a drink and then return to her music, unless she felt compelled to stay longer with the other three.

They all went to the dining room where Augusta opened the drinks cabinet. She placed a bottle of port and one of sherry on the table, along with four glasses. 'What would you like, George?' she said, pointing to the bottles. 'Or would you prefer a beer?'

44

'I'll have a glass of sherry, please, if I may.'

They all followed George's choice and within moments were chatting about his recent visit to Munich.

'I just adore the place. I have wonderful memories of it. One of my first concert performances was there. I sang the part of Hans Sachs in a concert performance of The Mastersingers of Nuremberg. Must have been nearly ten years ago. I was only eighteen!'

Hmm. He's older than he looks, thought Ethel.

'We've performed there a few times, too,' said Thekla. 'It's a wonder we haven't sung there with you!'

'We can't sing together everywhere. People would start talking about us! But I enjoyed your London, Ethel. Especially, as Thekla and Augusta sang with me there. Augusta tells me you were in the audience when we sang the Liebeslieder Walzer. And you went to see them at their flat a week later?'

'Yes, that's when we became friends and the girls suggested I stay with Thekla's aunt in Leipzig. So here I am!' Ethel decided not to bore the man with the dreary story of her father's constant objections and eventual surrender.

'Tell Ethel you know Brahms, George,' said Thekla.

'I shouldn't, really. It would sound as if I was elevating my abilities to those of the great master, himself... when I am mainly a singer and only a modest composer.'

'Not so,' said Augusta. 'You know him as a friend and there is nothing at all immodest about talking about friendships, is there Thekla?'

'None whatever.'

'How did you meet Brahms, then?' said Ethel. 'I love his music.'

'I first met him in Cologne at a music festival. I was singing in Handel's Samson. That was about three years ago. He came up to me afterwards to praise my singing. We then we adjourned to a tavern for a few beers and we've been good friends since. He often sends me examples of his music to ask for my opinion.'

'What's he like as a person?' said Ethel.

'I like him, but he can dismiss what he regards as poor work. I remember when we both sat and listened to a composer playing one of his piano sonatas. Afterwards, he went up to the man and put a page of his music paper between his thumb and first finger. "What excellent paper," he said. "From whom can I buy some?" The poor man just looked at him in total dismay! I didn't know what to say!'

'That strikes me as being very mean and not amusing,' said Ethel.

'In his defence, he is very self-critical. Last winter, while we were working together in Koblenz, he was the soloist in a public rehearsal of Schumann's A minor Piano Concerto. He missed quite a few notes and was utterly distraught. So he spent the whole of the following morning at the piano, putting himself right. He wasn't that pleased to see me when I interrupted him! In the event, he must have solved the problem because he gave a masterful performance the following day. We had quite a party that night to celebrate.'

Thekla and Augusta listened in awe at what Henschel said about Brahms. These stories were as new to them as they were to Ethel. She had done well in coaxing them out of him.

'I hope he would like my music if he heard or saw some,' she said.

'He would be amazed to know a woman had composed music,' said Henschel. 'You are a rarity. It's mainly us men who write music. He has a weak spot for young women and would like you very much!'

'I hope I meet him some time,' said Ethel, not sounding sure.

'We'll arrange for you to meet him, sooner rather than later,' he said. Ethel said no more on the subject.

The following morning, after another typical German breakfast, and while all four were still sitting at the breakfast table, Thekla posed a question. 'This is our first day together... Do we have any detailed plans for today? I'd like a swim!'

Ethel squirmed, wondering if she might be expected to swim in the nude again, not that they asked her to the last time.

'I would also like a swim. My costume is dry now,' said Augusta.

Thank goodness for that, thought Ethel, knowing full well that Augusta's costume was dry only because, despite swimming every day, their costumes hadn't been used. It sounded as if they would be, with George looking on!

'You go for your swim and Ethel and I will play some of her music. Do you agree, Ethel?'

'Of course,' said Ethel, smiling to herself.

'Fetch some of your music, Ethel, and I'll meet you in the drawing-room.'

Ethel immediately pushed her chair back, stood up from the table and dashed out of the room. Moments later she appeared alongside the piano where George was already sitting. She was clutching a sheaf of her music.

'Would you like to play a piece?' said Ethel.

'That's why I'm sitting here,' said George, raising his hands. 'You choose something for me to play.'

Ethel shuffled through her music and found the piano sonata she completed before she came to Leipzig. 'Try this,' she said as she placed the score on the music stand on the piano.

He read the first page, at the same time beating out a rhythm on the top of the piano, then flicked over to the next page, then the next. Then he returned to the beginning. 'You can turn the pages, as I play,' he said.

Ethel took a chair from the side of the room, put it by the piano and sat on it with him next to her. He played. The hairs went up on the back of her neck. Other than Mr Ewing, no one had played any of her music before and here was one of the century's famous young composers doing just that. It sounded better to her than it sounded in her own head when she wrote it. He played the first movement. She thought he would stop there, but he played on, through the second movement and to the end. He stopped and paused, looking up into the air. Then, without the merest sign of what he thought of it, said he wanted another of Ethel's pieces.

'How about a song?' said Ethel.

He nodded, expressionlessly.

She fumbled through her papers again and found the song she had written for Lady Sitwell. Again, she placed it on the stand. He played and sang it at the same time. His voice sounded quite different from the way it sounded at the concert at St James Hall. Somehow it was softer, as if he wanted to put the maximum expression into her song. Again, he did not indicate what he thought of it. He played several others of Ethel's works, a chant and the first movement of her latest piano sonata.

'Well?' said Ethel, with a quiver of anxiety in her voice.

'This is what I think, Ethel. The quality of your compositions is variable. Your best works are the piano sonatas. Your first sonata is near to perfect. So you are a talented composer in the making. All you need is teaching by a competent teacher. It's up to you to do the rest. That's all. I'd love to help, you but I travel all over Europe and could not dedicate the time to you. But at the Conservatoire…'

Ethel turned towards him and hugged him awkwardly while he was still sitting at the piano.

'I am so pleased you think that, George. I'm delighted. You have given me more confidence that I can accomplish my goal as a composer.'

'Make no mistake, Ethel. It will take hard work. But you have an advantage over many: you have a natural talent. You are a born musician. Quite rare in anyone, let alone a woman.'

Ethel was grateful and disappointed at this construction. She was pleased that he recognised her natural talent but couldn't see what being a woman was in any way relevant. She suddenly realised that this was an obstacle she would probably have to surmount unless, by some miracle, there became a plethora of women composers. Unlikely, she thought.

'Let me tell you something, George.'

'Please do, Ethel!'

'I have heard nothing to compare with your singing, even of my modest songs. You have the most incredible voice. I love it! You sounded wonderful in London, but standing here next to you, I can really appreciate the greatness of your singing!'

'You are kind, Ethel. I hope my voice lasts!'

They spent the following days enjoying themselves collectively or separately, walking, swimming and listening to music. They went on many forest walks, mainly in twos and threes. They frequently gathered around the decrepit piano singing or listening to George's and Ethel's compositions and the works of other composers. George delighted Ethel in his incomparable singing of Schubert, Beethoven and Brahms. He sang her Schubert's Gruppe aus dem Tartarus, which she had never heard before and loved from that moment on. She thrived in the friendly, musical atmosphere and wondered why she had been so fearful about the imminent arrival of George Henschel, who had turned out to be a thoroughly pleasant, friendly and decent individual. He was constantly encouraging Ethel in achieving her ambitions.

Ethel even took herself into the forest to find a place to work on her new sonata, away from the laughter and general conviviality of the others. After three days she had completed the third movement and, that night, played the whole sonata to the others.

'It's a lovely piece, Ethel. Well done!' said Augusta, breaking into applause. Thekla and George followed her lead.

'That is your best work, so far, Ethel' said George. 'It is truly very good! I'd have trouble in improving on that. It has a strong energetic and emotional content and stands as a work individual to you. No one else could have written it!'

Ethel shed tears of joy. A composer of the stature of George Henschel, heaping praise on her work. Thekla took out a handkerchief to wipe away Ethel's tears.

'I'm happy, really,' said Ethel, struggling to regain her self-control.

At breakfast on the day before they were to leave this haven in the forest, they did something together. They struggled to decide, but decide they did: they would go for a long walk in the forest, despite the early signs of a hot day to come.

'How do we prepare for this?' said Ethel. 'I have no walking shoes, only what I'm wearing now.'

'We don't need special shoes. The ground will not be too dry or too wet, and it won't be very soft because of the dry summer,' said Thekla, whose idea it was. No such minor obstacles were going to deter her.

They each donned what walking gear they wanted and met in the hallway.

'One of you two will have to lead the way,' said George, looking in turn at Thekla and Augusta. 'I don't know these woods half as well as you.'

'What if I go first?' said Thekla. 'Then you can take over, Augusta, after a few kilometres.'

Hmm, thought Ethel. Yes, they were about to embark on a long walk if they were already talking in terms of kilometres. Ethel had not before walked around the south side of the lake, so the start of the walk was quite new to her. She looked up at the pine trees. Each competed with its neighbours to be the most perfect in symmetry. Breathing in deeply, she could savour the rich perfume of the oils emanating from the branches. She had never experienced such heat in a forest before and was subtly intoxicated by it.

Thekla and Augusta were twenty metres ahead of her and George, so Ethel made the most of the chance to talk more to him.

'So where is your next engagement, George?'

'Didn't I tell you? In Leipzig. At the Gewandhaus. The Dresden Staatskapelle are playing Beethoven's Leonora and I'm a soloist. Julius Rietz is the conductor.

He took over from Krebs and is very conservative. He hates Liszt and Wagner and just won't play them. They are far too modern for him. He's quite at home with the master, though! I'm not sure I appreciate his views but they are paying me well so I keep my opinions to myself.'

'You can trust me, George. I won't say a thing!'

'And what about you, Ethel? Do you have any specific ambitions, like writing an opera or a symphony? Or should I say operas and symphonies?' He chuckled and smiled at her.

'Yes, I emphatically do,' said Ethel. 'I want to write an opera and have its first performance here… in Germany!'

'I have a feeling you will achieve that, Ethel. I hope I am in the audience. You may even let me sing one of the parts. A minor one, of course!'

They both laughed.

'You are far too modest, George. Disarmingly so!'

After about two hours or more of following the lead of Thekla and alternatively Augusta, Ethel felt thirsty. None of them thought of taking any water or beer with them, regardless of the summer heat.

'I'm not sure about you, George, but I'm thirsty.'

'So am I. Let's catch up with the others and tell them. They will know somewhere to stop for a drink and perhaps some lunch.'

As they approached Thekla and Augusta, George shouted out. 'Hey, you two! We're dying of thirst back here. What about you?'

They stopped and turned around. Thekla spoke. 'We have a confession. We are totally lost and have been for about half an hour or more. I thought we were heading for one of the taverns, but it wasn't where we thought!' Her head hung low as she admitted they were thirsty too.

George's eyes drilled into them. He raised his voice. 'I thought you two knew where you were going. Ethel and I have been oblivious to our directions because we thought we could rely on you. How much more wrong could we be?'

'We are really sorry, George. We didn't lose ourselves deliberately.'

'Who would?' glared George.

'Please don't be angry with us,' said Augusta.

'I've calmed down now,' said George. 'We need to work together to manage ourselves out of this mess. Otherwise, who knows what the consequences could be. Let's see. Which direction is south?'

George worked out from the position of the sun that they were heading in a south-westerly direction. Judging from the time they had been walking, it was as if they had completed half a circumference of a large circle, about ten kilometres in diameter.

'So where was the inn, in relation to the cabin?'

'More or less north-east, about three kilometres away.'

'That means we need to walk about four kilometres in a south-easterly direction if we want to reach that inn.'

They started again with the shamefaced Thekla and Augusta in the lead.

'I feel I'm going to die of thirst if I don't have something to drink soon.'

'Don't worry, Ethel. You can go two full days without water, so you have plenty of time yet. The trick is not to panic. I'm sorry I snapped at our leaders back there!'

'If you hadn't, I would have!' She felt sure these were empty words, but at least they showed some mettle.

Ethel was feeling ill. 'I'm not sure I can walk much further,' she said, as they reached the bottom of a steep incline. The thought of struggling up the other side was becoming too much to bear.

'Hold my hand, Ethel. We mustn't fall behind the girls. On no account must we become separated from them. You'll be fine.'

Ethel was becoming delirious. She reached the point where she didn't know where she was. All she knew was her throat hurt, and it was like walking in an oven. George put his arm around her waist. 'Come on, gal. You must keep going. Stay awake!'

After about twenty minutes of almost carrying Ethel and with sweat pouring off him, he shouted out again. 'Slow down in front. Ethel is becoming ill!'

They looked around in horror as George could no longer hold her and Ethel collapsed to the forest floor.

'Now what do we do?' said Thekla on the point of tears. 'We can't leave her here.'

'You two stay with Ethel and I'll go ahead. I'll come straight back with directions as soon as I find the tavern.'

George gave them no choice and raced on.

'Wake up, Ethel,' said Thekla. 'We are nearly there. It's very near now,' she said, more in hope than reality.

'Thank you, Mama. What are you doing here? I thought I left you in Frimley.'

Augusta and Thekla looked at each other, wondering where this would lead and what to do.

'If I die, Mama. Please bury me next to Johnny. You will, won't you?' At least Ethel was still conscious, if in a frightening state.

'You will not die, Ethel,' said Augusta. 'You are with good friends and we are looking after you. Just stay awake.' With Augusta's words echoing in her head, Ethel closed her eyes. Her breathing almost stopped. Looking quite sad, Thekla sobbed.

'It's over here!' shouted George from a hundred metres away. 'I've found the tavern! It's open and they've got beer! I've brought a bottle to share!'

With a bottle at her lips and George pouring it into her mouth, Ethel soon recovered. Minutes later, all four were guzzling back a half litre of cold beer each. Nothing could taste better. They each had another glass accompanied by a few slices of German sausage.

'This is the tavern we visited a few days ago, Ethel. Remember?' said Augusta.

'Of course I do. I recognise the barman.'

'Augusta and I know our way back to the cabin from here, so we cannot become lost again.'

'I hope you are right,' said George, downing another beer.

Ethel's apparent near-death experience marked the virtual end of her holiday in Thuringia. While she was sure of her judgement of George Herschel, and would like to remain good friends with him, she remained unsure about Thekla and Augusta. She felt a tinge of excitement every time she thought of Augusta. And it was not related to the woman's ability as a singer.

Each said goodbye to the others at Leipzig Central Station and went their separate ways, Ethel back to the Frau Professor's apartment, Thekla and Augusta to Thekla's mother's and George to a hotel near the station.

# CHAPTER 6

## The Conservatoire

Ethel still had a week to spend in Leipzig before starting the autumn term at the Conservatoire. She spent hours walking unaccompanied in the streets of the city. She swam in the public pool and spent some afternoons exercising her skills as a skater. Occasionally, the garrulous Joe would escort her, something she avoided if possible, but only if she could manage it without being overtly rude to the lad.

On one of her solo missions, she spotted a notice in a shop window. It announced that Heinrich Hoffman's Serenade was to be played in an open-air concert that night at the Rosenthal, the expensive restaurant to which Harry had taken her before he returned to England. Ethel knew of the piece and decided she must hear it played.

'Frau Professor, I won't be dining in tomorrow night because I'm going to a concert at the Rosenthal restaurant.'

'Who will escort you, Ethel? You cannot go there alone, not to a place like that. You will attract all kinds of unwelcomed attention.'

Ethel realised exactly what she meant.

'I would go with you, but tomorrow is the monthly great wash. I have a mountain of dirty linen in the cupboard, many of your things amongst them. They are beginning to smell so I cannot delay any longer.'

Ethel was determined not to miss this enthralling work and instantly came up with a plan.

'What if I went in disguise?' she said. 'As a wrinkly, stooping old woman, much older than you, Frau Professor. I would hire a wig and maybe you would lend me one of your veils and a gown? Please!'

'I'm not as certain as you, Ethel. If they uncovered you, they would throw you out and that would bring shame on you and me… Oh, go on! Let's try it!'

Ethel spent at least an hour in front of the mirror constructing her new persona. She had hired grey, tightly corkscrewed curls and borrowed a pair of heavy, horn-rimmed spectacles. To ensure the Frau Professor's gown fitted reasonably well, she tied several layers of newspaper around her waist. She painted some convincing wrinkles on her face and, smiling with excitement, left for the Rosenthal. With a pronounced stoop, she slowly hobbled in.

She needed to work out where to sit, so picked out a table for two near the back. She took out some knitting the Frau Professor had lent her, solely as a prop and, using the deeper voice of an older woman, ordered a beer and a ham roll from an unsuspecting waiter. The concert put Ethel in a state of ecstasy. Just what she expected in this wonderful country, the Germany of her dreams. A resounding round of applause greeted every piece the little orchestra played. The audience, some still holding their cutlery, stood in appreciation and many stamped their feet.

During the interval, Ethel looked around. Here we have the musical elite of this city, she thought. Could some of them be famous performers or even composers? Then she spotted a familiar face, that of Joe, sitting at a table with some rotund German youths, of about his own age. She stumbled over to speak to him.

In her disguised voice, she spoke. 'Tell me, my dear young sir, how far is it to the Gewandhaus from here?'

'Not far, madam, probably about four hundred metres.'

'Bless you, my boy,' she said and shuffled, unrevealed, back to her table.

Then they played the Serenade. Ethel just loved it. It exceeded her wishes. The orchestra played it with great energy and sensitivity. She was delighted that she had spotted that shop window notice.

By eleven o'clock, the little old lady had hobbled her way back to the apartment and soon tucked herself in her bed. For a moment she was disappointed that the Frau Professor had not stayed up for her, but soon realised that this was a compliment. She was evidently familiar with the strange behaviour of the English.

At lunch the next day, in her voice of the night before, Ethel asked Joe a question. 'Tell me, my dear young sir, how far is it to the Gewandhaus from here?'

For a moment, Joe looked completely puzzled. Realisation dawned. He promised to keep her secret. But when Ethel joined the Conservatoire, she discovered she was already famous because Joe did not keep to his word. At least the story never reached Frimhurst.

***

The following Monday, Ethel enrolled as a pupil at the renowned Leipzig Conservatorium. She walked to the imposing building from Professor Heimbach's house. She had planted a gentle kiss on her cheek and wished her good fortune. The structure proudly displayed itself as a masterpiece of post baroque architecture. Its three stories were crowned by a frieze in the style of a Greek Temple. Ethel's eyes shone as she contemplated the sources of learning within. The genius Mendelssohn had created it. Would it hold the golden key to her career as a composer? She couldn't wait any longer. She walked through the middle arch, pushed open the massive door and stopped in front of a Spanish looking individual at the reception desk.

'Yes?' he said, with the welcome a house owner would give a burglar.

'I'm Ethel Smyth from England. I enrol today. Could you tell me where I should go in order to do that, please?'

'For a modest consideration, I will take you there, Miss. It's on the second floor.'

'In which case, I'll find my own way there.'

She later discovered that this tired old Castilian would not move from his desk without some form of tip, not even to accept a letter for delivery. After loping, gazelle-like, up the two flights of stairs, she soon found the registration desk. She joined a queue of about ten students, an equal mix of boys and girls, all of about her age.

'Yes, Miss. What can we do for you?' said a pleasant, plump lady, sitting behind the desk and looking over her *pince-nez*. Ethel smiled at this friendlier welcome and explained who she was.

'Oh, yes,' the woman said, looking through her glasses to her list of students. 'Here you are, from Frimley in England.'

'Correct.'

'You need to sign some papers and pay your first term's fees.'

'Can I pay tomorrow? I totally forgot to bring the money!'

'That will be fine, my dear. Just sign here... here... and here,' she said, handing Ethel a pen she had freshly dipped in an inkpot. 'This is the course timetable,' she said, passing Ethel some printed sheets of paper. 'Most of your lessons will be here, in the Conservatorium, but some will be at Professor Reinecke's flat, which is along the road. You should now make your way to Herr Weissman's. He is the Admissions Director and likes to meet all the students. He is three offices to the right, along the corridor. His name is on the door. Just knock and wait outside.'

So far so good, thought Ethel, as she stepped along the passage. She knocked on the door and waited. Less than a minute later, a pretty girl emerged, looking red-faced. Ethel thought she saw a tear or two.

'Thank you! Thank you!' said the voice of a much older man within. 'I hope you do well and enjoy the course.'

The girl turned her back and dashed back along the corridor, as if her life depended on escaping. He then summoned Ethel. Wondering what to expect and sharing some the pretty student's anxiety, she entered the room. He stood.

'Welcome to the world-famous Leipzig Conservatorium,' said the director, slurring his words and dribbling down his beard. His shirt collar was up on one side and down on the other. His bow tie pointed to his left shoulder. A belt with no buckle barely secured his trousers. The man was a wreck.

His eyes traversed every part of her body. They rested at her breasts. Ethel feared for her safety. What next?

'Allow me to introduce myself. I am the Director of Admissions,' he said, with drops of spittle falling from his chin. He held out his hand.

Ethel wondered what to do. Should she take his hand? She had no choice. She took it and immediately felt it move to touch her breasts. With all the strength of a fit and strong sportswoman, she tore his arm away from her and cast it to one side.

'I was just testing your strength,' he said. 'You're a tough one! Good to meet you!'

'And you,' said Ethel who turned and dashed to the door, opened it and sped away in the direction of the frightened girl. She wondered if the friendly lady at the registration desk knew of this man's exploits and was complicit. This wasn't the start she expected. She caught up with the girl.

'Hey, hey! Can I have a word?' shouted Ethel, as she caught up with her. She was about to go into what looked like some form of café or restaurant.

The girl looked around. She seemed to be in a state of shock. She was shorter than Ethel and slightly built: an easy victim for the director.

'Yes, what do you want?' she said, with a suspicious glower.

'I saw you before I met the director and you seemed seriously upset when you came out.'

The girl burst into tears. 'He tried to rape me,' she said. 'I feel horrible. He forced me over his desk, tried to take off my drawers and was ready to do me. Then you knocked on the door.'

They sat at a table in the refectory and continued.

'He's a sexual aberration,' said Ethel. 'He tried it on with me, too. Tried to touch my breasts, but I pushed him off.'

'You look stronger than me, so could defend yourself better. I feel better now I've shared the experience,' said the girl. 'And knowing I wasn't his only victim.'

'Let's buy something to drink. By the way, my name is Ethel Smyth. I'm from England.'

'Mine is Theresia Hueber. I'm from Austria. A town called Linz. Yes, let's drink some coffee. We can leave our timetables here.'

They sat back down at their table, coffees in their hands, and carried on talking. 'So presumably you are here to learn about musical composition,' said Ethel.

'Yes, I'm dying to be a composer. An uncle on my mother's side is a composer, but he is not well known, not like Brahms or Wagner.'

'What's his name?'

'Anton Bruckner. You've probably never heard of him.'

'No. And no one I know has mentioned him, except you! Like you, I'm also desperate to be a composer. In fact, I've already written quite a lot of music, a couple of piano sonatas, some songs and some liturgical chants.' In uncharacteristic modesty, she resisted saying Ewing and Henschel had enjoyed listening to her music.

'My God, Ethel, you have made a start! I'd love to hear some of your music, when we have a chance. I haven't put a note to paper yet, so I'm a complete beginner. But I play the piano and love listening to and playing music. So I can read music reasonably well.'

Ethel liked Theresia, the more so as they talked together. But for some reason, she could not see her as one of her 'passions'. Maybe it was her youth and that she was so petite. Ethel's passions were mainly girls or women older than her. She did not attract Ethel in the same way as the dazzling and voluptuous Augusta Redeker. Even so, she and Theresia could well become good friends and support each other's ambitions to be professional composers. Having each other as an ally could only be good for each of them.

They spent a few minutes looking at the course timetable.

'That's a surprise. Our first lesson isn't here at all. It's at Professor Reinecke's flat along the road. Number 16,' said Ethel. 'It's on musical theory, one of my weaknesses.'

'Are you going?' said Theresia.

'Definitely. I'm gasping to meet one of our illustrious professors. And if it's at his flat, that could add an interesting dimension. There won't be many of us there. That must be a certainty!'

'Shall we meet here tomorrow, Ethel? Say, at nine o'clock?'

'Let's do that. Until tomorrow then.' The girls shook hands and went their separate ways.

*** 

'Shall we have a coffee before we go?' said Theresia, as they met.

'Good idea. We've plenty of time,' said Ethel. 'I've hardly slept with the thought of going to the first of Reinecke's lessons.'

'We must refer to him as Professor, Ethel. Otherwise, we could be in trouble. I've been wondering about him, especially after my encounter with Weissman yesterday. I wonder if Reinecke's married and has a family. At least if he's alone, there will be two of us.'

'How are you feeling today? Weissman nearly raped you, the dribbling monster.'

'I'm not sure, really. He terrified me, but your knocking on the door saved me, and talking together made me feel much better. I am really grateful to you, Ethel, for following me down the corridor! I admit, I still feel badly abused... taken advantage of. I've been wondering about reporting him. What do you think?'

On their way along the road, they discussed the attacks on them committed by Weissman. They quickly concluded that, because of the man's position of power, there was little they could do, other than report him to the police. The Conservatorium authorities would surely do nothing. It would be their word against his. They decided not to do anything about him, at least for then.

They knocked on the door of No. 16. A tall, thin woman with a mop of black, frizzy hair opened the door. Two small children stood inquisitively behind her.

'Hello,' she said, with a smile. 'Are you students for Professor Reinecke? I'm his wife.'

They each felt relief that another woman would be present in the house.

'Yes,' said Ethel. 'We are both his students and are so wanting to meet him!'

'Do come in. Some of you are already here. There will be ten of you, altogether,' she said, holding the door open. She led them into a room set out with three rows of four chairs facing the rear wall. The two children followed her in. The students already present were three boys. Two of them were chatting as if they knew each other and the other sat at the back at the end of the row. They looked like students, each with longish hair and unkempt beards.

'Sit where you like,' she said. 'The professor will be with you shortly.'

Ethel and Theresia sat in the front row. Before them stood a desk, strewn with music paper, some of which had been written upon. A pen leant out of an inkwell. It was as if they had interrupted the professor in mid-composition. There was another knock on the front door and within a minute or two, four other students came in. None of them appeared to know any of the others. The frizzy-haired woman took her children from the room, whereupon the professor himself entered and plodded to the front, with the desk behind him, to face his audience. His smiling face, which shone out of the beard around its edge, captivated Ethel and Theresia.

'Permit me to introduce myself. I am Professor Doctor Carl Reinecke. I am the chief conductor of the Leipzig Gewandhaus Orchestra and a full professor at the Conservatorium. I have been teaching here for seventeen years now and have a first-class reputation in that role. I taught Grieg and Svendsen, both of whom have become distinguished composers in their own right. My job is to make you equally famous. And you will be, if you follow my instruction.'

The boy at the end of the row at the back, clapped.

'Little early for that, young man,' said Reinecke and continued. 'I have written over two hundred works, including two symphonies, two operettas, three piano concertos, a cello concerto, a violin concerto and many chamber works, including sonatas for various instruments. Many of my works have been performed here in the Gewandhaus and in other countries in Europe, including France, Sweden and Denmark, where I was chief pianist to the King.'

I hope he stops elaborating on his own success, thought Ethel. This is just self-promotion. He's convinced everyone here he's a famous composer and conductor, but how do we fit into his scheme? He says he's going to make us famous, but not at his expense, I'm sure. She nudged Theresia in the hips and raised her eyebrows at her. Theresia reciprocated.

At the moment he completed his speech, the door sprang open and four children raced into the room, shouting and pulling at each other. The professor reacted strongly.

'Get out, children! How can I give a lesson with you chasing about?'

The children, laughing and shouting, left the room.

'I apologise for that interruption. I hope there won't be many more like that during our work together. There are two things I want to do in this lesson. First, I want you to say who you are, where you come from and why you are here. Then I want to go around again and you can tell each other what your career aims might be. And you will tell me, of course! Let's start with you two ladies at the front.'

Ethel sat at the end, so spoke first. 'I am Ethel Smyth, from a small village in England called Frimley. I am here because I want to become a professional composer.' One of the boys in the second row chuckled. Ethel responded.

'Frankly, I don't care what your ambitions are,' she said, pointing and stabbing her finger at the offender. 'The difference between us is that I have proven and substantial ability. I seriously doubt yours.'

'I am Theresia Hueber. I am from Linz in Austria. I want to follow in the footsteps of my uncle who is the composer Anton Bruckner. He's written a great deal of music, including six symphonies. You probably haven't heard of him but that doesn't worry me.'

'That's an interesting start,' said Reineke, which it was in more ways than one. 'What about you boys?'

Each of them said their names and where they were from. None were from outside Germany and five were local lads living in or near Leipzig.

'Now tell me what your interests and ambitions are, starting again with you, Ethel.'

'I intend to become a successful composer, like you, Professor. I am constantly longing to write music. My chief ambition is to write some operas and I want my first one performed here in Germany before I'm forty. I have written a number of compositions already, including two piano sonatas and some songs.'

'You must bring some of your music to our next class so I can look at it, Ethel. I'll tell you how you are progressing. What about you, Theresia?'

'I want to write symphonies, like my Uncle Anton. That's my ambition, and I want to see them performed. Unlike Ethel, I haven't written a note of music yet but I'm here to learn.'

None of the seven boys could say what they wanted from the course they were about to embark upon. They all said they hadn't decided or that they might want to teach. None showed any enthusiasm or real ambition. Ethel wondered why they had bothered to enrol. Had they come to the wrong course, or had over-demanding parents forced them there? Ethel, and Theresia, were mystified by their contempt, both for what they had said and what Reinecke himself was saying.

'Well, that's all for today. More of an introduction. Actual work next time we meet,' said the Professor. 'You may go now.'

As they left the room, Ethel looked behind her only to see the Professor take his pen from the ink-well and resume his composing. It was as if he couldn't rid the room of his students soon enough.

Their first lesson with Solomon Judassohn was equally farcical and shockingly awkward. He arrived at the lecture room fifteen minutes late, laughing all over his heavily bearded face.

'I'm freezing,' were his first words to the students, as he stood open-legged in front of the stove in the corner. 'I suppose you are expecting me to teach you... but you are going to learn by working through exercises I will be setting. Don't worry because I have done them myself so I'll be looking to you to improve on my answers. That shouldn't be too difficult, I should say!' He was a striking contrast to the formal Reinecke and seemed to be more of a joker than a professor. He had no intention or interest in presenting himself as the distinguished and prolific composer the girls subsequently found he was.

'Any questions, so far?' he said, casting his dark eyes around the thirty or more students there. 'If not, we can all go home! I am jesting, of course.'

'I've written various compositions,' said Ethel. 'Could you have a look at them for me, please?'

'Of course,' said Judassohn. 'I'd like to see one of your pieces... to begin with. We might even play it. What have you written?'

'Some songs and a couple of piano sonatas. And a few other works.'

'Bring me your second piano sonata... next lesson.'

'Thank you, Professor. I'm so grateful.'

A girl that Ethel and Theresia had not seen before asked Judassohn a question. 'Tell us, Professor. Are you Jewish?' Some other students, but Ethel and Theresia were not among them, reacted with muted laughter.

'Is that relevant to my position as your Professor? I am a Jew, and it is with great pride I say so.'

'Yes, it is relevant. I've not come here to be taught by a Jew,' said the girl. She stood up and left the room. About ten of the others followed her.

Judassohn's reaction was extraordinary. 'We don't want anti-Semites here, polluting our class with their disgusting views. So we are well rid of those people. If any of you others hold similar views, I invite you to leave now.'

No one moved. A few students applauded. Within seconds the applause had grown to a crescendo with a shouting and cheering accompaniment. Judassohn held up his hand. 'Much appreciated,' he said. 'I look forward to our next lesson.' He then left the room.

Ethel and Theresia headed for a refectory lunch. 'What did you think about that?' said Theresia.

'It proves that anti-Semitism is not dead, even among the intelligentsia of Germany. Many people, like that girl, can't accept Jewish emancipation, despite its early beginnings. It's probably because of the bad influence of their parents. Old prejudices die hard.'

'I'm sure you are right, Ethel. It's probably the same in Austria. But I haven't experienced it in Linz.'

'I hope we receive better quality teaching than we've had so far. Here we are, hoping to learn composition and we haven't learnt to write a solitary note.'

The following day, Ethel met Louis Maas, her piano teacher. Of her three main instructors, at least he had something to tell her.

'I want you to play me this piece,' he said, placing some music on the stand of a new looking, upright piano. 'It's a short piece by Mozart. Let me explain. I want to watch the way you use your hands, listen to the feeling you put into playing it, and assess your ability to sight-read.'

'When should I start?' said Ethel as she adjusted the height of the piano stool.

'Whenever you are ready!'

Ethel put her hands to the keys and her eyes to the music. Her fingers worked hard to strike the right notes in which they succeeded, despite the Professor standing right over her like some threatening cloud. She managed to turn the page without interrupting her rhythm and completed the work with a flourish, stopping with her hands in the air.

'Not at all bad,' said Maas. 'Your sight-reading is excellent but we need to make your hands move easier. I shall teach you to develop a more gentle touch but we can work on these areas. You are a good pianist and we will develop a practice routine to raise you to a high standard. What are your ambitions as a pianist?'

'I have none really,' said Ethel, realising that this would disappoint the Professor. 'My aim in being here is to be a composer. I will use the piano as a tool to aid my composition, but I have no aims to be a concert performer.'

'You don't wish to become a piano teacher then?'

'Definitely not. Just to play with a good level of skill.'

'You are unusual,' said Maas. 'You are one of the very few women I have known who wants to be a composer. You are at the right school though!'

From what Ethel had seen so far, she was wondering. And the question of being a woman had emerged from the rafters yet again. Ethel could not understand it.

Ethel played parts of her second piano sonata to both Reinecke and Judassohn. Neither seemed impressed. Their reaction contrasted savagely to what George Henschel and Alexander Ewing before him had said. Neither took the trouble to examine the work for mistakes and claimed not to have time to read it or listen to it through to the end. Ethel protested. 'You are not the only student here you know,' said Reinecke. 'Have you thought of a career in teaching?' said Judassohn, echoing the words of Maas.

# CHAPTER 7

## Various distractions

Ethel and her new friend Theresia reached the same disappointing conclusion. The Leipzig Conservatorium failed to match up to its international reputation.

'They aren't interested in teaching us,' said Ethel, as the two of them sat at their usual table in the refectory. 'They are living off the reputation of Felix Mendelssohn. We enjoy better service here than in their lectures. At least the staff here do what we ask of them. If you ask for a *bratwurst*, that's what they serve, and a tasty one at that. If you ask Reinecke to read one of your scores, he complains that he'd really love to, but that he's a busy man and he hasn't that much time to spare.'

'Yes, he just turns his face away and carries on with his own compositions. Not much use to us.'

'Same with Judassohn. Prefers to crack silly jokes than to teach.'

'The only serious teacher is Maas,' said Theresia. 'Dry though he may be, but I've definitely learnt from him over the last few weeks.'

'I agree. He's helped me, too. But none of them remotely fits the brilliant image I've had of the place. It was my dream for seven years to be taught composition here. Now I feel cheated, robbed. What we should do, Theresia, is make the most of Leipzig and go to the concerts at the Gewandhaus, try the theatre and soak ourselves in other cultural experiences. What do you think?'

'All the concerts at the Gewandhaus are conducted by Reinecke... or so he told me... so we'd just be putting more money in his pockets. We could try the theatre or even the opera house.'

'I disagree about funding for Reinecke. He'll be on some sort of stipend and won't be paid by the size of the audience... or by their gross weight! Come on... let's try some concerts!'

Within a few days, the two students made their status known at the Gewandhaus box office and retrieved their free tickets for the morning rehearsal. As they predicted, Reinecke conducted it and, from the rostrum, saw them sitting a couple of rows back.

'Aren't you two supposed to be at classes, this morning?' he hollered.

'No, Professor. Dr Judassohn suggested we could learn much from watching you conduct, so here we are!' fibbed Ethel.

'I see,' he said, not believing a word of it.

Although Alexander Ewing had taken her through the score of Schubert's Unfinished Symphony, she had never heard it performed before and was quivering with excitement at the prospect, just like a child about to unwrap a Christmas present.

'Are you all right, Ethel? You are trembling and your hand is hot.'

'I'm fine, just dying to hear this great symphony… for the first time!'

'Can't be that good!'

'Your Uncle Anton will surely know it well… and love it with a passion!'

Reinecke's conducting style surprised Ethel. While he overtly spent much time on his own compositions, he let the works of others speak for themselves. There were no Reinecke touches, he did not change the composer's markings of pace or emphasis. It was as if the music passed directly from the pen of the composer to the mind of the listener. His approach enthralled her. Pity about his method of teaching.

The two girls enjoyed many of the Gewandhaus concerts, all conducted by Reinecke. His performance of Beethoven's Symphony No. 7 brought Ethel to tears.

Theresia showed no actual interest in the theatre, so Ethel attended several plays on her own. Part of her aim was to improve her German. She went to plays by Shakespeare, Goethe, Schiller, Racine and even a few of Calderón de la Barca's. In some of them, the tragic heroine was played by Marie Geistinger,

69

whose career appealed to the young Ethel. By then she had retired from being a famous operetta singer to acting the parts of these unfortunate women. She had enjoyed amazing success as a singer and had been courted by archdukes, dukes and princes of various nationalities. Despite her age - then about fifty - heavily made up and with a wig piled high, to Ethel she looked simply gorgeous, and captivated her as the latest in a long line of passions.

The woman's stage presence enraptured Ethel, and not least her incredible ability to bring the fictional heroines to such a level of reality they seemed more lifelike than many living people. Her public loved her. Ethel wanted to meet this goddess of a woman. So after several of her performances, she attempted to see her at the stage door. She would wait outside in horrible weather, even slushy snow, just to have a fleeting glimpse of this female paragon who, on every occasion, pressed Ethel's heart into pumping faster and harder. She rapidly disappeared into a waiting cabriolet without even a passing acknowledgement of the infatuated Ethel.

After a good dozen of these empty encounters, Ethel bribed the doorkeeper into giving the Geistinger a signed note of extravagant appreciation. Distraught at receiving no response, Ethel took to buying tiny posies of flowers to tie to her fervid notes and bribed the doorman to deliver them to her dressing room. Eventually, one freezing night, on leaving via the theatre door, the Geistinger handed Ethel an envelope before vanishing into the cab. Would it be a rejection of her constant pestering? Or, by some miracle, did the actress want to know Ethel better? Ethel tore it open and, by the light of a street lamp, read the letter. She cheered out loud. The Geistinger wanted to meet Ethel at her house in the Judastrasse. She gave a date and time and the exact address, which was superfluous as Ethel, by her own researches, had discovered it for herself. She had even posted flattering notes under her door, ever hoping to see her idol.

At the due time and date, Ethel rang the doorbell of the Geistinger's house. It reminded her of her visit to Thekla and Augusta's house in London. The thought that this dowager lady might appear naked flashed into her mind but quickly vanished. A servant opened the door and, once Ethel had shown him the letter, invited her in. The lugubrious adjunct took her into a cold but immaculate drawing-room and left her perplexed, sitting on a sofa. He disappeared at the moment the Geistinger entered, in front of a shy, slim man whom she introduced as her new husband. He then retreated to a corner of the room to leave the actress sitting on the sofa next to Ethel. She wore a low-cut, pink dress and an extravagant curly wig, as if she was about to appear on a stage rather than to meet an invited visitor.

At first, Ethel just looked at her and breathed in the nascent perfume of this beautiful if aging creature. She quivered at the closeness of this human epitome.

'No need to be so shy, Ethel... if I may call you by name!'

'I have been idolising you for weeks. Now I am here with you, my words have deserted me!'

'Well, just relax. You can call me Marie. So I seem to have entertained too well?'

'You have entranced me and I now love you like no other,' said Ethel, recovering her composure but still shaking.

'Oh! You are too kind! I wish some others in the audience loved me as much as you,' she said, assuming Ethel's love was of her, rather than of other performers, and not of the deeply emotional variety. Little did she realise.

Ethel was still in that frozen state of working out what to say to the human deity, who had one leg up on the sofa and was almost facing her. Should she start with the weather? At that point a small, white, yapping dog appeared through the door, having apparently pushed it open. 'This is my Bonnie, a little poodle. It travels everywhere with me!'

Ethel put out her hand to stroke its head. 'He loves you, too!' said Marie.

'I love dogs,' said Ethel. 'But I prefer the bigger varieties.'

'Oh, these are far easier to manage in the towns. Larger dogs are for hunting in the country.'

'You may have a point there. So when are you next on stage?' said Ethel, by then feeling quite conversational.

'Tomorrow, I'm in de la Barca's The Mayor of Zalamea at the Stadt Theatre. I play the part of Chispa who is suspected of being a whore! What a lady! Do you know any of Calderón's plays? He was the Spanish Goethe or Shakespeare, depending on where you are from!'

'Yes, I know about him. I saw Life is a Dream a few weeks ago. You were in it!'

'Yes, I played Rosaura in that one! It's a wonderful play, don't you agree?'

'It's truly entertaining, one of the best of the plays I've seen so far.'

And so the conversation continued until the gracious lady invited Ethel to visit again, which she did after about a week. Such was her infatuation that she went there again and again. She enjoyed just being with this woman, probing into her career, especially as a renowned singer, and her latter time in the theatre. Ethel told her about her own interests in music and the works she had composed. She told her about her bitter disappointment at the poor teaching at the Conservatorium.

'Ethel, my dear, I have heard reports of their indifferent teaching. It's hard to know what to do about it.'

'My friend Theresia and I were thinking of raising a complaint but have our doubts. We feel it could rebound on us. They could strike us off their student list and that would mean no tuition at all.'

'Let me think about it, Ethel. Maybe there is an alternative solution. Perhaps I and some of my colleagues could write to the Director of Music to tell him what we have heard. I'll let you know next time we meet.'

Ethel thought about telling the Geistinger about the Director's assault on Theresia and the lesser one on her. She decided against it.

\*\*\*

Before Ethel travelled to Leipzig, Mrs Schwabe's mother-in-law, the philanthropist and eternally energetic, Madame Schwabe, gave Ethel a letter of introduction to a Frau Doctor Brockhaus. Just before her first Christmas in the city, Ethel stumbled across the letter and decided, in a fit of curiosity, to visit her. Much to her delight, she discovered she was a well-connected woman of incredible dynamism and one of the influential ladies of Leipzig.

'I am so pleased you called on me, Ethel. I have heard a little about you from Madame Schwabe, who I'm sure knows your mother.'

Within half an hour of intense and convivial discussion, the Frau Doctor had persuaded Ethel that she should stay with the Brockhauses for Christmas and that after Christmas, and on return from her New Year holiday at her country retreat near Dresden, she would introduce Ethel into her huge and powerful circle of contacts and friends in the city. Among the grandees Ethel met were the Tauchnitz family, founders of the Tauchnitz Edition, under which English novels, such as those of Dickens, could be legally printed and distributed on the continent. To the relief of the Frau Doctor, who could not fail to notice Ethel's attraction for her, Ethel fell for the Tauchnitz's gorgeous daughter-in-law, Edith. It wasn't long before Edith discovered Ethel's friendship with the Geistinger.

'So how long have you known Maria Geistinger, Ethel?'

'Since October.'

'How well do you know her?'

'Very well. I've visited her many times. We have spoken about both of her careers, as a singer and now as an excellent actor. And I've met her husband, He's quite young and quite new, she says.'

'Do you know about her lovers?'

'Lovers?'

'Yes. She's had no end of them. She's made herself available to many men, from dukes to cabriolet drivers. I wouldn't say she's a whore, but she leads an odd kind of life. Yes, that man is her new husband. He's her fourth or fifth. She discards them when they no longer attract her interest. She's insatiable.'

'Hmm! I don't know what to say.'

'Just tell me you'll never see her again. She could destroy any reputation you have. Simply by association.'

'I'll write to her.'

So Ethel wrote to the Geistinger saying she had little choice but to abandon the friendship for reasons that, if she cared to reflect on her past life, she would readily understand. Ethel received no reply to this abominable letter and had told the Geistinger that she did not want one. She thought many times about how she might have reacted, but came to the view that it didn't matter to her a jot. Ethel forever regretted sending that odious letter.

*** 

A few days later, her landlady, Frau Professor Heimbach, knocked on the door to Ethel's bedroom. It was about ten o'clock and Ethel had no classes that day, so was working on her third piano sonata.

'I have a gentleman visitor for you, Ethel. He didn't give his name but sounded English. He's in the drawing-room.'

She had no idea who this 'gentleman' could be. Obviously, not Joe who still lived there. She put down her pen, went over to the mirror to smooth out her hair, and then descended the stairs. She pushed open the drawing-room door and there, sitting on the settee, was none other than George Henschel, smiling at her as she entered the room.

'George, what a lovely surprise,' said Ethel. She stepped over to him and kissed his cheek. 'You are the last person I expected to see!'

'Well, I've found you at last. I went to the Conservatorium, and they told me you had no lessons today, so I took a chance and came here to see if I could find you! Luckily, you are here!'

'I still can't work out why you've come!'

'I've got some interesting news for you. You remember we spoke about Brahms when we were on our holidays in Thuringia. I told you I knew him reasonably well. The news is that he's coming here for the first performance in Germany of his second symphony.'

'I saw it on the programme for the Gewandhaus!' said Ethel.

'Yes, but you didn't know that he will conduct it himself. And that I've got you a ticket.'

'That's amazing and so kind of you, George. Bless you!'

'Yes, it was his idea to conduct it. At first, the Gewandhaus director refused but gave in when Engelbert Röntgen, the leader, persuaded him to change his mind.'

'How amusing,' said Ethel. 'I imagine Brahms was none too pleased with the refusal!'

'He was furious. There's an odd relationship between the Northerners, such as Brahms who is from Hamburg, and the people in this area who speak with a different accent. They just don't like each other so, although they didn't object to him being there… they couldn't possibly… they did not want him conducting the work. They don't like new works. So it's a wonder they agreed to perform it at all. They loath Wagner and won't even play his overtures if they can avoid them!'

'Has there been an announcement about Brahms conducting?'

'Not yet. Reinecke was to have conducted it, and he's not thrilled at having to step down.'

'Actually,' said Ethel, 'he's an excellent conductor. I've heard him direct Schubert's Unfinished and Beethoven's Seventh. Both really touched me. I'd not heard them before. Pity he's as bad as he is at teaching.'

'Really?'

'Yes! Told me he was a busy man and didn't have time to read my scores right through! I'm not impressed with the Conservatorium so far.' She decided not to tell him about the assaults perpetrated on her and Theresia.

'I've heard similar stories. All the way from England, too. I'll see if I can help you, Ethel, but it won't be directly as I am away so much, as I've already said. By the way, Brahms is staying with an interesting couple who you must meet. They are the Herzogenbergs, Elizabeth and Heinrich. She is a total delight. If you think Augusta Redeker is beautiful, you will be drawn into the whirlpool that is Elizabeth, or Lisl as we know her. She is as intelligent as she is good looking, and is a wonderful musician in her own right. She is shy and difficult to know. But you are just the type to succeed. You will love her. Brahms stays with them every time he is in Leipzig.'

'I'm fascinated already, George. I must meet her!'

'And her husband. He is a composer in his own right. Brahms doesn't rate him, but he's actually very good. His second symphony is a treat. You'd love it. He spends nearly all his time composing and pleasing his wonderful wife!'

'I should meet both of them, by what you say. And I'd probably see more of Herr Brahms, if he's staying with them!'

'I'm sure we can arrange that. I'll see what I can do. I should go, Ethel. Oh, before I forget. Here's your ticket!'

\*\*\*

Ethel was at the same time entranced and mystified by Brahms second symphony. She was struck by the contrasting melodies and the way Brahms had developed the major themes. What did not impress her was Brahms' strange style of conducting. It reminded her of the strange rendition Wagner gave of Lohengrin in St James Hall.

The audience gave the work a good reception, but not what a first performance in this musical city might expect. The applause was strong but not rapturous. It was far from clear whether this was due to the symphony itself or Brahms' conducting.

As Ethel stood up from her seat, two men came towards her. George Henschel was one and he smiled in her direction. She didn't recognise the other attractive young man who was clean-shaven and had the most startling blue eyes.

76

'Allow me the introduce you, Ethel. This is my friend Johannes. He conducted his second symphony tonight. I hope you enjoyed it and so does he!'

'In fact, I did. An intriguing work. Congratulations.'

'So this is the young lady who writes sonatas and doesn't know counterpoint.'

Ethel was unsure how to interpret Brahms' comment. Was it a compliment which acknowledged her ability, or was it a sarcastic remark? She took it as a compliment, at least for then.

'Many thanks, Herr Brahms. I'm flattered,'

He smiled and turned towards the stage. George Henschel followed him.

A few days later, in mid-afternoon, Ethel met George again, this time by coincidence, in the Conservatorium refectory.

'I didn't expect to see you here, Ethel. I thought you'd be in a class.'

'No. I've had a piano lesson with Professor Maas. He's trying to change my hand movement, but I'm having trouble doing what he suggests. It seems so unnatural! What about you, George?'

'I'm here to see another of your professors, Carl Reinecke, about a rehearsal we are supposed to be doing next week. I'm not sure what he wants exactly, so I've arranged to see him.'

'I hope he's got more time for you than he has for me!' joked Ethel.

'I hope so, too! What did you think of Brahms? I couldn't resist introducing you two!'

'Well, I loved that symphony. The tunes have been swirling around in my head ever since. It's a fresh, what I call a green work, if a symphony can have a colour! I was quite flattered by his recognising me as a composer.'

'I have something interesting to tell you about that. Before he went to Berlin, I showed him the scores of those two songs you wrote. There were three of us in the conversation, me, Johannes and Engelbert Röntgen. He thought they were excellent. To the extent, he couldn't believe a woman had written them. So he turned to Engelbert and said we'd been chiding him and that I had written them all along. I really struggled to convince him they were yours. I'm not sure now that he believed me!'

'I don't know how to take that, George. But it's a barrier I shall have to break through many times as a composer. And, as you know, a composer I shall be!'

# CHAPTER 8

## Lisl

Ethel waited to see the paragon called Lisl. She pestered George more than once to arrange a meeting, hopefully to meet husband Heinrich, too. But he seemed able only to find empty excuses for not doing so. So Ethel continued enjoying the musical delights of this enthralling city, between tolerating the mediocre lectures and tutorials dished out at the Conservatorium.

By this time, Ethel had worked out the complexities of the social structures in Leipzig. Although there was some overlap, the four main strata were: the Burgher Aristocrats, themselves divided into the urban and rural; the Professorial; the Artists; and the Artisans. The rural Burghers centred themselves on the Gewandhaus Society, which comprised about forty families who had intermarried for generations and owned most of the land in and around the city. A code of unwritten rules and laws, which passed from father to son, governed their existence. During the summer, each family decanted to its country house, usually on a sprawling estate, or to a dilapidated castle.

At the head of these families were the Limburgers, who had made their fortune from wool. The father, Julius Limburgher, whom Ethel found to be a charming man, was the President of the Gewandhaus Concert Committee. While Ethel had no special fondness for his wife, Ella, they had the type of relationship that fitted well with her being a young woman and Ella being a woman of the world. She was kindness personified.

The Professors claimed intellectual superiority. They thrived on being envious of the position, emoluments, pension rights and the qualifications of each other. They hated their friends even more than their enemies.

Ethel regarded herself as an Artist. This class, as did the Artisans, relied either on each other or on the Burghers for their work and income. Because of her elevated social position in England, Ethel felt rightly that she could socialise freely with each of these strata, except of course, with the Artisans who served the others.

One night, at the beginning of February, she and Theresia enjoyed the good fortune of being allocated seats in a box at the Gewandhaus for a concert at which the orchestra, as usual under Carl Reinecke, were to play Schubert's Symphony No. 5, another of the many works she had studied under the tutorship of Alexander Ewing. So she already felt she knew it and would enjoy it immensely. The box had the strange title of the 'Frege Box' appended to its entrance. As Ethel and Theresia sat there chatting, an old lady entered, went up to a seat at the front, removed the 'reserved' notice, sat there and began reading the programme. The woman had the air of an upper-class lady about her. She wore a gown that must have cost a small fortune, and what appeared to be a diamond studded tiara in her silver, grey hair. Having studied the programme, the lady turned to the girls.

'With whom will I be enjoying the concert tonight?' she said, in a high-pitched but friendly voice.

'We are students at the Conservatorium,' said Ethel, as usual taking the lead. 'My name is Ethel Smyth. I'm from England. And this is my friend Theresia from Linz.'

'I'm pleased to meet you,' said the lady. 'It's very good to know that our Conservatorium still attracts students from abroad.'

'May we ask your name?' said Ethel.

'My name is Livia Frege,' she said.

'Ah! The box here carries your name!' said Theresia.

'Yes, it is my box, actually. Well, I part own it!'

'I didn't even know you could own a box,' said Ethel. 'Would you mind telling us how you came by it?'

It was at that point that Ethel realised she was talking to another of the wonderful, if slightly mysterious women who inhabited the musical scene of Leipzig, evidently one of the burgher class. It emerged not much further into the conversation that Livia Frege was, in her past life, none other than the famous singer, Livia Gerhardt, to whom Schumann and Mendelssohn had dedicated many of their songs. Livia exuded a rare gentleness and generosity of spirit which Ethel found entrancing. She was captivated by Livia's blue eyes, which shone like the diamonds in her tiara. Ethel immediately felt the urge to befriend the woman and was so absorbed by her that the Schubert became a passing irrelevance.

'We must meet again,' were her parting words. 'I'm free tomorrow at lunchtime. Let's meet at the coffee shop in the Fielderstrasse.' She then vanished from the box.

'I'm not sure about you, Ethel, but I don't think I'm interested in seeing her again. Are you?'

'Of course,' said Ethel. 'You never know where a new relationship with someone who has the past of such an incredible woman may take you.'

Lunchtime came. Ethel sat by the shop's window and ordered a coffee. As usual, it looked like coffee but was weak and almost flavourless. She sat there waiting for more than an hour. She had finished her second cup and was about to pay the waiter when Livia appeared at her table.

'I'm so sorry, Ethel. It was Ethel, wasn't it? I completely forgot until about fifteen minutes ago. But here I am now. Many apologies again. Let's have something to eat.'

The two of them sat there and told each other about their respective lives.

'I'm so impressed that you have fulfilled your ambitions to come to Leipzig, Ethel. You have seriously beaten the odds against you!'

Ethel could not help adoring this much older lady for whom she felt a wish to protect despite learning she was married, was profoundly wealthy and probably commanded the respect and admiration of old and young alike.

'Are you a religious person, Ethel?'

'I was brought up in the Church of England so I respect the Church and what it stands for, but I'm not a deeply religious person and have difficulties with the faith which comes so naturally to many others.'

'Astonishing, Ethel! It was surely by the influence of God that you found your way here.'

Ethel admired her simple approach to religion, especially when compared with the gushing, highly demonstrative type often seen in those parts of Germany. Livia was essentially a simple woman who, for example, decided not go to a Wagner opera because she wanted to be musically pure in the sense that her beloved friend Mendelssohn's music was pure, even if it was being displaced by the music of the new and rising Brahms, as well as 'that man Wagner', as she described him.

Ethel found it flattering, if not entirely comprehendible that these older women, although knowing her only a little, invited her into their homes. Livia Frege fitted well into this pre-cast mould. A few days later, Ethel found herself in the Freges' house, listening excitedly to a new quartet of young musicians playing a piece which one of them had composed.

'You must meet my young friend, Lili, Ethel,' said Livia, after the quartet had finished playing. 'She is too modest to tell you she is Felix Mendelssohn's youngest daughter.'

Ethel immediately discovered a soul mate. Not that Lili Wach was a composer, but that she possessed an unerring calmness and a delightful, outgoing personality. For a person compelled to carry the burden of a famous father on her slim shoulders, she was incredibly normal.

'And now I want to introduce you to Elizabeth von Herzogenberg. You will love each other, Ethel and Lisl. You both have an intense love of music.'

The polite greetings dealt with, Ethel asked a question.

'I gather you are a friend of Johannes Brahms?'

'I am, in fact. I know him well,' she said, coolly and displaying not the slightest trace of emotion. It was as if she was being interrogated by a tax official.

'I was utterly smitten by that wonderful performance of his second symphony the other night. It is an amazing work. I was less sure about the master's conducting, but it was received well. Especially for a work not performed here before.'

'I see,' said Lisl, with a neutral, almost dismissive expression.

'Yes, I thought it a brilliant work. It inspired me to write something as stunning as that myself.'

'Oh, really.'

Realising that she was failing in her efforts to converse with Lisl, Ethel took a different line of questioning. 'Were you ever a student yourself?'

'In fact, I was. I studied with Brahms for a time.'

'You are a composer then?' said Ethel, smiling widely.

'Not really.'

Again a minimal answer that left no clue where Ethel should go next in her exploration of this so-called paragon of womanhood.

'Well, it was good to meet you and I hope we meet again at some point,' said Ethel, giving up on the conversation. She turned to the members of the quartet and talked to them about what they had just played.

That night, lying in bed, Ethel could not stop thinking about Elizabeth - Lisl - von Herzogenberg. The woman interested Ethel enormously. Her fine-cut features which were quite stark, sculptured almost, and her remoteness appealed to Ethel in a way she found unusual. Her almost complete reluctance to engage in conversation puzzled Ethel. Could it be that she was simply shy and unable to talk to people she had only just met? Or could this be the manifestation of an underlying personality issue, caused by some unfortunate past encounter? Her immediate ambition was to see the woman again and to penetrate the armour of mystery that encased her. Perhaps George Henschel or Livia Frege could help.

She had known George for much longer than Livia and thought he might understand her request better. The easier route would be via Livia because she knew where she lived. Despite this, she persisted with her aim of asking George. Her first task was to find him. She did not know his address. She knew he was in contact with Professor Reinecke so, after yet another of his almost pointless lessons, asked him a favour.

'You may or may not know, Professor, that I am a friend of George Henschel, the famous singer. We holidayed together in the summer, before I enrolled at the Conservatorium. He told me not a week ago that he was working with you on a forthcoming concert. Could you please help me with a huge favour?'

'Come on, dear girl, out with it!'

'Could you please ask him to contact me? I want him to help me arrange a meeting with someone whom I understand is a friend of his.'

'Can I ask who that friend may be?'

'It is a woman by the name of Elizabeth von Herzogenberg. I'm sure George Henschel mentioned her to me.'

'May I ask why you wish to meet her?'

Ethel hesitated, only because she felt disinclined to confess she had, on first encounter, all but fallen in love with this goddess of a woman.

'I understand she is a wonderful musician, and I simply wanted to make her acquaintance.'

'I don't see why I should help you. You are merely a student and have no right to move in such circles.'

'I thought we students were here to learn from people we admired and could help us in our endeavours, independently of social standing. I merely thought that it would be useful to meet her. If you will not help, I'll locate George Henschel. I'm confident he will help if he can.' Ethel turned towards the classroom door.

'Wait a moment, Ethel. It is Ethel, isn't it? I'm seeing Heinrich von Herzogenberg in a day or two. I'll ask him to pass your message on to his wife.'

Ethel was stunned by this sudden change of attitude. 'Professor, I'm so grateful. How will I know whether she will meet me?'

'I'll see you in class and tell you then,' he smiled, realising that he had corrected a mistake that could have affected his reputation as a teacher.

***

Ethel needed to economise. Although the tickets for concerts at the Gewandhaus were free to her and Theresia, the meals out and the drinks, aside from the cabriolet fares, were putting a strain on her budget. She had no capacity to earn her own money so thought about how to reduce her expenditure, perhaps by finding a single room and forgoing the luxury of full access to her lodgings and all meals, as provided at Frau Professor Heimbach's. After taking coffee at the Frau Dr Brockhaus's one morning, and as she walked to the Conservatorium, she noticed a sign in the window of one of the Frau Dr's neighbours, a French-looking house Ethel had frequently admired, advertising a vacant room. She made immediate enquires and within two days, much to the Frau Professor's disappointment, had moved into her new lodgings in the Salomonstrasse. The two rooms with a piano were a form of heaven.

The arrangements she agreed with her new landlady, Frau Brandt, were unusual. She would always have her evening meal at her own dining table, but at lunchtime she would eat at the Conservatorium, at a restaurant or with her landlady, depending what suited the two of them on the day. As for her evening meal, Ethel would buy a quarter of a pound of ham and some butter which she would store in a larder, which was a birdcage she had attached to the sloping roof outside her window. One day she saw a robin fly up to it but go away again, probably realising it was a form of prison. Ethel would often come home late. Because the gate to the property was closed at 11 o'clock, she would have to scale a fence at the back, climb up the sloping roof and enter her room through the window, an interesting sight to any passing policeman.

True to his word, Professor Reinecke spoke to Herr von Herzogenberg about Ethel's wish to see his wife and, within days, reported back to Ethel who, that afternoon, waited patiently in his class for him to finish.

'I have some news for you, Ethel. Elizabeth von Herzogenberg will see you. She wants you to go to their house in the Humboldt Strasse for coffee tomorrow morning. She has another meeting but can spare you the time for a coffee but little more. I told her you had no lessons tomorrow, not that I was aware of.'

'I'm so pleased, I could kiss you. But perhaps I shouldn't.'

They both laughed at Ethel's spontaneous response.

The Herzogenberg's house, at the top of a small hill, dominated leafy grounds of such beauty they could only have been designed by a knowledgeable and expert gardener. The hedges were trimmed to mathematical precision and the shrubs and trees planted in military order. Ethel stopped at the foot of the drive simply to admire the geometrical symmetry. She pulled the bell chord by the door. Seconds later, Elizabeth von Herzogenberg herself opened it and invited Ethel inside.

'I believe we have met before,' she said, smiling with her intense greenish-brown eyes. 'Come through to our drawing-room and I will arrange for us to have some coffee. Maybe, an Englishwoman would prefer tea!' Her effusive welcome contrasted strongly with the frosty encounter at the Freges'.

'Please, could I have a coffee? Yes, we met at Livia Frege's house about four days ago.'

'Of course,' she said, lifting her head to reveal perfectly white neck, just like an egret's. She invited Ethel to sit on a settee, picked up a bell from a small table and gently rang it. As if she had been waiting outside, a woman with a white cap appeared to take the coffee order. 'That piece by the quartet was not brilliant, but they played it with gusto. Don't you think?'

'I quite enjoyed it, too. But as you say, it was hardly inspiring.'

'Before we go further, please call me Lisl and I'll call you Ethel. All right?'

'That's fine! I'd umm... appreciate that,' said Ethel, as usual beginning awkwardly and nervously while in close proximity to women to whom she had taken a fancy.

'So where are you from in England? And tell me about your family and why you have come to Leipzig,' she said, adjusting her position next to Ethel on the settee and in doing so wafting some perfume in Ethel's direction.

The maidservant placed their drinks on a small coffee table while Ethel answered Lisl's questions.

'So you are learning to become a composer under the tutelage of Professor Carl Reinecke and others at our Conservatorium. Is the teaching up to your needs?'

Ethel took this as a loaded question to which she needed a circumspect reply. 'The professors are excellent musicians. There is no doubt about it. But I am having difficulty attracting their attention. I'd like them to have a close look at the compositions I've written.'

'We should let my husband know. As you know, he is a friend of Carl Reinecke. So you have written a number of works then.'

Ethel gave her account of what she had written.

'I do some composing, too, but mainly for children and I transpose pieces for my husband and I to play on our piano. My husband is a much better composer than me. I'll show you a recent piece I've worked on.'

She stood up and walked over to a neat pile of music on top of the grand piano on the far side of the room. As she returned with a sheaf of music, Ethel noticed she stooped slightly, but gracefully, almost as if to reduce the effect of her height and to lower herself to Ethel's level. She sat next to Ethel and showed her the first page.

'This is Brahms' second symphony arranged for piano duet.'

'Did he lend you the score?'

'Yes, but after I wrote this.'

'Do you mean to say you committed the symphony to memory and wrote this when you returned home from the concert?'

'Something like that. I wrote it over about three days. It's quite an easy symphony to reproduce because many of the themes are related to each other.'

'I'm absolutely staggered. I've never come across anyone with such amazing musical ability. You are a musical genius!'

'Please don't flatter me! Let me play some of it to you. You can see if you recognise it. I must improvise because Heinrich isn't here!'

Lisl went back to the piano, shuffled herself on the stool and looked around at Ethel. 'Ready?' she said and started.

Ethel immediately recognised the undulating horn theme at the beginning of the symphony. She sat back on the settee and allowed Lisl's playing to envelop her. She stopped before the recapitulation, raising her hands in the air, as if she was the soloist at a concert, which to some extent she was.

'That was incredible, Lisl. It was as if I was playing the symphony in my head and you reminding me of it as you played. I've never had such a musical experience before. I am truly amazed at your musicianship. You have a natural ability, but to harness it as you have is astonishing! Where did you learn or are you self-taught?'

'I couldn't learn these modest skills without much help and practice.'

'So where did you learn?'

'In Vienna… under the master himself, in '64. But I became very sad when he dropped me and passed me, like a left-over piece of sausage, to Julius Epstein. Johannes confessed only three or four years ago that he did that because he was afraid of falling in love with me. He had problems before with some women… and didn't want another relationship to end in disappointment...'

'Sorry to hear that.'

'Don't be. Please. I learnt a great deal from each of them. The next thing, Ethel, is to meet my husband Heinrich. You will love him. He is your type of man. I can tell because of your love of music and your aim to be a composer. He is quite a well-known composer here and has great skills as an instrumentalist as well.'

'I'd love to meet him. But I could not love him more than you love him!'

'I shall see to that,' said Lisl, smiling. 'I heard the front door close a quarter of an hour ago, so he's probably back from his appointment. Let's see.'

Heinrich von Herzogenberg looked to be a few years older than his wife, possibly because of his luxuriant growth of beard and his Bohemian style hair, tied in a braid which extended midway down his back. He wore a *pince-nez*.

'My wife said you'd be here today. I'm so pleased to meet you. A fellow composer, I gather,' were his delightful first few sentences, which contrasted sharply with his wife's initial reticence. Ethel could instantly feel she would like him.

'Yes, but I am nothing more than a beginner at this craft of composing,' said Ethel with surprising modesty. 'You are well known in this field!'

'Only locally. I've yet to reach the international scene, if I ever do,' he said, with a broad smile and eyebrows raised. It was as if he above all others knew the limitations of his talents.

'Ethel tells me that the professors at the Conservatorium are not interested in her works and just refuse to read them or play them. She is quite disappointed,' said Lisl.

'If Lisl agrees, I'd like you to return to see us tomorrow, at about the same time. But bring some of your compositions with you, and we can go through them together. I may be able to help you… at least to supplement what they are doing!'

Once again, Ethel's excitement about the following day's events damaged what could have been a good night's sleep. She contemplated a deep and lasting friendship with this woman of incredible talent and beauty, the likes of which she had never encountered before. She could also see some strong possibilities for befriending Heinrich, from whom she might actually learn something about composing. As agreed, she arrived their house in the Humboldt Strasse at exactly 10 o'clock, carrying a large bag of her music.

'Let's sit in the drawing-room by the piano,' said Heinrich. 'Which of your works would you like me to look at first?'

'Could we look at my second piano sonata?' Ethel dug into the bag for the score which she had put in a labelled folder. 'Here it is.'

Heinrich, sitting at the piano with Ethel by his side, opened the file and started to read it. He moved his hand to the rhythm Ethel had shown on the first page. Ethel could detect that he was playing it in his mind.

'Well, that's the first movement,' he said. 'Ethel, you are a talented and real composer. You have great potential in this field. Have your professors seen this sonata?'

'Yes, but they haven't given me their views, so I don't know what they think about it.'

'I have to tell you though, it's full of errors, some bigger than others. Some scream out loud, a bit like a frightened magpie!' he said, making light of her mistakes.

Lisl then appeared. 'So how are you two progressing?' She smiled, quite enjoying the fact that Heinrich was giving Ethel a private tutorial.

'Very well, my sweet. Ethel has written this wonderful piano sonata. However, I have detected some errors which her professors failed to point out and I was going to share with you an idea which has only just occurred to me.'

'Go on,' she said.

'Ethel is learning virtually nothing at the Conservatorium. They are not teaching her. They are certainly not correcting any of her errors. Frankly, I'm not surprised. Their reputation has dropped recently. Several people have told me so. The problem is that they are not full-time teachers. Reinecke is the chief conductor of the Gewandhaus… Judassohn is a composer… Maas is a professional pianist. So they don't have the time for the likes of Ethel.'

'So what's your idea, my love?'

'To become Ethel's teacher myself!'

'But you hardly know me, Herr Herzogenberg. We only met yesterday!'

'Please call me Heinrich! That doesn't matter. You have passed your entrance exam through your piano sonata... and I admire your ambition to become a professional composer.'

Turning to Lisl, he dropped in another surprise. 'Also, my sweet, you often complain at your lack of knowledge of counterpoint and the writing of fugues, so I will teach you and Ethel at the same time. I will be teaching myself to teach as we go along!'

Ethel immediately agreed with this extraordinary and unexpected proposal. She could not believe her luck. She thought Heinrich might give her some tips after reading a score or two, but for him to offer to become her 'professor' was a total surprise. He had handled the suggestion well with Lisl. He would avoid any marital jealousies by involving her in the lessons, too. Lisl readily agreed. Clever man.

'I still can't believe you have made this wonderful offer, Heinrich. I insist I pay you, if only to preserve my honour.'

'Let's not worry about such things, Ethel. At least not for now. Maybe later. There are things to arrange such as a mutually agreeable timetable!'

They needed to work out a schedule. There were three of them to please, so inevitably it stretched all three to confirm some dates.

'It's only Mondays when all three of us are free,' said Lisl. 'So as Ethel is clear then and Wednesdays, let's settle on those two days. I will try to make myself available on Wednesdays, if I can. If not, you two go ahead without me.'

'Yes,' said Ethel. 'I still have a commitment to the Conservatorium so my dates should fit in with my classes.'

'Try a few of my lessons before you stop attending the Conservatorium. I can understand you putting me on trial. I just hope you don't find me guilty and give me the death sentence!'

Ethel pondered for a few seconds. 'No. I just won't attend again, not regularly. I've paid until the end of the summer term and I'll formally leave then. So a trial will be unnecessary!'

Within a few days, Ethel began with her new teacher. It was a strange start as Heinrich gave just Ethel a lesson in musical appreciation.

'How familiar are you with the works of J. S. Bach?'

'Not at all. I've not heard any and I've not studied any Bach scores.'

'You won't know that about three years ago, my friend Philipp Spitta and I founded the Bach Society in Leipzig. Did none of your professors mention Bach?'

'No. Not one of them.'

'We must introduce you to him. We will use many pieces of his music in our lessons, so it is important that you become familiar with some of his works. The first step is to enrol you in the Society. Lisl is a member, so it's not just men who join.'

'Why did you set it up?'

'Philipp is an expert on Bach and felt that with the emergence of modern composers like Schumann, Mendelssohn and our dear Brahms, Bach's music, in particular his cantatas, was becoming neglected. It seems to have paid dividends because in Leipzig at least he is becoming more popular.'

The following weeks of lessons were far more conventional, as she expected. Both Ethel and Lisl attended and learned the intricacies of counterpoint, mainly from the works of Bach, and how to avoid simple errors. They learnt that 'Three Blind Mice' and 'Frere Jacque' were an accidental two voice counterpoint and that the final bars of Mozart's Symphony No. 41 was an example of a five voice combination that Heinrich admired greatly.

After about six months of enjoying and learning immensely from Heinrich's lessons and deepening her relationship with Lisl, Ethel and Lisl attended the birthday party of one of Lisl's female friends. While holding a glass of beer, Ethel collapsed onto the floor, dropped the glass and severely dampened the host's carpet.

'My God, Ethel. Whatever is the matter?' said a panicking Lisl who knelt beside her, only to wet her dress in the spilt beer. Within a few moments Ethel came to.

'Where am I? What's happening?'

'You passed out, Ethel. I'm calling a cabriolet to take you home. Tell me your address,' said Lisl.

Ethel could just about tell her. Within half an hour, Lisl was helping Ethel up the rickety stairs into Frau Brandt's house and Ethel's rooms. Poor Ethel was suffering from a severe illness, probably a nervous breakdown, brought about by overwork, her unrequited love for Lisl and probably a degree of unexpressed homesickness. Lisl and Heinrich were about to leave Leipzig for a holiday, but on the insistence of Lisl, they delayed it, at least until Ethel had recovered sufficiently to be safely left.

Despite not being very well, the following two weeks counted among the most delightful of Ethel's entire life. Ethel realised that Lisl, while keeping her feelings to herself, had fallen in love with Ethel, at least in the way a mother loves her child, and quite possibly deeper. Every morning at eight o'clock, Ethel would hear Lisl climbing the stairs to the house. She would wait in anticipation until Lisl entered her bedroom.

'Good morning, Ethel. How are you today?' she would say, as part of this delightful routine.

Ethel would reply that, although not fully recovered, she felt somewhat better.

'I have brought you some breakfast,' she said, on the first day of Ethel's confinement to bed. 'Here is some soft white bread, some mild cheese and a few slices of ham. I thought we would have our breakfast together. I hope you feel like eating!'

'You are so kind, Lisl. I didn't expect such wonderful nursing.'

'I'm here to help you conquer this, Ethel. I cannot rest until you are properly recovered. You are my child and I shall mother you.'

At about midday, somebody knocked on the front door.

'Who's that?' said Ethel. 'Frau Brandt is at her sister's today and won't be home until later.'

'I'm sure I know,' said Lisl. 'It's probably one of my maidservants. I asked her to bring us a little lunch.'

'You think of everything, my dear friend!' said Ethel, still lying in bed.

Lisl opened the door to her maid and brought her in. Ethel recognised her immediately and thanked her. The two of them ate their lunch together while the maid looked on. After they had eaten, Lisl gave the maid an instruction.

'I want you to go to the kitchen and bring me a bowl of hot water.'

A few minutes later she returned and placed the bowl on a table.

'Now go outside and wait outside the bedroom door.' She went and closed the door behind her. 'Now climb out of bed and take off your nightdress, Ethel.'

Ethel did as Lisl told her and sat on the edge of the bed.

'I'm going to wash you. Please pass me that flannel and stand up.'

Lisl dipped the flannel into the water and rang out the excess before washing Ethel. She started with her face and neck and gradually worked her way down Ethel's body via her breasts and down to her intimate area which, without inhibition, she also washed. She then worked her way down from her thighs to her feet.

'Now turn around, Ethel.'

She then washed Ethel's back and bottom. Ethel could not believe this beautiful woman was treating her with such tenderness, care and feeling. She was enraptured by what Lisl was doing. She then took one of Ethel's towels and gently dried her entire body.

'Now you can climb back into bed and rest, Ethel. How are you feeling?'

'Much refreshed, in fact. I just feel cold and shivery.'

'I can help you with that.' Lisl undid the buttons on her dress and eased herself out of it. Ethel watched, her eyes wide open and her lips apart. Still not fully better, she felt a shiver of excitement. Lisl stepped towards a chair and placed her dress over it. Ethel could smell her womanly perfumes. Lisl then undid her corset. She placed it on the chair over her dress and climbed completely undressed into bed next to Ethel. 'Cuddle into me and you will soon warm up.'

The bed was not wide, so Lisl moved herself onto her side, facing Ethel in order to remain in it. Ethel did likewise, so she faced Lisl and each pulled the bedclothes over themselves. Lisl gently pulled Ethel towards her so their bodies were in close contact.

'There. Is that better?' said Lisl.

'Not just yet, Lisl, but I can feel your body heat. You are so generous to help me in this way.' That this paragon of a woman was lying naked in the bed and pressing her body up to hers was unbelievable. She could feel her excitement growing. She placed a kiss on Lisl's lips. Her exhilaration raised itself to a frenzy. Then a shudder went through her body. It left her breathless.

'What was that, Lisl? I nearly passed out,' she said, shocked at how her body had reacted.

'It's perfectly natural, Ethel. You are not used to being so close to an unclothed woman.'

Within about ten more minutes, Ethel fell asleep. Lisl could feel that she was much warmer so, trying not to disturb Ethel, eased herself out of the bed and pulled the covers back over her. She then put her clothes back on, opened the door and closed it behind her.

'Is everything all right, madam,' said the maid. 'I thought I could hear your friend crying out.'

'Everything is fine. I can assure you. She is sleeping now. I'll open the door and you can take the bowl of water to the kitchen. Let's try not to wake her. Then you can go back to our house.'

The maid left and Lisl returned to sit in a chair next to Ethel. She picked up a book next to Ethel's bed and read. About an hour later, Ethel woke up.

'You are still here, Lisl. I've never known anyone as kind as you. You should go home. I am warm now and rested.'

'I am mothering you, Ethel! I will stay until your landlady returns. Then I'll go, but I'll return tomorrow at the same time, eight o'clock.'

Each day, for the two weeks, followed a similar pattern. As she promised, Lisl would arrive at the agreed time with a modest breakfast. Her maid would arrive at about midday with something for lunch. While Lisl undressed Ethel and washed Ethel, she would stand guard outside. Lisl would fuss over Ethel, tucking her in bed and making sure she was comfortable. She would read to Ethel or sing to her. Much to Ethel's delight, she even sang some of Ethel's own songs to her, reading directly from the sheet music. The high point was Lisl playing her piano transcription of Brahms second symphony.

'This is stunning,' said Ethel. 'I recognised it straightaway from when you played it before. I'm right, Lisl. You are a musical genius.'

# CHAPTER 9

## Back Home

After that fortnight of Lisl's tender nursing, Ethel recovered sufficiently for Lisl and Heinrich to depart for their holiday in Austria. So upset at the departure of her new and fondest love, Ethel cried herself to sleep every night for a week. The only compensation was the constant stream of postcards, boxes of chocolates, books and flowers delivered to Frau Brandt's house. A token of Lisl's love arrived every single day. The disappointment was that Ethel could not return her love for Lisl: she didn't know where she was staying.

The postman delivered one letter after another, each declaring eternal love for Ethel. One recalled the delight she had shared in Ethel's presence over the fortnight of her illness, and the undeserving way she had calmly accepted the thanks that 'poured from your mouth'. Another that they would 'belong together inseparably' and regretting her initial reluctance to engage with the charming Ethel.

In the middle of June, Ethel began the journey home to England. She had bought the tickets well in advance, so Lisl knew the timetable for the journey. Telegrams, letters and yet more postcards bombarded Ethel at virtually all the intervening stations.

She almost missed her train at the inter-change she made in Cologne. As her train was about to depart for Calais, she realised she was waiting on the wrong platform. She rushed over the bridge and scrambled aboard just moments before it departed. The train started to creep away as she shoved her way into a compartment adjacent to a corridor, only to discover it was occupied by a stout, clean-shaven gentleman, with baggy trousers and an oversized collar, sitting next to the window on the far side. He was much older than her, about fifty she guessed.

Ethel let out an 'Oh!' not expecting to see anyone. 'Do you mind if I join you, sir?' Not that he had a choice, as she was already dumping her case and two bags onto the luggage rack.

'Not at all. I'd be pleased if you did,' he said, in a strong accent which Ethel recognised as Austrian.

They sat in silence for a good hour while Ethel read a book which Lisl had sent her. Ethel, also sitting facing the engine, glanced across to what the gentleman was reading. Her eyes almost jumped from her head as she noticed it was a hand-written musical score. Moments later, he took a pencil from his jacket and put some marks on it.

Ethel looked away. Then paused for a few minutes. She could not contain her curiosity for any longer.

'I see you are working on a score, sir.'

'Yes, I am.'

'May I ask you, what is the piece?'

'It's my fifth symphony. I am revising it, quite substantially.'

'Has it been performed?'

'I pray it will but no, not yet.'

'Have any of your other symphonies been performed?' By then, Ethel was becoming utterly fascinated by the untidy-looking composer.

'It's a coincidence that you ask because my fourth was performed for the first time in Vienna only two weeks ago!'

'That's amazing. Congratulations!'

'I'm obliged,' he said, looking her straight in the eye.

'I am a composer, too,' she said, thrusting her chest forward and smiling all over her face.

The man smiled back. 'A woman composer? Really?'

'Definitely, I have been studying composition under Carl Reinecke at the Leipzig Conservatorium. Do you know him?'

'I know of him. But I've never met him.'

'Are you a professional composer or an amateur?'

'I call myself a professional because it is the only way I earn a living. Well, not quite. I also do some teaching.'

'We should introduce each other. My name is Ethel Smyth. I'm from London.'

'My name is Bruckner... Anton Bruckner.'

Her mouth fell open as she stared unto his eyes. Two seconds elapsed before she spoke. 'Anton Bruckner?'

'Yes.'

'I've met your niece at the Conservatorium!'

'What, Theresia? I know she is there, and I'm so pleased you know her! That is good news. Music to my ears, if you'll excuse the pun!'

'Yes, we've become good friends. We've been to concerts together and had many meals together in the refectory. We've also been exploring the city... so where are you heading, Herr Bruckner?'

'London. I'm playing the organ at the Royal Albert Hall and at The Crystal Palace.'

'I must come to listen to you.'

'I'd be delighted, Miss Smyth. You will enjoy it, I'm sure. I believe Queen Victoria will be at my Albert Hall recital.'

'I'll try to go to that one!'

So this extraordinary conversation continued. Ethel told Bruckner about her childhood, her ambitions to be taught at the Conservatorium, her compositions and her lessons with the Herzogenbergs. He told her about his childhood, his work at St Florian and his composing. He said by coincidence he was a professor at the Vienna Conservatorium. Before they left the train at Waterloo Station, they exchanged addresses and Herr Bruckner gave her the dates of his concerts in London.

Her joyful welcome home enthralled Ethel. Mother exploded into a flood of tears at the sight of her standing on the doorstep. Even her father was pleased to see her. Nina, Violet and Nelly helped take her things up to her room. The bitter feuding and arguing before she went appeared to be over.

'I have missed you so much, my dear Ethel,' said her mother, wiping her eyes with her handkerchief. 'I'm so glad you took time to write to me. I will cherish those letters forever!'

'How did the allowance work out?' said the General, as they sat around the dining room table.

'You will be pleased to know, Papa, I even have a few pounds left of what you gave me. Because I needed to economise, I changed to some cheaper lodgings and cut down on meals out, but I managed within your budget. I cannot thank you and Mama enough for funding me.'

'In your latest letter, you said you had been quite ill, Ethel. How are you now? You must be much better to travel here from Leipzig.'

'I'm fully recovered now, Mama. It's because of the nursing I received from my friend Lisl.'

'You must tell us about all the people you met out there, Ethel.'

'My only regret is that I signed an oath with my doctor that I won't play tennis, skate or do anything at all strenuous over the holiday.'

'You can probably ignore that. You seem in excellent spirits to me!' said the General.

So Ethel ignored the document she had signed with Dr Langbein and Lisl and began to ride, play tennis, dance and go hunting again. Her favourite sporting pastime was to climb up on her treasured mount, Phyllis, and ride her hard over the local downs. She loved this little filly, despite the fact that one day she threw Ethel at a hedge she refused to jump. Ethel got up, brushed herself down and, having gently told her not to do that again, rode her back to their stables and gave her a good feed.

Ethel made a point of visiting many of her old friends and saw her sisters Alice and Mary, by then settled into comfortable and affluent married lives.

She spent many happy hours playing the piano to her family, often playing her own songs and encouraging them to sing along to the words which Ethel had diligently written out on various bits of paper. She even played them some works by Brahms, Schubert and Beethoven. Hammered out in her usual style of hitting the keys.

After six weeks, the joy of being home faded. Her mother became quite jealous of the stream of letters, at least one of which arrived every day. While Ethel didn't read them out in full and kept a number solely to herself, her mother objected to Ethel taking instruction from Lisl.

'I am so glad you have found such a deep friendship in this Lisl,' she said one morning at breakfast, just after the postman delivered two more of Lisl's missives. 'But you seem to follow her instructions almost to the letter. You are on your vacation yet you are spending hours and whole days in your room composing and writing poems. Just what she has told you to do. You can finish writing your Variations when you return to the Conservatorium.' Ethel could not possibly tell them she'd resigned.

'I'm not sure how to answer that, Mama. Please understand that I am doing these things because I want to. If I didn't, I wouldn't do them. She's also told me not to do sport but I'm riding, hunting, playing tennis or rackets. Have I satisfied you?'

'Hmm. I'm still not sure and can't say I'm especially happy with the situation.'

A few days later, her father had an announcement to make. 'We are living beyond our means and, if Ethel is to return to Leipzig, we must economise.'

'Why discuss such things in front of all the family when you are directing them solely to me?' her mother shouted. 'I'm the only one who can economise and I will. Ethel must return to complete her studies. If that means we all have to live on cabbage soup, that's fine by me!'

'Calm down, my dear. You are talking in extremes. But we must learn to live with the furnishings we have and not change them at a whim.'

Mrs Smyth slammed her breakfast plate so hard on the table it broke into a dozen pieces. She sped from the room and slammed the door behind her. The General picked up his Times and continued reading.

Such an atmosphere made Ethel ache to return to Leipzig. Family life was becoming far more stressful than anything which happened in Germany. She left home with the completed Variations under her arm.

# CHAPTER 10

## Brahms

Ethel woke up early after her first night back in Leipzig. She wanted to see Lisl as soon as possible. She was dying to deliver a kiss to the gorgeous lips of the goddess. Immediately after dressing, she climbed down the rickety stairs out into the road and walked to the Herzogenberg's.

'My God, it's you, Ethel!' said a startled Lisl, as she opened the door to the unexpected guest. The colour instantly drained from Lisl's face, as if she had just seen Banquo's ghost. She staggered and almost collapsed on the doorstep. Ethel wondered if this was a symptom of a heart problem that Ethel was aware of. She quickly recovered, put her arms around Ethel and gave her the most passionate kiss. It was as if the two loving friends had been compulsorily separated for years rather than the few months of the summer vacation.

Ethel wasn't expecting such a physical reunion. 'Careful, Lisl! I've brought the score of my Variations. You're crushing it!'

'Oh, I'm sorry, Ethel. I'm simply overwhelmed to see you again. It seems so long, even considering the many letters we have written to each other. You must come in. We are about to have breakfast. You must join us!'

Heinrich was equally shocked to see Ethel, if less effusive in his greeting. It was difficult to know whether he fully subscribed to his wife's loving relationship with their young student. There was nothing to show that he didn't. Perhaps he also saw Ethel as the child that, between him and Lisl, they could not create.

'I must see your Variations, Ethel,' he said. 'Straight after breakfast.'

He sat at the piano and played the eight individual parts, one after the other. 'What a marvellous job you have made of these. We will work through them and I will suggest some minor changes, but they are a delight. I especially like number five, the one you have called Phyllis. Not another of your lady friends!'

Ethel laughed. 'No! Phyllis is my pet filly at home. She's as frisky as a gazelle in spring. Once she threw me over a fence, but I'm sure she was very sorry she did!'

'We have a little project for you,' said Lisl. 'It is to copy out one of Brahms' latest compositions… his Capriccio, Opus 76 Number 2. You will love it. He played it to us a few weeks ago, and I so liked it, he lent me the score. He has to send it to his publisher, and I'd like a copy. Would you do that, please?'

'Of course. Anything for you, Lisl. Give me some music paper, some ink and a pen and I'll start it straightaway.'

So no sooner than she returned, she was back in the thick of the music the three of them shared and would continue sharing. What could possibly go wrong? Within two days, Ethel had made a flawless job of the copying and Lisl sent the original back to Johannes Brahms with a note saying how she continued to enjoy the piece and that Ethel Smyth, whom he had already met, also enjoyed it. She sent him Ethel's compliments and good wishes. Lisl wrote frequently to Brahms and often sent Ethel's regards, which were often acknowledged. She didn't know whether to laugh or cry one day, when Lisl gave Ethel a piece of paper with his autograph inscribed upon it, which Brahms had specially written for Ethel. She treasured it for years; until she lost it.

Ethel continued to enjoy her lessons with Heinrich and enjoyed the company of his wife, whom she worshipped. She soon found her way back into the routine of being tutored through listening to pieces Heinrich played and testing herself through completing various exercises he set.

Less than a week after Ethel's return, and just before the day's lessons began, Lisl and Heinrich wanted to tell her something important.

'Ethel, Lisl and I have been thinking,' said Heinrich. 'Sometimes we finish our lessons so late in the day, it seems far too much to expect you to walk back to your lodgings, so we've come up with an idea. We would like to lend you a room upstairs that you can call your own as long as you want to use it. It's already furnished. There is a bed and an armchair, a smaller chair and a wardrobe, as well as a washbasin. And our maid will look after it for you. What do you think?'

She was so grateful, she hardly knew what to say. The real comfort she took from this immense generosity towards her was that Heinrich was so keen on the idea. She had until then wondered how he saw her relationship with his wife. So they were offering their adopted 'daughter' the opportunity to be more closely integrated into their family.

'I am really touched that you are making me so welcome in your lovely home. I'm delighted to accept your amazing generosity. Now I can work harder and longer. I insist on making a payment.'

'You will do no such thing, Ethel,' said Heinrich. 'It is partly us being selfish. While you are here, we won't worry about you having to face the dangers of walking home.'

Ethel spent her second Christmas in Leipzig, not with the Brockhauses but with the Herzogenbergs, and thoroughly enjoyed the fun. She provided much of the entertainment and much of the noise, singing at the top of her voice and hammering away at their piano, accompanying her own music, Heinrich's and some of Lisl's. They each had a session of playing Brahms' Capriccio No. 2, but Ethel played it fastest and loudest and laughed all the way through it. Then, on the day after Boxing Day, Lisl made an announcement.

'I should have told you, Ethel, that Johannes is coming today. He will be here into the New Year. He is conducting the first performance of his Violin Concerto at the Gewandhaus on New Year's Day. It will be quite an event.'

Not an hour later, the doorbell rang. Lisl went to open it, with Ethel on her trail.

'It's you, Johannes. I wasn't expecting you yet.'

'The train was early, so I thought I'd come straight here. I hope that's all right, Lisl.' She looked a little irritated but could hardly turn him away.

'Of course, Johannes. We are more than pleased to see you. Where is your luggage?'

'Just inside the gate at the end of the drive.'

'I'll ask Maxim to bring it in. Is there anything I can prepare for you now?'

'I'd love one of your ham rolls and a glass of beer. Is that all right? Do I recognise your assistant?' he said, smiling and looking at Ethel.

'You should. She is our fellow composer, Ethel Smyth from England.'

'Oh yes, with the counterpoint problems!'

'Not now! Heinrich has been teaching counterpoint to Ethel and me for a good few months now. She is becoming very good at it!'

'I'll have to test her myself!'

'Ethel will take you through to the drawing-room while I prepare you a ham roll.'

Ethel led the way and invited Brahms to sit on one of the sofas. She didn't quite know what to say to this acclaimed musical genius, so said nothing, hoping he would speak first. He didn't say a word to Ethel and spoke only when Lisl appeared carrying a tray which she handed to him.

'Lisl, you are a faultless delight. I asked only for one roll and you have brought me two. The ham is pouring out of them. And a lovely large beer!'

'You constantly flatter me, Johannes. We are longing to hear your Violin Concerto, aren't we, Ethel?' It was as if she had noticed his silence, while in the kitchen, and wanted to bring Ethel into the conversation.

'Yes, if it is as brilliant as your second symphony, it will be a real treat. What else will be on the programme?'

'So you want something other than my concerto, do you? Hmm! You've touched a nerve there, my girl. Joaquin has been a pest about that. You won't believe this, Lisl,' he said, redirecting the conversation her way. 'He insists he should play that damned violin concerto by Beethoven before mine. All right, it's brilliant, but why play it against mine? The man's an egotist. He just wants to show off playing the Beethoven. I had the devil's own job to persuade him to play mine. He wanted this changed and that changed. He said he wouldn't play it otherwise. And I've dedicated the blasted thing to him. It should have been to you, Lisl! You'd have deserved it more!'

Lisl didn't know what to say. She paused for a few minutes. 'Ethel, you mustn't breathe a word about this conversation… not to a soul. Understand?'

'Of course!'

'At least your concerto will end the programme, Johannes, and that will be the work everyone will remember,' Lisl said. 'I'm afraid you'll have to live with that now. And Joseph is a good friend of yours, remember. Is Reinecke conducting?'

'No. I am.'

'We shall enjoy it that much more then,' said Lisl.

'So where is Heinrich this morning, Lisl? Is he still churning out those pieces fit only for deaf, old widows to listen to?'

'You've got a nerve. My dear husband is a good and competent composer. He may not have reached the heights of fame that you have, but if that sort of remark is the price, I'd rather he didn't.' She promptly burst into a flood of tears.

Brahms was on the verge of crying himself, realising what a clumsy, insensitive remark he had made. He went over to Lisl and prostrated himself at her knee. 'I'm sorry, Lisl. That was evil of me. Your man is an excellent composer and deserves some fame. I deeply, deeply apologise. I do upset people and you are the last I would want to upset.'

Ethel could not believe what she was witnessing. This genius on the verge of tears, pleading for the forgiveness of a woman. Were all geniuses like this? Was Lisl right? Is this the price they paid for fame? She said nothing.

There are ugly things that one person can say to another that cannot be forgotten, whatever attempts the offender makes to withdraw or unsay them. They might diminish in intensity over a period, but they remain indelibly etched in the victim's mind. Such was this clumsy remark by Brahms. It annoyed Lisl, just like a chronic ulcer.

'I forgive you, Johannes, when many wouldn't.'

He stood and crept back to the sofa, like a chastened puppy, sneaking back to its basket.

'You are going to have to behave yourself tonight! We've invited Clara and her daughters and Lily Wach to dinner.'

'It will be wonderful to see them,' he said, with a renewed smile.

'I agree with Johannes,' said Ethel. 'I haven't seen Frau Schumann and her daughters since I met them in London.'

Lisl directed the cooking and, between her and her cook, produced the meal. They all sat around the Herzogenbergs' dining table with Brahms at the far end, Frau Schumann next to him, both flanked by her daughters, Ethel next to Marie and Heinrich next to Elise with Lisl at the head and closest to the door.

'Let me take your drinks order,' said Heinrich. They each elected to have wine, except Johannes, who said he'd prefer a beer. Heinrich served the drinks as Lisl and her maid took a serving spoon each and dished out what the two of them had created, venison stew with roast potatoes and beans.

'You are the chief guest, so you may start first,' said Heinrich to Johannes.

'I'm honoured,' said Johannes. He dug his fork and spoon into the thick stew. 'This is truly wonderful. Congratulations, Lisl!'

'Concocted by my maid and me together,' said Lisl.

'I agree,' said Clara. 'It's so tasty.'

'Reminds me of your second symphony,' said Marie.

'Really?' said Johannes. 'What an interesting analogy!'

'It's better than your second symphony,' said Clara. 'The tunes are a delight, especially that opening theme, but there is no orchestration… not to speak of. Did anyone teach you orchestration, Johannes?'

Ethel looked into Brahms' eyes and detected anger, if not fury. He was utterly outraged. Then, as quickly as his fury had risen, it subsided. Something brought it under control. Could it be respect for this clever woman, a brilliant composer in her own right?

'I'm sure there is something in what you say, Clara. I'll have another look at it. It's never too late to revise a work like that. You know, and I know that we composers are always fiddling with our works.' Again, Ethel could not believe what he was saying. Her eyes darted around the table. None of the others could believe it either.

'Not that bad, surely,' said Lisl. 'I really enjoyed it. I even wrote a piano duet based on it. Heinrich and I have played it many times.'

'You have confirmed my point, Lisl. That you could make sense of it on one instrument makes the orchestration poor,' said Clara, giving the symphony yet another thumping.

Brahms tried to change the subject. 'How is your writing, Clara? Have you written anything recently? I'd love to hear!'

'Not for public hearing. I tend to write for my own enjoyment now. I have become an ordinary woman who is more interested in the works of others than her own.'

'Talking of ordinary women, I can relate several stories to you all,' said Brahms. Ethel was not the only one who wondered what he would say. Would he praise these ordinary souls and admire them, or would he deride and kick them while they were down? Ethel had already learned from George Henschel how dismissive he could be of the work of others.

'It was after a performance of one of my string quartets. I forget which one. This lady, in her fifties I would say, came up to me and said, "How wonderful your composition, Herr Brahms... You... you are a true master. Not a schoolmaster... a genius, Herr Brahms." Such a squeaky voice. I wondered where that gracious lady had such feelings for my poor quartet... where did they lodge? Beneath the little blue shawl? Or perhaps under the cockyolly bird on her hat.' He let out a guffaw of uninhibited laughter.

109

'I hope you didn't say that to the lady,' said Lili, entering the conversation for the first time.

'Of course not,' said Brahms. 'But there was no harm in thinking it! Then there was a musical old lady who murmured half to a cloakroom attendant and half to herself that she felt so stupid having spoken to me because, in her excitement and nervousness, she referred to the *andante* when her remark was meant for the *scherzo* so was totally out of place. I overheard her. Incredible how people react to us artists!'

'The fact is, Johannes, you are well known,' said Heinrich. 'Many people have seen pictures of you or even seen you in the flesh and when talking to an exulted figure can be a little nervous or even overwhelmed. Perhaps you could be a little more sympathetic! But don't take me too seriously!'

At that point, Lisl's maid came in and cleared the dinner plates from the table. She and Lisl then brought in eight individual dishes of lemon mousse and placed them in front of them all.

'This looks delicious,' said Frau Schumann. 'Far too good to eat.'

The dinner over, Lisl made a request. 'All we need now is a little entertainment. Do we have any volunteers?'

'Having behaved a little clumsily, I shall make my recompense by playing the piano, if you agree,' said Brahms. Applause greeted his offer.

'Could you play one of your latest compositions?' said Lisl. 'One or two of your capriccios from Opus 76?'

'I'd love to, if only to show those of you who have not heard them yet.'

They all got up from the dining table and adjourned to the drawing-room. 'I'll play, numbers one, two and three and if you want any more, you must tell me.'

Brahms played the piano as if he could make it speak. His head held back and his blue eyes half-closed, he touched the keys with the fingers of a master. The veins on his head stood out and his hair fell back onto his shoulders. The piano obeyed his every move, responding with the softest of tones or blasting out as if

110

he was beating it. Just to watch him play was an entertainment. He and the piano were as one.

'There we are. I hope you all enjoyed it!' he said, after finishing.

'Bravo,' shouted Elise. They all joined in chorus.

'It's good to be appreciated. They are little pieces and will never be as popular as a Bach organ fugue or a Beethoven bagatelle. Still, I enjoyed writing them,' he said, with unexpected humility.

'It's my turn now,' said Elise. She and Brahms exchanged places, and she launched into a piece her mother had written and dedicated to her daughters. Clara smiled with pride.

***

The day of the premiere arrived.

'I feel so nervous, Lisl,' he said while she, Heinrich and Ethel were sitting having breakfast.

Ethel found it difficult to understand how this accomplished, famous composer and performer could be nervous. After all, he was then in his mid-forties and at his peak in skill and achievement. He could write music as quickly as dashing off a letter.

'You'll be fine, Johannes,' said Lisl. 'It's not a bad thing to be nervous before a performance.'

'I'm more worried about how the orchestra will respond. They may object to my conducting the concert. They'd prefer Reinecke. At least I felt that yesterday at the final rehearsal.'

'I'll give you a tip,' said Heinrich, unexpectedly. 'Smile at them from the moment you walk into the auditorium. Smile at them as individuals. Pick them out and look them in the eye. Bow to them once you are on the rostrum. Then bow to the audience!'

111

'Do you know? I'm going to do that,' he said. 'What excellent advice. I've never thought of that before,'

'Treat them as if you love them and they will love you back!' said Heinrich. Lisl and Ethel kept out of this brief exchange.

Ethel, Heinrich and Lisl looked on from the middle of the second row. Brahms did exactly as Heinrich suggested. The orchestra applauded as he beamed at them, or tapped their bows on their music stands. He turned to the audience and bowed. Then he raised his baton and the concert began.

The Violin Concerto was greeted with a standing ovation.

'A brilliant piece of music,' said Ethel to Lisl. 'Pity the man is such an oddity.'

It took many months for Ethel to put the genius Brahms to the back of her mind. She didn't like him. She thought if she were a man, he would more than appreciate her sonatas and her songs. Just in the way Alexander Ewing, George Henschel and now Heinrich Herzogenberg did. Alas, she lived in the body of a woman and there was nothing she could do about that. She thought he could at least acknowledge she had written her works. He could even say they showed promise or even say he admired them, even if he thought them banal or germinal. After all, she was unlikely to compete with him at any stage in her life. But no, he hardly recognised her existence, except to take any praise she might give to his works. Brahms saw women, such as Clara Schumann and Lisl, to be respected; or to be disrespected, such as the likes of Ethel or those women he leered at as possible sexual conquests. His gluttony didn't impress her.

# CHAPTER 11

## A Word of Warning

It took a few more years for Ethel to find the routine of counterpoint examples from Bach and others, followed by exercises Heinrich marked, less than interesting. She hankered for a change. So one morning in the summer of 1882, just after the teaching session with the three of them, she spoke.

'I have something to say, Heinrich and Lisl. Please don't think I am in any way ungrateful. Indeed, I have utterly enjoyed our joint lessons with Heinrich, but I now want to do something different.'

'Such as what?' broke in Lisl.

'I am thinking of going to Italy... to spend the winter there. The country has so much to offer, as the seat of opera, through the works of many famous artists to its magnificent architecture. St Mark's, for example. I am twenty four now and want for something completely different.'

'Makes no sense, Ethel,' said Heinrich. 'You are reaching a critical stage in your learning and are becoming an accomplished composer. You've written some excellent pieces recently. The Trio for example and your second piano sonata. You just need that little more time to finish your studies. Please stay, at least to see the winter through. Go there later, in the spring perhaps.'

It said a lot for Heinrich that he was prepared to have Ethel in their home for even longer, despite her boisterousness and her constant attempts at seducing Lisl. He evidently could see her potential as a composer, regardless of Brahms, whom he didn't like either.

'You are too ready to be distracted from your composing, Ethel,' said Lisl. 'What with your constant indulgence in sports of all kinds... your cricket, your tennis, your swimming... and dancing. You aren't giving your composing a chance. I've said that for years now and it's still true.'

After several days of friendly but firm argument, Lisl and Heinrich could see that she was determined to go, and nothing they could say would make her change her mind.

'Well, Ethel, if that's what you want to do, who are we to stop you?' said Heinrich.

'I have an idea, Ethel,' said Lisl. 'I've spoken to you often of the sister I revere. Julia lives in Florence with her husband, Harry. I'll write to them and ask if they can put you up in their house for a time. They will love your energy and temperament.'

'You are so helpful, Lisl,' said Ethel and stepped over to her to kiss her cheek.

'In fact, Ethel, we have another friend in Florence. He is the sculptor, Adolf Hildebrand. I'll write to him, too!'

Ethel could not believe the way the Herzogenbergs had changed from being so adamantly opposed to her going to Italy to actively supporting the idea. What luck to have such close and helpful friends, she thought.

By going home first and spending the end of the summer and the autumn there, she took a distinctly indirect route to Florence. She played tennis, hunted and indulged in many activities, including visiting Mary and Alice. She then made her way to Florence, having spent a time at the Wachs where she went mountaineering and fell over, almost breaking a leg. The incident left her in great pain and limping badly.

\*\*\*

'Who is this woman?' said the man who opened the door to her, on that unseasonably mild January morning. Ethel wondered if she had misread the address on the copy of the letter Lisl had given her.

'Oh! I may be at the wrong house. Is this the house of Adolf von Hildebrand?'

'Yes, I am Hildebrand,' said the man. 'To whom am I speaking, young lady?'

'I am Ethel Smyth, a composer from England. I believe you have a letter from Lisl von Herzogenberg, introducing me to you and your family.'

'Irene,' he shouted. 'There's a young woman here. Says Lisl sent a letter of introduction to us. Says a lot about her, apparently. You heard anything of it?'

'Oh, Adolf! I should have told you. One of the children opened it by mistake and I forgot to tell you. Better let her in. Does she want to stay? Will have to double up with Sylvie if she does.'

Ethel stood on the doorstep of the none too salubrious looking building during this awkward exchange. It looked like a convent which had been converted to a block of flats. She didn't know whether to feel welcomed.

'You'd better come in, Miss Smyth. You know Lisl do you? Great friend of ours. Sister lives few streets away. Julia.' He must have been about thirty five or so. Other than Brahms, he was one of the few clean-shaven men Ethel had seen since leaving for Leipzig, five years before. He'd obviously been shaved that day.

'Give me the letter,' he said to his wife. The untidy looking woman pushed it into his hand.

'Oh, yes. Known them for some time then. How's old Heinrich? Composer, too. No kids. Not like us. Place seething with 'em! Hope you like 'em!'

'I love children,' said Ethel. 'I'm one of eight so have little choice!'

The sculptor led Ethel down the narrow hall into a huge open area which looked more like an artist's studio than a place to live in. Several children were playing games on the floor and teasing each other.

'This is my wife,' said Hildebrand, as a child grabbed his leg.

'Pleased to meet you, Miss Smyth. Sorry about the confusion. Would you like to stay with us for a time? Lisl said you might. In her letter, that is.' She was a short, plump, motherly figure with deep brown eyes.

115

'I don't want to impose,' said Ethel, recognising chaos that confronted her. 'But if I could stay with you for just a couple of days, that would be wonderful and I would be so grateful. I can entertain the children. I love playing with them and will sing and play the piano!'

'Stay long as you like, in that case,' said the sculptor, almost with a growl and with his eyebrows pointing upwards.

It was clear to Ethel that he didn't want her to stay long, which was why she asked to stay for just two nights. He readily agreed, even though his wife looked as if she would have liked Ethel to spend longer there, if only to amuse her children.

'I'll show you Sylvie's room. It has two single beds.' The woman escorted Ethel up a long flight of stairs which matched the enormous ceiling height of the cavernous rooms below. She pushed a door open to let Ethel enter.

'What an incredible view!' Ethel almost shouted. 'What a beautiful city you have.' She walked across to the window simply to gaze in wonder. 'My goodness, I've never seen such a huge dome before!'

'It is amazing, isn't it? It's our cathedral. The church of Santa Maria del Fiore. It had the biggest dome in the world for centuries! And that building over there is the Basilica of San Lorenzo. I love its symmetry. Michelangelo designed the sacristy, and it's one of the oldest churches in Florence.'

'I must look at them in more detail.'

'You'll have plenty of time if you are spending the whole winter with the Brewsters.'

'That's certainly my plan.'

'Let me give you a word of warning. Please don't misunderstand me. They are lovely people, and through Lisl we know them quite well. But they have an odd relationship with each other. They believe they're free in their marriage to go with other people, if the fancy takes them. She's eleven years older than him and didn't want to marry him. It was only by her mother's insistence, the old dragon, Baroness Stockhausen, that they decided they would. Both of them treated the

116

whole ceremony as a joke. They even decided they'd permanently reject each other if one of them found somebody else. So take care, Miss Smyth. There could be danger lurking in that house.'

'I appreciate the warning,' said Ethel.

Irene pointed to the bed furthest from the window in this large room, which was clearly not designed to be a bedroom. Ethel placed her two bags next to the bed, as if to lay claim to it.

'Let's go back down. Adolf will want to show you his studio.'

'I'm dying to see it,' said Ethel, smiling at this strange welcome. She'd half expected them to offer her drink. Maybe this was more of an English trait that she could not expect in Florence.

Adolf was playing with a group of the children as Irene and Ethel entered the room where they had all met.

'Now I'll show you my studio. In the next room.'

She'd never seen such chaos. Three hefty workbenches bore half completed sculptures of various sizes. Stone chips and rubble scattered the floor.

'Problem with me being a sculptor is there's a maximum size to any work I can do here,' he said, straight-faced and as they walked in. 'It's about weight and access. The floors here are built on oak rafters so they will take a large load, but you can only bring a stone of a limited size into the studio and take out a limited size statue once you've made it. Much of my work is on large structures like fountains and other commissioned objects. But you can see, I have a number of ongoing projects here.' He lifted his arm and pointed it around the room. There were incomplete statues of arms, two hands, apparently in prayer, several busts, one of an army officer of senior rank, the head, arms and wings of an angel, more of the heads of men than of women.

Ethel didn't know quite what to say. Then a thought occurred to her.

'Who is the army officer? My father was in the army. He achieved the rank of Major General in our Royal Artillery.'

'Must have been a good soldier to hold that rank!'

'Yes, and intelligent!'

'Man's a general in the Italian army. His regiment commissioned this sculpture to commemorate his award of a distinguished service medal. You can see, it's almost finished! Want him back again so I can sort out his neck.'

'Why are so many unfinished? I can't do my composing like that. I have to see a piece through to the end before I start another one,' she said, lying somewhat and taking the risk that she might annoy the man.

'It's just the way I work,' he said, unperturbed. 'Sometimes, I cannot see what I'm looking for in the stone. I come back, look at the piece and there it is. I take the tools out and quickly find it. "Quickly" may mean an hour, even longer! All day, sometimes!'

Ethel enjoyed talking to this famous sculptor. She could hold her own in conversing with him, despite being much younger and at an early stage in her career as a composer. They were both artists and could relate to each other as creative individuals, even though they used radically different media.

'Adolf!' came a shout from a nearby room. 'If you want some lunch, you'd better come now!'

'Better go. Before the children eat our food!' he said, grinning at Ethel as if they were being naughty children. 'We can resume after lunch.'

The meal was as chaotic as everything else about this family. The children constantly left their chairs and vanished to some other place in the house, got down from the table to tease and fight each other. It was as if they could do whatever they wanted, independently of what their parents said or did. Ethel delighted in the freshly made pasta and Bolognese sauce, enjoyed with a glass of Tuscan beer.

'Going back to the studio, Irene,' said Adolf, having had enough of the lunchtime pantomime. 'Follow me, Miss Smyth.'

Ethel wondered what he wanted to show her or discuss. He took her to the far side of the studio and lifted a sheet from a complete statue of a woman in a long gown, about five feet tall, a little under life-size. 'This is a commission I recently completed of a Puglian countess. What do you think of it?'

Ethel couldn't understand why he was asking her, someone who knew next to nothing about his art, about this masterpiece of a statue. He had captured the woman's look of majesty on her elegant face. It reminded Ethel of a portrait she had once seen of Isabella of Castile.

'It's brilliant. The only thing is that the right arm looks too long to me. Otherwise, it's perfect.'

'Aha! Fact is, the arm is too short. It would have looked ridiculous if I'd used the full length of her arm. It's a matter of what looks right to the observer when the reality could be quite different!'

'I see,' said Ethel, not sure if she did or not.

Adolf and Ethel spent much time in conversing about sculpture, even to the extent of him letting her try a chisel on stone for herself. It was on a piece he had not yet finished.

'The chisel goes in easier than I thought it would!' said Ethel. 'What do you think about when you are sculpting?'

'Depends on the hardness of the stone. Think about? One of the children asked me how to sculpture an elephant. I said, you first find a piece of stone bigger than the elephant. Then take a hammer and a chisel. You then chisel off all the pieces that don't look like the elephant. You are then left with an elephant! So the piece you are making is in your mind. It's like the quartet you are composing. It's in your head somewhere. You have to drag it out, note by note!'

'What an interesting explanation, Adolf. Writing music is just like that! Let me ask you a simple question. Who is your favourite sculptor?'

That is difficult, Miss Smyth. I admire Rodin. But he's very commercial. He looks at every chance to make money. Don't blame him. Age of Bronze is a masterstroke. And he is very popular with you English. Probably my favourite is

Michelangelo and the utter masterpiece, David. But there are a few others, too. Giambologna and Samson Slaying a Philistine is one of the most dramatic sculptures of all time. Then there is Bernini… Probably the greatest sculpturing genius who ever lived… in Italy or anywhere else. Neptune and Triton is superb. Unbelievable! And his Saint Peter's Square in Rome.'

Adolf needed to work the following day, so Ethel spent her time playing with his children. She showed them how to play cricket in their overgrown garden. They gave up when they lost several balls in the undergrowth. She danced with them, played their piano and sang with them, so loud that Irene asked her not to be so noisy. Despite the pain in her leg, she showed them how to jump over a table and land on two feet. The children thought she was crazy but loved her all the same.

Each member of the Hildebrand family kissed her before she went. The children especially demanded her return, 'as often as you like,' said little Sylvie.

'I'll probably name one of my compositions after you,' she said, as she left and waved to them.

# CHAPTER 12

## The Brewsters

Adolf told Ethel exactly where the Brewsters lived, so she found their house with surprising ease.

'Yes, we are expecting you,' said Harry Brewster as he opened the front door of their house in the Via de' Bardi. Ethel didn't know quite what to make of this handsome figure of a man. His blue eyes didn't quite look straight at hers. It seemed as if he was shy and unused to speaking to strangers, especially not to women he didn't know. He had the prominent forehead some might associate with a deep thinker. He had grown a moustache that more than covered the width of his face and an unkempt beard to match. 'Is that all you have for baggage,' he said, looking down at her two, not very large cases. 'You are staying for the winter?'

'Yes, that is the plan. I understand Lisl will have said as much in her letter. I believe I've got enough here, provided I can do some laundering!'

'Of course! Come and meet Julia.'

Julia looked stunning, even more beautiful than Lisl's description of her. Ethel immediately fell for her amazing statuesque features, the high cheekbones and pale yellow hair. She lived in the body of an athlete, trim, fit and agile. How could Ethel entice this goddess into liking, appreciating, or even loving her? She would soon discover.

'Hello,' she said, with surprising coolness and no hint of a smile. 'You might as well come in.' Was the alternative to go away? Ethel was shocked by what seemed to be indifference, verging on rudeness. It was as if she was compelled to take Ethel in, simply because her sister had asked her to do so.

'Thank you so very much,' said Ethel, so effusively that she counteracted Julia's unwelcoming tone.

Ethel found dinner with the two of them a painful experience. They hardly spoke to each other, so she could hardly expect them to speak to her. So much of it passed in all but total silence. The only intervening sounds came from their two young children, Clotilde, the older, and Christopher, who evidently ate separately from their parents. They were playing each other in a board game and celebrated loudly when one or the other won a piece. So Ethel tried to make conversation.

'It was good of Lisl to offer to write to you about my visit to Italy.'

Neither responded. She tried another line.

'I've spent the most interesting couple of days, also at Lisl's suggestion, with the Hildebrands. Isn't he the most incredible sculptor?' They had to answer such a positive question.

'Not as good as he thinks,' said Julia. 'He's never made a lot of money at it, and some of his work is distinctly odd.'

'If he did better, he might clothe his wife better and that hoard of children. How many has he got, Julia?'

'Don't know. Five, I'm pretty sure.'

'He is working on several commissions, one from the Italian army for a general they've just awarded some high honour.'

'Oh, that one. He's taking an age to finish it. If he doesn't finish it soon, they'll go to someone else.'

'My father was a general in the British army.'

'Really?' said Julia.

'Yes,' said Ethel, making whatever she could of the discussion. 'He was in a regiment called the Royal Artillery. He and our family spent much time in India. We left because of the mutiny. That was back in fifty seven.'

Neither of them responded, so Ethel took a different tack. 'I do like your house,' not that she'd seen much of it. Her bags were still in the hall and they had shown her directly into the dining room. 'How long have you been living here?'

'Since we got married, what nine years ago now. That's right, Julia. Isn't it?'

122

'Ten actually.'

'Where were you married?'

'In Germany, near Munich. We never intended to marry, but it was at my mother's insistence. As a baroness, she wasn't having her daughter living with a man and not in wedlock. The good thing was that she and my father paid the bill! As far as we were concerned, it was nothing more than a party.' At last, Ethel had touched on something that Julia felt she could speak about.

'Amazing! You must be almost unique. Most couples who live together are married, at least they are in England. To do otherwise is regarded as living in sin!'

Neither replied to Ethel's comment, so all three ended the meal in silence, but for the competitive noises from the children. Ethel wondered if she really wanted to be in this dreary place. As Julia cleared away the dishes, Ethel hit on an idea.

'Do you have a piano?'

'Yes,' said Harry.

'Wonderful. In that case, I shall provide this evening's entertainment. I'd like to freshen up first so would you mind showing me where I shall sleep?'

'I can do that. I'll carry your bags.'

He took Ethel upstairs to a pleasantly furnished room at the end of the landing. The view was nothing like as enticing as the one from her room at the Hildebrands' but it looked homely enough and large enough for Ethel to be comfortable for the winter, especially as she had spotted a large pile of blankets in the wardrobe. A washstand stood by the wall opposite the bed and one of her hosts had the foresight to provide a jug of water.

'I'll be back down in a few minutes,' said Ethel, closing the door.

She was soon sitting in the drawing-room at their colourfully decorated piano, ready to announce her programme.

'Good evening, everyone!' By then Julia, Harry and the two children were sitting in anticipation of the coming recital.

'I will start with a couple of songs I have written and follow that with my first piano sonata. Then I will play a short piece by Johannes Brahms.'

None of them had ever heard anything like it before. Ethel pounded away at their piano, so hard it tried to escape along the floor on its castors. She sang at the very top of her voice. At first, the children looked terrified at this strange woman, generating this astonishing tornado of sound. Then they enjoyed the performance and even applauded as Ethel finished the various pieces, usually with a flourish.

Neither Julia nor Harry knew what to make of Ethel's performance. She could obviously play well and sing well. But was all this noise necessary? Has she been sent by Lisl to destroy the peace and tranquillity of this little family? Or was she naturally boisterous and full of energy? They could not work out then whether they would enjoy her company or regard her as a bothersome nuisance.

At that point, Ethel preferred Julia. She had a cloud of mystery surrounding her, which Ethel found to be a challenge. Harry seemed so shy he avoided communicating where possible.

The stiffness of the first day spilled over to the second and third but showed signs of breaking on the fourth when at breakfast Harry posed a question to Ethel.

'So what do you think of the works of Shakespeare?'

'I love them, the language, the characters, the morality and the marvellous stories. I fully intend to read more of this genius's work. When I can find the time!'

'Genius, did you say? A hack, if you want my view. He can hardly put a sentence together and as for all those pretentious sentiments. I'm surprised you English have made him such a hero!'

Ethel was quite shocked and felt the pain of what he was saying.

'So who is the world's greatest playwright if it wasn't William Shakespeare?'

'Racine, Moliére, Verlaine in French. Goethe, Schiller in German, de la Barca and Lope de Vega in Spanish. They leave Shakespeare in the dark!'

'Apart from Goethe, I've studied none of them! But I've seen some de la Barca's plays.'

'I'll lend you some, if you are interested.'

'Yes, I'd love to read some. Seems like I'll have time. I want to do some composing while I'm here, but a few plays would be a pleasing distraction.'

'Come with me and we'll find a few.'

Julia looked distinctly troubled as the two of them got up from the table and left the room. She didn't especially enjoy listening to the exchange on the playwrights. This was the first time Harry had successfully conversed with another woman for years. She was tempted to follow them, but resisted.

Harry picked some volumes from the shelves, A Baudelaire, a Racine and a Schiller.

'You are an incredible woman, Ethel. I don't know how I feel about you.'

Ethel was astonished and didn't know what to think or say. Was he falling for her or was this just an awkward comment on her personality?

'Well, there you are, Harry,' she said, as neutrally as she could. She didn't want to give him any impression that any feelings he was developing towards her were even slightly reciprocated.

'Start with the Racine. This one contains Andromaque and Phedre. I hope you can read in French!'

'Of course. All part of my education!'

The two of them returned to the dining room to finish their coffee, a much better brew than the weak offerings Ethel didn't much enjoy in Leipzig. After he had drained his cup, Harry excused himself, saying he needed to go to a meeting at his bank and wouldn't, for various other reasons, be back before lunch. His

125

departure left Ethel alone with Julia for the first time in the four days. What a wonderful opportunity to know her better, thought Ethel.

Ethel helped Julia tidy away the breakfast things and dried the dishes as Julia washed them. What a contrast with the servants that were at the beck and call of Lisl and Heinrich.

'So, other than looking after your two lovely children, do you have any major preoccupations, Julia?' Ethel asked while wiping a plate.

'Hasn't Lisl told you? I am a great believer in metaphysics and I apply it constantly to everyday life,' she said, actually showing a spark of interest in the question which was so different from her attitude at dinner the nights before.

'I'm not sure I know what metaphysics is.'

'It's a branch of philosophy which studies and applies the relationships between mind and matter… cause and effect. Things like that. I try to find the reasons for events and whether there is any metaphysical cause. It utterly fascinates me. While Harry is reading his French writers, I am reading Aristotle's thoughts on the subject and the works of other philosophers, including Buddha.'

'Hmm. Not something I've actually thought about before. How did you become interested in it?'

'Like most of these things, it's a long story. It was before Harry and I got together. My mother is a very domineering woman and while I was at home she was so demanding, I became quite introverted and miserable. I am still introverted despite being married to Harry. So I went to a library and just by chance came across a couple of books on the subject. I borrowed them and found a great release in reading them. The subject has fascinated me ever since.'

Ethel stood there with her arms crossed and her eyebrows raised, listening intently. What she said about Baroness Stockhausen fitted completely with what Irene Hildebrand had said.

'I'll stick to my music. I have so many interests, I don't think I could entertain any others. That being said, I would like to know you better, Julia, if not through the medium of metaphysics. I would like to think we could become good

126

friends. After all, we have a common link through Lisl, whom I love unconditionally.'

'My problem, Ethel, is that I am not an affectionate person. That means I do not give affection very well. I know Lisl adores me, but I have difficulty in returning her feelings. In fact, I have no particular wish to see her or Heinrich. You will have seen I am not especially loving towards Harry or to my children. Harry and I regard each other as good friends who live together as man and wife, which by the insistence of my mother we actually are!'

Despite this explanation, if that is what it was, Ethel still found Julia attractive and someone she could readily love. She saw her as being at least as attractive as Augusta Redecker, in some ways more so, as what she was saying made her more of a challenge. She thought she would try to clarify the situation.

'Would you rather I saw less of you and your family? I could easily stay in lodgings for the rest of my time in Florence, or maybe go back to stay with the Hildebrands?'

'I won't hear of such a thing, Ethel. You are welcome here. You are so energetic. The children love playing with you and enjoy your piano performances. And Harry and I enjoy having you here, too. Please believe me and stay.'

So that's what Ethel did. Although her leg was still giving her pain, she taught the children to play cricket and took them to the swimming baths. She showed them around some art galleries and took them to the opera. She even persuaded the Brewsters to buy some bats and balls, so they could play table tennis, and a violin which Ethel would teach them to play. The children adored her.

It did not surprise Ethel that Harry was so willing to converse with her about a vast range of subjects from seventeenth century French literature to the history of the American Civil War. He was partly American, so knew about such things. And he was a great admirer of many cultural aspects of France. The main language spoken in their family gatherings was French, which challenged Ethel's fluency and understanding. Apart from his toxic opinion of Shakespeare, he had a poor opinion of German culture. He didn't like Germans as a race, especially the

Prussians, whom he regarded as arrogant. He and Ethel enjoyed these rich and varied conversations, which sometimes included Julia but frequently didn't.

What Ethel failed to realise was that Harry was falling in love with her. He wanted to spend every available minute with her and couldn't stop himself. It is hard to conceal such feelings from your wife, even if she treats you only as a close friend. But Julia could see and feel what was happening to her man in the presence of this pretty, clever and vivacious young Englishwoman. He was emerging from a shell which he had quietly inhabited for many years. Julia's observations prompted serious discussion.

'Harry, I need to have a conversation with you,' she said, while Ethel was working in her room.

'Really? What's the problem?'

'Ethel.'

'What's wrong with Ethel?'

'Nothing. It's the effect she's having on you.'

'I'm not sure what you mean.'

'You should be. You are falling in love with her. It is so obvious from the way you look at her and involve her in the things you do, especially these conversations about many aspects of culture. But it's the way you look at her which is the most obvious. The way you look at her breasts and into her eyes… and at her bottom when she is walking away from you. You'd love to have her in bed with you. To have sex with her.'

'I hate to admit this, Julia, but you are right. I cannot deny it. I just don't know what to do about it. I love you above all others and I need to cure my feelings towards Ethel. I'm sure it's just an infatuation. I haven't made love to her, I can assure you.'

This was a tough conversation for each of them, but Julia's courageous challenge had at least produced a result, if an uncomfortable one for Harry. They discussed various solutions to Harry's problem.

'We should ask Ethel to find somewhere else,' said Harry.

'That is out of the question, Harry. I've already told her she can stay. She asked me if she should find somewhere else and I said no. I'm not sure what she feels towards you but I haven't noticed her falling for you.'

'Maybe I should move out, Julia. If only until I've got over her.'

'That won't work either. The apparent reasons do not suit me. No. We need to find another option.'

'What if I go abroad for a fortnight? I could go to France on study leave or Algeria on the pretext of improving my Arabic, which is not as good as it could be. I'd like to know more about the country… especially Algiers. And their Islamic history.'

'You are going to Algeria, Harry. I'd be worried that you'd fall for another among those charming women in France, Paris in particular. But Algeria…'

Within a week, Harry had packed a suitcase and was at the quayside waiting to board a ship to Algeria. Ethel couldn't understand why he had gone there - they presented it as Harry's decision and his alone - especially as Ethel was a guest in their house. It seemed rude to Ethel that he was leaving, just as she was learning more about him and enjoying their conversations. It made no sense to her. In favour of his departure, however, was the opportunity to become closer to his wife.

The strained atmosphere between Ethel and Julia, in Harry's absence, was obvious to each of them. Although domestic matters, such as who should cook the evening meal, were uncontroversial, virtually anything else was a cause for strife. At the first weekend of Harry's absence, Ethel offered to take Clotilde and Christopher to a play by Racine. Julia realised this was a play to which Harry had introduced Ethel and expressed extreme reluctance to them going. Her resorting to a metaphysical solution, however, led her to give in. Ethel imagined that metaphysics told her how irrational she was becoming. Ethel didn't think the children understood the play.

Julia noticed a significant change in him from the moment he returned. He no longer fawned over Ethel. As she moved around their house, he spent less time in her wake. He devoted more time to Julia and expressing his love for her. Julia was delighted. Ethel was as puzzled as she was before he went.

The amicable relationship between the three of them continued. Harry was still keen to converse with Ethel over matters of culture, and he behaved in a more relaxed way towards her. Ethel in all innocence persuaded him to go back to playing his cello, which he had neglected during his marriage. Julia and the children were much amused at the recitals the two of them put on after dinner, especially when their father produced a sequence of wrong notes. So Ethel's break in Florence ended and apparently all was well. The three of them agreed she would return the following year when her foot would be better and she could see more of the city.

# CHAPTER 13

## Work and pleasure

The year passed quickly, but not quickly enough for Harry. Ethel spent it visiting and composing. She was in no hurry to go back to Frimley. She completed three string quartets, started on another she called 'Hildebrand' but left it incomplete, wrote a string quintet and started several other works which she never finished.

She went from Florence to Germany to visit Lisl and Heinrich who were in Berchtesgaden, near the Austrian border where they were having a modest holiday home built. They had rented a small house almost next to the building site.

'My dear Ethel, you are limping, my darling,' were Lisl's first words to her friend, as they met her off the train. 'Whatever have you done to your leg?'

Ethel explained.

'Have you seen a doctor?' said Heinrich.

'I saw one in Florence, but he was almost useless. He just told me to rest it. He couldn't find anything wrong.'

'How long has it been like that?' said Heinrich.

'From not long after the mountaineering accident, when I was with the Wachs.'

'I have an idea, Ethel, my sweet,' said Lisl, as they were having dinner, as usual, prepared by Lisl. 'There is a spa town near here where there is a mud bath. Apparently, it has wonderful healing properties. You and I could go there while we leave Heinrich in charge of the building work. I've been terribly bored with the whole thing. I'll be glad when it's finished! It will do us both good!'

So before Ethel had any chance to settle in, Lisl had hired a coach and four horses, and the two of them were on their way for a few days in Aibling. It was much further away than Ethel imagined, so they stayed the night in a hotel *en route*.

'The only room we have left has a double bed,' said the pretty, young receptionist. Ethel couldn't believe her luck. A night in bed with Lisl! She remembered with relish those days and nights she and Lisl spent together over five years before when Lisl was helping Ethel recover from her sickness.

'I'm not sure about that,' said Lisl. 'Is that the best you can do? Doesn't the bed separate into two singles?'

'I'm afraid not, madam.'

'In which case, we must sleep top to toe,' said Lisl, not wishing to betray any secrets. 'And I hope you could give us a reduction accordingly.'

By then it was late in the day and the two of them settled into the dining room ready to order a meal.

'So what do you think of Julia?' said Lisl, as she was browsing through the menu. 'Did she meet your expectations?'

'I'm still bewildered by her. I'm wondering if she's actually human. She is so lacking in emotion, even to her own children. There's no kissing good night. They don't eat with her and Harry. She even started an argument with me when I offered to take them out. And as for her obsession with metaphysics… well, it left me completely cold. I told her I didn't know what it was, and that I didn't want to become interested! But she loved my first piano sonata and my songs. I admire her for that!'

'Hmm… She is my sister and I will love her to the end of the earth. But what irritates me is the way she sneers at our conventional marriage. Hers is odd, but they have lived in their ivory tower for about ten years now, and they seem happy with each other… in their quiet way.'

Ethel was shocked at Lisl's criticism of Julia and the oblique swipe at her and Harry's marriage.

'I can't see much wrong with their marriage. They seem to have what they want. It struck me as strange that Harry left for a fortnight in Algeria when I hadn't been their guest for two weeks. I was completely puzzled, especially as he and I had so many interesting discussions on German, French and English drama and literature. His attitude to Shakespeare really annoyed me and I let him know it!'

'Let's leave the subject, Ethel. It's time we were in bed. I've told the coachmen that we want to depart by nine o'clock at the latest.'

The loving relationship that Ethel had with her darling Lisl contrasted vividly with her cool and distant one with Julia. Lisl helped Ethel out of her clothes and into her nightshirt. Ethel did the same for Lisl. The thought of cuddling up in bed to the warm, beautiful body of her best friend sent shivers down Ethel's spine. She had been aching for this to happen from the moment the receptionist said the only room available had a double bed.

Aibling stood out as the most picturesque little town in Bavaria. Wooded hills and mountain tops surrounded it, and a river valley divided it. A different architect appeared to have designed each house. Lisl directed the carriage to a hotel close to the spa which seemed to be the focal point of the town.

'Shall we share a room, Ethel? Not to sound mean, but it will be quite a saving. Hotels here are quite expensive because it's a spa resort.'

Ethel agreed. She loved every second she spent with Lisl, so spending a few nights cuddling up to her would be a kind of bliss.

'Of course, Lisl. I love sharing with you, my second mother!' said Ethel, beaming broadly.

***

Ethel didn't know quite what to expect of the mud baths. As they walked in, the lady attendant directed them along a corridor to some steps which they were to descend. They would then go into a changing area, undress and place their clothes in a locker which they would secure with the key the lady gave each of them. They would then go down another flight of steps to the baths. The lady said they could either go into the baths and immerse themselves in the hot mud, or splash it on themselves using a kind of ladle.

'What shall we do? Go into the bath or splash the mud on each other?' said Ethel, by then completely disrobed.

'Let's try the mud with our hands. If it's too hot to go right in we can put some on each other with the ladle.'

Each with a towel around their middle, they went down the lower flight of stairs. A huge cavernous space, which smelt of sulphur and was clouded in vapour, confronted them. Around it circled a wide path. They were surprised to find no one else there. The mud came right up to the level of the path.

'Now what do we do?' said Ethel.

'Drop your towel and I'll ladle some mud onto you. Where do you want me to put it?'

Ethel took off the towel and put it on a wooden bench. 'On to my foot,' she said, not expecting an especially pleasant experience.

Lisl took a ladle from a nearby box, dipped it in the mud, filled it and moved it towards Ethel's foot. 'Are you ready for this?'

'As ready as I can be!' She gently poured a small volume on to Ethel, starting at her toes.

'That feels so strange. It's like having some weird creature crawling over you. It's not boiling hot. You can pour some further up my leg if you wish!'

Lisl poured more of the warm, dirty looking fluid onto Ethel's thigh. 'It doesn't feel too bad, actually... once you familiarise yourself with it. Shall I pour some on you?'

'No. Let's just climb right in. There are some banister rails over there we can use to lower ourselves in.'

'You lead the way then!'

They lowered themselves completely into the mud and sat there, covered in it and facing each other. Ethel laughed.

'What is so amusing, Ethel? This is a serious business.'

'I just can't believe we are doing this. Sitting here stark naked in a pool of filth. I feel like a pig on a farm.' She laughed again. Then she picked up a handful of the mud and threw it at Lisl. It fell short but, as it landed, it splashed onto Lisl's face.

'You're a demon,' shouted Lisl, who then broke into laughter and retaliated by slinging a handful back. It hit the middle of Ethel's face.

Ethel waded over towards Lisl, dipped her hand in the mud and smeared it all over Lisl's cheeks. 'That's got my own back on you!' said Ethel, roaring heartily and with her head all but concealed by the mucky fluid.

Lisl's justifiable response was to smear mud all over Ethel's hair. Ethel shouted. 'Don't do that, you wicked minx!' Then burst out laughing again.

Lisl stood and grabbed Ethel by the arms to pull her over. Ethel resisted and pushed back, making Lisl topple and fall headlong into the bath. It was like a wrestling match, but in mud. Lisl eased herself up onto her haunches. Ethel put her arms around Lisl and pulled her towards her. The mud was so slippery she failed to grip Lisl's body. Lisl tried to grab Ethel, who was too slippery to hold. Each of them laughed so much, tears ran down their faces, making clear rivulets on their mud bespattered faces. Neither would let the other stand until they both tired of this frenzied activity. The warm, smelly slime completely covered each of them.

They ended this raucous game by giving each other an affectionate, muddy hug.

'I love you, Lisl,' said Ethel, still chuckling. 'That was such fun and totally amazing.'

'Likewise, I love you too, Ethel. That was one of the funniest things that has happened to me for a long time. I thoroughly enjoyed it, even though we got rough with each other!'

Totally besmirched with the smelly fluid, they staggered out of the mud bath and made their way to the washroom. It was behind a closed door near the stairs they used to enter the bathing area.

'I've never seen a shower like this before,' said Ethel.

'Nor me!'

Continuously running chutes delivered the water from a height of about ten feet on to a sloping marble floor. The washed-off mud and water then poured into a drain.

'If we stand under the same chute, we can help wash the mud off each other,' said Lisl.

Ethel had never made such intimate contact with another woman's body. She took pleasure in moving her hands over the whole of Lisl's beautiful form. Lisl returned the favour, but seemed to treat it as if she was helping wash the mud from a recalcitrant daughter.

'It looks as if we've cleaned it all off now,' said Lisl.

'Turn around and I'll check.'

They each inspected the other only to discover their feet were still dirty, but soon cleaned them. They then dried themselves with large towels from a pile.

'Well, how do you feel after that, Ethel?'

'Wonderful… but I don't know what effect it will have on my leg!'

They made their way out of the building, found their coachman and began their journey back to Berchtesgaden.

\*\*\*

Heinrich greeted them at the door. 'I have a surprise for you two!' he said.

He led them into the lounge where an oldish woman in an extravagant, full-length dress was sitting on a sofa.

'My God,' said Lisl. 'It's you Clara. We haven't seen you for a good few years.' Lisl couldn't understand what made Frau Schumann appear at the Herzogenberg's rented house. Then it became clear.

'I invited Clara to come for a few days. I wrote to her the minute you and Ethel drove off to Aibling. Did I do the right thing?'

'Yes, my dear. Exactly the right thing. It's wonderful to see you, Clara! You've met my friend and composer, Ethel Smyth from England?'

'Of course' said Frau Schumann, as she slowly stood up to hug Lisl and to shake hands with Ethel. 'We first met in London. Then at the party you gave for Johannes the night before he conducted Joachim in his Violin Concerto. The premiere on New Year's Day '79.'

'Yes, it was a delightful experience,' said Ethel, remembering how badly Brahms had treated her before the party. She didn't really want to think about it, but willingly forgave Frau Schumann for mentioning it. 'I have something of a surprise for you, Frau Schumann. I have written a piece which follows your style of piano playing, which I know is most unlike mine. It's called Prelude and Fugue for Thin People. I wrote it only a few weeks ago and I have the score with me, somewhere upstairs!'

'Find it, Ethel,' the Frau said, smiling with her entire face. 'My fingers are so fat it cannot possibly relate to me!'

Ethel soon retrieved the score and passed it to the Frau, who sat back down and read it right through. 'I love it, Ethel! It is amusing and so well crafted. I could play it now!'

'I am so pleased you like it, Frau Schumann. May I dedicate it to you?'

'Yes, of course you may. And you honour me by doing so! Please call me Clara, Ethel. I detect we are becoming the greatest of friends. I've always said that a friend of Lisl's is a friend of mine!'

Little did Ethel know that, up to that point, Clara Schumann had not liked Ethel whom she regarded as garrulous and an unfitting friend to Lisl. She upset

Lisl by expressing such a view. Lisl dismissed what she said and attributed her view as jealousy of one friend for another.

***

Ethel headed for home, straight after staying with the Herzogenbergs. Her family seemed even more dysfunctional than usual. A financial crisis, almost certainly brought about by her mother's ceaseless extravagances, clouded the air.

'I have some bad news for you,' said the General, at Ethel's first breakfast with the family. 'We will soon have to move out of Frimhurst. We can't afford to live here much longer. Our debts are piling up and my pension is all we have to live on.'

Mother's face immediately flooded with tears which dripped into her porridge.

'So how much longer have we got?' said Nelly, by then eighteen.

'Between two and three years, I'd say,' he said, looking at his wife as if puzzled she was crying.

'So what's the cause of the problem?' Ethel ventured to say.

'Living beyond our means,' he said, glaring angrily at her mother.

'How can we make some savings?' said Nina.

'Let's cut down on our sugar and butter usage,' said Violet.

'That won't save tuppence a week,' said the General, his eyebrows raised. 'You must do better than that.'

'I shall stop buying extravagant gowns,' said mother. 'I'll start wearing old ones to parties instead of turning up with a new one every time.'

'That will certainly help,' said the General.

***

Ethel's mother had a habit of collecting friends. She had far more than she could actually remember, one of which lived in Farnborough, only a few miles from Frimhurst.

'I want you to meet one of my new friends,' said Ethel's mother.

'Who's that?' said Ethel.

'A lady who has recently moved into the area and whom I've got to know. She is expecting me for tea this afternoon and I'm sure she will have no objection if you come, too!'

They tied the pony and trap to a rail outside of the lady's large house, walked up the front drive and knocked on the door. Ethel stared in amazement as one of the most striking women she had ever seen opened the door. She was in her late fifties or early sixties and carried herself like a princess. Her hair, tied into a braid, was dark, almost black, and she had the most penetrating brown eyes. She could even have been Spanish.

'Permit me to introduce you to Empress Eugénie of the Second Empire of France, Ethel. And Eugénie, please meet my daughter, Ethel.'

Ethel could hardly say more than a shy hello.

'The Second Empire is confined to history now, of course,' said the Empress, modestly.

'Eugénie ruled France while her husband, Napoleon the Third, was fighting the Franco-Prussian war.'

'You mean losing the Franco-Prussian war,' she laughed. She didn't challenge what Ethel's mother had said about ruling the country.

Ethel recovered. Her mother had totally surprised her with her new aristocrat of a friend. She hadn't known who to expect, a nice but unexceptional woman maybe, but not the wife of Napoleon the Third.

Eugénie brought in a tray with a teapot, three cups, a jug of milk and an elegant bowl of sugar. She placed them on a low table in front of the settee where Ethel and her mother were sitting.

'Let me pour. Help yourselves to sugar. Tell me about yourself, Ethel.'

Ethel told her about her time in Leipzig, the Herzogenbergs, and even about the mud baths in Aibling. She told her about the range of music she had composed and that she intended, beyond anything else, to be a professional composer.

'You are a remarkable woman, Ethel. I've known no one like you before. Have you had any of your works performed in public?'

'Not so far and I haven't earnt a penny from them yet! I've entertained many people by playing them and that has sufficed up to now! My primary ambition is to have one of my operas performed in Germany before I am forty. But I haven't written it yet!' she chortled.

'You sound so ambitious and enthusiastic, Ethel. I'm sure you will have some of your work performed sooner than you might think.'

'Could you tell me more about what you did when you were the ruler of France?' said Ethel, with her curiosity roused and having dispelled her shyness.

'It's a long story, but I shall keep it short. It was after the outbreak of the Franco-Prussian war in '70. My husband was away at the front and left me in charge as regent. We soon lost several notable battles, and when news reached Paris, the people took to the streets in their thousands. Any excuse and the French will riot... not like you English who will just pour another cup of tea!'

All three laughed at the Empress's frivolity.

'The people of Paris were seeking a scapegoat or two. Prime Minister Émille Ollivier and the chief of staff of the army, Marshal Leboeuf both resigned, so I took it upon myself to appoint General Cousin-Montauban as Prime Minister and Francois Achille Bazaine as head of the army. Neither was that brilliant, but I had a limited choice. All was to no avail, as within a month we lost at the Battle of Sedan, which effectively cost us the war. My husband and thousands of our troops were captured. I was so angry, I wished the Prussians had shot him. I now regret ever having such evil thoughts!'

'I'm utterly staggered by your story. You amaze me,' said Ethel. 'So what happened to your husband?'

140

'They eventually released him, and he came back to Paris. And that was the end of the Second Republic. My husband and I fled to England and lived for a time in Chislehurst. Then a few years later, not in good health, he unfortunately died. Then in '79 our loving son died, would you believe, fighting for the English in the Zulu War? I miss them both, dreadfully,' she said, with a tear rolling down her face.

'Please don't be sad, Eugénie,' said her mother. 'You now have good friends around you and none of the pressures you were under before.' Not that what she said could do much to quell the lady's tears.

'Let me pour you another cup of tea,' said Ethel. 'And I'll wipe your tears away.'

'You are kind, Ethel. I'm fine now.'

Shortly after the Empress had related her story, which enthralled Ethel, she and her mother bid their farewells to this incredible woman, who said she'd love to see Ethel again, and drove back to Frimhurst. After another visit to Mary and one to Alice, Ethel made her way back to Florence.

# CHAPTER 14

## Return to Florence

Ethel had three aims in going back. She wanted to take up the kind invitation that Harry and Julia had given her to return. She still saw Julia as a challenge and badly wanted her to become a genuine friend, despite her reluctance before. Third, she wanted to see more of Florence and other parts of Italy now that her leg was completely better.

'Welcome back to the Via de' Bardi,' said Julia, as she opened the door to Ethel. 'You are travelling light again!'

Ethel beamed at what seemed to be a genuine welcome. 'Yes, I rely on being able to wash my things. It's wonderful to see you again. I hope you are both well and got my letter all right.'

'Yes, we were expecting you today or tomorrow, Ethel, and it's great to see you, too.'

Moments later, Ethel was giving Harry a hug and a kiss. He was obviously pleased to see her, even more so than Julia.

'I'm absolutely delighted you've come back to see us, Ethel,' he said, after their embrace. 'Much has happened since you were here before. We can discuss it over dinner. Let me take your bags up to your room.'

Ethel wondered what could deserve the announcement of a discussion over dinner. Had he taken up a professorship at the university? As before, was he about to go abroad? Had they had a disastrous falling out with the Hildebrands? Were they moving to France or somewhere else in Italy?

'Well, Ethel, we have spent a lot of time talking about you in the last year. Do you remember I went to Algeria for two weeks, shortly after you came to see us?'

'I do and I thought it very odd! Especially as I was supposed to be your guest!'

'There was one simple reason for my absence. It was that… and I'm now going to shock you, Ethel… I was beginning to fall in love with you!'

'My God. I'm incredulous! What, me?'

'Yes, you.'

'Julia and I discussed the problem which, as my wife and friend, she had noticed. We decided a period of separation would cure me. So I went to Algiers, as you know, on the pretext of improving my Arabic.'

'No, I don't know if I knew that,' said Ethel, with eyes wide open and quivering at what he was saying.

'During the year of your absence, both Julia and I have realised that although I felt the stay in Algeria had the desired effect, I still love you. I am deeply and irretrievably in love with you. That is why we need a discussion. I simply don't know what to do about it… and neither does Julia.' What Harry did not reveal was that he desperately wanted a strong physical relationship with Ethel and the sooner he could have her the better.

'I agree with everything Harry is saying,' said Julia. 'We have, as I explained to you, an open relationship. This means that either can break away, whenever they please. After all, we married only because my horrible mother insisted. So, but for that, we are friends living together.'

'Not that any speedy action is needed by any of us,' said Harry. 'What do you think, Ethel?'

'The simple answer is, I don't know what to think. I have to tell you both that I am especially fond of Julia. I'd like to have a closer, more loving relationship with you, Julia. That's one reason for my return. Unlike most women, I don't have a lot of time for men. I love women and I've had some wonderful and satisfying relationships with them. For example, Lisl. I've loved other women before her. The singer Augusta Redecker. The actress Marie Geistinger. I like you, Harry. We've had many interesting discussions, but the fact is I'm not in love with you. And I never will be!'

Julia's lips formed a partial smile, relieved at what Ethel was saying. She fully realised, from Ethel's attempts to become closer to her, that she loved women more than men. It was a well-known phenomenon, but little publicised or discussed. Julia thought that while the trip to Algeria failed to dampen Harry's attraction for Ethel, prolonged exposure, hour by hour, day after day in front of this noisy torrent of argument and energy, he might just realise how much better off he would be to leave things as they were and let thoughts of Ethel fade into oblivion.

For days, Julia's idea worked well. For much of the time, she could hear the two of them arguing and shouting at the tops of their voices about some principle or other: the merits or otherwise of 'King Lear', whether Racine was a homosexual, whether Lope de Vega or Calderón de la Barca was the greater playwright, who was the world's greatest sculptor, whether Beethoven's ninth symphony was the greatest ever written. Julia thought they were virtually coming to blows over these opinionated arguments. Fists struck tables; feet stamped on the floor.

Even their children became bored with her. They tired of the sonatas she had written, played on the piano as loud as she could. And her songs, sung at the top of her voice. They lost interest in playing card games with her, and sighed at her excuses when she lost. Her charging around their tiny garden, jumping the bench and a table, failed to amuse them. She wanted to play cricket with them, but they refused after one attempt. Against their wishes, she took them to places in Florence they had never seen before. They became exhausted by her.

After a couple of weeks of ignoring these issues, Ethel decided she would go to Puglia and spend a week there. Then she would go to Rome. So, much to their relief, except of course Harry's, the family had a welcomed break from the hurricane that was Ethel. Knowing she was skilled at using a gun, she bought herself a revolver to protect herself. Having visited all the major towns there, she left Puglia with the impression that the Italians were the most wonderful people on Earth. She fell in love with Rome to the extent that, if there was another city in the world she could easily live in, this was the one. Its architectural beauty astounded her.

While she toured these regions of Italy, Harry and Julia had much to say to each other about the future of the relationship between them.

'So what are your intentions, Harry?' said Julia, at lunch one day, smiling in such a way as to mock his vulnerability to his feelings about Ethel. It was as if he was the victim.

'Frankly, I don't know. I love Ethel and I want her. I want to live with her and go wherever she wants to go.'

Julia laughed. 'Why didn't you decide to go to Puglia with her then? You could have shown her the sights of Rome.'

'The problem is that although I love her, she doesn't love me. I don't know how to persuade her.'

'She can't love you, Harry. Can't you see? She loves women. I've told you! She's told you! And if she changed her mind and fell in love with you, the relationship could go nowhere. You are a married man, like it or not. An affair with you would destroy the relationship with her family. Imagine what the general would think. She would become an outcast. She would wreck her career as a composer. Can't you see it?'

'I would not leave you, Julia. We would behave discreetly. We would write to each other. If we met we would meet in cafes in side streets and book into different hotels.'

'Now you're being stupid! No such relationship exists. You said you want her. That means you want to sleep with her. What would she think about becoming pregnant? Even more shame on her family. You've always been a dreamer, Harry, but never to this extent.'

'It's pointless discussing this because she doesn't love me.'

'If she changes her mind, I shall not give in. We made a solemn pledge of marriage and have lived under that pledge for eleven years. I know in our youth we did not want a marriage, but here we are married and I intend to stay that way. Whether you like it or not.'

She walked out of the room and slammed the door behind her. Harry was not the man to give up. He had enough of living in the confines of life with the colourless Julia. He wanted new pastures, adventure and freedom. Ethel had extracted him from his shell. She would be his saviour, the key to a renewed future. And he wanted her in bed with him.

Ethel could detect the tensions between Julia and Harry from the moment she returned. She ignored it and carried on as if everything was normal. She reported back on everything she saw and told them at the dinner table about the wonderful people she had met.

'At one point someone told me if I went up the Apennines to a certain spot, I could see both the Adriatic and the Mediterranean. I did as exactly as I was told and sure enough, I could see these great seas.'

'Really,' said an indifferent Julia.

'Amazing,' said Harry. 'I'd love to do something like that myself. Not just now but in the future!'

'Not only that, while I was up there, I met this odd character who claimed to be a baron. He was at least twenty years older than me. He told me I'd have a better view from another place, near where I met him. So, armed with my revolver, I decided I could do more harm to him than he to me, so I followed him.'

'A revolver? Where did you find a revolver? You don't know how to use a revolver, do you?' said Harry.

'Yes, I learnt to shoot when I was younger, at home. I bought it at the gunsmiths in the market square. He let me have it for a good price, as it wasn't new.'

'So did you see that better view?' said Julia.

'No. The mist came down and we could only see the Mediterranean. But the baron really looked after me. He made some wonderful picnics with a tablecloth, cutlery and glasses and we sang long into the night, then slept on the side of the mountain. It was an adventure! He gave me his card, and it's in my rucksack.'

Ethel's break in Florence with the Brewsters continued. She was as boisterous, energetic and just as noisy as she was before she went to Puglia. The tension between Julia and Harry remained.

Suddenly, for no obvious reason and not prompted by anything any of them said or did, Ethel came to the sudden realisation that frightened her as much as confronting an alligator. She was falling in love with Harry. The thought stopped her from sleeping that night and made her toss and turn in bed. She couldn't understand what was happening in her mind. She loved women. How could she suddenly discover she loved a man? Could she love men and women? There could be nothing but shame in taking a man from his wife. And the thought of having a man penetrate her body. Could she stand the pain? She shivered in fear. The ineluctable fact was she was falling for him.

She needed to think clearly. Unlike the situation of a single woman falling in love with an unattached man, there were four people involved in this. Her, Julia, Lisl and Harry. She didn't want to steal Harry from Julia. It was Lisl she loved and didn't want to lose her. She would have to discuss this with Harry and Julia. Breakfast presented the opportunity, difficult though it would be.

'I'm furious with you, Ethel. We invite you into our home… something we have built up over ten years… and now you are attempting to steal my husband,' she said, shaking. 'And I'm even angrier with you, Harry. Because you started all this,' she shouted. Then burst into tears.

Harry went to the other side of the table to put his arm around her. She pushed him away.

'I don't know what to say, my love,' said Harry.

'Don't you "my love" me! If you think you can escape from our marriage, you can think again!'

Ethel didn't know what to say. She had caused a rift between a man and his wife. Things may not have been perfect between them when she first arrived a year ago. But because of her, the two of them were at loggerheads.

'Let's try to deal with this calmly,' said Harry, trying to take the heat out of the discussion.

'How can we?' shrieked Julia. 'Calmly? When this woman wants you, now she tells us, as much as you want her.'

'Put it this way, Julia. I am a decent man and basically kind. So I propose Ethel leaves and that we never see each other again.'

Before Julia responded, Ethel spoke.

'I agree with Harry. I am much in love with your sister, Lisl, and I don't want to lose her. I will not demean myself by being a married man's mistress. That would put me to shame, and I couldn't accept it, nor would my family and friends. And I don't want to hurt either of you. So I shall leave, wash Harry out of my thoughts and we shall never meet again.'

\*\*\*

Ethel headed for Berchtesgaden to open her heart to Lisl. By then, she and Heinrich were living in the modest new house being built during Ethel's previous visit. Lisl greeted her with the passionate embrace to which she had become accustomed.

'My dear Ethel, your brief letter arrived yesterday so we are expecting you. You looked distressed and you have a worrying story to tell me, so you say in your missive.'

'Can we discuss this in private, Lisl? It is not something I especially want Heinrich to know about, before we have spoken.'

'We will discuss it in our third bedroom, Ethel. The one I have furnished for you.'

Lisl tucked her legs under her thighs on the bed while Ethel tried to relax in an armchair that was a little too small. She related the whole story, starting from her visit to Florence the previous year. She calmly told her about Harry falling in love with her and her eventually falling for him. Then she explained they had parted never to see each other again.

'I know all about it, Ethel. Julia has told me the entire story. Her letter arrived on the same day as yours. I fully understand.'

'It is you I love, Lisl, not Harry. I have put him out of my mind.'

'Don't worry, Ethel, I still love you as my little daughter and always will. I attach no blame to you over a situation my brother-in-law created. We are as close now, if not more so, as we were before.'

'I am so relieved, Lisl. I could never be that man's mistress any more than I could love the devil. You are the love of my life.'

***

So Ethel went back home to England knowing, or at least believing, that her relationship with Lisl was still intact and even stronger. Her family was delighted she had returned, especially her mother.

Ethel told them all about her stay with the Brewsters - but not about the extraordinary eruptions over her relationships with them. She told her family about her adventures in Puglia and Rome, that she had bought a pistol in Florence, about the baron with whom she had picnicked on the Apennines, how utterly faultless the Italians were as a people.

'Do you mean to say you slept with this baron fellow?' said the General.

'For one night on the side of a hill. If he'd tried anything physical with me, I'd have shot him in self-defence.'

'I see,' he said, unconvinced.

She had them laughing in unison when she described the health resort and that Lisl and she had enjoyed a friendly wrestling match in the mud. As usual, there were discussions about how close they were to living in poverty and that their finances were still in a state of irretrievable chaos.

A few weeks after Ethel's homecoming and while in her room working on a new string quartet, there was a gentle knock on her door.

'Are you in there, Ethel? I have a letter for you. It looks as if it's from Italy.'

'Yes, bring it in, Mama. Please.' Several thoughts flashed through her mind. Could it be from Harry, again declaring his love for her? Or telling her that something bad had happened to Julia. Could it be a letter from Julia condemning Ethel again, or telling her some bad news about Harry?

'You look worried, Ethel, and you haven't opened it yet.'

'I am worried, Mama. Maybe, not good news.'

Ethel's mother left her to open and read it. It was from Harry. Its content almost knocked her off her feet. It said that Julia and he had been discussing his relationship with Ethel and that the two of them were wondering whether it was morally right to end it. They had agreed that they should continue the relationship through correspondence to see if it was merely an infatuation. If so, it would peter out. If not, Julia had agreed that they should meet socially from time to time. It said that Harry felt then that he loved both of them and that he didn't want to give up Julia any more than to give up Ethel.

Seething with rage, Ethel screwed up the letter and threw it into the rubbish bin. She couldn't believe the nerve of the man. By some corrupt means, he had persuaded his wife that they had got it all wrong and that door, which less than a month ago they had slammed shut, was now open.

Her first thought was that he was lying, and that Julia knew nothing of this letter. It was a fabrication, crudely designed as the first step in his renewed efforts at her seduction. Then she thought again. Harry seemed totally honest to her. She had no evidence of him lying. The letter demanded a reply. She bent over and retrieved it from the bin.

She would have to be careful about what she said. Julia or Lisl or both could see any reply. She would tell Harry that she wanted nothing to do with him. She said she didn't believe Julia would accept their meeting. It would undermine their marriage. He should take it that this would be the last letter in their correspondence. She took the letter to the post office and posted it.

Mainly to satisfy her continuing curiosity about what Lisl thought, she would write to her to express her ardent love for her and to tell her about the letter Harry had written and her reply. She told Lisl she would return to Leipzig for the winter.

Harry must have written a reply the moment he received Ethel's letter. It reiterated what he claimed to be their agreed position and there could be no harm in their meeting occasionally or in continuing to correspond. Ethel did not reply. She continued working and engaging with her family until her return to Leipzig.

# CHAPTER 15

## Agony shared

Lisl greeted Ethel's return to Leipzig for the winter of '85 with a more muted welcome than the uninhibited outpouring of affection that she usually gave her. Heinrich put his hand out to her in the friendly way he always had. The three of them settled into a similar routine to the one they adopted before Ethel went to Florence. The differences were that Ethel spent more time composing with Heinrich checking her work and less time reading Bach counterpoint, and Lisl spent less time in Heinrich's tutorials. Ethel stayed in her room in their house but spent days at a time in her lodgings, on her own, writing her music. She enjoyed this greater independence but the perceptibly cooler atmosphere in the Herzogenberg's house troubled her. She decided not to discuss it with them and hoped matters would improve. However, after a couple of months of the three of them muddling along together, Lisl found the courage to tell Ethel what was troubling her.

'I can't help but raise the question of Harry Brewster,' she said, one morning while Heinrich had gone to a meeting with Engelbert Röentgen, the leader of the Gewandhaus Orchestra.

'Go ahead,' said Ethel.

'How did the situation arise exactly?'

'I told you before I went back to England. He fell in love with me. A fortnight before I left Florence to come to see you, I thought I was in love with him. There was no joy because he was in a marriage and I was already in love with you. I wrote to tell you about the exchange of letters with him. There is nothing more to it than that, and nothing more to say.'

'Well, Ethel, Julia has written to me several times while you have been away, accusing you of interfering in their relationship. She suspects you of committing adultery with her husband.'

This accusation shattered Ethel into pieces. 'I'm totally staggered by that, Lisl. It is totally untrue. She's lied to you!'

'I believe you, Ethel. Truly, I do. I don't know why she wrote such a thing.'

'I do, Lisl. It's jealousy of the loving relationship that we have.' She got up from the chair, went to Lisl and kissed her. Lisl was, however, still not satisfied.

'Julia tells me you are still writing to Harry. Is that so?'

'My dear Lisl, I told Harry as I told you, I never wanted to have anything to do with him after I left Florence. I left early because I wanted to forget him. I could see that to do otherwise would damage their marriage. And I feared any physical contact. The idea of penetration terrifies me.'

'I believe you, Ethel. Don't worry about our relationship. I am wholly confident in that. I have no reservations about your love for me.'

The door opened, and Heinrich appeared with a mischievous smile on his face.

'You two look serious. What's happened?'

'Nothing,' said Lisl. 'I was just telling Ethel about our move to Dresden and your work with the orchestra there.'

Ethel could hardly contain her surprise. She thought they would never move from Leipzig, not in a thousand years.

'And I've got good news for you two! The Gewandhaus have agreed to play my symphony. I'm absolutely delighted. Thrilled. And they are going to pay me!'

Lisl rushed over to him and put a kiss on his lips. 'Wonderful, Heinrich! Congratulations. When will they play it?'

'Not until the autumn. So there will be quite a wait!'

'Fantastic news, Heinrich. Well done!' Ethel kissed him, too.

153

Lisl remained unhappy about the situation between Ethel and Harry. She needed to speak to Ethel again about it, before they left for Dresden, mainly because she had received a letter from her brother.

'I'm sorry to go back to the problems with Harry, Ethel. I've had a letter from my brother. It talks about you breaking up the marriage between Julia and Harry. It's not a pleasant letter to read. But I will always support you, believe me.'

Ethel was almost in tears at this fresh revelation. 'That is simply untrue, my dear Lisl. Harry and I spoke a lot about many cultural matters, and all I can think is that jealousy crept in somewhere. I never as much as hinted I wanted any relationship with him. He did with me, but that wasn't my fault. I rejected him.'

'Don't worry, my dear Ethel. Let's drop the subject now. I won't bring it up again.'

Later that day, Ethel arranged for a bouquet of red roses to be sent to Lisl. Lisl glowed at them and sent a note to Ethel's lodgings thanking her. She said she had a heavy heart and that 'I still enjoy having to fight for you, my loyal child. Don't distrust me when a word seems sometimes to contradict me! I believe in you!'

Ethel was unsure of what to make of these words. Did Lisl really believe in her, or was there doubt in her mind?

*** 

At the beginning of May, Heinrich and Lisl departed for Dresden. Ethel accompanied them to the station and waved frantically, as the train slowly pulled way. Lisl and Heinrich waved back. Little did Ethel realise she would never see Lisl again.

Ethel and Lisl usually corresponded with each other once a week, so a week after Lisl left, Ethel wrote to her saying how she had enjoyed their recent meetings in Leipzig and that she would soon return to England. It was not until the middle of June that Ethel received the reply. The gist of it was that their relationship could no longer continue in the way it had, at least not for the present. Ethel was distraught and saw the love of her life fading. The exchanges between them over the following few months were bereft of joy, aching with regrets and scattered with reproaches. Then Lisl's letters ceased completely.

The effect on Ethel was catastrophic. This was territory she had never entered before, not even when Johnny died. She stopped composing and became ill with remorse. It was as if she was grieving for a woman so emotionally distant that she may as well be dead. She became a child again, attempting to grasp at the apron strings of her mother. But her mother had aged, had become deaf, arthritic and aggressive. So she could not give Ethel the emotional support she craved.

***

As the wife of the Archbishop of Canterbury, Mary Benson enjoyed living in luxury in the ancient and historical Lambeth Palace. As befitting of her husband's position, the palace abounded in servants and lackeys, engaged by the Church to make their lives comfortable and relatively easy. She married Edward, her second cousin, when eighteen and when he was thirty. He had fallen in love with her when she was eleven. While a good and loving mother, Mary lived a life which rarely overlapped with that of her husband. Six years after they married, Mary became completely enamoured with a woman called Emily Edwardes. The force of attraction sent Mary into a new world of human experience, of daring, experimenting and ecstasy. It engulfed her completely. Her attraction to women extended into her husband's time as Archbishop. They spoke about it and prayed together about it. Emily was not the only woman Mary fell for. In '71, after the birth of her sixth child, she became ill and went to Wiesbaden to recuperate. There she fell for an Ellen Hall with whom she had a madly passionate fling. She met, but did not fall for, a 'Tan' Mylne when she returned. Tan was a woman of strong religious views. Mary confessed her feelings for women to Tan, who helped her understand what Mary called this 'stain' on her life and tried to help her overcome it. She failed.

It was at about this time that Ethel needed help to overcome her depression. Mary Benson and Ethel met in the autumn of '85 at a party organised by Alice, Ethel's eldest sister, at the Deanery of Windsor. Alice's husband Harry was the brother of the Dean.

It was less than half an hour after they were introduced when Ethel and Mary were deep into a quite intimate conversation. Ethel told her about herself and her sadness over the disintegration of her relationship with Lisl.

'I can fully sympathise,' said Mary. 'I've had several such relationships. We should become friends, Ethel. That way I can probably help you overcome this.'

'That would be utterly wonderful, Mary. I am feeling better already!'

Mary explained that, as she had become older, she had turned to being a counsellor to people, mainly women, who needed the help she could give.

'I don't want you to pass this on, Ethel, but the Archbishop treats me like some chattel. So I've learnt tolerance and forgiveness. I've turned to women, partly because I didn't and don't want a relationship with another man. They're too demanding... in more ways than one!'

'I am so sorry about the Archbishop.'

'Oh, don't worry about him. I just go my own way. In fact, doing so has made me able to help others... such as you. Let's share ourselves with others while we are here, but I want to see you at Lambeth Palace. Are you free next Wednesday morning? I can see you at 10 o'clock.'

'That would be perfect, Mary. I look forward to seeing you then.'

***

Ethel walked from Waterloo Station down York Road and along Lambeth Palace Road to the Palace, at the foot of Lambeth Bridge. She walked towards the main door and knocked. A miserable man let her in and led her into a waiting room, just like a doctor's surgery. Ten o'clock came and went. It was almost half past when the door to Mrs Benson's office opened.

'Goodbye. So see you in a week's time,' she said to an emerging plump woman with a brimmed hat and no neck.

'It's so good to see you, Ethel. Do come in. Would you like a cup of tea?' she said and launched a kiss full onto Ethel's lips.

'No thank you, Mary. I'm happy just to talk.'

'The best place to start is the beginning, so let's start there, shall we?'

Ethel explained how the relationship with Lisl began, what wonderful, often amusing, times they spent together, such as in the mud bath as Aibling, her visit to Florence, Harry falling for her and its unfortunate aftermath.

'You're going to have to tell me more about the people involved, Ethel, if I am to help you overcome this. For example, what relatives does Lisl have? Could they have influenced her decision to break with you?'

Ethel told her more about Julia. She painted the sad picture of her unconventional marriage, which had frozen for ten years. Then she told her about Baroness Stockhausen, Lisl and Julia's mother, who could not stand Ethel's presence in the same house, let alone the same room. With tears welling in her eyes, she related the story of the nasty letter Lisl's brother sent, just before Lisl left for Dresden.

'I'm sure I can see what's happened, Ethel. It is this. Several sources have influenced Lisl. The letters she received from Julia, discussions with her mother, who, through jealousy of your relationship with her daughter, clearly loathed you. The brother's letter about you. And who knows who else influenced her. With this background of forces against you, Lisl, who is not as strong as you, sided with them. She probably feels as devastated as you. So you are not at fault. You may have got a little too close to Harry, as far as Julia was concerned, but she could have stopped that if she wanted to do so.'

'You make me feel so relieved,' said Ethel, with tears running down her face. 'I haven't felt better since I left Leipzig. I'm so grateful, Mary.'

'There may be even more to this. Are there any more people in this drama who may have played a part?'

'On my way to Florence, at Lisl's suggestion, I called in to see the Hildebrands who also live in Florence. They are friends of Lisl and her husband. He is a moderately well-known sculptor. I spent quite a lot of my time there talking to him about sculpture, art and music. I was never sure what his wife, Irene thought…'

Mary interrupted. 'That's it, Ethel. She was jealous, and she has also influenced Lisl. That's almost certainly what added to her misery!'

'You're brilliant, Mary. I've truly not felt better! Just through speaking to you.'

'I'm so glad I could help. We should meet again soon, next week maybe? I would like you to meet my family. Come to dinner next Tuesday. Let me know if you are free! There is probably someone else waiting for me outside. I am running late today!'

'I'm sure I'm free then, Mary. Yes, I'll come!'

Mary kissed Ethel on the lips again and opened the door for her. Sure enough, there was another customer waiting outside. She looked tense and troubled.

*** 

Ethel looked forward to the dinner with Mary Benson and her family. She pondered for many days what it would be like to meet the daunting figure of the Archbishop whom she had barely glimpsed at the party at the Deanery. And she wanted to meet her children, the eldest of which was only two years younger than her and the youngest a mere fifteen.

'So you are the woman composer, are you?' was the awkward welcome the Archbishop gave her.

'Yes, I am actually. I can play you some of my music, if you wish.'

'Not really,' was the starchy reply.

Mary witnessed this exchange and, if only to manage Ethel's escape from her husband, promptly introduced her to her daughter, Maggie.

'My mother has said so much about you, Ethel, so I'm very pleased to meet you. We have a good deal in common. We are both artists in our different ways. I

158

paint and you write music. At present, I'm a student at Oxford. So I have little time for painting.'

'You must show me some of your paintings,' said Ethel. 'It's something I haven't tried yet but I might. Who knows?'

'And despite Papa, I would love to hear some of your compositions.'

Maggie seemed very intelligent to Ethel. They conversed on a range of subjects, including the place of art in society and politics, and the mischief caused by Mr Gladstone.

'I'll introduce you to my brother, Robert. He's the youngest of us and is the cleverest by far!' said Maggie.

Ethel heard no one speak as quickly as young Robert Benson. He was only fifteen. Occasionally, he stumbled over his words. It was as if his brain was working faster than he could speak.

'I really like school,' he said. 'I especially like mathematics and am the best in my class at algebra and trigonometry. But what I want to do when I grow up is to be a writer. I spend quite a lot of time writing short horror stories and science fiction. But I love writing about horror more than anything else!'

'So you don't want to follow your father into the Church?' said Ethel.

'No. I'd rather do something creative! Writing sermons doesn't appeal to me!' he said, the only one up to then who betrayed a sense of humour.

'So where are you at school?'

'Eton College actually,' he said, in a tone Ethel interpreted as an apology. But she couldn't see why.

'So you are my mother's new friend, Ethel,' said Nelly, a cheery lass who looked a few years older than Maggie but seemed equally intelligent. 'I'd love to hear some of your music, too. I don't think I've met a composer before!'

'And there isn't always a first time,' quipped Ethel. 'We are a rare breed, you know!'

'What else do you do? You don't compose all the time!'

'I ride, play cricket, swim and play many games, mainly with my brothers and sisters, even though they've all grown up now. And I have a strong sense of adventure. I toured Puglia nearly two years ago and I've been all over Bavaria and Saxony.'

'We have a lot in common. I love adventure too and sport and playing games. I can see we'll be good friends, Ethel.'

She also spoke to Edward and Arthur, but neither seemed interested in her.

The dinner was what Ethel regarded as an excessively formal occasion which started with the Archbishop delivering a never-ending grace which sought redemption for every soul on earth, virtually one by one. He led what brief conversation there was, and rebuked Mary at least twice, once for mispronouncing the name of one of his archdeacons. Mary simply ignored his poorly timed remarks.

'You must stay the night,' she insisted. 'There are plenty of furnished rooms in the palace. We've entertained you for far too long and I won't have you going home this late.' Ethel was grateful and relieved. She was surprised when Mary came unannounced into her room, just as Ethel was climbing into bed, to kiss her goodnight.

That room became Ethel's permanent mooring at Lambeth Palace, in the sense that it was available any time she wanted to use it; and use it she did. The Archbishop, however, strongly disliked Ethel and couldn't stand the sight of her. Even to glance her through a window brought on an attack of anger verging on rage. So, while he was in the Palace, Mary would smuggle Ethel in through a side entrance or up through the Palace gardens. It reminded Ethel of the way the overbearing Baroness Stockhausen treated her, even though she never understood why. The reasons for the Archbishop's dislike of her were obvious enough to Ethel. His wife fell for many women she met and, to the Archbishop, who was all too familiar with his wife's dalliances, Ethel was yet another. So he was fearful and jealous of young Ethel, some forty years younger than his wife, but a possible new lover all the same.

Mary became a steadying rock for the troubled Ethel who, from meeting her, gradually climbed out of the abyss which was opened solely by the break with Lisl. She gave Ethel the confidence to return to Germany and the motivation to restart her composing.

# CHAPTER 16

## The Master Criticised

Knowing that the Herzogenbergs had left Leipzig, Ethel returned to her digs in the Salomonstrasse. She knew few people in the English musical scene and, rather than penetrate what seemed a dusty, introverted scattering of individuals, she decided Germany was by far the better option. Not only that, by then she had cultivated an impressive circle of friends and contacts, not least the Wachs, the Freges, the Limburgers and Frau Schumann and her daughters. She had also met Dvořák and Grieg at one of Lisl's gatherings, so vaguely knew them, too.

Ethel did not live alone for long. In February 1887, her loyal friend, Ella Limburger, while strolling through a street market, saw a huge yellow and white puppy. The seller claimed it was a cross between a St Bernard and another breed he could not identify. Frau Limburger immediately fell in love with the handsome creature and took him home. Julius, already the owner of three dogs, fumed the moment he saw him and demanded she take him back. An impossibility because the market stall would have closed by then and the seller returned home. Ethel heard about all this and, almost on her knees, begged Ella to let her have the dog. Ethel called it Marco and took it everywhere she could. She loved Marco and while he didn't replace her human loves, made an amazing and sometimes embarrassing companion.

Not long after acquiring Marco, Ethel was invited to a rehearsal at Brodsky, the violinist's, flat at which Brahms would play in his Piano Quintet.

'You turn over the pages, Ethel, as I play the piano parts,' said the great man. 'Brod, are you ready to go?'

'Yes, Jo. When you are.'

All was going nicely until the door burst open and Marco bounded in, knocking the cellist's stand to the floor. He sidled up to Ethel to lick her face. Ethel wondered how Brahms would react.

'My God, Ethel, that reminds me of the pantomimes of my youth when the harlequin bursts in. He rarely knocked the music stand over though!' said Brahms, laughing all over his face. Ethel was much relieved.

\*\*\*

To her great pleasure, the Griegs invited Ethel to dinner in their flat near the Gewandhaus. As usual, she dressed in her tweeds and had asked them if she could bring Marco to which they readily agreed.

'What a nice present, Ethel! Praise be to you,' said Nina, his pretty wife, as she accepted the bouquet of white roses which Ethel brought her. 'Come and say hello to Edvard.'

Grieg was sitting at their piano, his hand holding a pencil with which he was making some changes to a piece he had written. Ethel stopped so as not to disturb him.

'Oh, come in, Ethel! I'm just fiddling about! I'm having a real problem with my fourth book of Lyric Pieces! It's the cursed third one! I've called it Melody, but something less like a melody you will never have heard! You might like to look at it for me!'

Ethel could not believe that this famous composer was asking her to help him with his composition. 'I'm flattered you ask me,' she said in an outburst of modesty. 'Yes, of course!'

'Not before we've had dinner, though!' said Nina. 'I can leave you two composing then!'

Nina had prepared a typical Norwegian meal. They started with pickled herring, which was followed by venison steak and red cabbage.

'I just love venison,' said Ethel, tucking in heartily. 'It's something we rarely see in England.' Marco sat under the table next to Ethel, who surreptitiously passed him the odd morsel.

'We have venison often. There are many deer in the forests around here and many Germans like to hunt.'

'I am amazed you two look so similar,' said Ethel, gazing at the beautiful features of Nina, although not tall, a typical Norsk blond.

'There is a reason for that,' said Edvard. 'Nina is my first cousin. We simply fell in love and married!'

For reasons she didn't understand, Ethel felt embarrassed at her question, so promptly changed the subject.

'I saw you two performing recently at the Gewandhaus.'

'Yes, the Romances and Songs. I just love singing them. The lovely words are by Hans Christian Andersen,' said Nina.

'And I enjoy playing them,' said Edvard. 'I know I shouldn't say that because I wrote the music!'

'Has Edvard told you about the time we first met?' said Ethel.

'I don't think so,' said Nina.

'Do you remember, Edvard?'

'No, I'm not sure I do!'

'It was at Heinrich Herzogenberg's house, a good few years ago, seven or eight, maybe.' She couldn't bear to mention Lisl. 'We were discussing Liszt's music, which was out of favour then, if it isn't now. I said I didn't like it either and you, Edvard, snapped back at me, asking what a beginner like me could know about it!'

'I couldn't have been that bad, could I, Ethel? Not to a lovely lady like you,' he said, with his eyebrows raised and his moustache twitching a little.

'You came over to me afterwards to say how sorry you were, so all ended well. You were right, though. I spoke out of turn!'

'I remember now. You had just finished studying at the Conservatory. I believe you had resigned or were just about to! I told you then that I thought I had wasted my time there, too!'

164

After dinner and with Nina's blessing, Edvard and Ethel returned to the piano to see if they could solve the problem Edvard was having with the third movement of his Lyric Pieces. Marco followed.

'I fancy I can see what's wrong, Edvard!'

'Go on... tell me!'

'You need to repeat some bars, say from here to here,' she said, pointing at the score with a pencil. 'That will give the listener a sense of familiarity and a better sense of melody.'

'Good thought, Ethel. I'll play it now.' Edvard pulled up the piano stool and tried it.

'My goodness, Ethel, it works! Composing comes easily to you! I'll do that all the way through, wherever it makes sense. I'm so glad I asked you!'

Ethel slept well that night in the comfort that she had quite impressed Edvard Grieg with her idea.

***

A dog the size of Marco needed several walks a day so Ethel often took him to the Johanna Park, which was a short walk from her lodgings. On this particular day, not long after her dinner with the Griegs, she was walking along the main path through the park when she passed a man sitting on a bench. He responded to her glance at him by briefly looking back at her. She went through one of those moments of possible but uncertain recognition of the face of another. She had seen him before, or someone who looked remarkably like him. It may have been in a restaurant, a tavern, or even at the Gewandhaus concert hall. She carried on but overcome by curiosity, and after about another hundred yards of walking and puzzling over this individual, turned around to have a closer look.

She stopped in front of him. Marco seemed put out by this sudden interruption. Never a shy or reserved person, Ethel asked the man straight out.

'Good morning, Sir. Do I recognise you as Pyotr Tchaikovsky?'

'Well,' said the man. 'I'm not sure I want my privacy invaded by a young woman and her bodyguard,' he said, smiling cheekily.

From that moment Ethel thought she was right and broke into a smile.

'I admit, I am the person you have surmised I could be!' He laughed as if he was enjoying this interruption. 'How do you know it's me?'

'I often attend concerts in the Gewandhaus, and I listened with great interest to your fourth symphony only a few weeks ago. You conducted the work, and I was near the front, so got an excellent view of you as you faced the audience. Perhaps I shouldn't tell you this, but I too am a composer, yet to be well known.'

'You must tell me more, young lady. But let us find a place more conducive to conversation. If you agree, I shall buy you a coffee at the restaurant at the entrance to the park.'

The two of them were soon enjoying a typical Leipzig coffee, and each other's company as Marco sat, apparently listening in.

'So I've met another composer today,' said Tchaikovsky. 'I'm delighted to meet a fellow tunesmith!' Ethel was pleased that he didn't mention, as did many, that she was a woman and women rarely composed music. 'So tell me, what have you written so far?'

She told him about her songs, the piano sonatas, the good many quartets she had written and the quintet.

'Have you written for a full orchestra yet?'

'No, but I should because I want to write opera,' she said, stressing the urgency.

'We must see what we can do to speed that along,' said Tchaikovsky.

The conversation continued in this vein for longer than the two of them imagined. Marco was becoming restless and growled gently.

'What was that?' said Tchaikovsky, furrowing his brow.

'Only my dog. His name is Marco, by the way… and I am Ethel Smyth. He's becoming impatient, so I need to take him for another walk. I hope that's all right.'

'Of course, Miss Smyth. We must meet again soon. Within the next week, if we can.'

'I am a passably good cook and would love to prepare you a meal, lunch maybe. Just an idea. I live in Salomonstrasse. Would you be free for lunch around midday on Friday?' Just after she said it, she couldn't believe she had. What a cheek, inviting this famous composer to eat with a mere beginner.

'I accept your kind invitation, Miss Smyth. We will talk about writing for orchestras!'

Ethel gave him detailed instructions on finding her digs. They shook hands and parted. A relieved Marco took off at such a pace that Ethel had trouble holding on to his lead.

*\*\**

'It smells good, whatever it is!' said Tchaikovsky, as Ethel opened the door to her little lodgings.

'I hope it tastes as good,' said Ethel. 'Welcome to my modest home in Leipzig.'

'I'm so pleased you invited me. I have few friends here, if any really. So it's really nice to have someone I can talk to.'

Ethel found it difficult to understand how this world-famous composer could be so lonely in this city of music. She would do her best to befriend this charming, gentle and sensitive individual. He was so different from the many loud, self-centred German musicians she had become used to tolerating. Most of them had never moved from Leipzig, their city of birth, but here was a genuine man of the world. He knew his way around Vienna, Munich, London, Paris and this city, and St Petersburg and Moscow.

They soon started discussing their respective musical interests, as they dug into the roast gammon that Ethel had cooked.

'This is good, Miss Smyth. Do you mind if I call you Ethel? It is Ethel, isn't it? I'd be pleased if you call me Pyotr.'

'Well remembered, Pyotr. Yes, Ethel it is!'

'So where do we start?' said Tchaikovsky. 'Which composers do you admire most?'

Ethel reeled off a list of them and their works she liked most. Tchaikovsky replied.

'Schubert. I love his music. Beethoven. Another perfect genius. Heinrich Hoffman. Well. Very good. Wagner another master. But Brahms? Overrated. What do you see in his music?'

'He's brilliant. I love his second symphony, that rolling theme at the beginning. In fact, one of the Herzogenbergs has written the whole thing as a solo piece for piano!' Again she couldn't say the name, Lisl.

'There is a lot wrong with that symphony, Ethel. Do you know what it is?'

'No. No idea.'

'Nice tunes there are, but it almost totally lacks good orchestration. And this is where I can help you. I may not be brilliant. I wouldn't dare elevate my ability. But I have worked hard on orchestration. I will tell you more!'

'Do you have the same views on any other composers?'

'Hmm! That's a tricky question. Let's say some are better than others at orchestration. But Brahms is not good! I can tell you some who are good: Bruckner and Richard Strauss. I've heard none of their music, but I've studied their scores. They are true orchestrators!'

'How can Brahms be that bad? I really don't understand you. You just don't like the man. I don't like him but I do like his music!'

'I can't say I like him either. He's self-inflated. Let's go to your piano. I'll show you what I mean about his music.'

Ethel took him into the sitting area and opened the lid of the piano.

'Here is something from one of his Piano Trios. It's in C minor. It's fairly new, opus a hundred and something.' He played a passage from memory.

'Isn't that hideous?' he said. 'It's awkward and it goes up a blind alley. Can't you see that?'

'I don't agree. It sounds relaxing to me. I can't see anything wrong with it!'

'You must be under some hypnotic influence. It's talentless!'

'I thought you were going to talk about orchestration!'

'I am, but not now. Reinecke wants to see me about something. I'm not sure what. I'm meeting him in half an hour, so I'd better go. Let's meet up again soon?'

'That would be excellent. I'm dying to learn more about orchestration!'

'You are a wonderful cook and I much appreciated the lunch! I'll treat you to a meal at the Rosenthal. Two days' time. Twelve o'clock. Must go!'

'No trouble. That'll be great!'

'Bye, Marco!'

The dog let out a minor gruff.

And he'd gone. Ethel couldn't remember a conversation like it. She thought he was wrong about Brahms, dislikeable man that he was.

*\*\**

The following day, just for a change, Ethel went to lunch at the refectory in the Conservatorium. She sat there drinking a coffee and eating a biscuit when she felt a tap on her shoulder.

'Hello, Ethel. I haven't seen you for ages!'

'My goodness, it's you, Theresia. How are you? I was only thinking of you yesterday!'

'I'm upset, really fed up and angry. But why were you thinking of me yesterday when we haven't seen each other for at least five years? Sounds like we were destined to meet today. What a coincidence!'

'You'll never believe this, but I met Tchaikovsky in Johanna Park. To shorten the story, I cooked him a gammon roast in my lodgings. Would you believe he mentioned your Uncle Anton? He said he'd heard none of his music but had studied his scores and thought his orchestration was very good!'

'You amaze me, Ethel! I didn't know Tchaikovsky knew about my uncle. And as for you entertaining him in your flat. Incredible!'

'I wouldn't lie to you, Theresia. So you must believe me! I'm having lunch with him tomorrow!'

'Of course, I believe you, Ethel!'

'So why are you so angry and upset, Theresia? I hate to see you unhappy.'

'I'm sure you remember, an official sexually assaulted me and tried it on with you. You fended him off. I didn't. Well, several years later, I still felt bad about it. After you left. So I lodged a formal complaint.'

'That's very courageous of you, Theresia,'

'That's the reason I was here today. To attend the hearing. I was the only witness. It was his word against mine. The tribunal didn't believe me. So he got away with it. That's why I am so angry!' She burst into tears, which ran down each side of her face.

Ethel got up from the table and went around to give her a hug. 'Please don't cry, Theresia.' She took out a handkerchief and gently wiped Theresia's eyes. 'You should lodge an appeal. I could act as a witness. I can tell them what he tried with me.'

'You are a marvel, Ethel. Let me think about it and let you know. The thought of having to go through all that again fills me with utter dread.'

'So what are you doing, now you've left the Conservatory?'

'I am a music teacher in a school in Austria, Ansfelden, in fact. And I compose in my spare time. I'm still single! What about you?'

Ethel told her about her time with the Herzogenbergs, Harry Brewster, and how she and Lisl broke up. She told her about the music she had composed and her visits to England and Italy. And about her saviour, Mary Benson.

'So I'm still single, too. I shall never marry. I'm too selfish… and I'm not impressed by men!'

They sat chatting and exchanging experiences until Theresia said she needed to catch a train back to Austria. They exchanged addresses. Theresia agreed to write to Ethel if she appealed the tribunal decision.

\*\*\*

Ethel wasn't sure she had seen dogs in the Rosenthal, but took Marco anyway. As a precaution, she took him for a long walk on her way to the restaurant but was still on time. She looked around the restaurant for Pyotr but couldn't see him. So she walked through to the gardens at the back. He wasn't there either. So she sat at a table in the garden and waited. She watched as a robin landed near her feet, and pecked at something before it flew away.

'Ethel, I apologise. I meant to be here earlier because I didn't like the idea of you being here before me and sitting alone. But I was delayed at a rehearsal. And you've got your bodyguard, anyway.'

'Please don't worry, Pyotr. It is truly not a problem!' said Ethel, smiling and obviously meaning it.

'To make up for my failure, you can have anything you like on the menu!'

'You are too generous, Pyotr!'

The waiter came to the table and Pyotr ordered a fillet steak. 'I am setting an example! You can have one, too, if you wish.'

171

'I will then,' said Ethel. 'Could we ask for some off-cuts of meat for Marco? He will behave himself, I promise! I will pay for his meal!'

'No, I will and delight in it, although he does scare me, I have to admit. Why did you buy a dog the size of Marco? He's not a town dog!'

She told him the story of Ella and Julius Limburger's disagreement over Ella buying him.

'That is so funny. So you got all that dog for free!'

'Exactly! So when are we going to talk about orchestration, Pyotr? I'm becoming impatient!' Ethel said, just as the steaks arrived.

'Now, if you wish! We can start with a very simple idea. Orchestration is about colour. Making your music chromatic, more colourful. I know we were only talking about that Piano Trio the other day, but it was lacking in hue, except for grey. For colour you should also read emotion. When you compose, you must paint with the entire orchestra. Do it for all you are worth. In ordinary conversation with live people there are inflections in the voice… that is orchestration for you. There's not much more to it, really!'

'Amazing. I shall take notes of orchestral effects at the next concerts I attend!'

'Good idea. If you can learn from them, you will improve as a composer. I hope I've inspired you to write for an orchestra now!'

'You have, Pyotr, and I will!'

From then on, Ethel took a profusion of notes at each concert she attended. She filled one notebook after another, taking his advice to heart. She regarded the sounds at least as important as the direction of the music. At his inspiration, she wrote, both at the same time, a Serenade in four movements and an overture, Anthony and Cleopatra. She hadn't realised what a colossal effort she needed to write for an orchestra, but she loved to do it. It gave her a glowing feeling of achievement. She was determined that these works would be performed and to satisfy her wish to be known as a real composer. She went to bed exhausted after every day spent composing these pieces.

172

# CHAPTER 17

## Pauline Trevelyan

Ethel needed a change from Leipzig. She had enjoyed her latest period in the city, especially meeting the Griegs and even more so her inspiring meetings with Pyotr Tchaikovsky. Her Serenade and the Anthony and Cleopatra Overture remained unfinished, but she couldn't face completing them in her digs. She felt Marco needed to experience somewhere different, too. So she packed her bags, said her farewells to Frau Brandt, and she and Marco headed for the station to catch a train to Munich. Eventually, and after almost a whole day searching, she found digs suitable for both her and Marco.

She spent the first two months there, continuing work on her orchestral pieces and, in her breaks, taking Marco for walks around this wonderful, buzzing city. Once she had almost completed them, she badgered many conductors to perform one. Hermann Levi was far too pre-occupied with the coming Wagner Festival to look at her incomplete manuscripts. However, she became friendly with August Manns, the conductor of The Crystal Palace Concerts, also in Munich then, and showed him one of her String Quartets. She hesitated to show him an unfinished score after Levi's reaction. To her astonishment and relief, the work impressed him. He told her if she let him have the complete orchestral score of one of her new works by January 1, he would consider conducting it in London in the spring of 1890.

\*\*\*

Over the past six or seven years, Ethel had become a serious admirer of Wagner, despite many others loathing his music. She had watched and heard him struggle to conduct a performance of Lohengrin in London. She loved this opera, as if it was a friend, and attended a performance being held that night in the city. So after an early dinner, she took Marco for a walk, left him settled in her digs and headed off to the National Theatre. Because she enjoyed this work so much, she had bought quite expensive tickets, the price of which the General would certainly not have approved.

173

Ethel sat in a seat in the tenth row. Hermann Levi conducted. He'd turned down both of her recent works, so she had nothing to thank him for. She was utterly entranced, especially by the looks and the amazing voice of the soloist who played Otrud, who reminded Ethel of what Marie Geistinger could have sounded like at her peak. Somewhat to the annoyance of those on either side of her, she scribbled a quick note on her pad whenever she heard something worth jotting down.

Ethel could hardly conceal her joy when she stood up to take a break after the first act. There are pieces of music that make the listener glow, become incandescent, such is their impact on the psyche. For Ethel, this first act was one of them. She turned around, for no particular reason, perhaps just to look in the opposite direction for a moment. What she saw almost knocked her off balance. The Trevelyan family, sitting only six rows back on the other side of the aisle. She would try to meet with them in the interval after the second act.

So she made her way along their row, knocking a few knees on her way. 'Lady Trevelyan, it's Ethel Smyth. Do you remember me? And you two, Pauline and Beatrice. We've met several times at my sister Mary's parties!'

Lady Trevelyan frowned at the sight of this strange woman, dressed in tweeds and wearing a circular brimmed hat. Then realisation struck.

'Of course we remember you, Ethel. Fancy seeing you here!' she said, breaking into an endearing smile.

Sir Alfred gave Ethel a frosty look. Pauline and Beatrice couldn't believe their luck in seeing Ethel again. Equally high spirited, they were overjoyed that Ethel had spotted them. She could provide some relief from their unexciting parents. They all agreed to meet in the foyer after the performance.

'So why are you in Munich?' said Ethel, directing her question to all of them but looking at Lady Trevelyan. 'Surely, you haven't travelled the vast distance here just to see Lohengrin?'

'No,' said her ladyship. 'We are here because of our health. Alfred, I and the girls all suffer from various aches and pains. We are heading for Bad Wörishofen, where Herr Kneipp gives his famous treatment.'

'I have to confess my ignorance,' said Ethel. 'The fact is though, I suffer from various issues like that. I damaged my leg some years ago, and it still isn't completely right.' She put her hand down and touched her knee. She wondered then whether she would be audacious enough to invite herself along with them.

'Where is Bad Wörishofen?' she asked.

'A very long way from here, high in the Bavarian mountains,' said Sir Alfred, in a tone designed to discourage her from wanting to go with them.

Ethel remembered her intense attraction to Pauline when they first met at Mary's house, only a few years before. Whether the attraction was mutual was an unanswered question. One certain way to explore the relationship further was to go with them to this health spa. It would anyway be good to have a break from composing for a week or two, having just finished both the Serenade and Anthony and Cleopatra.

'This may sound extremely impertinent, but may I make a request?' said Ethel, humbly.

'Please do,' said Lady Trevelyan. Sir Alfred, anticipating the question, raised his eyebrows and manufactured a glare.

'Please, may I come to Herr Kneipp's with you? I would pay my own way, of course… but say no if you would rather stay together as a family and not take me along with you.'

'Do you mind us discussing this in private, Ethel,' said her ladyship, recognising the mood of her husband.

'Not at all,' said Ethel.

All four Trevelyans slinked off to the far side of the foyer and stood there for a full two minutes. Then all but Sir Alfred came back. Lady Trevelyan announced the answer. 'Ethel, we'd be absolutely delighted to have you join us!'

Pauline and Beatrice applauded.

An excited Ethel skipped back to her digs. She had two days in which to pack. She'd travel light, as usual. Her only worry was Marco. She'd take him with her. She'd arrive at the station with Marco on his lead and a supply of food for him. The Trevelyans could hardly say he couldn't come!

Ethel was surprised by the sheer volume of luggage the Trevelyans had brought with them. As she walked along the platform, she could see them supervising two porters who were loading their many trunks into a first class van. She had bought only a second-class ticket. So with Marco on his lead, went back to the ticket office for an upgrade. She then made her way to where the Trevelyans were piling onto the train.

'I didn't know you had a dog, Ethel!' said Beatrice. 'Isn't he sweet?'

'Nor me!' said Sir Alfred, his eyebrows raised in anger. 'Did you have to bring him?' He stressed the 'have'.

'He goes everywhere with me, Sir Alfred. He's very well behaved and will cause no trouble, I can assure you,' she said, with conviction.

'Have you bought your ticket?' he said.

'Yes, first-class, of course!' said Ethel. The question implied that if she hadn't, he might just suggest she didn't go.

He turned to Lady Trevelyan. 'We have to let her come… and with the dog.'

'I'm extremely grateful,' said Ethel. She was sure Marco smiled.

***

They travelled the last few miles to Bad Wörishofen, along the snow-covered streets, in a coach and four. As Sir Alfred had said, the tiny village sat high up in the Bavarian mountains. Ethel was glad she had worn her winter coat.

'You are lucky, Ethel,' said Pauline. 'We have reserved a suite of rooms and there is a room that you and Marco can use, assuming the hotel will take Marco!'

'Hmm. He's never stayed in a hotel before.'

The receptionist argued about Marco. She refused to check him in. Lady Trevelyan complained. She'd rather taken to Marco and insisted on seeing the manager who sided with the receptionist.

'In which case we shall go to another hotel. That will cost you a significant amount of money!' she said, despite any move being a major operation, given the amount of luggage.

'Just a minute,' he said, realising he could incur a serious loss. 'I am not happy about the dog staying in your suite, which is luxury accommodation. Would you accept a slightly less well-appointed room which you can use with my compliments?'

Lady Trevelyan turned to Ethel. 'Would that be all right for you, Ethel?'

'Of course, if the hotel can provide food for Marco.' There can be no harm in asking, thought Ethel.

'Yes, madam. That will be fine,' he said.

***

The manager, by then quite friendly, directed the five of them to Herr Kneipp's treatment centre, which was only about four hundred yards from the hotel. Ethel had fed Marco and taken him for an early morning walk in the snow which had fallen overnight. He seemed happy to stay in the room. They carefully picked their way there through the whiteness. Whether Herr Kneipp expected them, Ethel would never know, but he was standing at the entrance to his spa. Ethel had difficulty in taking in what she saw. The spa was nothing more than a collection of large, barn like wooden huts, each covered in snow which broke away from the eaves in small avalanches. Each looked badly run down and in desperate need of repair.

Herr Kneipp wore a clerical collar, so was some kind of priest. A dapper looking man with closely cut hair and a clean-shaven face, he welcomed them with a smile.

'I'm sure you realise what we do here,' he said. 'We give water treatment in these buildings.'

Ethel wondered exactly what he meant. She hoped the water wasn't too cold.

'At this point we divide the ladies from the gentleman,' said Herr Kneipp. 'So you, Sir, should go to that shed over there and you ladies go to the far one. Just go in and the person giving you the treatment will meet you.'

'Off you go!' said Lady Trevelyan to Sir Alfred. He didn't look amused.

The women made their way in the snow to the shed Herr Kneipp indicated. Beatrice pushed the door open. It fouled on the ground so it needed a forceful shove. Inside, several naked women were lying on what looked like marble tables. A woman was standing over each of them and treating each by pouring water over them from a bucket. Some of those being treated were lying on their backs, some on their front and some on their sides. As they watched from inside the door which Lady Trevelyan had closed behind them, some women manoeuvred themselves off the marble slabs and went to the bench where they had left their clothes and put them on over their wet bodies.

'Good morning, ladies,' said a plump, short-haired woman who could be Russian. 'Please find a bench and take off all of your clothes.'

The four of them found a couple of benches which would accommodate all of their garments so they didn't need to separate.

Each stripped off. They were all naked together and trying to avoid looking at each other. Each of them laughed at this extraordinary ritual. Pauline laughed the loudest. Lady Trevelyan clearly felt embarrassed at being undressed with the others, all much younger than her. They each found a vacant slab and sat on it, awaiting their treatment.

A slim black woman approached Ethel with a bucket of water. 'Where do you need treatment, madam?' she asked.

'Mainly on my legs,' said Ethel.

'You have whole body treatment for legs,' said the black woman, speaking flatly.

'I see,' said Ethel. 'You'd better go ahead then.'

Ethel shivered as the woman poured the bucket of cold water over her.

'I have to do that three times,' said the woman, who left Ethel to join a queue at a water pump. Within five minutes, the woman returned and poured another bucket of water over her. By then Ethel was so cold that she didn't feel like any more of this.

'That's enough! No more, thank you!'

'I have to pour another bucket of water over you.'

'No! I've had enough, I tell you.'

'I have to, madam. Those are my instructions. The treatment only works after three buckets. I am under strict instructions from Herr Kneipp.'

'I don't give a damn about Herr Kneipp's instructions! I am telling you, I've had enough of this,' shouted Ethel.

All the others being treated looked around at Ethel's noisy protestations.

'Calm down, Ethel,' shouted Pauline. 'Do what the young lady says!'

Not wanting to upset her, Ethel relented. 'All right, then. Bring some water and pour it!'

The woman joined the queue again. Ethel was so cold she shivered. It seemed an age before the woman returned. She lifted the bucket and poured the water over Ethel, making sure she wetted Ethel's hair.

'Now you can dress,' said the woman, 'but don't put your shoes on.'

'Why not?' retorted Ethel.

'That's part of the treatment. You must leave your shoes and stockings off and walk in the snow.'

'May I have a towel, please?'

'No. You put your clothes on while you are still wet.'

'Ridiculous!' said Ethel, but not wishing to draw further attention to herself, reluctantly complied. Having had similar treatment, the other three were dressing at the same time as Ethel.

'What do we have to do next?' said Ethel, addressing none of them in particular.

'According to our water diviner, we have to walk in the snow, barefoot.'

'Whose idea was it to come here?' said Ethel.

'You asked to come with us, Ethel,' said her ladyship, laughing and standing in her soaking clothes.

The wind was blowing, not strongly but enough to make it freezing cold outside.

'I'm not sure I'd have come if I'd realised I'd have to suffer this,' said Ethel, as they all crept into the snow. Her Kneipp greeted them as they came out of the shed.

'I hope you are not too cold, ladies. But you should be cold, and that's how my cure works. When you have walked out here for twenty minutes, you go back in to put your stockings and shoes back on. Your body temperature will rise and this will cure your ailments.'

'I hope you're right,' said Pauline. 'I have to admit, I'm frozen.'

'Follow me,' said Herr Kneipp. He led the way on a snow covered route around and between the run down huts. They were so cold they didn't say a word to each other. Sir Alfred, not looking especially happy, was also walking one of these paths. After this traverse and while putting her shoes back on, Ethel gradually felt a pleasant warm feeling. Her fingers positively glowed, as did her feet.

'Do you know, Pauline, I think experiencing the bitter cold was worth it for the warm feeling I've got now. I hope my aches and pains are cured, too!' said Ethel, as the four of them began walking the short distance back to the hotel. Sir Alfred was about five minutes behind them.

'Let's see if we can order some coffee,' said Beatrice, as they walked into the restaurant area. 'And some biscuits. I'm starving after all that!'

While her ladyship found a waitress to take their order, Sir Alfred walked in with a frown embedded on his face. 'I don't care what you decide to do, but I'm not going through that again. Several people have died being treated in this place, and I will not be one of them. I've brought some work with me so tomorrow I'll be labouring over our revised plans for the coal mine.'

'You are a disappointment, Father,' said Beatrice. 'When we saw you walking in the snow, it looked as if you were enjoying yourself,' she said, lying about how he actually appeared.

'No such thing. The whole thing was designed to humiliate. So whatever you say, I'm not going back tomorrow.'

'I didn't realise we were expecting more of the treatment,' said Ethel, her hands and feet warmer than they felt since first going there. 'I'll fall in with you girls.'

'I'm keen to go through to the end of the course. How many treatments would that be, Mama?' said Pauline.

'Five,' said Lady Trevelyan, coolly and with no expression on her face. It was difficult to see whether she had seriously had enough of this or was still annoyed with Sir Alfred's unenthusiastic reaction.

'I'm going to follow Pauline,' said Ethel.

'Me, too,' said Beatrice.

'I agree with you three. I'm going to see the course through, too. You can do what you like about the coalfield. I'd hoped you'd left all that in England,' said her ladyship, glaring at Sir Alfred.

The four of them became better used to the cold as day-by-day their treatment continued. Even Ethel enjoyed it, in a masochistic way. The thrill she had a problem concealing was what she felt in the presence of Pauline. She'd love to kiss or cuddle up to this beautiful creature. From the way Lady Trevelyan looked at her, Ethel wondered if she had detected her feelings towards her daughter. She said nothing to Ethel about it, if she had. Ethel didn't know what to do about what she felt. Pauline had a certain aloofness about her. Puzzle as she did, Ethel couldn't work out how she could break this barrier to her heart.

At the end of the treatment course, Sir Alfred became more sociable, and they all spent a couple of days exploring the little town of Bad Wörishofen. Marco joined them on these jaunts and seemed to enjoy the company of the Trevelyans, all of whom, including Sir Alfred, delighted in his amusing antics, especially when he ate the snow.

The journey by train back to Munich seemed an anti-climax to Ethel as she realised that, after two days in Munich, the Trevelyans were to travel to Cannes for a further holiday. The thought of being separated from the albeit remote figure of Pauline caused Ethel much pain. She had become intoxicated by her and couldn't bear the thought of having to say goodbye to her as she went.

Ethel felt miserable and low. That Marco relied on her for everything kept her going. She felt even lower than she had felt over the break with Lisl. At least with Lisl, she knew what she thought of her. She'd made it clear enough in her letters. Pauline had given no sign at all what she thought of Ethel. When they kissed, there was no flow of feeling from her, even when Ethel put her arms around her. It was a purely mechanical act. Pauline and her family were staunch Roman Catholics. Pauline often spoke of her strong, unbreakable belief in God. Ethel wondered if her love for Him had distorted her feelings towards people. One reassuring fact was that even when men looked longingly at her stunning figure, she seemed totally indifferent.

Many days passed by with Ethel in this state of languor. Apart from walking the ever spritely and cheery Marco, she spent most of the day lying on her bed in a state of misery. She felt awful and sorry for herself. Whenever anything, even slightly unpleasant, occurred to her, she broke into tears. She cried when she thought of home. Her muscles ached. She felt unwell and wished, but for seeing Pauline, she'd never had the Kneipp treatment. It had completely failed as far as she was concerned. The thought of composing filled her with dread. She thought she'd never write another crochet or quaver again.

After just over a week, her Munich landlady stopped her as she came in from walking Marco and handed her a letter. Ethel took it and dashed up to her room with Marco still on his lead to open it. The postmark was Cannes. Her heart beat faster and hammered in her bosom. She tore it open. It was from Pauline. She read it as fast as she could. It said she had left a copy of 'The Imitation of Christ' at their hotel and asked Ethel if she could go to retrieve it. She signed it with a kiss, but nothing else. What an anti-climax.

So on her next walk with Marco, Ethel called in at the hotel the Trevelyans were staying at and went up to the reception desk.

'Excuse me, but my friends were staying here less than two weeks ago and one of them believes she left a book here called The Imitation of Christ. She asked me to see if anyone had found it or handed it in.'

'Not to my knowledge,' said the receptionist. 'If you'd like to take your dog and sit over there,' she said, pointing to some luxurious armchairs, 'I'll look in the room we keep lost property.'

Ethel sat in a chair and instructed Marco to sit on the floor. She shuffled the cushion to make herself more comfortable. Whatever is this, she thought to herself. Under the cushion, and half pushed down between the seat and the arm of the chair, was a book. She eased it out. Unbelievably, it was the one Pauline had lost. She stood and went back to the reception desk, arriving as the young lady also reached it.

'No. It's not in our lost property store,' said the lady, before Ethel could speak.

'Here it is. I've found it,' said Ethel, looking embarrassed.

'Really? Hard to believe,' said the receptionist. 'One minute you are asking me to look for it, and the next you say you've found it.'

'It's completely true! I sat in the chair, moved the cushion and there was the book, stuck between the seat and the arm. So many thanks for telling me where to sit!'

The woman looked puzzled as Ethel and Marco left the hotel. She took some comfort from retrieving Pauline's book but still felt utterly miserable. She would keep it until she saw Pauline again, but would write to her about the miracle of its discovery. Giving it to her directly would at least present another opportunity to speak to this angel of a person and tempt her into liking her.

Once back to her digs, she went straight to her room to lie on the bed. Marco looked up at her as if he could see she wasn't very happy. He sat on the floor and eventually fell asleep. She couldn't think of anything creative or constructive to do. She lay there, staring at the ceiling. Then, overcome by boredom and while Marco was still asleep, went over to the dressing table, picked up Pauline's book and took it back to the bed with her. She read some of it, if only to solve the mystery of Pauline's indifference.

What she read amazed and shocked her. The message of this extraordinary little book, written by a fifteenth century monk, was plain. A life without God was pointless, it said. It stressed the importance of humility, compassion, patience and tolerance. Its effect Ethel on was profound. From being an unbeliever, she changed her life completely. She would live for God and put others first, something she had never even dreamed of before. She would become a member of the Anglican Church, not a Catholic, as were the Trevelyans. That night she went to the English church and prostrated herself before the altar. She shed tears, right through the communion service.

This revelation lifted her from the depths she was in. She smiled again and realised how well off she was compared with many women of her time. Suddenly, she wanted to compose and be once again creative. Ideas flooded into her mind. She would write a major work, a symphony, a piano concerto, an opera or perhaps a religious work. All she needed to do was to decide and begin this important project.

She would give her aging parents first priority and return to see them. So she would leave Munich, return to her lodgings in Leipzig, pack and head home.

# CHAPTER 18

## Ethel redefined

Ethel felt better still when she and Marco arrived back in Leipzig. She often thought of Pauline and wondered if she might dedicate her upcoming major work to her, especially if she could convince her to be at least a close friend.

Frau Brandt opened the door to her. 'It's wonderful to see you back here, Ethel. Come in. You look freezing! I hope you've had a successful trip. How are you and how is Marco?' she said.

'Marco is fine and so am I, bless you. I've not been very well, but I am much better now. I went with some friends to a health spa in Bad Wörishofen but ended up worse than when I went there! It's good to be back, but I shall be off again soon, back to England. I'm just dying to see my family!'

'You will come back, won't you?'

'Of course!'

'Oh! Here's a letter for you,' she said, as she picked up an envelope from the hall table.

With Marco in tow, she sped through to her rooms. She opened the envelope. The letter was from Theresia, saying she agreed with Ethel's idea to appeal the Conservatory tribunal's decision to drop the charge against the official who assaulted her. She asked whether she could meet Ethel in the refectory again on 8 January, when she would return to lodge the appeal. She said it would take months, possibly years, to arrange the hearing and that if Ethel wasn't available, then perhaps she could attend the new tribunal, if they gave Theresia leave to appeal.

Ethel grinned. She felt sure she could help Theresia. There was no point in replying, as Theresia would soon be back in Leipzig, well before she received any letter. So Ethel's departure to England would have to be delayed, but only by a few days.

'It's so good to see you, Ethel,' said Theresia, as she went up to her in the Conservatorium refectory and kissed her.

'And to see you, Theresia,' said Ethel. 'I'm so glad you are going to appeal. Have you brought your letter?'

'Yes, please read it. I can always rewrite it, if we think I need to.'

'You say you have asked me to be a witness. That needs strengthening to "has agreed to be a witness". Also you should say, "Miss Smyth will present evidence to the effect that this individual attempted to attack her, but she fought him off."'

'You are so generous, Ethel. I'll rewrite it now.'

'While you do that, I'll buy some coffee!'

Theresia was still rewriting her letter when Ethel returned with two steaming cups of coffee. Theresia gave her the revision.

'That's excellent,' said Ethel. 'If that doesn't win you a hearing, nothing will! If I can find anything about this man from my friends and contacts here, I shall.'

'I'm indebted to you, Ethel. You are a brilliant source of encouragement!'

'When they tell you about their decision and give you a date, you will write to me, won't you?'

'Of course.'

'Please send two letters, one to my lodgings here and one to my home in England.'

'Definitely. That will be fine.'

They stood up from the table, hugged and kissed each other and left the refectory.

Two days later, Ethel and Marco were on a train, heading for England. She was carrying a bag of raw steak for Marco and a bottle of brandy for herself.

As usual, Ethel let herself into Frimhurst. She walked up the hall into the lounge where her mother and father were sitting in adjacent new armchairs. Probably purchased in another of her mother's uncontrollable spending sprees. At least she recognised the rest of the furniture and the carpets.

'Not a dog, Ethel? A stray you picked up on your way home?' said Ethel's mother as she stood up to give her a welcoming kiss.

'No, Mama! This is Marco. I've had him for nearly two years now. He goes everywhere with me. My friend in Leipzig, Ella Limburger, gave him to me.'

'He's beautiful!' said her mother, as Marco went up to her and licked her face.

'How can you afford to look after a dog, Ethel? A big one like that,' said the General, by then having dropped his Times into his lap to join the conversation. 'So what brings you home this time? You don't want more money, do you?'

'No, Papa. I have come home to help you and Mama, especially as you are becoming a little older now. You might appreciate my help in running this house, the finances, the staff and the garden. I can also do the shopping for you and help with the horses.'

Ethel's mother could not believe what she was hearing. What had happened to their daughter? The self-centred, self-opinionated and over-confident woman who went back to Leipzig two years ago. She turned to the General. He couldn't believe it either. Both were in a state of shock.

Mother spoke first. 'My dear Ethel, that is so kind of you. You are an absolute darling to think of us in this way. Of course, we are thrilled. You could not have returned at a better time. We are both becoming old and tired. Any help you can give us will be well appreciated.'

The General was less effusive. 'Yes, I agree,' he said. 'The longer this lasts the better. You can start by looking at the finances.'

'Take no notice of your father, Ethel. You must settle in and relax for a few days before you do anything.'

'I will, Mama. I can also do some thinking about a new composition. I'm thinking of writing a mass.'

'A mass, Ethel? Have you taken to religion? Never!' said the General.

'I have, Papa. I recently read The Imitation of Christ and I am now a believer. I never have been in the past and it has been a great influence on me.'

'Good for you, Ethel,' said her mother.

'I'm surprised but pleased,' said the General.

True to her word, Ethel made great strides in managing the household and taking charge where she could. At the General's suggestion, she first dealt with the finances. They couldn't afford their three gardeners, so she laid off the middle one, keeping the oldest and the apprentice. They owned too many horses, which they couldn't ride all at once, so she arranged for some to be sold. She kept Phyllis, which was, of course, her favourite. She broke off several arrangements the General had organised to have various individuals on a kind of paid standby 'in case we needed them'.

***

As agreed at their meeting in Munich, Ethel took the scores of Anthony and Cleopatra and the Serenade to August Mann's office in the St James Concert Hall.

'I'm sorry, I'm a few days late, August, but I've been putting the finishing touches to each of my new orchestral works. Here they are,' she said, dumping the untidy bundle of music onto his desk. 'I'd be so grateful if you would play one of them at The Crystal Palace. It would be a huge step forward in my career as a composer if you did, and I'd be forever grateful to you.'

'Please don't worry about being late, Ethel. I've been so busy since returning from Munich. How many are there here?'

'A Serenade and an Overture, Anthony and Cleopatra.'

188

'So which would you like me to play?'

'Preferably the Serenade. Pyotr Tchaikovsky inspired me to write it. I've tried to follow his advice on the orchestration. So I've made it as colourful as I can but not overly so, I hope!'

'Find the start for me, Ethel, and I'll have a look.'

She untied the bundle and found the first page. 'This is it.' She handed him the whole score.

'You are not a tidy writer, Ethel, but we can handle it.' He quietly looked through the first few pages. 'It's a remarkable piece, Ethel. Sometimes when a piece is inspired by a particular composer, it sounds like one of his works. But this isn't like Tchaikovsky. It sounds like Ethel Smyth!'

Ethel could not contain her emotions. She hugged him with tears rolling down her cheeks. He kissed her face and could taste them.

He chuckled. 'Please, Ethel, don't cry. Your tears will stain my jacket. It really is good. My Crystal Palace regulars will love it!'

'So you're going to play it then, August?'

'Of course. It's too good not to!'

Ethel wiped her face with her handkerchief and just about managed not to cry again. 'You are so kind, August. It's simply impossible for me to tell you how pleased and grateful I am.'

'Let me warn you now, Ethel, I may need to make some changes to it. The Crystal Palace is a large, odd-shaped venue and I may need to double up on some instruments. I may even need to add more. I doubt it. But I thought I should tell you. It is your work and yours alone. If I think you should add to or subtract from it, I'll discuss any changes with you and we can decide together what we are going to do. Is that all right?'

'Yes, August. I'm in your hands entirely. I've never been there so don't know about its acoustics.'

'I'll let you know if we need to make any changes and we can meet to discuss them. Let me have your address, please. Performance in the spring. Probably towards the end of April. I'll confirm the date when I can.'

Ethel kissed August, shook hands with him and made her way to Waterloo Station and home. Glowing within and unbelievably happy, she was almost too excited to tell her parents about her success.

'I have some incredible news for you,' she said. 'I'd like to invite you to The Crystal Palace to see and hear the first public performance of one of my works, my Serenade!'

Her mother pushed herself up from her chair and went over to kiss her daughter. 'Ethel, we are so proud of you. You are a proper composer now and it's time you enjoyed some success. And to believe we were quite reluctant for you to go to Leipzig to learn to write music!'

'I hope they are paying you for this,' said the General. 'I suppose I must come. It's not the kind of event I've been to before.'

'I hope it won't be your last, Papa,' she said in quick response. 'No, I forgot to ask about the money! I'm more interested in being recognised as a composer of merit. And I say that with due modesty!'

*** 

Days later, the Trevelyans returned from their continental travels. Pauline came to see Ethel, partly to retrieve her 'Imitations of Christ.' During her absence, she had thought a lot about Ethel. She had heard Ethel performing her works on the piano at their hotel in Bad Wörishofen, and her abilities as a composer impressed her. They chatted for a while about their respective times in Cannes and Germany and their homecomings.

'My dear Ethel, it's wonderful to see you. I owe you an apology. I'm sorry if I seemed so off-hand with you in Munich. There were so many things going on in my mind. But I've thought a great deal about you while we have been in Cannes and I would like to know you better.'

Ethel's eyes lit up. 'Pauline, I am so pleased with what you are saying. I have thought much about you while we have been separated. You are right. We have much in common and we must become closer.'

'We must start by seeing each other more often!'

'Here is your copy of The Imitation, Pauline.' She told her what a profound effect it had on her.

'So we have even more in common, the love of God, our Redeemer. Do you know, Ethel? I thought you sounded calmer and more at peace when we started this discussion. What good news.'

'Yes, I am transformed. I am deeply engaged in helping my dear parents, especially helping them economise in managing this house. It is far too big for them, but they are staying. They love it too much to move!'

'They must be very pleased you are back from Germany. They would have been constantly worrying about you.'

'I can safely say I have thrilled them. They can relax while I carry more of their load.'

'I'm just as pleased for them as I am in seeing you, Ethel. I don't think you have been to our house in Camberley. Come tomorrow for afternoon tea.'

Over the following months, Ethel and Pauline became more devoted. They swam together, walked together, and even played board games together. They saw each other at every opportunity. Then one afternoon, while the two of them were sitting on a settee in one of the Trevelyan's three drawing-rooms, Ethel announced she had something important to tell Pauline.

'You may not be aware of this, Pauline, but I've been writing a new composition. It is a Mass and I am dedicating it to you. The Mass will celebrate my love of God and, just as important, my love for you. I cannot say how much I love you, Pauline. You have inspired me to write this work, of a kind I have never even attempted before!'

'I am so pleased and flattered, Ethel. Surely, you could find someone more deserving, your parents or one of your sisters. And question whether your love for me is equal to your love of God. Thank you, Ethel. I could never contemplate that the work of a composer would be dedicated to me!'

'I have thought a great deal about the dedication, Pauline, and it will be to you.'

Pauline slid across the settee to be closer to Ethel, put her arms around her, held her tight and kissed her firmly on the lips. Ethel reciprocated. The two of them enjoyed a passionate and lasting embrace.

'My goodness, you two,' said Lady Trevelyan, as she pushed open the drawing-room door and went over to the two of them. 'I didn't realise you were that fond of each other!'

Taken completely by surprised and blushing with embarrassment, Pauline felt obliged to attempt an explanation. 'My dear mother, Ethel is dedicating her new Mass to me and I was just giving her a kiss as a gesture of my profound gratitude.'

'I see,' said her ladyship, looking as if she was wondering if a far deeper relationship was emerging between the two of them. 'I thought you were in here and I've just popped in to see if you would like a cup of tea.'

'I'd love one,' said Ethel, sounding out of breath.

'I would, too. We'll come into the kitchen,' said Pauline, as if she wanted to leave the site of their being caught in such a passion soaked embrace.

'I didn't know you were writing a Mass, Ethel,' said Lady Trevelyan. 'How exciting! Is it a commissioned work, maybe by Archbishop Benson?'

'No. I have been thinking of writing a religious work ever since becoming a believer. All credit to Pauline leaving The Imitation of Christ in your hotel in Munich.'

'Yes, Pauline told me, just a few weeks ago, about your conversion and about the wonderful work you are doing for your parents.' She poured each of them a cup of tea from a silver teapot and the three of them sat at the kitchen table drinking it. Ethel tried to inject some humour into the conversation by describing some of Marco's recent antics but failed to remove the stiffness and artificiality from the discussion. She thought Lady Trevelyan was still in a state of shock at discovering her daughter in such a delicate position with Ethel. She drank her tea and decided she should go.

'I've several things to do at home, Pauline. Do you mind if I go now? Why don't we meet at my house on Friday morning? I'll be in for the entire day, so I'll welcome you whenever you arrive.'

'I'll see you Friday then,' said Pauline, as she held the front door open and gave Ethel a farewell kiss.

***

'I don't know what to wear, Ethel! What would you suggest?' said Mrs Smyth, as they were preparing for Ethel's premiere.

'You look lovely in your purple dress, Mama, the one you wore to your granddaughter's Christening.'

'I'd prefer something a little more cheery.'

'What about the green one with the yellow braiding? You look especially good in that!'

'Come on, you two! We need to be at the station in thirty minutes,' said the General who had taken charge of the travel arrangements. 'And we need to change trains at Clapham Junction.'

'Five minutes, darling. Then we'll be ready!'

All three of them scrambled from the coach and four at the entrance to Farnborough Station. The General almost lost his top hat in the *melee*. They rushed onto Platform 1 and clambered on board the train which was just blasting out a head of steam.

'We made it!' said Mrs Smyth.

'No thanks to you two,' said the General, breathing through his moustache. 'Just as well I bought the tickets in advance.'

They were much calmer when they stepped out of the train at Crystal Palace Low-Level Station. Ethel was longing to know what her Serenade would sound like in this magnificent glass building. She had agreed with August Manns several changes to her score, the main ones being the enlargement of some sections, in particular the woodwind and French horns, to take account of the size of this colossal building.

'I can't believe the enormity of this glass structure. It's like a giant greenhouse!' said Mrs Smyth.

'I was lucky. I saw it when it was in Hyde Park, before they moved it,' said the General. 'It is huge. It must have been a massive undertaking to bring it here.'

'I hope the people at the back will hear it,' said Ethel, as they walked through the building to the seats they had been allocated near the front. The building was gradually filling in front of an empty concert platform. Most, like the General and Mrs Smyth, were formally dressed. The men looked regal in their top hats and tails and the women gorgeous in the long colourful dresses and pretty bonnets.

'Ah, I knew these were your seats,' said August Manns, as he suddenly appeared near Ethel. 'I had to make a few more changes, but only to put in another rank of violins. Otherwise, it's the same as we agreed.'

'I'm sure I would have approved,' she said.

'I hope you all enjoy the performance,' he said, turning to the General, Mrs Smyth, Mary, Alice and their families, Violet and Pauline, who by then was sitting next to Ethel. He vanished as quickly as he had arrived.

The members of the orchestra assembled themselves and applauded as the leader stepped in from the side. Further applause greeted August Manns, who bowed to the audience before raising his baton to begin. A solemn performance of Beethoven's Egmont Overture started the concert and then Mozart's Clarinet Concerto.

'Your work is next,' said the General.

'Yes,' said Ethel. 'After the interval.'

They all remained in their seats chatting to each other in the break, which the ringing of a bell closed off.

'The conductor is taking a long time to come back in,' said Pauline.

'There is still a fair bit of noise in the audience,' said Ethel. 'He won't enter until it is quiet enough.'

Ethel felt nervous. Never had a work of hers had such an enormous audience. There must have been at least four thousand there. Could she have made a better job of writing it? How well would the orchestra play it? How would the audience react? And what would be the reaction of the press?

With the orchestra at the ready, August Manns ran in and hopped onto his podium. He raised his baton, and the orchestra started to play. She was in raptures. This was the culmination of her career. She had waited a long time for this, up to the age of thirty two. She should concentrate on every note of the tumultuous first movement, in case she wanted to change anything. August was living up to his excellent reputation. She was thrilled at the sheer quality of the performance. She breathed a sigh of relief at the end of the movement. A small ripple of applause broke out. Ethel was grateful for this premature appreciation.

Ethel could detect a minor commotion along the row. The General was attempting to stand up. He had a piece of paper in his hand. It looked as if he wanted to send a telegram. By the tails of his coat, Mrs Smyth pulled him back down again. 'Not now!' she said.

The second movement started as Pauline put her hand onto Ethel's lap and Ethel held it there. She could feel the pace of this fast movement. It sounded and travelled just as she had imagined it. A shudder of excitement went down her spine, which she was sure Pauline also felt. Her father again attempted to stand at the end of this section, but Mrs Smyth dragged him back down.

The third movement started. Ethel glowed at the tunes she had composed. They delighted her even more than she expected. She was pleased, too, with the orchestral effects, just as Tchaikovsky had suggested but not sounding remotely

195

like him. She could not believe she was hearing her music live and not just reading it in her score. Once again the General rose from his seat, clutching the same piece of paper. 'Sit down,' said her mother as quietly as she could while ensuring he heard her.

The fourth movement pleased Ethel just as much. It sounded like no other composer's work. She gave herself full credit for originality. It was hers and nobody else's. The audience exploded into applause at the end. She could not believe the reception. The General stood again and rushed out of the auditorium, carrying his piece of paper. August Manns beckoned to Ethel. She didn't understand him at first, then realised he wanted her to appear on the stage. She couldn't move fast enough.

'Take a bow, Ethel. You deserve this wonderful reception.'

'Thank you, thank you,' she said to him, then turned to the audience and bowed. The applause became louder.

'Again!' said August. 'And again.' On the third bow, Ethel looked over to where her family and friends were sitting. She couldn't believe what her eyes were seeing. There in the row behind them, sitting immediately behind her mother, was a familiar figure. He had grown a beard, but the fluffy hair and calm brow were still in place. Harry Brewster was smiling and applauding. Ethel thought he looked like the man in Titian's Portrait of a Venetian Nobleman.

Harry came to join her family group. She introduced him to her parents, to Mary, Alice and their respective husbands, to Violet and to Pauline. Pauline's face turned from a smile to a grimace and her heart almost stopped. She was shocked at the joy she saw in Ethel's eyes at meeting this man. She wondered how his reincarnation would affect her relationship with Ethel, whom she loved intensely.

Ethel noticed the sudden change in Pauline. She took her slightly to one side as Harry and the General were talking to each other. 'Please don't worry about him, Pauline. We are just friends. We are not lovers and never will be. I love you too much for that.'

Pauline raised a slight smile. She thought there must be more to this relationship. Otherwise, why did Harry Brewster come to this performance? 'I'm not worried, Ethel, honestly,' she said, not believing her own words.

'I'm as puzzled as you at seeing him, Pauline. I must have a coffee or something with him to find out what exactly he is doing here. I'll let you know when we next meet, at your house on Monday?'

Ethel explained to her family that she was going to have a drink with Harry and told them she'd be on a later train. They went to a café in Sydenham for a reunion chat.

'You totally knocked me out, Harry. I'm still in a state of concussion. So what's going on?'

'Well, Ethel, it's a fairly short story. I'm on my way to Liverpool to catch a liner to New York. I have business to attend to there.' He didn't elaborate, and Ethel felt she couldn't ask. 'I'm here because I saw this concert advertised on a hoarding for today, 26 April '90. I simply couldn't resist coming to see your Serenade. The wonderful thing though is that we have met again, what after six years?'

'We must keep in touch by letter, Harry.' She could not forget that he was behind her rejection by Lisl. But that was in the past.

'I don't agree, Ethel. I want you. You are the only woman I have loved, other than Julia. I still want you after all these years. I have published my second book, The Prison. It's about the prison of the mind. I have written it in English and I intend to become involved in the literary scene here, not in Italy, France, Germany or America. So I'll spend much more time here and I want to spend as much of it with you as I can.'

'I'm very flattered, Harry. I really am. But how would Julia react if she knew we were seeing each other, even if our meetings were not frequent?'

'She wouldn't know. Don't misunderstand me, Ethel. I have no intention of abandoning her. That is the last thing I would do. But she is stuck in the metaphysical world she had inhabited since I met her. She has become more contained within herself while I have broken free. And I need to spend my freedom with you.'

'I'm not sure where this is going, Harry… and definitely not where it will end. You know full well I love women more than men. I have a new friend in Pauline whom you met only a half an hour ago. She loves me and I love her. How that will survive her forthcoming marriage, I do not know. But I have other women friends too, and I could never marry you. Never could I become a wife. And you don't yet know about my dog, Marco. I don't know what he would make of you!'

'I would respect all that, Ethel, for your occasional love. I am not seeking your exclusive attention. Far from it. I would not want to compel you into anything you were in the least bit uncomfortable with.'

'In which case, I suggest a compromise. I am prepared to see you in London, or even elsewhere, but only if Julia agrees to our meeting and if nothing improper happens between us.'

Harry had tried for this long to entice Ethel into his bed. He was a patient man, so agreed with what she was proposing.

'I'll write to her, while I'm in America.'

'Write to her if you will, but I forbid you to put our agreement to her until you see her face to face.'

'You are right, of course, Ethel. I must be more patient.'

'I have no objection to meeting you on your way back from America though,' she said as an afterthought.

They parted with a peck on the cheek and Harry left for Liverpool.

# CHAPTER 19

## Where next?

Ethel saw her parents before dinner that evening.

'Congratulations, my darling Ethel. We are so proud of you!'

'Yes, Ethel. Your piece was wonderful. I truly enjoyed listening to it,' said the General, sounding unsure if he had.

'I'm delighted and I'm glad you were both there to celebrate this huge step forward in my career as a composer. It will be interesting to see what the papers say tomorrow! And Papa, why were you standing up between each movement?'

'I just wanted to send your brother Bob in India a telegram to tell him about your astonishing success.'

'I forgive you, Papa!'

The following day, the General stepped through the doorway carrying a huge bundle of papers.

'What have you been doing, John? What's all that?' said Mrs Smyth.

'I've been to the shop and bought a copy of every newspaper. I want to see the reviews of Ethel's Serenade.'

'I'd never have thought of that,' said his wife. 'Let's see.'

It didn't take them long to see what incredible reviews the Serenade had attracted. Not one of the national newspapers disapproved of it. The Times claimed Ethel was the best composer to emerge in these lands for years. Ethel spilled tears of joy when her parents told her. Surely, more of her works would be performed from here on.

***

Ethel felt uncertain about meeting Harry. Without Julia, it would be perfectly legitimate, but she had caused Julia enough agony without causing more when it was Harry who was so keen to resurrect the relationship, less so Ethel. Her love for him had returned, almost from the instant of seeing him in the audience, but she had no intention of becoming his mistress. So she went to Lambeth Place to seek the wise counsel of Mary Benson.

'I'm surprised you are asking these questions, Ethel. Especially now that you have given your soul to God. "Thou shall not commit adultery". And you are on the brink of just that. You told me when we first met that you had given up completely on this man who had caused you such pain and the break in your relationship with Lisl.'

'You misunderstand me, Mary. I have no intention of becoming the man's mistress. I just want to be friends with him. That's all. The thought of having a man inside me fills me with horror. I'm still a virgin and intend to stay that way.'

'I find it difficult to see how you could allow him to be your friend without knowing what he actually wants of you. He wants to take you to his bed. No doubt about it. Can't you see that?'

'He is a man of great honour, Mary. He wouldn't force me to do anything I didn't feel entirely comfortable with.'

'It strikes me as a man of endless patience. He'll become closer and closer to you until you can't resist his sexual advances. It might even take years. You cannot put his totally innocent wife in the position of having to decide whether the two of you should meet in London or elsewhere, occasionally or frequently. It's immoral to expect that of her.'

'It's simply that I am in love with him and he is with me. But I love him as a friend and not as a mistress.'

'So you say you love him. That makes it many times worse. Love needs consummation. You will suffer eternal damnation for this Ethel, believe me. And before that, the awful social consequences. What will your parents think? No. And if you became pregnant. You would be an outcast. Your career as a composer would be wrecked… finished. Despite your success at The Crystal Palace.'

'I'm sorry, Mary, but I find it difficult to subscribe to what you are saying. Perhaps the best thing, for now, is for me to go home, reflect on what you are saying and meet again with you in a few weeks. Does that sound reasonable?'

'Let's do that, Ethel. Let me look at my diary. I can see you in two weeks on Friday at ten o'clock in the morning. Would that be convenient to you?'

'Yes, Mary. That will be fine.'

Not satisfied with her ideas being rejected by Mary Benson for a second time, she took her a copy of Harry's latest book, The Prison. Her idea was to convince her she should meet him and therefore discover what a thoroughly decent man he was. She even suggested that she could meet him on her annual sojourn to France. Ethel detected a cooling off in their relationship, even though she protested that her love for Harry was love as a friend and like-minded individual... not as a physical lover. Mary Benson rejected the idea entirely. She even wondered how she had become on such intimate terms with Ethel. As the wife of the Archbishop of Canterbury, she again insisted Ethel should not renew her relationship with this married man.

\*\*\*

Harry took Ethel's advice and decided not to write to Julia about meeting Ethel. So he discussed the idea with her on his return home from America. Julia's reaction startled him.

'My dear, Harry, you utterly surprise me! I've told you she's a lover of women, not men! She's probably told you in no uncertain terms that she won't let you penetrate her... not just because you are married but... and she probably didn't admit to this... because she prefers the fairer sex! Don't think you will be the one to break down this barrier. You will never persuade her into your bed... not to do what you want to do to her! Not even if you make her drunk!'

'You're wrong about this, Julia. I love her purely as a friend, not as a woman I want to conquer sexually. She and I have an enormous amount in common. Our love of literature, music and adventure. I love you, too, Julia, and I'll be your husband as long as we are both living. Let there be no doubt about that. I'll never desert you for her.'

201

'You are talking nonsense, Harry. You're making me angry. While you're with her, you're not with me. I could understand better if you had a group of male friends and wanted to spend more time with them. But you have no male friends. More's the pity.' She sobbed, deep sobs, as if she was giving up on this argument when she seemed in control of it when they started.

Harry took out a handkerchief from his pocket and handed it to her. She wiped her eyes.

'I cannot stop you seeing this woman, Harry. If you decide to see her, so be it. But I am not giving you my blessing, even though I know you won't succeed with her.'

Although this was the first of Harry's attempts at persuading Julia to agree to him seeing Ethel, it was far from the last. Over the coming months, he broached the subject many times, but each time Julia gave him the same answer. Why should she agree? Just to ease his conscience. She resorted to her metaphysics for help. The answer was simple: not to give in.

Harry wrote to Ethel telling her of Julia's decision, saying there was only one way forward: to meet, regardless of Julia. The letter referred to the failing health of his mother-in-law, Baroness von Stockhausen. He said she was not much longer for this world. She was gradually succumbing to her heart disease, an affliction from which Lisl also suffered, as Ethel was aware.

Ethel's reply was ambiguous. She neither agreed nor disagreed with his proposed encounters. Although she opposed Mary Benson's rigid condemnation of their relationship, platonic though it would be, she could see serious difficulties in regularly meeting him. She did not want the rumour machine to swing into her life.

*** 

The Christmas after Ethel's success at The Crystal Palace was a true celebration for Ethel and her family. She had persuaded her parents to invite George Henschel and his wife, Lillian, to join them. The General's dislike of artists had collapsed by then and had vanished into the recesses of his failing memory. He even regarded George, who was becoming well known in England, as a 'good fellow'.

'I do like, Lillian,' he confided to his wife, as they were dressing for dinner on Christmas Eve. 'She is a very attractive woman and intelligent, too.'

Luckily, Ethel's mother could see the amusing side of his infatuation. 'You are stuck with me now, John. So don't like her too much.'

'Your daughter is one of the most interesting people I know,' said George, while they were at the dinner table. 'I met her in Thuringia a good few years ago now, twelve or more maybe. There were two other singers enjoying a holiday with us, Thekla Friedländer and Augusta Redeker, and Ethel showed us some of her amazing abilities. None of us knew what to admire most. She showed us how to play lawn tennis, how to jump over fences, over chairs and even tables. I'd never come across a woman as energetic as Ethel. And could she play the piano? I knew then she'd be famous one day, and she's already had an enormous success at The Crystal Palace. Well done, Ethel. Congratulations!'

'You flatter me, George. I don't remember doing half of that!'

'Now who's being too modest?'

'I agree! That couple of weeks in the forest with Augusta and Thekla was a real treat. They were so generous to me! Do you hear much of them now?'

'They are becoming better known, too. I heard Augusta is married now.'

'Incredible,' said Ethel. 'I thought she preferred women to men!'

'She must have changed her mind!' said George.

'Changing the subject,' said the General. 'How do we propose to go to church tomorrow? Who will walk and who wants to ride?'

'I will go to your church tomorrow, General,' said Lillian, who was sitting next to Ethel's father. 'But you might like to know that I'm a Unitarian.'

The General's tone became unexpectedly serious. 'Well, Mrs Henschel, I've often said this, and I'll say it again for your benefit. Some of the best fellows I have known in my long life were Mohammedans!'

They all laughed, but Lillian Henschel laughed the loudest.

The joyful atmosphere surrounding Christmas suddenly vanished on New Year's Eve, after Ethel's mother made an extraordinary pronouncement.

'I've had enough of Frimhurst. I no longer want to live here. We must sell up and go to live in London.'

'Surely not, my dear,' said her father. 'What has brought this upon you?'

'We both need a change and, at our time of life, we may not have much time left to do it in.'

Ethel looked worried. So did the General. They looked at each other and then back at her mother. 'Let's think about it,' said the General. Ethel could not remember seeing him in such mental pain. He realised, as did Ethel, that this shocking statement meant that something strange and unwelcomed was happening in her mind.

'Ethel,' she said, a few days later, as Ethel was in the kitchen, working on the home finances. 'Can I have a word?'

'Of course, Mama. By all means.' She wondered what she was going to say, after the surprise she had given them only a few days before.

'I've completely given up the idea of going to London. I've decided I'm happy here. I've told Papa, and he is quite relieved.'

'To be utterly honest, Mama. So am I!'

\*\*\*

On a dark, dreary morning, a few days later, Ethel was in her bedroom struggling on her still unfinished Mass when her father came in. 'I have something terrible to tell you,' he said, with tears running down his face. 'Your mother is dead. She's on the bed in our room.'

204

Ethel broke into tears, got up from her chair and put her arms around her sobbing father. She could not remember hugging him like this before. For a moment, her mind failed her, and she became confused. Was this real? Otherwise, why was Papa crying?

'I'm so sad, Papa. The doctor said she was all right yesterday.'

'I know, my dear. She had a dreadful night last night… but now… I was so surprised when she blew me a kiss and closed her eyes. That was the end.' He sobbed again.

'I'm angry with the doctor, Papa. I didn't know she was that bad and, obviously, nor did you.'

'No, my dear. He made a serious error. We could have called a surgeon to see her within an hour. Who knows?'

'Papa, I am so glad I am here for you, and was with her for that wonderful Christmas. Let me make us a cup of tea,' she said, wiping tears from her eyes.

As they went into the kitchen, Ethel clasped her father's hand. She filled a kettle from a large jug of fresh water and put it on the hob. The mere act of doing something helped ease their misery, if only marginally.

'I must tell the staff,' said the General. 'We must write to your brother and sisters. We have to arrange the funeral.'

Ethel could hardly take in the word 'funeral' being used in relation to her mother. They had their bad times, but she knew well that her mother loved her and had given Ethel her unfailing sympathy and support. She was proud of her achievements, too. She'd even cut out all the favourable reviews of the Serenade and sent them to Bob. Ethel would never forget that.

'We must let nothing affect your health, Papa, or put you under strain. I shall arrange the funeral. I shall bicycle to the undertakers in Frimley and set things moving. Would you like Mama removed today?'

'No. Tomorrow. I shall cover her and sleep in Nina's room tonight.'

'Are you all right for me to leave you, Papa? Perhaps I'll go after we've had our cups of tea.'

'Yes, I can write the letters. I'll draft a telegram to send to Bob. Then I can tell the staff. I feel quite prepared for that, or will be.'

After calling at the post office, Ethel rode to the undertakers, parked her bike against the brickwork and went straight in. A dark haired, clean-shaven man in black welcomed her from behind a desk. 'Can I help you, madam?'

Again, she broke down in tears. Clearly used to such reactions, he offered her a clean, white handkerchief. 'There, madam. You are welcomed to use this.'

She wiped her eyes and put it in her trouser pocket. 'I'm grateful to you,' she said, recovering her composure. She couldn't believe she was choosing a coffin for her poor mother, flowers to put on top of it, the type of hearse which would bear the coffin, how many horses would draw it, the number of pallbearers and all the other things that she could decide there and then.

'Obliged, madam,' said the undertaker, with not a shred of emotion. 'I'll send a carriage around right away to collect your mother.'

'We'd rather you didn't. Would it be possible to send a carriage around in the morning? That's what my father would much prefer.'

'As you wish, madam. At what sort of time?'

'Let's say eleven, or thereabouts.'

On her way back home, she couldn't stop thinking about her mother. She often questioned whether her mother loved her. She remembered her kicking her bedroom door when she was a girl and shouting the most horrible things to her. But then she thought her mother loved her intensely. She was the chief ally in her fight against her father at the time she dreamt of going to Leipzig.

Her funeral was, as are all funerals, a sad event. There were two mitigating features. One was that both her father and Ethel believed her mother's death was something of a relief. She was finding life a constant struggle and, apart from her physical illness, her mind was fading. The other was that Ethel's relationship with The Empress Eugénie changed significantly.

'There is something I would like to ask you, Ethel,' the Empress said at the wake, while picking up some quarters of a ham sandwich.

Looking somewhat quizzical, Ethel wondered what this powerful friend of her mother was about to say. Surely, there was little that Ethel could give her, especially as they differed in age by at least thirty years. She was a woman of incredible beauty, considering her years, unattached, wealthy and a woman with whom Ethel could easily form a deep friendship.

'Please go ahead. You can ask me anything, Eugénie. Absolutely anything you wish.'

'I would be honoured if you would take over where your mother left off,' she said, with no trace of emotion.

'I'm not sure what you mean by that, Eugénie.'

'You are obviously much younger than I, but your mother was a great friend of mine. I have been thinking of asking you this since learning that she had passed away. Would you care to be my friend in the same way your mother was?'

'My dear Eugénie, of course I would. Equally, I'd be honoured, and absolutely thrilled,' she said and placed her arms around the Empress. They both cried.

'This is such a sad day for each of us, Ethel. But now you have said that, I feel significantly better.'

'I do, too,' said Ethel.

# CHAPTER 20

## Harry resurgent

Ethel was having serious problems balancing her work on the Mass with her duties as the General's daughter. She wanted to help her father, whom she admired even more since her mother's death, partly because he became more supportive of her and even took back some duties she agreed to take over, or at least wanted to share some. One morning later that January, her father appeared at Ethel's bedroom door.

'What are you doing, my dear? You look deep in thought.'

'I am, Papa. The Kyrie of my Mass is giving me real trouble. The text just won't mesh with the music. I really don't know what to do. I'm sure I'll find the answer, though, even if I have to pray for it,' she said, smiling and devout a believer as she had ever been.

'I have this telegram for you from Germany. I hope it's not bad news, my dear.'

Ethel held out her hand and took it. Her father went to leave her.

'Papa, would you stay, please? If it is bad news, you will be here to comfort me. If it is good news, you will be here to celebrate!'

Ethel took a letter opener from the drawer of her desk and slid the tip into the top of the envelope. She took out the telegram page and unfolded it. It was dated 15 January,'91. It shocked her into silence.

'What is it, Ethel? Please tell me! I can't stand not knowing!'

'Lisl is dead, Papa. I never expected this,' she said. She didn't know what to feel. This woman had been the love of Ethel's life, a passionate and intimate friend, until she froze her out.

'You have suddenly turned pale, Ethel. Is there anything I can do to help?'

'Probably not, Papa. As you know, she and I were the very best of friends until she turned against me. I don't know what to think. But I'm glad Lili told me the news. She is also a friend of mine in Leipzig. Mendelssohn's daughter, in fact.'

Ethel found it difficult to recover from this second death, so close to her mother's. She became overwhelmed by an amalgam of sadness and relief. A strange awareness of finality made her feel empty and lonely. She couldn't bring herself to confide in her father about her state of mind, but wrote to Harry about it and what she was enduring. Harry replied saying that they must start meeting again and, without one of the barriers between them, there was no actual impediment. He ignored the views of his wife, who so strongly objected.

\*\*\*

'I am overcome with the sheer joy of seeing you,' said Harry, as they met in the March, for the first time in just under two years, at the agreed venue, a not especially salubrious café in Bressenden Place, Victoria. He was sitting at a table drinking a cup of coffee when Ethel arrived.

'You haven't changed a smidgeon since I last saw you at The Crystal Palace,' said a smiling Ethel. 'At long last, we are together again.' She hugged and kissed Harry as if they were lovers, which she had determined they would not become.

'Julia still doesn't agree with our meeting. I've begged and pleaded with her. I've told her I'm here for a literary festival. There is one here and I will have to attend it, at least to provide her with the evidence I've been to it.'

'I'm disappointed with her attitude, but I'm not surprised. I'm sure you have made it clear that we are not and will not become lovers.'

'Of course, Ethel. But she doesn't believe me and never will!'

'I have a certain sympathy for her, but she is being unreasonable towards you. We all have friends of the opposite sex, but that doesn't mean we have to bed them! And you have good, professional reasons for being in London. She cannot deny that.'

'If you agree, Ethel… and I will not be the one to push you, we shall meet regularly, here or elsewhere in Europe.'

'I agree. We should next meet in Paris, say in about two months.'

The meeting with Harry and the promise of future encounters lifted Ethel's spirits. There is nothing like feeling wanted to make you feel happy with your lot in life. No doubt Harry wanted her, but this was an agenda that Ethel was determined to control.

*** 

Ethel told Mary Benson about her renewed relationship with Harry, which had advanced beyond letters between them.

'I'm disgusted, Ethel. I really am,' she said, sitting at her desk in her 'consulting room' at Lambeth Palace. 'You will incur the wrath of God. You have taken a further step towards the furnace of Hell and eternal damnation. It is not too late. Write to him, I beg you… and break off this sinful arrangement.'

'I can't, Mary, and I won't. You know that, like you, I am a lover of women, not men.'

'That was a phase in my life that has long since passed. I now dedicate my life to helping women who have mental problems, of the kind which you had when we first met. I have to say, Ethel, your mother would be quite ashamed if she knew about your renewed relationship with this man.'

'I am appalled that you say that, Mary. Disgusted! You are a disgrace to your mission. You wouldn't say anything as hurtful to any of your other women,' Ethel broke down in tears, sobbing uncontrollably.

'I'm sorry, Ethel, but I am telling you as a friend, not just as one of my clients. I am feeling you may soon be a former friend, the way you are behaving. Whatever you say, you and your man will be seen as lovers, regardless.'

'In which case, it is time to end our friendship. I will go now.'

Ethel stood up, walked towards the door and, without looking around at Mary, stepped out of her room.

***

Ethel became closer and closer to Empress Eugénie. They met regularly, mainly at Eugénie's house in Farnborough. Ethel would ride her bicycle from Frimhurst to Farnborough, dressed in her cycling clothes, change into more formal dress behind some bushes and push her bike the few yards to Eugénie's door. It wasn't long before the Empress discovered Ethel's routine in the undergrowth and allocated her a room in her vast house, which she could use whenever she wished. Ethel regarded her as a kind of mother figure and a substitute for her recently deceased Mama. She loved the Empress, the more so as their friendship developed.

'I'm so glad we have become friends, Eugénie. You impressed me the first time we met when my mother brought me here to meet you,' she said, during Ethel's third or fourth visit, as they both sat on one of Eugénie's settees.

'I am equally pleased that you agreed to be my friend, Ethel. I have some good friends and contacts that I will introduce you to, in due course, but your mother was my main friend near Farnborough and I will be eternally grateful to her for befriending me.'

It was not surprising to Ethel that, as Napoleon III's wife, she had a certain aloofness about her. She seemed so remote and cool that she betrayed little in the way of emotion. After all, she was in her time the most powerful woman in France. Ethel could feel herself falling in love with this idol of a person. She was still a woman of incredible beauty and attractive to Ethel, who felt strongly that she needed the love of a woman.

'I have an idea for you, Ethel. A week on Friday, I am having a little party here and I invite you to come. I will introduce you to a few of my friends. One lives in Windsor and another in Chelsea. You will love them! I would like to tell them you are a composer, so it would be wonderful if you could play them some of your music on my piano. What do you think?'

Ethel leant over towards Eugénie and pressed a kiss onto her cheek. 'That would be a great honour for me, Eugénie. I'd absolutely love to do that.'

'If you could bring along some of your songs, a piano sonata or two and some music from the piece which was such a success at The Crystal Palace that would be wonderful!'

As Eugénie had suggested, Ethel arrived early for the party, so she had plenty of time to prepare herself and arrange her things in the dining room.

'I would like you to accompany me in welcoming my guests,' said Eugénie, as Ethel appeared downstairs, having changed out of her cycling clothes into a cream blouse and green skirt. 'They will be here in about twenty minutes. They are coming by train and I've sent my carriage to meet them at Farnborough Station.'

'I'd enjoy that,' said Ethel. 'That will still give me time to set up my music!'

The guests arrived slightly earlier than expected, but Eugénie was well prepared.

'Welcome back to my home, Sir Henry and Lady Ponsonby. Permit me to introduce you to my good friend Ethel Smyth who lives nearby.'

'Delighted, I'm sure,' said her ladyship, looking first at Ethel and then at Eugénie, as if to wonder at the difference in their ages. Ethel's heart missed a beat as she glanced at Lady Ponsonby. She became immediately attracted to her. Who was this beautiful and mysterious looking woman? She would surely find out soon.

'And this is William Waddington and his wife Mary. William is the French Ambassador to Great Britain and Mary is an author.'

'I'm pleased to meet you, Miss Smyth,' said the ambassador's wife. 'It will be good to speak to a fellow artist!'

Over dinner, Ethel discovered that Henry Ponsonby was the Private Secretary to Queen Victoria and that the Ponsonbys lived in Windsor Castle. Ethel hoped that, in the fullness of time, she would become better acquainted with Mary Ponsonby. She also learned that the other Mary, Mary Waddington, was an American by birth and had written a book about life as an ambassador in London.

212

She suggested Ethel write a book, telling the tale of her travels and of her composing.

Not long after two of Eugénie's maidservants had cleared the table, she announced they would all adjourn to one of the drawing-rooms where Ethel would entertain them.

'I would like to begin with two of my piano sonatas,' she announced. 'The first is an early work which I completed before I first went to Leipzig.'

With her usual flair and energy, she set about the piano as if she was playing a drum. She hammered at it and gesticulated wildly. She even stood to inflict greater force on the forbearing instrument. It was as if she wanted to destroy the poor thing. She stood to take a bow at the end. With only five in the audience, the response was hardly rapturous, but it was heartfelt for a committed performance. She then proceeded with her second piano sonata, played with equal vigour. The result was another well-meant round of appreciation.

Then, accompanying herself on the piano, she sang some of her songs. They loved her singing. The two Marys gave her a standing ovation and asked for more. The men remained seated but clapped in unison. Ethel obliged with more songs, some of them others had written and more of her own. She concluded by playing some of her incomplete Mass, improvising the orchestral parts on the piano and singing so loudly, she sounded almost like a full choir. They each applauded and Ethel beamed at the enthusiastic reception they gave her.

'You should come to Windsor Castle and perform for the Queen,' said Lady Ponsonby.

'Hear, hear!' said Sir Henry.

'And come along to the Embassy and perform for our guests there,' said Mary Waddington.

'I'm for that,' said Mr Waddington, in such a tone he may well not have been.

'You were wonderful,' said Eugénie, after her guests had left. 'You made the evening. Dinner parties so often degenerate into playing cards, empty silences and sleeping, but you kept us all awake, Ethel. Well done! We must invite a larger number of guests so you can give a proper concert!'

'For your sake, I'm glad it went so well,' said Ethel. 'Yes, I wouldn't mind doing it again!'

***

Ethel's efforts at tempting Eugénie into a more intimate relationship, even if limited to a warm hug or the occasional kiss on the lips, were failing. Ethel realised it was not her fault, but simply that Eugénie was not thinking of something more familiar, even if she was emotionally able to be that much closer. The fact was that Eugénie was much older than Ethel so may not need the warmth of another individual, especially a younger woman. But when Eugénie said she wanted to be friendly with Ethel, she meant it.

Ethel was fascinated, if not overawed, by the character of this incredible woman. She was an original for sure. She had a sense of humour, but Ethel thought it childlike. Her little jokes were crude and often repeated. She owned a number of works of art, mainly from Germany and France. None was by an artist of note, but Eugénie regularly launched into exaggerated praise for them and the people she bought them from. She had even named some rooms in her palatial house after the artists. Fully accepting that the Second Republic was dead, she closely followed French contemporary politics through reading The Times. She admitted to Ethel that although she enjoyed listening to her music, she had no interest in the subject and would be reluctant to attend a concert.

'My dearest Ethel, you tell me you haven't finished your Mass and are struggling with it. Well, I have an idea that might help you. I own a rather nice yacht which is moored at a place called Cap Martin, near Monte Carlo. I'd like you to be my guest on the yacht. Your time on board would be your own. You could work on your Mass, if you wished. Apart from the crew, there would be just the two of us. We could sail the Adriatic, partly because I'd like to see more of the Dalmatian Coast.'

'You own a yacht, Eugénie?' Ethel's face lit up and her eyes shone. 'What sort of yacht? And you have a crew?'

214

'Oh yes, you'd love it! It has six berths, three masts, and is two hundred feet long. It is steam-driven, so we won't be at the mercy of the wind! I bought her in Amsterdam nearly two years ago. I have a crew of five and that includes a cook who is also the maidservant. Do come, Ethel. We'll have a wonderful time.'

'I would love to, Eugénie. But I don't know what I'd do with Marco.'

'It wouldn't be good to have him on board. It would be dangerous for him. Maybe your father and the household could look after him. We'd be away for about four weeks, I'd say, maybe just a little longer.'

'Four weeks! I simply can't leave him for that long! So, I'm afraid I won't be coming, Eugénie. I really am sorry. Really.'

'Not to worry, Ethel, but I'll be going, anyway. You can use your room here while I'm away, if you wish. And as usual, Marco can stay, too!'

On her way home, Ethel thought about Eugénie's generous offer. The primary reason for not having yet finished the Mass was that she was so involved in various household tasks. Surely, Marco would still recognise her and love her just as much when she returned from a yachting trip. What would her father think? She would ask him as soon as she arrived.

'Papa, I have a serious question to ask you.'

She explained in full. She dreaded his reaction.

'I knew she had a yacht but didn't know it was that impressive. Go, Ethel. Please. You have been wonderful to me and your mother, ever since you came back from Leipzig. You deserve a rest and a holiday. Marco loves me and will survive without you! Go! Take her up on her offer, before she changes her mind!'

Ethel positively glowed at her father's reaction.

'That's wonderful, Papa. I'll go right now!'

She knocked on the Empress's front door.

'Come in immediately. What's happened? You are out of breath!'

215

'I've spoken to Papa about your utterly brilliant and generous offer. Are you still willing to take me because he's made me change my mind?' she said, still holding onto her handlebars.

'My dear Ethel. I'd be thrilled for you to come with me! And Marco?'

'Papa is sure he'll survive without me!'

'Wonderful. Prop your bicycle against the post and give me a hug!'

Ethel couldn't believe this uncharacteristic outburst of affection. She did as instructed and opened her arms to the Empress who hugged her with surprising passion. 'We just need to do some planning, Ethel. I'll write to my crew to forewarn them and we'll go in about a week. We can stay in my favourite hotel in Paris on the way!'

They took a train from Victoria to Dover, a channel steamer to Calais and the fast train to Paris.

'I am the Empress Eugénie and have two rooms booked for one night,' said Eugénie to the handsome receptionist at Le Grande Hotel. Three porters were standing behind them, minding their luggage.

'Yes, I am aware, Your Highness. Take the Empress to room 201,' he said to a flunkey, as he gave each of them a room key.

Ethel was just a little disappointed that Eugénie had booked two rooms. She thought it would have been nicer to share.

Ethel's eyes lit up at seeing room 201. It was an enormous suite with a dining area, a dressing room, a bathroom and a bedroom in which the typically French canopied bed seemed lost. Ethel's was quite modest but, as Eugénie was paying, who was she to complain?

A full day after they left the Gare du Sur, the train was pulling into Monte Carlo Central Station.

# CHAPTER 21

## The Thistle

'My God, Eugénie! What an amazing ship! It's enormous. I can't believe it's so long. It looks fast and powerful!' Ethel said, as the crew was loading their luggage from the jetty onto the vessel.

'It's a yacht, not a ship, my dear friend! She's called The Thistle. But you are right, she is fast and I must teach you the safety drill. You do not want to fall overboard! Come with me and you can choose a cabin! Oh… and can you swim?'

'Yes, I've been a reasonably good swimmer since my youth!'

'Only we must swim ashore in some places we'll be stopping!'

Ethel chose a cabin next to Eugénie's, but on the opposite side of the boat. She had never been on a yacht before and smiled broadly at the quality of the fittings and the overall level of luxury. The cabin walls were made of varnished mahogany, as was the bedside table, the wardrobe and the wash-stand. All the safety rails were in polished brass which glistened at every flash of sunlight. The bed looked as comfortable as anything at Frimhurst and had bars at the side, presumably to prevent the occupant from falling out in rough weather. She could see the world through a choice of two portholes, separated by about six feet.

'We are going to head for the Adriatic,' she told the captain, a tall Frenchman, Ethel guessed in his mid-forties, standing by the wheel and in the middle of pre-embarkation checks. 'I want to go up the Dalmatian coast as far as we can, stopping off at the major ports but still return within four weeks.'

'That will be fine, Your Highness. I'll tell the navigator to plot a route for you. Have you made any arrangements for dinner?' he said.

'No, but we are planning to go to the restaurant in the Hotel Cap Martin.'

'I'll send one of the crew to book you a table.'

'Much appreciated, Henri.'

Early the following morning, to make the most of the off-shore air currents, the yacht left its berth with the captain at the wheel. The movement of the vessel woke Ethel, who dressed and went up on deck. The rising sun almost blinded her. Fully extended, the yacht's sails were straining in the wind which howled over them with a low-pitched, vibrating hum. Ethel couldn't hear the engine so imagined they were running on wind power only. Taking up Eugénie's safety advice, she harnessed herself to the side rail and walked around the deck, breathing in the fresh sea air. What a way of life, she thought, sailing the seas of the world!

There was no one else on deck, except the captain, so she went back below. She had plenty to occupy herself and started by writing to Harry to tell him where she was and what she was doing. She told him her primary aim in being at sea was to complete her Mass, but that Eugénie had some interesting ideas of where they should go, including the Adriatic. Proud of her new-found faith, she spoke of her continuing and transformative belief in God and that she had truly found salvation. She asked him about his religious views and whether he was also a believer, a subject that neither of them had touched on before. She ended by saying she would write to him when she was on her way home to suggest their next meeting place, whether it would be Paris or elsewhere, said she loved him and asked him to give her regards to Julia.

The cool breeze on deck, and having Harry in her mind for half an hour, inspired her to write more of the Mass. So she took out her music papers and placed them on the dressing table. She decided the yacht was moving too much to place her ink on the surface, so used a soft pencil. Starting on the Agnus Dei, she would make it sound like a celebration for Christ taking away her sins and those of the rest of the world. Yes, it would be a celebration, irrespective of its purpose in the more conventional masses of other composers.

She had been writing for about half an hour when there was a knock on the cabin door. Ethel opened it.

'Good morning, Ethel,' said Eugénie. 'How was your first night aboard?'

'Good morning to you, too, Eugénie,' said Ethel and kissed her on both cheeks. Eugénie looked wonderfully relaxed in a long, white, loose-fitting dress. She seemed more at home on her yacht than in her palatial mansion in Farnborough. 'Honestly, Eugénie, I slept like the proverbial log. That beautiful wine at the Cap Martin Hotel probably helped. I woke about an hour and a half ago and went up on deck. I have written a not very long letter to Harry and would like to post it where we first stop.'

'According to the navigation chart the captain showed me a minute ago, that will be in Bastia, a port on Corsica. Depending on the weather, we may dock there for the night. In the meantime, Monique, our cook and maid, has prepared us some breakfast. Do come along to eat.'

Ethel followed her to the galley, where the maid had set the table for two.

'This is Monique. Let me introduce you.'

To Ethel, she seemed about thirty three, the same sort of age as she was. She had the most striking green eyes and black hair, almost down to her waist. Ethel could not take her eyes off the surprising area of cleavage she was exposing.

'What would you like for breakfast, Madam?' said Monique. She recited the various options.

'I'll have what The Empress is having.'

Monique brought them some French bread, some sliced ham, some soft cheese and a cup of tea each.

'That's perfect!' said Ethel gratefully.

'I must tell you something, Eugénie. You are so generous in inviting me to come with you and stay on your yacht. You have paid for everything so far and I feel guilty. Please let me pay for something, perhaps the next meal we have onshore?'

Eugénie chuckled. 'Ethel, please don't worry about such mundane things. I am grateful to you for deciding to come with me. Have I told you I was a supporter of women's causes in France before we lost the war? I helped quite a few at the start of their various careers and, apart from us being the best of friends, I am doing the same for you. Of course, you can buy a meal if you wish… but only for reasons of conscience!'

Just as they were finishing their breakfast, Eugénie asked a question. 'What are you intending to do today, Ethel? I have a special place on deck at the stern where I sunbathe. I'd be delighted if you'd joined me. You want to work on the Mass, I know, but maybe an hour in the morning sun before it becomes too hot might be good for you.'

'What a tremendous idea,' said Ethel. 'I'll just sort my room out and then join you.'

'Don't worry about making your bed. Monique will see to that. I'll see you up there soon, Ethel. Just walk to the back of the yacht. You won't walk past me. If you do, you'll end up in the Mediterranean Sea!' She laughed at her not funny joke, so Ethel laughed, too.

Ethel decided the only option was to dress in her cumbersome bathing costume, so, slim as she was, squeezed herself into the thing. It was a little tight, but she managed at a pinch. The ship was rolling in the breeze, but not to the extent of making it difficult to walk on the deck, as long as the harness was secure.

Ethel made her way aft. Sure enough, there was Eugénie, sunning herself, face down on a low deck chair. Were Ethel's eyes deceiving her? As she slowed down and moved closer, she realised the Empress was completely undressed. Ethel hadn't seen a naked female body since trying to divert her attention from Pauline's nakedness at the spa in Bad Wörishofen. The Empress's bottom, in all its creamy glory, was facing the sun while her breasts were pressed out at each side of her as they bore the weight of her upper half. Ethel cast her eyes over Eugénie's beautiful form. Even to a much younger woman, she was in excellent condition. She looked up as she heard Ethel's footsteps.

'Join me, Ethel. You can keep your costume on or take it off. Entirely up to you!'

'I have to say, you surprise me. I didn't expect you to be completely unclothed! Aren't you concerned the crew will see you?'

'They are under strict instructions to look away as soon as they see me undressed. Each of them knows I walk the decks without clothes and that they will be dismissed if they don't immediately look away! They also know that they must divert their attention if any of my guests are partly or completely undressed!'

'You reassure me, Eugénie!' Thinking that sharing their nudity might help in becoming closer to the Empress, she announced her decision.

'Yes. In which case, I'll join you.' Making no attempt to be modest, Ethel heaved herself out of her bathing costume and climbed onto her deckchair.

'My goodness! You are a beautiful woman, Ethel.'

'You flatter me!'

'No. Truly you are! You have a lovely figure!'

'You, too, Eugénie. I am having trouble taking my eyes off your gorgeous body!'

'Don't be ridiculous. I'm over seventy years old!'

It was true. Ethel would love to have cuddled up to the naked Empress and kissed her with a passion.

'Tell me, do you bathe naked every day?' she said.

'It depends on the weather. And on the state of the sea. It can be so rough, the sea washes right over you. With any luck, you'll experience some rough sea, Ethel. I love it. I enjoy it so much I've sometimes got the captain to tie me in a chair to the mainmast, that one in the middle.' She pointed to the mast. 'It's totally exhilarating. He comes to check on me every ten minutes. Once he forgot and I was dying to do a pee. I waited and waited. In the end, I just let it go. I was soaked anyway, so a half litre of pee made not much difference. You are honoured, Ethel. I've told no one else that story. But it's true!'

'Were you dressed or naked then,' said Ethel.

'No. I wouldn't embarrass the captain by showing him everything I've got, not that close up anyway!' She roared with laughter, so Ethel laughed just as loudly.

'I must do some work, Eugénie. Do you mind if I leave you?' said Ethel, after about an hour and a half of this relaxing indulgence.

'In fact, I must go below now. You have written your letter and I've yet to write mine. Mary Ponsonby asked me if I'd write to let her know we were safe and having a good time. Would you mind helping me climb onto my sea legs?'

'Of course. I'm more than willing.'

The Empress manoeuvred herself into sitting on the low deck chair. She held out her arms so Ethel could help her. Ethel put her arms around the Empress's waist and, with the Empress's arms around Ethel's neck, eased her up on her feet.

'I can't help saying this, Eugénie, but you are in superb shape. You have the breasts of a thirty year old, no sagging in your tummy and a nice firm bottom!'

'You truly flatter me, Ethel. I'm going to walk below like this. You can follow me now or put on your costume. Either way, let's meet for a little lunch around one?'

'I don't mind following you as I am... and a one o'clock lunch will be fine.'

Ethel tried not to look at Eugénie's undulating rear. The sight of a man in such a state would leave her stone cold.

The Thistle stopped for the night at Bastia where the Empress instructed Monique to post Ethel's letter and hers. At five o'clock the following morning, the crew untied the yacht, the high seas beckoned, and they were on their way.

Ethel settled nicely into the routine of sunbathing with the Empress for an hour or two, before the summer sun became too hot, then going below to work on the Mass. They would have lunch, either on deck or below, before falling asleep or reading a book, and dinner was spent on board, if at sea, or, if not, in a local hotel or restaurant. They thrived in each other's company.

\*\*\*

It is not always possible to predict what will happen when travelling on the high seas on a not especially large vessel. As they approached Sicily, they sailed into a violent storm. The crew quickly lowered the sails and fired up the engine.

'Everyone below!' shouted Captain Henri over a megaphone. 'And batten down the hatches.' He locked the wheel so that the yacht sailed straight into the wind.

Ethel made her way to her cabin to lie on the bed. The yacht flung itself from side to side and up and down as it tried to cope with the gale. Ethel could just about hold on to the bed rails. It was like trying to ride a bucking stallion. She felt terrible and afraid. The strength was going from her arms. The cabin door flung itself open with a crash. Her various things fell off the dressing table onto the floor. She could hear her case rattling inside the wardrobe. How would all this end?

Then a horrible thought occurred to her. The Mass! How could she keep it dry and safe? It was strewn all over the floor. Water was coming in under the door, not much, but enough to wreck the score. She climbed out of her berth, despite the violent movement of the vessel, and picked up the pages. She took a chance so released the grip of her hand, then stepped onto the floor. The yacht took a lurch to port. She lost her balance and had to let go with the other hand. Her head hit the dressing table. She saw stars but was still conscious. Bending down onto her knees, she grabbed the music sheets. She timed her next move with that of The Thistle, unlocked a drawer on the dressing table and pulled it open. Luckily it had stops so could not be separated from the table. Still kneeling, she shoved the pages in random order into the drawer and locked it.

The movement of the vessel was becoming more violent. She was in a contorted heap on the floor. She felt as if she was going to heave. In a state of panic, she grabbed the jerry pot and was violently sick into it. Some of it went on the mat. She tasted the residue in her mouth. It seemed like a dead frog had putrefied there. She wiped her face with a towel. Almost totally exhausted, she pulled herself back into her berth and hung onto the sides to save herself. At least she'd rescued the Mass.

She lay on the bed. It seemed for an eternity. Her head ached where she had hit it. She felt as if she would pass out. She stayed just about conscious. Then, after about two hours, and as suddenly as it started, the storm subsided. Calmness joyfully displaced it. The vessel stopped its angry and violent movement. Suddenly, she felt much better, even well enough to think of Eugénie. How had this much older lady coped? Had she been sick? And what about Monique? And the rest of the crew?

She rushed out of her cabin along to the galley. Eugénie was sitting at the dining table calmly drinking a cup of tea.

'Eugénie! Are you all right? What a horrendous storm! I thought I was going to die!'

'I'm fine, Ethel! That was nothing! I enjoy these minor storms! We may run into worse weather than that! You haven't been sick, have you? You've got some of it down your front. Monique, please take her to the bathroom and help clean her up.'

Monique conscientiously attended to Ethel, to her blushing shame, and rubbed her down, as if she was a schoolgirl who had been playing in the mud.

\*\*\*

Ethel soon recovered from her embarrassment and settled back into the combination of holiday and work. The Thistle was moored by the quay in Dubrovnik when Ethel went up on deck to speak to Eugénie, who was on her deckchair enjoying the sun. Because she was quite visible to the many people walking by, she was wearing a loose-fitting, figure covering bathing costume.

'Eugénie, I have something exciting to tell you! I've completed the Mass! It's finished. I can relax a little more now!'

'That is brilliant news, Ethel. When are you going to play it to me?'

'Play it to you? Well… as soon as I can, when we are back home!'

'You haven't been into the aft saloon then, Ethel.'

'No, only the one amidships!'

'It's behind my cabin. It's not very large, but it has a piano, fixed to the floor.'

'I'm amazed, Eugénie. So I can play it to you! Well, I can play the various tunes and sing the words!'

'We are going to dine in the town tonight, so let's see how we feel when we arrive back. What do you think?'

'I'd love to play some or all of it, as soon as we can both enjoy it!'

The two of them had a delightful meal in Dubrovnik, but Ethel partook in far too much of the local beer to perform her Mass, so they delayed the recital until the afternoon of the following day. As they berthed in the port, Eugénie engaged some interest from the crew, so Ethel played to an audience of five, which included the captain and Monique.

'That was utterly brilliant,' said Eugénie, as Ethel ended the Gloria with a flourish. All five applauded. This minor gathering gave Ethel encouragement for its performance at a major concert, possibly in Germany and hopefully in England, too. The audience dispersed and the two of them adjourned to the galley, where Monique served them each a cup of tea and a slice of a cake she had made.

'That work proves to me beyond doubt you are a brilliant composer. I know you will say, "What do you know about music?" but I attended a lot of musical events in France and your Mass would not be out of place in any of them. Well done and congratulations on writing such a lovely piece. I like its celebratory feel and its cheerfulness. It's not like any other mass I've heard, Ethel! Have you ever thought of writing an opera? You clearly have the skill and we in Great Britain have few writers of opera. You could convincingly succeed in this area and I would help to promote you!'

'I'll be forever grateful for your generous praise, Eugénie. And for your extraordinary offer of help. I have put a tremendous effort into that Mass, and it is wonderful for me to know that you appreciated it so much. It's a pity I needed to improvise the orchestra! Yes, I've harboured the ambition to write an opera for many years now and I've said before I want it performed before I'm forty and in Germany!'

'So you've got a few years yet, my dear!'

From that moment, the idea of writing an opera burned Ethel inside. She felt desperate to write one as surely as if her life depended on it. There was nothing much she could do about it while she was on board The Thistle, apart from thinking of a few plays she could write an opera around. Something from Shakespeare, perhaps? She would leave the idea of an opera for now and, between relaxing with the Empress on deck and enjoying the culinary extravagances Monique produced, she would carry out some necessary revisions to the Mass. With Eugénie's support, she was confident she would see it performed.

# CHAPTER 22

## Royal patronage

Ethel returned home refreshed and exhilarated. Her beloved Marco gave her the most delightful welcome. That the General and household had looked after him well so gave her the confidence to leave him again, if the need arose. Two immediate tasks confronted her. First, to promote her Mass, abroad if need be. Second, she would write an opera.

She touted the Mass around the choral societies in England, but none showed the slightest interest in the first mass they had seen written by a woman. Undeterred, she thought of a different tack. She'd take it to Munich and show it to Hermann Levi who, the last time she visited him, some two years before, had immersed himself so deeply in the forthcoming Wagner Festival, he could hardly spare her three minutes. He might be less engaged than when she showed him her Serenade and the Anthony and Cleopatra Overture. If not, there were other conductors she could try, and Levi might suggest some.

Excited by the prospect of a visit to Munich, she wrote to Harry to say she wanted to promote the Mass there. She asked him if he would like to meet her in the city, not in Paris as they had earlier discussed, and suggested some dates. Unable to resist further philosophical argument, she again touched on the subject of God. Having given birth to the Mass, she said, her fervent belief in the Father had unexpectedly vanished such that, while still more able to help with the needs of others, especially her father, she was completely free of any religious persuasion. She said she was intent on writing an opera and would force herself to write one, as if her life depended on it.

His reply was instantaneous. He sent her a telegram agreeing on a date and said he'd meet her at the main station in the city. He met her on the platform, exactly as planned.

'Ethel, it's wonderful to see you. I hope you've had a pleasant journey,' he said, as he picked up some of her luggage to carry it along the platform. 'You are looking so well! We haven't met since we had coffee in that odd café in

Bressenden Place… and I love you just as much now, if not more so, than I did then. And that was at least six months ago! I've booked us into a comfortable hotel.'

'It's good to see you, too. You are looking well. I'm so glad you were free to meet me and not in America… or somewhere else on business! How is Julia?' She didn't reply to his declaration of love.

'The same as ever. Still wedded to her metaphysics. I haven't told her I'm seeing you. That would only cause trouble. I've told her I'm here on business and am seeing a publisher here about printing The Prison in German.'

'I'm not sure if I approve of that, Harry. But I leave you to decide on how to handle Julia. So you've booked us into a hotel. Separate rooms, I trust.'

'Of course, Ethel. I'd love to make love to you, as you know… but I don't want to do anything you wouldn't agree with.'

'Good!' was Ethel's blunt but sincere response.

They walked to the hotel, and Harry booked them in. A porter helped them take their luggage to their respective rooms, which were next to each other. By then it was almost time for dinner, so they agreed to meet in the hotel restaurant.

'I regard it as a real privilege to meet you here,' said Harry, looking longingly into Ethel's eyes across the table. 'So how are you intending to promote the Mass?'

'My first port of call will be Hermann Levi, conductor of the Royal Munich Opera Orchestra. I've met him before and although I don't like him much, he may just be interested. If not, he may help me find someone else for me, a choral society or another orchestra. It wouldn't be right to take you with me, Harry, so I'll go there on my own. I may need to arrange an appointment.'

'I understand that, Ethel. So you are thinking of writing an opera… yes?'

'Definitely. I'm dying to write one!'

'I've thought of a plot you could base it on.'

'Really?'

'Yes. It's a simple story in a novel called Thaïs by Anatole France. I've read it twice! It would make a brilliant opera!' He outlined the plot in which a hermit in the Egyptian desert goes to Alexandria to find Thais, a beautiful woman of pleasure whom he knew as a youth. Pretending to be a wealthy gentleman, he speaks to her about heaven and eternity; he converts her to Christianity. On their return to the desert, he becomes fascinated with her former life and makes love to her. She enters a convent to repent. He cannot forget the pull of her beauty, and he becomes confused about the values of life and the hereafter. Later, as she is dying and can only see heaven opening before her, he comes to her side and tells her that her faith is an illusion, and that he loves her. She passes into oblivion, in neither heaven nor hell.

'My goodness, Harry. What an incredible story. I'll buy the novel. Presumably, it's in French?'

'Yes, but there are various translations. I'll see if I can find you a copy while you are meeting Herr Levi!'

Ethel made her way to the Royal Opera House. Levi wasn't there. The orchestra administrator told her he was in Venice and would be back in three days. She offered Ethel an appointment, which she gleefully accepted. It would be for eight o'clock in the morning, his first meeting.

In the meantime, Ethel and Harry had several discussions about their future and Ethel's dereliction of faith.

'I'm with you, Ethel. I have to say, I was surprised at your conversion and I'm sure several of your friends and your parents were, too. What do you think happened?'

'I wish I knew. It suddenly vanished. At almost the moment I finished the Mass. I first felt bad about it, but now I feel a wonderful sense of liberation.'

'I've never been a believer, Ethel. The whole idea of a deity suffered badly from Darwin's Origin of Species. The Pope hated it. He'd have excommunicated him, if he'd been a Catholic. If I were alone on this planet, I'd never have invented the idea of a god.'

'You've some interesting thoughts, Harry. We have much in common.'

'I still want you, Ethel. Do not forget that.'

'You know the answer to that one, Harry.'

*** 

Ethel turned up a quarter of an hour early for the meeting with Levi. The secretary installed her in the outer office.

'Haven't I seen you somewhere before?' said Levi, as he bowled into his office, threw his hat at a hat stand and sat in his high-backed chair. 'Have a seat.'

'Yes, we met about two years ago when I showed you my Serenade and my Overture, Anthony and Cleopatra. You had a quick look at them and encouraged me… so I thought you'd like to see my latest work, a Mass for choir and orchestra.'

'Where is it?'

'In my bag.'

'Give it here. I haven't much time. I've another meeting at eight thirty with my old friend Anton Bruckner. Do you know of him?'

'Yes, I met him on a train well over ten years ago and I know his niece, Theresia Hueber.'

'What a coincidence!'

She dug her score out of her canvas bag, stood up and put it in front of him. He turned the pages over, starting at the beginning. He paused here and there and either whistled or sang the tunes, while conducting with his left hand.

'Do you know, it's very good, Miss Smyth. Better than I expected. I'm impressed. It has a sense of real drama which is rare in a mass. I wish I could perform it here but I've a full programme until the end of ninety two and into ninety three so I can't help you now. Maybe, the Gewandhaus could help or the Vienna Phil. But it is well worth an airing. It's so dramatic you should write an opera!'

'I'm delighted you think that,' said Ethel, almost in tears.

'Yes, and if you want anybody to confirm that, just ask them to write to me. I'm sorry, but I can't spare you any more time.'

'Well, all I can do is to thank you, Herr Levi. Thank you so much!'

She shook hands with Levi, turned and, both elated and disappointed, walked out of his office. Sitting in the outer office, wearing trousers that were far too wide for him, Anton Bruckner was turning the page of a newspaper. She recognised him immediately.

'Herr Bruckner, how are you? We met on a train from Cologne to Calais. I'm Ethel Smyth, an up-and-coming composer!'

He looked up. 'Of course! I remember you, Miss Smyth. You are a friend of Theresia's!' He smiled with his whole face. 'So I take it you've composed many more works since I last saw you?'

Ethel told him about the first performance of the Serenade and about her Mass, some of her other works, her hopes for other performances and about writing an opera.

'That's all wonderful news. I wish you all the best. And I hope we meet again!'

Hermann Levi opened his office door. 'Come in, Anton. I believe you two already know each other.'

***

'So is Levi going to perform it?' asked Harry, as they met in the hotel reception on the way to the restaurant.

'No, but he liked it. I am naturally disappointed that he won't, but that's because his programme is full... or so he claimed. He said he'd endorse it if anyone asked him. Also, and completely unprompted, he told it was so good I should write an opera!'

'Well done, Ethel! So an opera it will be! We could write it together. I could write the libretto and you the music. It would be a masterpiece!'

'What an interesting idea, Harry. I hadn't thought of that. And we could do it remotely, in correspondence, with you in Italy and me in England. But I'd need the words before I could set them to the music.'

'Yes, but you could write an overture and any incidental music.'

'And I could write some tunes to identify the characters. I'll start as soon as I arrive home!'

'I'll do the same. And here is a copy of France's Thaïs. I bought it in a bookshop today!'

Ethel read the novel on her train journey back to London. She liked the story and couldn't wait to tell Eugénie what she and Harry had decided. Within two days of reaching home and enjoying another wondrous reception by Marco, Ethel unlocked the door of The Empress Eugénie's sumptuous house and let herself in.

'My dear Ethel, it is so good to see you. You naughty girl! You didn't write to me while you were away as I thought you would,' said The Empress, as Ethel bounded into the Empress's favourite drawing-room. She put down the newspaper she was reading, stood up and gave Ethel a hug and a kiss on both cheeks.

'Sorry about the lack of a letter. I've no excuse, really.' She told Eugénie about her meeting with Levi and his suggestion, identical to Eugénie's, that she should write an opera.

'So one of your professionals supports my idea, then. I'm as pleased as you are! Have you chosen something for the libretto?'

'Yes, a novel by Anatole France called Thaïs. I read it on the train home and I just love it!'

'That one is not for you, Ethel. I hope you have wasted no time on it.'

'What do you mean? No, apart from reading it.'

'One of my closest friends in Paris is Émile Waldteufel. He's a composer and pianist. I wrote to him as soon as we returned from Cap Martin and brought him up to date with my life and told him all about you and our idea for you to write an opera. You must believe this amazing coincidence. He replied saying his friend Massenet was writing an opera. The shock is that it will be based on France's Thaïs. Isn't that terrible news for you? I'm so sorry.'

'I'm stunned, Eugénie. I need a cup of tea to recover from the shock.'
Eugénie called in one of her maidservants and asked her to brew some.

Typical of her wish to support and help Ethel, Eugénie came up with another idea.

'Another alternative might be a Musset play if you want something French. He wrote quite a number and you could do a lot worse than one of his! I quite like the comedies! I have copies of all of them in my library if you want to read them.'

During the next couple of weeks, Ethel read or skimmed through all the plays of which Eugénie had copies. There were so many to choose from and a number were quite amusing, so she became firmly committed to writing a comic opera.

***

That year, in the autumn, Eugénie invited Ethel to stay with her in the mansion on the Birkhall Estate, part of the Balmoral Estate which Queen Victoria had lent her. The Empress had her motives for asking her but had no intention of revealing them to the unsuspecting Ethel.

'I'm constantly staggered with what you do and whom you know, Eugénie. But having been the wife of Napoleon III, I shouldn't be surprised! Yes, I'd be absolutely delighted!'

'Bring some of your music, especially your songs, the piano sonatas, and the Mass.'

On her second day at Birkhall, The Empress presented Ethel to The Duke and Duchess of Connaught and Prince Henry of Battenberg. All three were keen on music and Eugénie asked Ethel to sing to them. Within a few more days, in the early afternoon, Eugénie dashed into the study where Ethel was reading a Musset play.

'Ethel, something interesting for you. The Queen wants me to present you to her. She sounds very keen to meet you and, according to her Equerry, is coming here at three o'clock, despite the appalling weather! Have your music at the ready. She may want you to sing or play some! The Connaughts and Prince Henry have told her about you.'

'I need to tidy myself up first, Eugénie. Just need to sort out my hair. I haven't combed it at all today!'

To make sure there was no one there, The Empress spent the next hour scanning the corridors and the storm-lashed garden. The Queen hated to come across unexpected people. The Empress and her unofficial Birkhall maidservant, Madame Arcos, received the Queen and Princess Christian at the front door. Moments before, they had rolled out the red carpet, but it was sodden before the Queen stepped onto it. The poor woman was soaked but could still smile.

The Queen, Princess Christian, and The Empress disappeared into a drawing-room. Ethel and Madame Arcos waited in another room. A few minutes later, The Empress reappeared and beckoned Ethel. She followed.

With a face exactly matching the photographs, a little old lady was sitting on an ordinary wicker chair. A white straw hat, tied by a ribbon around her chin, perched on her head. By the force of logic, Ethel should have been terrified by the Royal presence but the Queen's blue eyes and her captivating smile, 'the most entrancing I have ever seen on a human face', made her feel confident and unexpectedly relaxed.

Princess Christian did much to help Ethel's introduction. She explained she had heard much about Ethel, not only from The Empress but also from Mary Benson, the Archbishop's wife. Ethel hoped that Mary Benson had been positive with her remarks. The Empress also helped. She talked to the three of them in her own competent social manner, utterly befitting of a former head of state. Then the time came for Princess Christian to ask Ethel to sing.

'Your Majesty, I would like to sing a few songs in German. I wrote one of them myself.'

Ethel sang strongly. She deliberately exaggerated the contrast in the quieter passages. She put everything she could into the songs. To accentuate the words, she used her head, her arms, and her body. She even stamped her feet. She glanced several times at the Queen who, though impassive, looked as if she enjoyed the entertainment. Her Majesty kept eye contact with Ethel, which encouraged her even more. Ethel impressed the whole of this tiny audience.

Eugénie noticed that all of them seemed to enjoy Ethel's brief recital. So she took a chance. 'You ought to hear her sing her Mass!' she said.

Almost imperceptibly, the Queen nodded. Ethel instantly launched into a startling performance of the Sanctus and the Benedictus. Just as on The Thistle, but without the piano, she sang with commitment and power. She confidently tackled both the solo, choir and instrumental parts, using different voices for each. She improvised the percussion by stamping her feet and hammering her fists on the table. The sound she created filled the whole room, despite the storm outside.

The Queen enjoyed Ethel's unique style of singing, so she asked for a repeat performance at Balmoral. This delighted The Empress who realised her aim looked close to achievement.

# CHAPTER 23

## The Mass Performed?

The Empress took unprecedented trouble in organising Ethel's toilet for the big occasion. She arranged some outrageous headgear, shaped as a black viper, which she pinned in Ethel's hair.

'I simply cannot wear a thing like that,' said Ethel, as Eugénie picked it up from the dressing table and uncoiled it. 'It will look ridiculous!'

'Trust me, Ethel. I know what I'm doing. A lady must wear headgear in front of the Queen. You know I never wear a hat… but I'm sure you noticed that square of black silk on my head when I welcomed her and her ladies-in-waiting.'

'Yes, I did, in fact.'

'This is a very expensive piece of decoration I bought in Biarritz. It will be perfect. There you are,' she said, as she finished installing it.

Ethel looked in the mirror and grimaced. 'I hate it already. But it doesn't look as bad as it could.'

A carriage came to take them the eight miles to Balmoral. The lazy autumn sun shimmered above them. A smiling Princess Christian welcomed them to this magnificent castle. Two guards' officers flanked the main entrance, and the Princess led them in.

'I still can't believe this, Eugénie. I know I was born into a well-to-do family and was never poor, but I could never have imagined performing in front of Her Majesty… now for the second time,' Ethel said, as they sat down next to each other at dinner.

'Look at it this way. She has the same range of emotions. She can suffer the same problems as you. Not wishing to sound indelicate, she has the same bodily functions as you. And you have something she does not, which is the ability to perform music in the inimitable way you do. That's why you are here! That's why she wants to see you again.'

'You've made me feel more confident, Eugénie. I seriously love you.'

The sumptuous dinner over, the entire company, including legions of courtiers and royals re-assembled in the adjacent drawing-room. Once the Queen could see they were all settled and expecting spectacular entertainment, she gently gave Ethel her instruction.

'Now let us hear some more of your Mass.'

The Queen sat on one side of Ethel and The Empress on the other, while Ethel arranged herself in front of the keys of a huge grand piano. A piano! The unexpected component in this distinguished gathering! She played it as if she was a baker pummelling a lump of dough. It had never been so brutally thumped. She sang with verve and gusto, hitting notes as high as ever before and with such volume the window panes were on the verge of rattling. The serpent on her head was holding on, despite her thrashing movement. Her feet banged the floor. An enormous round of applause rang out as her arms flew into the air at the last note of the Agnus Dei. Once it had subsided, she launched into the Gloria, its most rumbustious and closing movement.

The performance was a triumph. At the end, the applause was even louder. The Queen graciously joined in. Who needed a choir or an orchestra when Ethel was performing at her peak?

'They must perform this Mass in London,' said Princess Christian. 'It must be... at the Royal Albert Hall.'

'Absolutely right,' said The Empress. 'It is an important original work!'

'How can we achieve it?' said the Princess.

'Let's talk to Ethel.'

The two of them brought Ethel into the discussion.

'If you want a professional endorsement, write to Herr Hermann Levi at the Royal Opera Orchestra in Munich. He saw the score and loved it so much he even suggested I should write an opera!'

Within a few weeks, the Princess received a reply that none of them could have expected: 'I know of no living German composer who could have written it', said Levi. She wrote to The Empress about it and told her she was going to send the letter to Sir Joseph Barnby, the conductor of the Royal Choral Society, along with the suggestion that he examine the Mass with a view to its performance. A few days later, Barnby invited Ethel to bring the score to him.

'May I come with you,' said Eugénie. 'It might just help if I did. Even though I know nothing about music!'

'A wonderful idea, Eugénie.' She went over and gave her a kiss. 'Do you know him?'

'No… But he may know of me!' The Empress felt her mission to have Ethel's Mass performed in public was bearing fruit.

***

Sir Joseph looked through the score.

'Hmm. It's original, but I'm none too sure about performing it. It's a little light, almost ungodly for a Mass.'

'Ridiculous,' said Eugénie. 'It's a celebration of God, not one of the usual supplicatory works.'

'I'll have a think about it.'

'I'm not letting him waste our time pondering it,' said Eugénie, on the train back to Farnborough. 'I'm going to involve Princess Christian. She'll help. She loved it and wants it performed. Didn't she suggest the Albert Hall? I'm going to write to her as soon as I'm home.'

'I'm so disappointed. But I'm so grateful to have you on my side. I really am.'

True to her word the Empress wrote to The Princess who replied saying Barnby's reaction surprised her. Eugénie told Ethel about the letter.

'She's made an incredible suggestion!'

'Go on. Tell me!'

'She's going to speak to her brother, the Duke of Edinburgh. Apparently, he's the President of the Royal Choral Society. She'll try to persuade him to ask Barnby to conduct it. If the Duke agrees, he will have to play, like it or not!'

Ethel jumped for joy. 'Hooray! Well done, Eugénie. You're a genius!'

'Don't let yourself become too excited, Ethel. We're not there yet!'

The Princess explained to the Duke how their mother had enjoyed Ethel's performance at Birkhall and the Balmoral rendition even more. The Duke was convinced. He immediately wrote to Barnby to suggest it be played by the Royal Choral Society no later than in the coming season. The Princess wrote to The Empress who set off to see Ethel.

'The Princess persuaded the Duke! Barnby has been told to perform it next season, at the Royal Albert Hall.'

Ethel went up to Eugénie and kissed firmly on her lips. Eugénie eased back a little. 'I am so grateful. Without you, it may never have been performed. You are such a wonderful source of support. I love you even more now.'

Within days, Barnby wrote to Ethel to say he would perform her Mass in the following concert season and had provisionally put it in the programme for 18 January, '93. He said that it would be a good idea to meet soon to discuss the score and issues about the venue. He gave her some dates to meet at St James Hall.

Ethel was not especially surprised that Barnby had become so enthusiastic about playing the Mass, even though he did not withdraw his misgivings about it. He didn't know that Ethel knew the full background.

'I'm really looking forward to playing your Mass, Ethel. It's certainly an interesting work. I understand you played a piano version of some of it to the Queen… at Balmoral? What an honour!'

'Yes, I think she quite enjoyed it,' she said. 'I've brought you the score again.' She pulled it out of her bag.

'Excellent. We must arrange for the individual parts to be printed, of course. But we should look at the orchestration first, in case we need to change anything. You have written it for a large range of instruments, so it will cost quite a sum to print it. Still, the Royal Choral Society can bear it!'

'There's no need for you to pay.'

'Not me. The Society!'

'No. The Empress Eugénie says she'll pay!'

'That is good news! We can spend what we save from the printing on promoting the concert!'

Ethel was not surprised at the possible need to change the score, from her experience just over two years before on the Serenade.

'What about the soloists?' said Ethel. 'I imagine you will want some outstanding performers.'

'I'll do my best on that front. There are two issues here. The most famous are not always keen to play an unknown work by a relatively unknown composer. But you are a rarity, Ethel. A woman composer. So the performance will be a unique event and many will grasp the opportunity. Another point is that, because of the nature of the event, several Royals will be there, probably including the Queen. She has already shown she likes it!'

'This is truly exciting. I'll help in any way I can,' said Ethel. She still felt apprehensive. She regarded the Mass as one of her loves, despite its imperfections, and didn't want Barnby to make any gratuitous changes, just to fit in with his idea of what a Mass should sound like.

The months up to the performance sped by. She wrote to Harry telling him the glorious news. He promised to come to give her support. She smiled and clapped her hands to see George Henschel at a rehearsal.

'George! George Henschel! What are you doing here? I thought you only came to these places to sing!'

'I was speaking with Joseph Barnby the other day, and he told me he was working on a new mass by a fairly unknown British woman composer. I guessed it was you! So I asked him when the next rehearsal was going to be. He said today… so here I am!'

'George, I'm so pleased you could come along. How is Lillian?'

'Very well, in fact. She is still telling her friends about that exchange with your father when she admitted to being a Unitarian!'

'I wasn't sure whether to be embarrassed or not by what he said!'

'Everyone laughed, so that was a good thing. So how are the rehearsals going?'

'I can't believe I've written such a poor piece of music. There are numerous silly mistakes. Honestly, George. The choir is having trouble with it. I hadn't realised I'd been so demanding of them.'

'Mistakes? What sort of mistakes?'

'One of the crassest is that I've scored one of the solo parts in the Sanctus for a quartet of soft horns. In the vast emptiness of the Albert Hall they sound like husky mosquitoes. I'm quite depressed about some of it,' she said, on the verge of tears.

'You are being too critical, Ethel. It will sound wonderful on the night. You must be more forgiving of yourself. Why not let me help you with the scoring?'

'George, you are a godsend. Yes, I'd truly appreciate your help.'

Ethel and Henschel spent many hours poring over the score, making changes and listening to them at the rehearsals. He knew Ethel would never be satisfied. Then came the final rehearsal. She arrived at the Albert Hall for a ten thirty start only to be told that Barnby was rehearsing Haydn's Creation, the work they were performing before hers, so he wouldn't be ready for the Mass for at least an hour. She wandered around backstage, losing herself in the maze of corridors, flights of stairs and blind corners. After ten minutes of panic, she found herself at the bottom of some stairs into the arena. The orchestra was playing a wonderful piece of music. Surely that wasn't Haydn? No. She suddenly realised it was from her Mass. It sounded better than she expected. She was overjoyed and almost broke into tears.

***

The night before the actual performance, the Henschels gave a party in Ethel's honour.

'Harry, I didn't expect to see you here!'

'I promised to come to the first performance!'

Ethel went up to him and planted a kiss right on his lips. She hoped it didn't raise his expectations. 'Come,' she said. 'You must meet my family.'

She held his hand and took him to the other side of the room. 'Papa, this is Harry Brewster, an old friend of mine who lives in Florence.'

The General looked at Harry as if he and Ethel were closer than she may be saying. He raised his moustache slightly, almost in protest.

'I'm pleased to meet you, Mr Brewster. So you've come all the way from Florence to see Ethel's Mass performed. That is exceptionally kind of you.'

'I'm pleased to be here. I've known Ethel since she came to stay with my wife and me, what, ten years ago, Ethel?'

'Yes, it must be about that.' Ethel was pleased that he'd mentioned his wife to the General. At least he acknowledged her existence. The General still seemed uncomfortable speaking to this bearded, arty looking individual.

Ethel and Harry had talked for long enough with the General and, because the conversation was touching on difficult ground, she took Harry to meet her sisters. They all rather took to him, even though their spouses were a little unsure and showed it by looking away from him during the introductions. Ethel half expected their reactions.

***

The performance was a spectacular success. Barnby, the Royal Albert Hall Orchestra and the Royal Choral Society put their all into it. The audience which filled the Albert Hall absolutely loved it. The sheer force of this energetic Mass thrilled them. They had heard nothing like it before. Hardly a soul had come for the Haydn. They were there for Ethel's Mass. The sheer volume of the applause astonished Ethel as it did the Empress who, as she had promised, made her first public performance there since the death of her husband. Every member of Ethel's family enjoyed the triumph as much as Ethel herself. Barnby forced her to appear on the platform to receive the adulation of the many.

Some of those who considered themselves better informed were less impressed. George Bernard Shaw remarked it was not as vulgar as the Salvation Army, but more like a crack military band. Archbishop Benson was equally dismissive. He reckoned God was not implored to have mercy in the way he expected, but commanded to in a way he may not appreciate.

The next question was, how had the press received it?

'Ethel, you must read this,' said Alice, two days later when the reviews were published. 'It's in Papa's paper… "The work definitely places the composer among the most eminent composers of her time, and easily at the head of all those of her own sex."'

Ethel was both delighted and disappointed. How did her sex come into the equation? She composed music. Surely, that was all that mattered.

'And "throughout it is virile, masterly in construction and workmanship, and particularly for the excellence and rich colour of the orchestration", it says. Congratulations, my dear sister!'

Ethel kissed her. 'Thank you for spotting that, Alice. I'm so pleased with the point on the orchestration. I learnt so much from Tchaikovsky. He is an exceptional orchestrator you know!'

Other newspapers gave Ethel's Mass faint praise. The Morning Star said it was seldom a woman composer soared to the heights of musical art. The Daily News attributed the performance of the work more to Royal patronage than to any merit the work might have.

Ethel's sister Mary organised a party to celebrate Ethel's achievement. She invited the rich and famous. Harry had become accepted in the family, so Mary invited him, too.

Ethel badly wanted to capitalise on her success.

'Harry, I'm going to Europe to promote the Mass. Maybe we could meet over there.'

'Do you have any city in mind?'

'I don't see the point of going back to Munich, but I might go there, anyway. I thought I should concentrate on Amsterdam, Cologne perhaps, Heidelberg and Leipzig. Could we meet in Leipzig? I'll write to you and keep you in touch with where I am.'

'We'll meet in Leipzig, Ethel! I look forward to that. As you know, I'm here only for your Mass so I'll be leaving for Florence tomorrow.'

# CHAPTER 24

## Theresia

Ethel went home to pack her bags. She bitterly regretted having to leave Marco again, but knew he would be in excellent hands. The General had decided not to attend Mary's party and greeted Ethel at the front door of Frimhurst.

'You must tell me who you met at Mary's and how it all went. I must give you this, Ethel. It came a week ago and I apologise for not giving it to you then. But everything was somewhat chaotic, with you going to London for the rehearsals almost every day!' He handed her a letter. 'It looks as if it's a German cancellation mark.'

'No, it's Austrian, Papa. I have a friend there, Theresia. She said she'd be writing to me.'

'Do you want me to stay with you, as I did with the letter about Lisl?'

'You can stay if you wish, but I'm not expecting bad news!'

'I'll go into the kitchen!' As he opened the door, Marco came bounding out to meet her.

'You lovely boy,' she said, as Marco licked her face and she patted his back. Flicking his head up towards her hand, he snatched the letter from her and with it firmly between his jaws charged back into the kitchen.

'Marco! Marco! You naughty boy. Come back here, this instant.'

Marco didn't respond. Ethel chased after him. She almost crashed into the kitchen door. Marco sat in his basket with the letter between his paws, chewing it vigorously. Ethel took it from his mouth. 'So this is the welcome you give me! And I've not been away that long!'

Ethel rescued the letter while it was still in a readable state. Most of the damage was to the envelope. She read the chewed letter. The Conservatorium had granted Theresia's appeal against their earlier decision. She was asking Ethel if

245

she could take up her offer of being a witness and coming to testify. Ethel's heart missed several beats. What about the date? Would she be in Leipzig when Theresia was there? She sped through the rest of the letter. Yes, she could arrange her schedule to be there at the hearing on Wednesday 15 March, 1893. That would give her almost two months. She would write to Theresia to say she would meet her the day before, and to Harry to tell him she aimed to be in Leipzig from the Sunday. Eugénie fully supported her plans and wished she could come, too, but for other commitments.

Despite identifying what she thought would be the most receptive choirs and orchestras in Amsterdam, Cologne and Heidelberg, her energetic and confident efforts to persuade them to play the Mass failed. With time to spare before meeting Harry, she tried the Staatskapelle in Dresden. Her efforts there also drew a blank, so she made her way to Leipzig.

'It's been a total waste of time, Harry,' she said after they had settled themselves into separate rooms in their hotel. 'I've visited the musical directors of four orchestras and seven choirs, all to no avail. I showed all of them the reviews in The Times and The Daily Telegraph, the letter from Levi to Princess Christian and the score. My only hope now is Carl Reinecke, one of my tutors when I was a student.'

'I'm disappointed for you, Ethel. You must have spent a fortune.'

'I'm lucky, Harry. The Empress Eugénie has been hugely helpful. She is paying for nearly all of this. She gave me enough to cover two months over here and my father has helped, too. Apart from what I earned from the Albert Hall performance.'

'So presumably you want to see Reinecke as soon as you can. Tomorrow?'

'Yes. I'd like to see him tomorrow or Tuesday. He may not be available then, if my experience with the other choirs and orchestras is anything to go by.'

At dinner that night, Ethel surprised Harry with an idea.

'I must tell you, Harry,' she said, as she cut a piece off her Wiener Schnitzel. 'I've read almost all Musset's plays and the one I'd like to use for an opera is Fantasio.'

'I've heard of it, Ethel. It's a real oddity. Are you sure?'

'Yes, I'm confident! The plot is quite simple and is about an arranged marriage that goes awry. You are right, though. The plot is distinctly odd. It goes something like this. Elsbeth, daughter of the King of Bavaria, is due to be married to the Prince of Mantua, whom she's never met before. Elsbeth is mourning the death of Saint-Jean, the hunchbacked court jester. Fantasio, a worker from Munich, adopts the jester's costume and gait in order to ingratiate himself with the princess, an odd thing to do, in itself. Meanwhile, the prince, anxious to discover her true feelings, has exchanged clothes with Marinoni, his aide-de-camp. When the court assembles, Fantasio, perched in a tree, removes Marinoni's wig. The insult has the intended consequence of deferring the wedding. Fantasio is gaoled for his outrageous behaviour. Elsbeth visits Fantasio in prison. After some confusion, she returns his love and helps him escape. War threatens. Fantasio's suggestion that the rulers fight it out between them is nervously rejected by the prince who withdraws. Fantasio wins his princess and is proclaimed the King of Fools.'

'The way you've summarised it, Ethel, it sounds good. So how do we make progress? I'll need a copy before I write the libretto. Presumably in French?'

'Yes, I agree. I'm sure there are copies everywhere. As we said before, I'll write an overture and some catchy tunes to identify the characters and we can finish it from there!'

'I'll start as soon as I return to Florence!'

***

On the Monday, Ethel visited Carl Reinecke in the Gewandhaus. She was not surprised he didn't recognise her, or at least he said he didn't. After all, she had left the Conservatory many years before.

'I'm glad you explained who you are, Miss Smyth. Exactly why have you come to see me?'

Ethel explained, took the score, Levi's letter and the other supporting documents from her canvas bag. He started with the score.

'Hmm. Not a bad piece at all. Not like a conventional mass, I have to say. It lacks somewhat in solemnity, don't you think?'

'You must understand, Professor Reinecke! I'm a modern composer and I've put a modern interpretation on it. It is a genuinely religious work. However, unlike most masses, I've tried to give it a celebratory feel, rather than plead to The Almighty. It is not supplicatory.'

He perused a few more pages. 'I can't help saying, you've written it well. Better than anything I've seen from a woman, up to now, for certain. It's got quite a masculine feel about it.'

Ethel was becoming irritated by these patronising remarks and showed it. 'I'm not sure what you are saying, Herr Reinecke. How does the fact that I'm a woman have anything to do with its merits? Are you saying that if a man had written it, it would be acceptable to put in your concert programme?'

Ethel had unsettled him. 'Hmm… I'm not thinking that but…'

'What are you thinking then?' she said, interrupting him with her voice raised and stressing the 'are'.

'I don't think it fits with what I can accept in the programme of the Gewandhaus.'

'Why not?' she bellowed. 'In one second you compliment its originality and in the next you reject it!'

'I don't feel I have to explain.'

'You are a disgrace to your profession, Professor Reinecke. Not only are you a useless teacher, but you are incompetent as a director of the Gewandhaus. It is a great orchestra and deserves better than you!'

She walked out of his office and slammed his door so hard it almost came off its hinges. She turned around and kicked it.

'I completely lost my temper with him,' she said, as she explained to Harry what happened. 'He rejected it because I'm a woman, not on its merits. I was furious. I cannot imagine he's had his door slammed louder!'

'What about going to Munich to see Levi?'

'Utterly pointless. That would be to go full circle! Levi sent me away to write an opera, and it's going to be Fantasio!'

'I understand that, Ethel. Sorry I mentioned it! So when do you meet Theresia?'

'Tuesday. Tomorrow. Her reply to my letter suggests we meet at lunchtime in the Conservatory Refectory. Noon.'

\*\*\*

'So we meet here again, Theresia!' said Ethel, as her eyes fell on Theresia sitting at a table near where they always sat. She was drinking a weak, Leipzig coffee. She dashed over to the table and hugged and kissed her.

'I can't tell you how pleased I am to see you, Ethel. You are so considerate.'

'I was coming here anyway,' said Ethel. 'I've been trying to convince orchestras and choirs here to perform my Mass.' She explained the background, that she had performed it to the Queen and that the result was its performance in London.

'Congratulations, Ethel. Well done. What an amazing story! So have you had any success here?'

'I'm afraid not. And Professor Reinecke was the most unreasonable. He basically refused it because a woman had written it. I was furious and slammed the door on him!'

'Brilliant! I wish I had been behind the curtain, listening! So what are you going to do next, try Paris or Munich?'

'No. I will probably leave the Mass for now. I am planning to write a comic opera so the Mass will have to wait. Enough of me, Theresia. We are here for you and you haven't said a word about the appeal yet!'

'I was amazed to read the letter agreeing the appeal. I thought it would be rejected. Here it is. All it says is they accept; it is to be held on 15 March… and for me to present my case, along with any witnesses. In one of the administrative offices, room 614 at 10.30.'

'How do you feel about it, Theresia? Are you nervous?'

'I was until you said you would come to support me! Are you still happy to say what this man, Weissman, tried on you?'

'Of course, Theresia. That's why I'm here!'

Theresia told Ethel about her teaching and about her family, especially about her uncle who had written his Symphony No. 8 and was working on a ninth, even though he was feeling his age by then. Ethel told Theresia about playing in front of the Queen in Balmoral and more about the press reception of the Mass and the reviews, even though some seemed biased against her being a woman. She said she saw her uncle in Munich about a year before when she went to see Hermann Levi. She said she was thrilled that he recognised her. They agreed to meet in the morning there in the refectory, but they would locate room 614 before they parted.

Ethel and Harry discussed the appeal over dinner in their hotel.

'I'm not sure how I should play this. Have you any advice?'

'Just tell the truth, Ethel. Say what happened and when. That's all you can do.'

'What if they ask questions of an intimate nature? Should I answer them or refuse?'

'My view is simple. Just be honest with them. There will be only three, and there is nothing to be gained by being less than frank. You sound confident when you speak, Ethel, and if you can stay confident, it will be a great help to Theresia.'

\*\*\*

The two of them hugged each other as they met at the same table in the refectory.

'Are you just as relaxed as yesterday, Theresia?'

'No… I feel quite nervous now. I must admit.'

'In fact, I am, too. My friend Harry said, just be yourself. So we should follow that advice. He says try to be confident in dealing with their questions.'

By the time they'd finished settling each other down, they found themselves outside room 614. They stopped and waited. The due time came and went. They were still waiting outside.

'What if we look in?' said Theresia. 'I wonder if they've cancelled it and not told us.'

'No, we stay here.' Ethel put her ear to the door. As she did so, it opened. She almost fell into the room.

'Do come in ladies,' said a clerk. They followed him. Professor Reinecke was sitting on the tribunal. Ethel scowled.

'Please sit over there,' said the bearded chairman, who wore spectacles and smiled reassuringly at them. He pointed to his left. They crossed the room and sat down.

'I am now going to ask the defendant to come in.'

The clerk went to a door at the side of the room and opened it. In came Herr Weissman, smiling smugly, as if certain he would win the appeal. He sat to the chairman's right. The chairman then introduced the other two members of the tribunal.

'This is Professor Reinecke. You probably know him as I understand you both studied music here. And to my right is Herr Bloch. He is a Conservatorium administrator.'

'I'm delighted to see you again,' said Reinecke.

Herr Bloch just nodded in their direction.

'Let me explain why we are here,' said the chairman, who sounded as if he could be a judge. 'In May 1886, Fräulein Hueber charged Herr Weissman with attempting to assault her sexually. An assault that could be interpreted as an attempted rape. The case was heard by the Conservatory tribunal in February 1888, when the case against Herr Weissman was dismissed. In a letter dated 11 January 1890 you, Fräulein Hueber, lodged an appeal against the decision. The letter claimed you had further evidence to support your case. You mentioned a Miss Smyth who had information to support your case.

'First, I must apologise for the delay in arranging this hearing. It was to do with various aspects of the administration here. I would now like to offer you both the opportunity to present the tribunal with that evidence. Fräulein Hueber, the reasons for your appeal are clearly set out in your letter. But is there anything you would wish to add? Please relax. You are not under any pressure from us.'

'No, Chairman. I have nothing to add to what I said in my letter of 11 January. Herr Weissman attacked me and tried to rape me. However, my friend Ethel here has also something to tell you.'

'Thank you, Fräulein. Would you like to give us your testimony, Miss Smyth? You can take your time.'

Ethel told them about the state Theresia was in as she came out of Weissman's office. She described her frightened appearance with the tears running down her face. Looking and sounding serious, she told the tribunal what happened when she went into his room. She reported the pathetic state of him with spittle dribbling down his face and his trousers not fully belted up. Then she described how she fought him as he went to touch her breasts. She said because she was stronger than Theresia, she could fight him off before he could assault her fully. She told them about catching up with Theresia in the corridor and telling Ethel what Weissman had done to her. In concluding, she said they had never met before then.

'Do you have anything to say in response to Miss Smyth's testimony, Herr Weissman?'

'It's a pack of lies. I've never assaulted anyone in my life. I was perfectly sober and in possession of all my faculties when I met the students.'

'Do you remember these two?'

'No. Why should I?'

'I thought it was your job to remember them, in case they needed you to help them. In fact, you met Fräulein Hueber at the earlier hearing. Don't you remember her?'

'Well... obviously. But you don't expect me to remember them all, do you?'

'No,' said the chairman. 'Do you remember any of them?'

'Of course, most, in fact.'

'But you don't remember these two, other than seeing Fräulein Hueber at the previous hearing?'

'No. Definitely not.'

'I put it to you it seems odd that you don't remember these two women, the two who allege you attacked them, when you remember most of the others.'

'I'm not sure how to answer that.'

'Do you other members of the tribunal have any questions?'

'Was Herr Weissman's behaviour influential in your resigning from the Conservatorium, Miss Smyth?' said Professor Reinecke.

Not wishing to give the impression she was biased against the Conservatorium, she chose her words carefully and said, 'Only marginally. I left because I was unhappy with the quality of the teaching.'

'Are there more questions or points to be made?' said the chairman, giving everyone a chance. 'In which case I declare this hearing closed. The tribunal will now deliberate on this fresh evidence and call you back in once we have reached our decision. Clerk, could you please escort Herr Weissman outside and then

Fräulein Hueber and Miss Smyth? Through the same doors by which they entered, please.'

The clerk stood and did as requested.

Ethel and Theresia hugged each other tightly as the clerk disappeared back in. 'That wasn't as bad as I thought it would be,' said Theresia. 'You did nearly all the talking!'

'It was I who had the additional evidence, so I needed to speak more than you.'

'You were excellent, Ethel. And so calm. I loved your last statement. You should have seen Reinecke's face when you said you left because of the quality of the teaching!'

'I did. He left me an open field with that one!'

The unsmiling clerk appeared and led them in. The chairman invited them to sit.

'Are you ready for me to give you our decision?'

'Yes,' they said in unison.

'The tribunal has reached its decision,' he said, reading from his notes. 'A certain Miss Smyth, who has travelled from England, in good part to attend this tribunal, presented it with additional evidence.' He summarised what Ethel had said. 'The important decision for us to make was whether what Miss Smyth said was an accurate account of what happened. We unanimously agreed that it was. We, therefore, uphold Fräulein Hueber's appeal. Herr Weissman will be dealt with in due course. I will write to you, Fräulein, with a statement of our decision. You may go now.'

The two of them couldn't escape fast enough.

'Ethel, I love you,' said Theresia. She placed a prolonged kiss onto Ethel's lips. 'You are a female wonder. You've turned this case right around. I'm so grateful. And you've come all the way from England for me. I am going to entertain you to a meal tonight. Will you have dinner with me at my hotel?'

'I'd be grateful to have less of the "female"! I've had enough of that with these damned orchestras! But a tremendous result, Theresia. I'm delighted for you. I must go back to my hotel and tell Harry I'll be dining with a lady friend tonight. That will make him think!'

Ethel arrived at the reception of the Fürstenhof Hotel at seven o'clock, as agreed. She expected to see Theresia sitting in one of the armchairs but she had not arrived by then so took one herself. After more than half an hour, there was still no sign of Theresia. She wondered if she had remembered the meeting time correctly, but was sure she had. She waited for another fifteen minutes, but when that passed, she went to the reception desk and asked the lady there if she would mind contacting Theresia's room.

'So why do you want me to do that? We prefer to respect the privacy of our clients, not to interrupt them for no reason.'

'But I'm concerned about her. We were supposed to meet here at seven o'clock. That was over an hour ago. We are close friends and the only plausible reason she hasn't met me is that something has gone wrong.'

'I'll speak to the manager.'

The woman was gone for what seemed an age. She came back behind a tall, thin man who took over the discussion with Ethel. She repeated word for word her concerns.

'What if my friend is ill in her room? It won't look good for this well-known hotel if something unpleasant happens to her just because of your intransigence,' she added.

The manager turned to the receptionist. He told her to go with Ethel to Theresia's room. They both ran up the stairs. The receptionist opened the door. Theresia was lying on the floor, unconscious.

'You stay with her. I'll call a doctor,' said the receptionist. Ethel knelt beside her and listened to her breathing. She held her hand. She stirred.

'What happened, Ethel?'

'I don't know. Did you pass out? Let me help you onto the bed. You are not bleeding, so you must have fainted.'

'I must have, Ethel. I have fainted twice before, at least. I just feel hungry and thirsty. What shall we do about that dinner? You are my guest, don't forget.'

'Let's not worry about guests. What do you think about having dinner here, in your room? We can order from the menu.'

Moments later there was a knock on the door. Ethel opened it.

'I am a doctor. I am here to check on a guest.' He walked into the room carrying what looked like an attaché case.

'She's over on the bed. I presume she fainted, but she's better now.'

'I'll be the judge of that, if you please.' He dashed over to Theresia, opened his case and pulled out a stethoscope. He placed it on her chest and listened carefully. Without saying a word, he took a thermometer and said she should open her mouth. He placed it under her tongue, left it for a quarter of a minute, took it out and read it.

'Can't find anything wrong with you,' he said. 'What happened?'

Theresia explained with Ethel's help.

'You've simply fainted. You may have had a difficult few days, and it has had a deleterious effect upon you. I recommend a few days' rest. Stay in this room and in bed, if you can and have no other commitments.'

'I certainly will, doctor. I'm grateful,' said Theresia. He left the room.

'I'm so glad there's not much wrong with you, Theresia. Good news, yes?'

'What a relief, Ethel. I was really worried. I'm still not sure what happened. All I remember is coming around and looking into your eyes. I don't remember passing out.'

'Don't worry, Theresia. Don't even try to work it out. The key thing is you soon came to… and the doctor couldn't find anything wrong. Now, what are we going to eat? You have a look at the menu first.' Ethel went over to the dressing table, picked up the menu and gave it to Theresia.

They each chose filet of salmon with sautéed potatoes and a glass of beer. Ethel went down to the reception area and asked if the meals could be brought to the room. The receptionist said in the circumstances they could, and within twenty minutes a waitress was knocking on Theresia's door with a tray of food and drinks.

'I wonder what will happen to Herr Weissman?' said Ethel.

'I feel sorry for him. He is almost certain to lose his job and everything which goes with it. Obviously his salary, his pension maybe. And he's too old to find another position.'

'I don't feel sorry for him. It's his family I feel for. The shame. Losing status and money. And what looked like a secure future.'

'Now I've eaten and had something to drink, Ethel, I feel tired. I ought to go to bed. Do you mind?'

'Not at all. Would you like me to go?'

'No. Not yet. I'm so tired perhaps you could help me into bed. These stockings are quite a challenge to roll down. Please help me with them, could you?'

Theresia sat on the bed with her dress pulled up to her waist while Ethel knelt on the floor. One at a time, she rolled down the stockings. She had never had any special feelings towards Theresia until then, but suddenly wanted to cuddle her close and kiss her. Surely, she wasn't falling for her, just because she was helping her out of her stockings. This woman of the same age, if not a little younger, though not conscious of the fact, was giving her the most pleasant feelings.

'Could you please help me with the rest of my clothes and into my nightdress?'

'Of course, Theresia. It will be a pleasure,' she said as she undid her bodice. 'I wish I were as petite as you!'

'You are good looking in my eyes, Ethel. I am feeling cold now. Could you hurry, please?'

Ethel slid Theresia's nightdress over her head. 'There you are, you can climb into bed now. I have an idea. If you are cold, I'll come in with you until you warm up.'

'Please do. I'm shivering a little.'

Ethel undressed herself down to her undergarments and clambered into bed beside Theresia. She snuggled up close and put her arms around her. Theresia didn't feel cold at all to Ethel but reciprocated by moving closer.

'That is just right, Ethel. I'm feeling warmer already.'

At that point, Ethel pressed herself into Theresia's back. It reminded her of being in bed with Lisl. A shiver passed right through her. Then she relaxed. They both stayed in the same position for a few minutes. 'How is that, Theresia? Are you at the right temperature now?'

'Oh, Ethel. Yes, I really am. You rubbing up against me helped. I'm nearly falling asleep. I'm lovely and warm now.'

'It's no good, Theresia. I have to leave you, I'm afraid. Harry will wonder where I am and I promised to see him, however briefly, before I went to bed. We've had an extraordinarily successful day and must do our best to stay in touch. We will always be good friends.'

Ethel climbed out of the bed and put her blouse and trousers back on, slipped into her coat and bent over to give Theresia a kiss.

'I'm sure we'll meet again, Theresia. We must! I'm determined my first opera will be performed in Germany and I'll let you know when! Goodnight!'

*** 

Ethel took a cabriolet back to the hotel where she and Harry were staying. She went up to Harry's room and, hoping he would still be awake, knocked on the door. He soon answered it. 'Where have been, Ethel? It's gone eleven o'clock. I

258

thought you were just going to have dinner with Theresia, not go to a concert as well.' He sounded angry and looked it.

'I'm so sorry, Harry. But it all went wrong.' She told him what had happened but stopped short of telling him she had undressed Theresia and had spent some time in bed with her.

'How was she when you left her, Ethel? Had she fully recovered?'

'She was in good health, if a little tired. I made sure she was settled for the night, before I left her.'

Ethel was pleased, if not surprised, that the appeal hearing had taken less than a day. She dearly wanted to return to England. She was feeling homesick and desperately in need of the company of her beloved Marco. So she and Harry decided at breakfast the following morning that they would spend no longer in Leipzig and leave the city that day. They discussed their plans for the new opera. It would be called Fantasio and written in French. Harry had started on the libretto and Ethel would begin work on the score. She would have the overture finished in a month. Then they would meet again.

# CHAPTER 25

## Mary Ponsonby

Ethel's train pulled into Farnborough station at the dead of night. She glanced along the platform and could see that she was the only passenger to leave the train. The duty porter helped her with her two cases.

'Am I too late to hail a cab?' she asked, as they walked out of the station.

'You might just be lucky, Miss. One of our regulars is usually waiting for a fare outside.'

He put her bags on the pavement by the entrance. 'You're out of luck, Miss. Don't know where 'e is. Mind you, it's a Monday and there ain't much call for cabs on a Monday. Not this time a' night, Miss. And you were on the last one through 'ere from Waterloo.'

Several rich obscenities passed into Ethel's mind, but she resisted uttering them.

'Like me to try and get 'im on the blower, Miss? Can if ya like. Only if 'e's 'ome a course.'

'What a good idea. Yes please, porter.' No sooner had Ethel spoken when a single horse cabriolet appeared from nowhere and pulled up at their feet.

'Looking for a cab, Miss? Climb in. I'll put your cases on the rack.'

Ethel took an enormous sigh of relief. She didn't fancy walking home lugging two cases, not that late anyway. Nor did she want to spend the night on a bench in the waiting room.

'That will be tuppence halfpenny, Miss,' said the driver, as he unloaded Ethel's cases. 'Thruppence if you want this lot taken to the door.'

He put the bags down, doffed his hat as Ethel paid him, and disappeared back down the drive. The house was in total darkness. Ethel unlocked the front door and went in, carrying one of her cases. Marco started barking.

'You've always been good at choosing your time, Ethel,' The General shouted from upstairs. 'That is you, I presume. For goodness' sake light a lamp!'

Moments later, the hall and landing glowed in a subdued, flickering light. Marco dashed out of the kitchen and almost knocked her over as he welcomed his long-lost owner. He jumped up and licked her face. He gave her the usual welcome for an absence of more than a few days.

'I'm going back to bed,' said the General. 'Catch up with you in the morning.'

Ethel related the whole story to him at breakfast.

'Bloody Teuts! Don't recognise genius when it stares them in the face. All they want to play is that Beethoven chap and his like!'

'It's not that bad, Papa. Really! What annoyed me most was the director of the Conservatorium turning it down. He said he thought it was well written for a woman. How patronising. Then he said he wouldn't play it. And I was one of his students! It was as much as I could do not to swear at him, in German, of course. I did have the pleasure of slamming his door so hard it almost dropped off its hinges!'

'And how did that appeal hearing go?'

'Theresia won, Papa. No one was more surprised than me! The chairman, whom I thought was a judge, was tremendous. He showed the accused was lying... or at least not a credible witness.' She didn't tell him about her own testimony for fear of upsetting him over the fact that the man tried to assault her, too. She told him she had met Harry in Leipzig and spent some time with him.

'Well, that's about it, Papa. Once I've tidied up, I'm going over to see Eugénie. She'll be dying to know what happened. She'll be as disappointed as you are!'

\*\*\*

'Ethel, it's wonderful to see you,' said The Empress, as Ethel put her head around the main drawing-room door. As usual, she had let herself in. 'I enjoyed reading your letters. You didn't forget me this time!'

'I couldn't possibly, Eugénie. I love you far too much to do that!'

'So, refusals in Amsterdam and Cologne, then. What about the other cities? Surely, your man in Leipzig would have accepted it?'

'No, Eugénie. I'm afraid not.' She described her encounter with Reinecke and her outrage at his decision.

'At least my friend Theresia won her appeal at the tribunal. They ruled against man who attempted to rape her. But I'm truly sorry that I couldn't engage any genuine interest in my Mass.' Ethel was on the verge of tears.

'Please don't upset yourself.'

'But you paid for it all and I've wasted your money.' A tear ran down her cheek.

'But the money means nothing, Ethel. You don't realise how wealthy I am. We left France with a fortune! It's nothing, believe me!'

'You are so good at making me feel better, Eugénie. You are my best ally and I truly love you.'

They both looked around as someone was knocking on the front door. 'That must be Mary,' said Eugénie.

'Not Mary Benson. If it is, I'll sneak out the back way.'

'No. Mary Ponsonby. You've met her. She's the wife of the Queen's Private Secretary.'

Ethel's heart almost stopped. She liked Mary Ponsonby when they met at Eugénie's party. To Ethel, she was one of the most beautiful women she had ever seen. Eugénie's maidservant brought her in.

'It's good to see you, Mary. I'm so glad you could come. You already know Ethel, don't you? She's my young composer friend.'

'Yes, of course. Ethel gave an astonishing rendition of some of her work at your party. What about two years ago? Is that right, Ethel?'

'Yes, and I'm delighted you liked my performance!'

'I suggested you perform for the Queen at Windsor, but you went to Balmoral instead and performed for her there, I believe.'

'She was wonderful with the Queen, Mary. You know that, as a result, we arranged for the Mass to be performed at the Albert Hall!'

'Yes, I am aware. I saw the wonderful review in The Times and, of course, I knew the Queen was there in person. Congratulations, Ethel. Have you plans to have it played elsewhere, in Europe say?'

Between them, Ethel and The Empress told her about Ethel's disappointing failure to convince the Dutch and Germans to perform it.

'I'm sad for you, Ethel. What are your plans for another composition?'

She told her about Fantasio and how she and her friend Harry were working on it together. The three of them spent the rest of the morning talking about Mr Gladstone, what the political situation was in France, and about the new extension to be built at the Victoria and Albert Museum.

'Before I go, Ethel, I'd like to invite you to visit me at Windsor. You will love our apartment in the castle and I would love to show you around.'

'What a tremendous idea, Mary. I'll take you up on that.' Ethel was as amazed as she was delighted. She was faintly surprised but moderately pleased that she didn't mention her husband, Henry. Here was an opportunity to further improve her relationship with Mary Ponsonby. She wondered if, by making such an invitation, Mary also wanted their friendship to develop.

\*\*\*

Three days later, Ethel rode to Windsor Castle. She left at about eleven. It was at least twenty miles From Frimhust and, apart from being a little breathless on arrival, she felt fine. She walked up the slope to the main entrance, which was flanked by armed cavalry officers.

263

'Excuse me,' said Ethel to one of them. 'I've been invited here by Lady Mary Ponsonby. Is there anyone who can take me to her?'

'Yes, Miss. Bring your bike and follow me,' he said with a slight smirk. He had never known any guest of Lady Ponsonby to arrive on a bicycle. He took Ethel through the entrance and handed her over to another guard patrolling the inside. Eventually, after a long walk, the guard knocked on a door to the tower. Mary opened it and kissed Ethel's face.

'I'm so pleased you came, Ethel. What did you use for transport?'

'I rode my bike!'

'My goodness. That is a long ride. You're not cycling back today, are you?'

'That was my plan.'

'It's too far, Ethel. You must stay the night. You really must. There are plenty of rooms in our part of the castle and you can have one to yourself.'

'You've convinced me, Mary. I'll stay!'

'I find it hard to believe you live here, Mary, in the Castle.'

'Yes, we have a place in London and in the town, but this is our primary residence. We have done much work here to make the Norman Tower our own. Let me show you.'

Mary guided Ethel from the entrance, up the stone staircase into the upper part of the Tower. Ethel could not believe what the Ponsonbys, mainly Mary, had achieved.

'Do you see that strange-looking graffiti? I must tell you the story,' she said, in her awkwardly pinched style of speech. 'When we moved up here from the cloisters, quite a few years ago, I proposed to the Queen and the Office of Works that I restored these two rooms which are over the gateway. I wanted to bring them back to their original medieval state. They weren't happy but eventually agreed and I set about removing the plaster, inch by inch.'

'Goodness, there must have been tons of it!'

'Yes! Tons! I needed help to remove it all! Eventually, I exposed these pieces of graffiti,' she said, pointing to some scribbled writing on the upper walls. 'These are signatures of prisoners held here during the Plantagenets and again in the seventeenth century. Royalists locked up after the defeat of Charles the First.'

'I'm absolutely amazed, Mary. And at you for taking on such a gigantic project.'

'I did most of it myself, as Henry is away so much with the Queen. He's at Balmoral at the moment.'

'I can imagine you have a lonely time while he's away,' said Ethel, thinking she might use his absence to increase her closeness to Mary, who seemed a very lovable person.

'Yes, it can be, but we constantly disagree while he is here, on almost everything we discuss! But we continue various dialogues by letter so keep our arguments going by post! Let me show you the second room I've restored. You see, there are more signatures here. I particularly like this one,' she said, pointing to a name in barely legible black chalk.

Ethel leant over to look at it. 'It doesn't say "Mary", does it?'

'Exactly. Well deciphered, Ethel!'

'You didn't write it yourself, did you, Mary?'

'Don't be ridiculous, Ethel! Of course not! And this one says "Thomas Piggott, Abbott of Chertsey". A rather arrogant Royal librarian rushed to the library when I told him about it to discover the Abbott lived in the 1400s! I'm not boring you with all this, am I Ethel?'

'On the contrary, I'm completely fascinated. You're taking me back centuries in our history, Mary. Actual history of actual people, not what you read in the history books!'

'You are just in time for some lunch, Ethel. I shall prepare you something. Would you like some scrambled egg on toast or a poached egg, perhaps?'

'I'd love scrambled egg, Mary. That would be lovely.'

'Come with me into the kitchen and we can talk there.'

Ethel followed her, still wondering how she could show her affection for this striking woman. She loved the way she spoke and was so impressed by what she had created in the Norman Tower.

'I have to say, Ethel, I am so impressed by the progress you are making as a composer. I was disappointed not attend the performance of your Mass, but I'm determined to be at the next public performance of one of your works.'

'You are so kind, Mary. I'm not sure what it will be. I remember telling you when we were at Empress Eugénie's about my work on a comic opera.'

Ethel told Mary about her and Harry's joint efforts on the opera and what difficulties they were having with him in Florence and her in Frimley, as well as telling her he had made a good start on the libretto but that she had hardly started her work on the score.

'Harry? Do I know about Harry?'

'I'm not sure. I might not have mentioned him to you, but Eugénie knows about him,' she said confidently, even though realising that Mary might see him as a barrier in developing their friendship.

'Would you mind telling me about him, Ethel? I'm sure he is a nice man.'

'I'll tell you the whole story, Mary.' She started with the holiday Lisl recommended with her sister Julia, her husband Harry's infatuation with her. Julia's beliefs in the metaphysical, Ethel's second visit. The arguments Julia and Harry had about her. His confession that he was in love with her and Julia. Her refusal to have a physical relationship with him. His appearance at The Crystal Palace at the premiere of the Serenade. The various exchanges of letters and meetings in Munich and Leipzig. His continuing attempts at seduction. Mary Benson's condemnation of her.

'So there we are, Mary. That's what it's about. I have to say I'm deeply fond of him, but as a close friend, not as a lover. It's easier for me to relate to women than to men. I will never marry, that's a certainty.'

266

'Well, if you are seeking my opinion, Ethel, I can't see what you've done wrong. You have a close friendship with Harry and nothing more. I can't be judgemental. I'm not surprised by Mary Benson's view. After all, she is married to the Archbishop of Canterbury!'

'I am reassured, Mary. I have to say, I'm enjoying working with him. We have similar views on many topics, religion, art, evolution to name only a few.'

By then they had finished their lunch and adjourned to the kitchen where the independent Mary washed the dishes.

'Would you like me to show you more of what I've been doing here, Ethel?' Mary said, as she put the lunch dishes away.

'I'd absolutely love you to.'

'Come this way.' They walked back down the stone stairs and, as they did, Mary pointed out the views of Eton College and the entrance quadrangle. 'You can see the Queen's coming and goings from here, Ethel. Not that I'm a spy!'

Mary took Ethel out of the castle through a door that led onto a small drawbridge by which they crossed what would have been a moat, had it contained water. She led Ethel to a garden which had its own shed, which she opened to reveal a full range of gardening tools.

'I had this shed built, Ethel, and here is my garden,' she said, moving out her hand as if to introduce it. There were a few vegetables still growing, some leeks and cabbages, and some herbs. She had dug the rest over, ready for planting. Their talking disturbed a robin, which flew off the handle of the spade she had left standing in the soil.

'I'm amazed, Mary! What a creation. Are you self-sufficient?'

'Don't be silly, Ethel. Of course not! We do a lot of entertaining so have to buy vegetables. We keep these for ourselves. They're too good to give away.'

'I won't ask for any then!'

They went back inside and continued the conversation. Mary suddenly launched into telling Ethel about her previous strong religious views.

'I used to be a devoted believer, and I much enjoyed church services and the ceremony of it all. Then about twenty five years ago, I became an agnostic.'

'Not an atheist, then?'

'No. I find the idea of atheism intellectually unsustainable. No one can prove that God does not exist.'

'So what made you change your mind?'

'Science. Subjects like physics, Darwin's theory of evolution. I no longer believe in the creation of the universe, as set out in Genesis. It's a fiction. And I'm inclined to think that God is an invention of man. And just think how many gods there are Ethel! Your parents were in India. The number of gods there!'

'I also used to be a believer, Mary. But no more. I was drawn to believe by what I read in "The Imitation of Christ". I was in an awful state at the time and it deeply affected me. So much that it made me less selfish than I was, and I became determined to come home to help my parents. By then I had made a start on the Mass and that was a product of my profound beliefs, but almost at the moment I finished it, my beliefs evaporated. Vanish they did. I've tried to remain less self-centred but whether I've succeeded is for others to decide!'

'Well, we have even more in common, Ethel. We are both former believers.' They both exploded into laughter. Ethel suddenly realised what a noise she was making and stopped. 'Can anyone hear us in here?' she whispered.

'Absolutely not! The walls are six feet thick!'

Their conversation continued through dinner and into the night. They were obviously enjoying their developing relationship, even though they did not see it from the same standpoint. Mary saw Ethel as a useful parry to her thoughts on the many subjects each could discuss. Ethel regarded Mary as a possible future love. Mary, although in her early sixties, while Ethel was a mere thirty five, was an attractive woman. Mary had looked after herself over the years. Her features were sharp and she had the appearance a woman who could command much respect. Some considered her to be fearsome. Even the Queen found her daunting.

'I don't know about you, Ethel, but I usually go to my slumbers at about this time. We've had a busy day and I've much enjoyed being with you.'

'Likewise, Mary. I'd love to become better acquainted with you and you must tell me about your family… and more about being married to the Queen's Private Secretary!'

'I agree with you. It would be good for both of us to see more of each other. In the meantime, let me show you some of the options for a room in which you can sleep.'

Mary led the way further up the Tower to a suite of bedrooms of various sizes. 'There is quite a choice, I'm afraid. There are twelve bedrooms up here, on two levels.'

'It's no surprise that you can entertain here… with all these guest rooms. Could you please recommend one? It feels quite cold, so a warmer one would be best.'

'This is the one for you, Ethel. There is a chimney stack next to that wall and it's never that cold, even at this time of the year.'

'It sounds perfect.'

'And the bed is already made so all you have to do is to undress and slide in! Oh… would you like a nightshirt?'

'That's a civilised idea, Mary. But I could sleep in my underwear.'

'That's not so good, Ethel. You will naturally perspire and that won't be comfortable tomorrow. You prepare for bed and I'll be back in a minute or two.'

Ethel removed each item of her clothing, neatly folded it, and placed it on a chair next to the bed. She was completely undressed by the time Mary returned with a pink nightdress.

'My goodness, Ethel. You have a beautiful body!'

'Not in the same league as yours, Mary. For a lady who is over twenty years older than me, you are a true beauty.'

269

'Quite wrong, Ethel. You haven't seen me in the state you are in. I'm all folds and wrinkles! Let me slip this over your head,' said Mary, with the nightdress already folded.

'That's perfect,' said Ethel, turning to give Mary a goodnight kiss and a hug. 'I'm so grateful to you. We've had a wonderful day together.'

Ethel extinguished the gas lamp and climbed into bed. She was in total darkness until her eyes adjusted to the small amount of light leaking through the curtains. Moments later, she fell asleep.

The two of them continued their discussion at breakfast the following morning. Mary told Ethel about her five children, Victoria Alberta, Magdalen, John, Frederick and Arthur, all of whom were at least four years younger than Ethel. Each had apparently inherited their parents' intelligence and had become successful in their chosen futures.

'You must be very proud of them, Mary. I didn't know you had that many off-spring!'

'We started producing early and after nine years we'd produced all five. It was a period of intense family activity, as you can well imagine.'

'Next time we meet, I'll tell you more about my family, Mary. They are interesting people, too. I really ought to go home now. My father and Marco will wonder where I am!'

'Can we fix a date, Ethel? I'm here alone until Henry returns. Would you like to come over next Monday? Stay the night again, of course, unless you come by carriage.'

Ethel couldn't understand how the mode of transport had anything to do with whether she stayed the night. 'I'll probably cycle, Mary. And I'd love to stay!'

Mary escorted Ethel into the courtyard where she had left her bike. She took her through the main Castle entrance, past the guards and almost to the road outside. They kissed each other and Ethel pedalled off into the distance.

***

270

Marco was as pleased as the General to see that Ethel had safely returned. Marco dashed down the hall to greet her with a slavering kiss.

'Good morning, Papa. I hope you didn't miss me last night.'

'Ethel, I've almost given up worrying about you. You've spent so much time away from here in the last fifteen years, is it? I've given up worrying about you. I half guessed you would have stayed with her overnight, after that twenty odd mile cycle ride.' If the General was concerned about where she had spent the night, he had no intention of showing it.

'Marco's missed me, Papa, so I'll put his lead on and take him for a walk.'

At the sound of the word 'walk', Marco started jumping up and down and making a nuisance of himself. 'Behave, damn you, boy!' she shouted.

She loved these walks, as did Marco. They gave her a chance to think about where she was going in life and how to arrive there. She was pleased that she had at least made a start on the score for Fantasio, if only to sketch out a few ideas for the overture. She would dream up some tunes to identify the characters, something fairly haughty and arrogant for the King of Bavaria, a presumptive and self-serving tune for the Prince of Matua, a soft, shy tune for Elsbeth and a confident, amusing theme for Fantasio. She would compose some variations on each of them.

She spent the next few days writing the opera and walking Marco in her breaks. She also worked on the home finances, something the General was more than willing to delegate to her. On the morning of the Monday she was due to ride to Mary Ponsonby's, a letter arrived for her.

'Here's another for you, Ethel, one from Rome this time,' said the General who was always first to pick up anything the postman delivered.

Ethel glanced at the envelope and frowned. She knew no one in Rome, so she quickly opened it. It was from Harry who said that he and Julia had rented a property in the city and were having a holiday there. He had completed the libretto for Fantasio. Ethel smiled. He was copying it, ready to send it to her.

What brilliant news and a stimulus for her to complete the score, she thought. But she needed that libretto before she could compose much more of it.

She took the letter to her room and prepared herself for the ride to Windsor.

*** 

Mary embraced Ethel strongly. They spent much of the day in Mary's garden. Again, they disturbed the robin which fluttered away from the spade. They planted some rows of vegetable seeds in the ground Mary had prepared, then went in and argued about British Politics for the rest of the afternoon. Mary had some strong, left-wing views while Ethel's were right of centre. Mary had no time for Disraeli, whom she regarded as almost totally lacking in intellect. She almost worshipped Gladstone. The Queen, she said, was aware of her views and hardly approved of them. She said that she'd seen Disraeli attempting to seduce Her Majesty who seemed to enjoy his advances.

Mary's views angered Ethel. She strongly disagreed with such a commitment to the left. She was staggered that her outlandish opinions had found their way to the Queen. They both raised their voices as they expressed their opposing views. Ethel's views angered Mary. They ended up shouting at each other. Then a stony silence descended, broken by Mary.

'I'm so sorry, Ethel, I shouldn't have shouted at you, a guest in my apartment.' She went over to Ethel and put a kiss on Ethel's face.

Ethel placed a hand on Mary's right breast and held it there. She shocked herself at this spontaneous, if awkward and probably unwelcomed gesture. They each froze. Mary had never been touched this way before, not even by Henry. She did not know what to say or do. She had just been groped by another woman. Ethel had to find her way out of this situation. So she moved her hand away from the warmth of the breast.

'I'm sorry, too, Mary. I should never have shouted at you. I'm a guest here, after all.'

Mary then overcame her shock and found some words. 'Well, Ethel. I can honestly say that has never happened to me before. What made you do that?'

'My problem, Mary, is that I am extremely fond of you. It was merely a spontaneous expression of my love. I hope you didn't mind. I didn't hurt you, did I? Somehow, having that row with you over politics made me more confident in my feelings for you.'

'No, you didn't hurt me, Ethel. But you did surprise me. I'm not an especially physical person, so am unlikely to reciprocate. But I love you as a friend and who knows how that may develop?'

Ethel detected a glimmer of hope in what Mary said. Perhaps their continuing relationship may lead to something in which Mary would feel more able to demonstrate greater affection.

Mary decided she'd had enough of this talk of love and changed the subject to something less intense.

'Would you like to play something to me on my piano, Ethel?'

'I thought you would never ask me, Mary!'

'In that case, come through to the other room.'

The relationship between Ethel and Mary Ponsonby continued in this emotional and temperamental vein. After each of their fiery arguments, they always made up and parted as good friends. Mary even gave Ethel free access to the Norman Tower and a room she could use any time. This did not entirely meet the approval of Sir Henry, who tolerated Mary, unlike Archbishop Benson who loathed her. Mary's grown-up children also got to know her and became immune to their rowdy arguments. After two years of trying to seduce Mary, Ethel gave up, but they remained close.

Having played some of her music on Mary's piano, she kissed Mary and rode home. Ethel was about to embark on another adventure.

# CHAPTER 26

## Fantasio

As he had promised, Harry's libretto soon arrived in the post. He'd written it in German. She couldn't believe it, especially because he said it would be in French. Was there a letter? Nothing but a brief note which contained not a word explaining the content or discussion of the manuscript. It took her an hour to recover from the shock before she took it to her room. She was pleasantly surprised to read the German so easily. He had taken a good deal of trouble to make it clear, even though the plot was complicated.

She spent the next eighteen months between writing the music, visiting Mary Ponsonby and Eugénie, and helping her father. All interspersed with taking Marco for his daily ration of walks. Ethel did much of the creative thinking about Fantasio during these outings. She enjoyed the challenge of planning and composing the music for what she regarded as an important work, the key to achieving her ambition.

'How much more have you got to compose on that perishing opera?' said the General, as he looked up from The Times at breakfast.

'I know you think I waste a lot of my time, Papa, but you may be surprised to know that I'm about two-thirds of the way through. I've completed writing the thematic material and am working on the orchestration. So I'm quite pleased with it… so far.'

'So what happens next?'

'I want Harry to see it, even in its unfinished state. Then I'll look for an opera house to perform it.'

'I suppose you'll try Covent Garden?'

'No, Papa. Waste of time. I'll be parading it around Germany.'

'Why not try Covent Garden?'

'My dear Papa, Fantasio is a light opera and Covent Garden doesn't perform light operas.'

'You are so sure of yourself, Ethel. I have to admire you for that. So what makes you think the Teuts will like it?'

'The simple answer is... I don't know, but the fact is they have fourteen opera houses where we have just the one. And I know many conductors in Germany.'

'Well, I hope they don't treat it in the way they treated your Mass! So Marco and I will again have to bid you fond farewells... while you go off to Florence or wherever he's living now.'

'Yes and no, Papa. He's coming to stay in London. Probably for about a year.'

\*\*\*

Ethel wrote to Harry to arrange to meet him at his hotel, the Savoy in the Strand. They met in the restaurant for afternoon tea. By chance, they arrived within a minute of each other.

'It's so lovely to see you, Ethel. Did you have a straightforward journey?' he said, bending over to kiss her cheek.

'Very easy, Harry. A train from Farnborough to Waterloo and an agreeable summer-time walk across Waterloo Bridge! I'm amazed you can afford to stay here, with your children as well. It's normally only foreign royalty who can afford the Savoy!'

'Well, I've had something of a windfall. My American publisher has given me an advance for my latest book, The Statuette and the Background. Much more than I expected. So we are staying here for a few days. Then we'll move to somewhere cheaper!'

'I'd ask you to stay with me, Harry. But I'm not sure my father would agree.'

'Oh please, Ethel. Don't even think about it. We can easily meet in London.'

'Let's talk about our opera, shall we? I have to say, your libretto is so clear, Harry. To say the least, I was surprised you'd written it in German! I thought we agreed it would be in French!'

'You're right, Ethel. Absolutely... but the more I thought about it, the more obvious it became to write it in German. The reason is simple. Where will it be performed? Not in France. Not in England. But in Germany. They'll love it, and they've always favoured works in their own language. That's why Wagner is so popular... in some quarters.'

'I have to admit, I hadn't thought of that. But I do like what you've written. I'd love you to see what I've done so far. It's a shame you don't read music, Harry. I've brought it along. I could whistle or sing it to you. I'm about three quarters of the way through, but I've more to do on the instrumentation.'

'I have a better idea. There's a piano over there. Why not play some on that?'

'We can't just use their piano, Harry.'

'I'll ask someone.'

A couple of minutes later, Harry came back, smiling widely. 'I've spoken to the deputy manager, and he says we can use it, as long as you don't play so loudly you annoy other residents.'

'Let's start then. First, I'll play you the tunes I've invented for the principal characters and then I'll sing some of the opera itself.' For once, restraining herself from making an excess of sound, Ethel played it. As she did, Harry took notes. She took nearly an hour. She finished with a flourish, but a less extravagant one than usual.

Harry applauded. 'You've made a magnificent job of the music, Ethel... and I recognise some of the words!'

'I should damned well hope so! You wrote them! That's as far as I've reached, up to the present. So, seriously, what do you think?'

'The music is strong and fits the text well. I like the way you have given the characters their own tunes. I just have one idea which we can discuss.'

'Tell me!'

'Why not have some words spoken, as in the Spanish Zarzuela? Alternate between the spoken word and words accompanied by music.'

'That's an interesting idea, Harry. My first reaction is to disagree. It wouldn't be an opera. And singers are renowned for not speaking well. Like ballet dancers walking. My second reaction is to rule it out. Our ambition is to write an opera. The German's wouldn't want to listen to some obscure Spanish construction.'

'Can we not rule it out completely, Ethel?'

'Just to please you, we won't. It would be easy for me to implement. I'd just chose where to remove the music. And I also have an idea. I'll ask Eugénie who is Spanish. She will have a view, for certain.'

'I agree. So let's move on to something else,' said Harry, eager to change the subject. 'How are we going to promote it?'

'I shall go to Germany. Straight to Hermann Levi. He suggested I should write an opera, having seen my Mass. I'll write to him and make an appointment to see him.'

'That's a brilliant idea. So you'd go to him first. If he refused, you'd try other conductors and opera houses?'

'Spot on. If you agree, that's what I'll do!'

'I agree, Ethel. That makes a great deal of sense to me. So when will you go?'

'As soon as I receive a reply from Levi. I'll do more work on the opera, but I probably won't have it finished by then.'

Ethel stood up from the piano and the two of them went back to their table to finish their afternoon tea.

'There is something else I ought to tell you. Ethel, I am deeply in love with you. I cannot hold back from telling you. I want you. I desperately need you.'

Ethel shrugged her shoulders and looked up towards the ceiling. 'Harry, we've been here many times before. I love you, too. I also need you. But I don't want to share you. And you are a married man. I'm not an adulterer and never will be! I regard myself as your loyal friend and long may that continue.'

'I hope you don't object to my continuing to try!'

'As long as you don't mind my continuing to say no!'

They parted with a hug and a kiss, and Ethel made her way back home via Waterloo. Her thoughts became clearer on the train. She would do no more on the opera until Levi had seen what she had completed. She would do everything in her power to secure a performance in Munich. If she failed, she would do the rounds of the other German opera houses. If that failed, she would try Amsterdam then Paris. She could translate it, if necessary.

She wrote a short letter to Levi. She reasoned he was a busy man, and if she elaborated too much on the plot, he would soon become bored. A summary of what the opera was about could whet his appetite. She was surprised at the speed of his response. He was utterly delighted that she had taken up his idea of writing an opera and wanted to see it as soon as she could come to Munich to show him. He suggested the following month, and the date, 17 September.

*\*\**

'My dear Ethel, it is so good to see you,' said Levi. He kissed her on both cheeks. 'I'm so sorry to have to ask you to come to see me. If I were anything of a gentleman, I'd have offered to see you in London. However, I have been overwhelmed with work. And to let you into a secret, I haven't been very well of late. So apologies for asking you to see me here.'

'I'm sorry you haven't been well, Herr Levi,' she said. She hesitated about using his first name. From what she recalled of their previous meeting, they were not on first-name terms then, so she would call him Herr. 'I hope you are fully recovered by now.'

'If not completely, I am much better than I was. Now, have you brought your manuscript with you? You said it was incomplete. I can't imagine you'll have

278

finished it on the train!' He chuckled at his own joke. 'But that doesn't matter. I'm sure I will be able to judge it as it is!'

Ethel walked around his desk and opened the score in front of him. She returned to the seat on the other side of his desk and waited. Gazing around his office, she hadn't realised how big it was. She had done this so many times, she thought, quietly wondering what these famous maestros were thinking as they were pondering her work. How did they reach their conclusions? How could they possibly know what it would sound like when they needed to examine up to fifteen or more staves of music, and that didn't include the solo parts or the choir?

'I must say something before I give you my opinion. I don't want you to cry this time or I'll end by crying myself! Are you happy with that proposal?'

'Yes, Herr Levi. I won't cry. I may chuckle instead!'

'Enough of the Herr Levi. Call me Hermann! Your opera will be brilliant when it's finished. The orchestration is excellent as it is, and you clearly haven't finished it yet. And I like the story. German audiences will love it!'

'I'm so pleased, Hermann. It was your suggestion I write an opera and I'm so pleased you like mine!' True to her word, she chortled.

'I have a great idea. We are running an opera competition here. Yours is a certain winner. I'm a judge so may help it on its way!'

'Please tell me more!'

'The prize is impressive. There is a lump sum, a guarantee of its production at one of the top opera houses in Germany, with a guaranteed number of follow-up performances, and a contract to publish the work. Does that sound good?'

'Unbelievable, Hermann. I shall definitely submit it! What is the closing date for entries?'

'The first of April, next year, '95. You must finish the work, of course, otherwise it will be rejected.'

'Understood, Hermann.'

'So you can work on it on the way home, Ethel.'

*** 

There was much work to do before Ethel could enter the competition. She started on the train, as Levi had jokingly suggested, but she failed to make any headway. The train was noisy and smelly and she became involved in too many conversations with other passengers who were fascinated by her English accent. Four days later, she put her key into the lock at Frimhurst.

'Where have you been, Ethel?' screamed her sister, Lily, as she opened the door. 'We've been trying to telegram you. Bad news, I'm afraid. Father had passed away. His funeral is tomorrow. So you are just in time.' Lily broke down in tears.

Ethel was completely taken aback. Her father seemed fine when she left for Germany. In fact, he was in excellent form and joked with her about the 'Teuts' as he waved to her from the front door.

Ethel cried and went to hug Lily. 'I don't know what to say, Lily. I'm in a state of shock. That is the last thing I expected. I'm so sorry I wasn't here when he passed. I feel bad that I was away. When did he die and what did he die of?'

'It was a heart attack, Ethel,' she said, then sounding less angry. 'He was barely conscious when the doctor came, but he died within two minutes of his arrival, apparently. One of the maidservants told me. She had the wit to telegram me and Mary. It was she who called the doctor and then the undertaker. She's been wonderful.'

Moments later, Marco came along to meet her. It is surprising how a dog can detect the atmosphere in a house. Marco usually charged down the hall to greet her, but that day he merely walked. He could not resist planting his usual welcoming kiss over her face.

'Is there anything I can do? Where are we holding the wake? I can help prepare sandwiches and serve drinks if needed.'

'Here at the house. Yes, some help tomorrow would be very useful.'

280

Just like her mother's funeral, it was a sad occasion, and many tears were shed. A military bugler played the Last Post. At least two hundred attended, mainly former Royal Artillery colleagues from Aldershot and a few from Woolwich.

Ethel benefitted substantially from the General's will. With her share of the proceeds from the sale of Frimhurst, she bought the lease on an eight roomed cottage, still in her old neighbourhood, which she called 'One Oak' after a single oak tree at the front of the property. Much to her delight, woods and fields surrounded this quaint house, which suited Ethel's character perfectly. As a welcomed bonus, Marco loved it, too. The sanitation was far from perfect since the two front rooms, up to Ethel's occupation, were occupied by a pony and a donkey. They stank.

By then, Harry had established himself in rooms in London, more affordable than the Savoy, and often visited her.

'So what's my task for today, Ethel?'

'I don't know about one day, Harry. Follow me around the back.' He did as instructed, wondering what she had in store.

'I showed you this plot before. What I'd like is for you to convert this piece of jungle into a flower garden I can plant out as a new hobby and sit out and admire.'

'You are joking, Ethel. That's a week's work for three labourers and I don't have the muscles of a navvy!'

'Who said you could do it in a day, Harry? Not me, I'm certain. Stay a few nights. I'll supply the food and the drinks and I can even help you. I'm as strong as you, I'm sure!'

So, thinking he may conquer more than the digging of the ground for his efforts, he stayed for nearly a week. He first dug a hole as deep as he was tall. Between them, they dumped what the donkey and pony had left in the front room and, along with a pile of other junk left by the former occupiers, buried it. While he was piling the detritus in the bottom of the hole, a frightened deer jumped clean over him and the hole and, in quick succession, the Queen's staghounds did the same. Marco watched this display and, since not the stag nor even one of the hounds took a blind bit of notice of him, went into a sulk that lasted two whole days.

Ethel struggled to manage One Oak, even with Harry's help outside, and wondered about engaging a servant. Luck came her way. A former cook at Frimhurst heard about the General's death and wrote to ask if she could 'do for you' what she did for Ethel's mother. Miss Ford loved Marco and Ethel, probably in that order, and became the cook, cleaner, dog walker and Ethel's general servant. She did not become one of Ethel's 'passions', but Ethel treated her with tremendous respect, well deserved by such an amiable and reliable servant.

'Can we discuss Fantasio?' said Harry, while he and Ethel were having a private Christmas party, dutifully prepared by Ford.

'It is Christmas, Harry. Do we have to?'

'Yes, Ethel. There are only three months left now before you have to submit it.'

'Yes, if you insist. I'm having some issues about the solo parts, but I'll be able to resolve them easily enough.'

'Can I help in any way? I could listen as you play them.'

'It's not that so much as the orchestration. The orchestra is overbearing in places and a slightly weak soloist would have trouble holding their own against it.'

'If you bring the score, Ethel, you can play the orchestral parts on the piano and sing the solos. I can judge the result.'

'Seriously, on Christmas day?'

'Seriously, Ethel. Unless you can think of some alternative.'

By then, Ford had settled herself into her own part of the house, so the two of them were free to do what they wanted. 'I know what alternative you have in mind, Harry.'

'Well, I'm not going to give up, Ethel.'

'I'll fetch the score!'

The two of them spent the rest of Christmas day, Boxing Day and most of the day after adjusting the orchestration and libretto. They argued and shouted at each other. Ethel hadn't experienced such strong disagreements with anyone since one of her routine rows with Mary Ponsonby.

'Well, that's that! I'm not doing any more to it now! Come what may! It's finished, completed, ended!' she bawled, just as Ford was coming in with cups of tea for the two of them.

'Sorry, Ma'am. Hope I haven't interrupted you.'

'No, Ford. Mr Brewster was just agreeing with me that we have now completed this opera that we've both been working on.'

'Yes, Ma'am. I've heard you discussing it.' The woman was far too discreet to say she'd heard them rowing, almost coming to blows over it. But smiled as she said 'discussing'.

'Do you intend to send Levi the manuscript or a copy?' said Harry.

'I hadn't thought of that! We can't possibly send the manuscript without making our own copy.'

'So that's the next major task, copying it!'

The two of them set about it. In between times, Ethel invited Eugénie, Mary Ponsonby and Pauline Trevelyan over to One Oak. Understandably, she was proud of her new acquisition and wanted to show it off to her friends. Mary was surprised at what Harry had done to clear such a large area in the garden, mainly to grow flowers and shrubs. She suggested Ethel allocate a patch to cultivating vegetables, much as she had seen in the garden Mary had created near the moat at Windsor Castle.

Ethel discussed with Eugénie, Harry's idea of changing the opera to make it more like a Spanish Zarzuela. The Empress was quite impressed with the idea and, despite Ethel's arguments against such an unusual form, came down firmly in favour of it. Ethel stuck with an opera. She 'forgot' to tell Harry what Eugénie had said.

'We really need to complete this, Ethel,' said Harry, one day in early March. 'Otherwise, we are going to miss the last date to enter it.'

'Point taken. Let's spend the next couple of days at it. We need to put it in the post with a clear fortnight for it to arrive in Munich.'

Three days later, they finished. Harry took the original to the post office in Farnborough and sent it off.

# CHAPTER 27

## Competition

'I wonder when we will hear from Munich,' said Harry, as he and Ethel were sitting in Ethel's flower garden enjoying an unusually warm, early April afternoon, supplemented by a gin and tonic each.

'I wish I knew. I'm just dying to know. Surely, they will want to publish the result as soon as they can. Mind you, it will depend on the number of operas entered.'

'They won't be biased against you, Ethel, because you are English?'

'No. Levi told me it would be a blind competition. So my Englishness shouldn't come into it. Our German shouldn't give too many clues away either!'

'May I drastically change the subject, Ethel? I'm going to Paris for a few weeks. Would you like to come with me?'

Ethel could read Harry's mind. His attempts to seduce her, here in England, in Florence, in Munich and even in Leipzig had all failed. She constantly refused to join him in bed. She would prefer to die a virgin than to commit adultery. 'Harry, I'm afraid I am going to have to decline. Much as I love Paris, I have other things to do. I have written one opera and I intend to write another. I don't see Paris as a source of inspiration.'

'I'm disappointed, Ethel, but I respect your view. I hope you don't mind if I go. I have some business to transact there and then I'll head back to Florence after a few days' holiday. I shall stay in my usual hotel in Montmartre, you know the one.'

'I have no objection to your going, Harry. While I love you dearly, we are still independent people, so you must go.'

\*\*\*

Ford looked after Ethel well. She loved Marco and did all she reasonably could to make Ethel's life comfortable. However, in Harry's absence, there was something missing. While she did not fall into the depression which followed the break with Lisl or over her relationship with Pauline, she was far from happy. Visits to Mary Ponsonby and Eugénie helped but did not solve the problem. It took her a full week of his absence to realise what was wrong. She would have to go to Paris. It became a compulsion. Two opposing forces were acting upon her. She did not want to become an adulterer, but wanted him to make love to her. The more she thought about the latter, the less important became the former. However painful it might be and whatever the consequences, she wanted to have sex with him. So she sent him a postcard saying she had changed her mind and was about to leave for Paris. Ford packed a bag for her, she kissed Marco and off she went.

\*\*\*

'Do you have a resident called Harry Brewster,' said Ethel as she arrived at about three in the afternoon at the reception desk.

'Just a moment, Madame, I will look at the register,' said the man at the desk.

'Yes, Madame, I have a person of that name staying here.'

'Would it be possible to call him?'

'We don't normally disturb our guests,' he said, looking down his nose at her.

'This is a special request,' said Ethel. 'Messr Brewster and I are madly in love with each other and I have come all the way from London to visit him, here at the hotel.'

'Do you have a reservation, Madame?'

Ethel was about to deliver this obsequious functionary a blast of her anger. She paused for a second. 'In fact, you may well find they have added my name to Messr Brewster's name in your register. Naturally, we stay in the same room.'

'In which case what is your name, Madame?'

'Ethel Smyth.'

286

He turned away to look again at the register. 'Ah yes, Madame Smyth. My colleague registered you to Messr Brewster's room for three nights. Does that sound right?'

'That sounds about right,' she said, pleased that she had chosen not to spar with the man.

'Would you like a key?'

'Yes, please. Do you know if he's in his room?'

'I don't know, but I can call him if you wish.'

'Please do.'

'Yes, he's in Madame and says he's expecting you. Here's the key. It's room 276 on the second floor. Turn left when you came out of the lift. The room is along on the left. It has a wonderful outlook over the street.'

Ethel couldn't wait to see Harry. She over brimmed with excitement. She unlocked the door. Harry was sitting on the bed, his back towards her, reading a French newspaper.

'Ethel!' he shouted, as he turned to see her come in. 'I'm so glad you changed your mind.' He stood up and with his arms outstretched rushed over to hug her. They stood by the door in a firm embrace.

'Harry, I'm desperate for you to make love to me. Shall we do it now? Or wait until dark?'

'Well… we can do it now, Ethel. We can draw the curtains, if you like. But it would be nice to see each other naked. We are far enough up, so no one outside can see us. And we can put a sign on the outside of the door.'

'Let's do it now!'

Just like a couple of youngsters, they watched each other undress. The sight of Ethel's wondrous breasts and her bottom had a profound effect on Harry.

'My God, Harry, I wasn't expecting anything as big as that! You'll kill me putting that thing inside me.'

'Don't worry, Ethel. Everything will be fine. You'll hardly feel a thing. And when it's home, you'll enjoy the sensations, I'm certain.'

'So speaks a man of experience.'

'Here goes then, Ethel. Just make yourself comfortable on the bed and we'll begin.'

Ethel let out a slight yelp but soon settled into the rhythm of the lovemaking. She wasn't sure which of them was enjoying it most, Harry or her. It surprised her she liked it so much. She thought of Julia, but only fleetingly and then of Eugénie, naked on her yacht. Harry was clearly an experienced lover and as gentle as he was firm. She wondered what he was thinking. Not of Julia, for sure. He was probably wondering whether she was enjoying the experience.

'How are you feeling, Ethel? Are you ready for me to finish?'

'Fine, a minute or two more. I'm quite enjoying this!'

'Thank you, Ethel, that was beautiful,' he said as he reached the conclusion. 'And I've waited eleven years for just that! You are a wonderful woman to make love to. I enjoyed your responses to my movements!'

'I don't think I responded to anything!'

They made love several more times before it was time for Ethel to go back to One Oak. The feeling of guilt persisted, but somehow she could cancel it by the feelings of pleasure and achievement. She pondered on the nature of this kind of love. A wonderful sense of belonging to Harry filled her mind. For this was sure to be just the beginning, a start to a more complete form of her love for him. At that point, she began to understand the intensity of the feelings that physical love could generate, equally for the man and the woman.

She could not wait to tell her lady friends what she had done. She had no idea what reaction to expect.

'Ethel, you are a naughty girl,' said Mary Ponsonby. 'I understand your feelings but I'm surprised at your cold blooded scheming.'

'Cold blooded? I'd say hot blooded, Mary! Need completely overcame me. So I went to Paris with just one thing in mind!'

'Hmm. I'm still surprised, despite what you say… and up to now your passion for women.'

'All I can say, Mary, is that I suddenly felt compelled to do it. That Harry didn't say he wanted me in Paris to go to bed with him, influenced me. Not that I felt he didn't need me. Nothing like that. He said he was going and that I could join him, if I wished. I said no and he went. Then the thought of going started to form in my head. It built up to a crescendo and completely overcame me. I had to go. That's the full story, Mary.'

'I forgive you, Ethel. Not that it's my place to forgive. So the forces of nature overcame you? It could be the best things you ever did. We'll see how things develop!'

Quite heartened by what Mary said about her exploits, she went to see Eugénie.

'Wonderful news, Ethel. I'm so glad you did it. Congratulations!' she said, after Ethel had explained it all.

'I'm so pleased you approve, Eugénie! Not that it would be possible to undo what we did!'

'I've been wondering for years why you didn't let him have his way with you. I put it down to your morality combined with your feelings towards our own sex.'

'Oddly enough, the thought of you crossed my mind while we were doing it!' confessed Ethel.

'I don't know why. I found the whole messy business disgusting after all the pain I went through giving birth to Louis-Napoleon. The Emperor and I never did it again. I wouldn't let him! I just turned a blind eye to his many paltry affairs!'

They both laughed.

Fearing the threat of eternal damnation, Ethel didn't tell Mary Benson. She would have been outraged.

Not many days after visiting her friends, a letter arrived from Harry. She wasn't expecting a letter so soon after their Paris encounter. She opened it slowly, not knowing what to expect. It said that Julia had died of a heart attack. Ethel didn't know what to think. She felt guilty. Had Julia realised that she and Harry had become lovers? Harry had said in Paris that she had not been well. Had the knowledge of their affair tipped her over the edge? Had it made her deteriorate to the extent of having the attack? Surely, Harry hadn't told Julia about their meeting in Paris. He couldn't be that unkind.

Harry didn't say he had told her. He made some poetical remarks about how he felt towards her now that she had gone, describing her as a villa in a 'malariously desolate country' such to stay in that place was to court death but it was impossible to escape. He said he loved her and hated her simultaneously.

***

One morning in July, Ford came into the dining room with Ethel's breakfast on a tray and a letter under her arm. 'Here you are, Ma'am and this letter was on the front doormat. And I've brought an opener.'

Ethel sliced the envelope open and eased out the content. It was from Levi. She read it rapidly. Fantasio had not won. It was among one hundred and ten entries and among the top seven highly recommended by the judges. There was no outright winner. At first, it disappointed her. Then she thought it was not her idea to enter it into this accursed competition. In fact, it had spurred her and Harry on to finishing the opera. So she should take comfort from the fact that it had done well in the competition, and the idea of entering it had made her complete it sooner than she probably would have.

***

Ethel and Harry met frequently. He suggested they stay again at the same hotel in Paris. Then they visited Florence and Germany. They made love. He enjoyed it more than Ethel.

'We have no choice but to marry, Ethel. That would be perfect. We could live together. All our friends and colleagues would accept the situation better than where we are now. I could even live in England. One Oak is big enough for the two of us!'

'I am confused, Harry. The only reason I can think of marrying is to enable us to meet openly. I don't want to change your life or mine. I don't want to move in with you and I don't want you to move in with me, much as I love you... and am no longer an adulteress.'

Continuous uncertainty shrouded the following months. They argued by letter and face to face about marriage. Although they raised their voices when they met and exchanged strong words on paper, they remained in love. Ethel dithered. He persisted. She consulted Mary Ponsonby, Pauline Trevelyan and Eugénie. None of them would commit themselves to the view she should marry him. She decided not to marry. A disappointed Harry gradually accepted her decision.

# CHAPTER 28

## Towards a performance?

Ethel couldn't believe what she was reading. It was incredible. It was a letter from Felix Mottl, Conductor of the Karlsruhe Opera, inviting her there to discuss performing Fantasio. Levi had recommended it to him. Mottl wanted to read her score.

'Ford, I must tell someone. This letter, dated June '96 but with no day, invites me to Germany to meet a famous conductor who wants to look at my opera!'

'My goodness, Miss Smyth. That sounds marvellous. How do you know he is famous?'

'I know his name well. Bring me the writing paper and a pen, please. I shall reply immediately. And would you mind posting the letter?'

'Of course not, Madam.'

Ethel scribbled a reply suggesting she leave in two days for Karlsruhe and meet Herr Mottl in ten days' time. That would give her time to settle in Karlsruhe and even a chance to look around the town. She promised to bring the score.

\*\*\*

At Karlsruhe, she found herself in that familiar position again, looking at a conductor who was examining her manuscript.

'I absolutely love it, Miss Smyth. We will perform it in our city!'

'I'm delighted, Herr Mottl. Do you have any idea when that may be?' Ethel didn't sound too excited by his apparent enthusiastic response. She'd had promises like this before.

'It critically depends on the consent of the Intendant of the opera house. But I see that as a mere formality.'

'Shall we take it to him now? It would be my pleasure to meet this important man.'

'I'm afraid he is away at the moment, but returning shortly. I'm not exactly sure when. Please stay in Karlsruhe and I will introduce you the moment he returns. You must let me and my wife entertain you to dinner, at least once. It will be my honour.'

'Yes, of course, I shall stay here,' said Ethel. 'I have already found a comfortable hotel, the Kaiserhof.'

'That's excellent, Miss Smyth. I will contact you there with an invitation and any information I may discover about our Intendant.'

Days went by with no news on the Intendant. Ethel dined twice at Mottl's house, somewhat awkwardly because of his wife's constant silence and his total ignorance of his Intendant's whereabouts. Ethel wondered if the man existed. After another week, she completely lost patience. Dressed in her tweeds with her hat jammed over her head, often smoking a cigar and with a determined look on her face, she started a tour of the opera houses of Dresden, Leipzig, Cologne, Hamburg and Wiesbaden. All was to no avail. With impressive displays of interest, all found one excuse after another for not adding Fantasio to their 'already committed' or 'purely conventional' programmes.

An exhausted Ethel missed home and Marco. It was a hot summer in Europe and she hadn't brought the clothes for such heat. Her health was deteriorating. Her hands were shaking and her heart was palpitating. She went back to One Oak disheartened, bedraggled and miserable.

'You look terrible, Miss Smyth,' said Ford, as she met Ethel in the hall. Even Marco seemed concerned about her down-trodden appearance. She told Ford what a disaster the whole excursion had been. By the time she finished, with Marco's head in her lap, she was almost in tears.

'It cannot be that bad, Miss Smyth. Someone will want to play it for you.'

While grateful for the sympathy, Ethel could only think that Ford knew nothing about such things. She didn't understand how difficult it was for a woman to have her work performed.

Ethel realised that she needed to rest. She needed a holiday. She had been working flat out since her father died almost two years before. Eugénie came to the rescue.

'You must stay at Farnborough Hill with me for a couple of weeks' rest. Then we will go to Cap Martin and join the Thistle for a little cruise. I'm thinking of going to Sardinia. Then go to see Harry!' she said, winking as she finished.

'You are truly a wonderful friend, Eugénie. But this time I must pay my way.'

'Don't be silly, Ethel. Buy me a couple of meals. It might surprise you how well off I am. The French Treasury is still feeling the pain we inflicted on them before we escaped,' she laughed.

Eugénie made her relax at her palatial residence. She worked her way through a good part of her prodigious collection of world literature. Plays by Goethe, Calderón de la Barca… more of Musset, Schiller, the scores of Schubert, Mendelssohn and some Dostoyevsky. Eugénie wouldn't let her near the kitchen or even make her own bed. It was idle luxury at the extreme. Her only given task was to take Marco for his daily walks. He'd never had so much attention from his owner.

'Now you are back to normal, it's time to go to France, so go home and pack a bag.'

They travelled to Monte Carlo via Paris and stayed a night in Le Grande Hotel. They took a carriage and four from Monte Carlo to Eugénie's new villa in Cap Martin, which the builders had completely finished.

'My goodness, I wasn't expecting anything as magnificent as this, Eugénie. It's huge!' said Ethel, as she took her bags from the coachman who had driven the carriage up the drive and stopped outside the enormous front door.

'I'm not sure what you expected, Ethel! I couldn't entertain your Queen in a three-bedroom place with one bathroom now, could I?'

'Of course not, Eugénie. I imagine from the size, it has several suites of rooms! Has the Queen stayed here yet?' Ethel wondered if she'd offended Eugénie by mentioning her surprise.

'No, not yet, but she's planning to come soon.'

A servant opened the door to them the moment they arrived. It was as if he had been keeping an eye out for them and wanted to be sure of opening the door himself.

'Good afternoon, Giorgio,' said Eugénie as they walked in. 'Could you please take Miss Smyth to the Royal Suite?'

'Delighted, Your Highness.'

Ethel followed Giorgio up the stairs. She wondered how the Queen would manage them. The suite was certainly fit for the Queen. They had gilded the furniture, including the posters on the bed. Even the taps on the sink and bath were gold coloured, if not gold plated. She unpacked enough for a few days there, came back down and went into one of the drawing-rooms.

'So what do you think of your rooms, Ethel?'

'I'm staggered, Eugénie. It is beautiful and it's so tastefully decorated. I'm surprised you put me in it!'

'I'll let you into a little secret!'

Ethel wondered what she was going to admit. She suddenly became quite anxious. Surely, she hadn't invited the Queen to visit at the same time as she was there. That prospect terrified her. She wasn't yet in that state of mind.

'I am using you as a guinea pig, Ethel. I want you to pretend you are Queen Victoria. In the next few days, I want you to be as critical as you can be about every aspect of that suite. Whether the curtains suffice to keep the morning light out, whether the water in the taps is hot enough, the thickness of the bedding, and the position of the chamber pot. Everything you can think of.'

295

'Do you mean to say, I will use the chamber pot the Queen will use?'

'No, Ethel. She will expect a new one that nobody else has used!'

Over the next few days, Ethel became more relaxed. That awful, rejected and dejected feeling she brought back from her disastrous trip to Germany had deserted her. She felt quite refreshed and was looking forward to her time on The Thistle with Eugénie.

'I've told Henri to head for Sardinia,' said Eugénie, as the two of them clambered aboard in the bright, early morning sunlight.

'Can I ask you an enormous favour, Eugénie?' said Ethel, once they were on deck.

'Of course, Ethel. And I shall do my best to comply with your wishes.'

'Before we left England, you mentioned my going to see Harry.'

'I did!'

'Harry is staying in Rome at present and will probably move there permanently now Julia has passed away. The favour I am asking is that, after we've been to Sardinia, could you please drop me off at Civitavecchia? I can then catch a train to Rome. You are already thinking what an audacious idea!'

'Actually, that would suit me well. I've brought some fabric with me and I was thinking of making some new curtains for the cabin the Queen will use. So yes, Ethel, we will go to Civitavecchia!'

Ethel hugged Eugénie tightly. Too tightly for Eugénie. 'My beloved friend, I'm so grateful!'

'Now turning to more immediate matters… would you like the same cabin you were staying in before?'

'Yes, please! It was perfect until we rode out that terrible storm!'

'I remember what happened to you, Ethel. Monique cleaned you up, as I recall!'

'Please don't remind me. I felt so embarrassed!'

'She'll be glad to see you again, I'm sure. I sent advanced notice to the galley to prepare us a substantial breakfast, which we can have before our departure.'

Captain Henri waited for the two of them to finish their coffees before he set sail. The Mediterranean was pleasantly calm, and the sun shone strongly. The morning kept its coolness until eleven o'clock when the two of them went to the stern to sunbathe. As if it was part of a familiar routine, they both stripped off their swimming costumes and lay undressed on the sun loungers.

'You have a beautiful body, Eugénie,' said Ethel, betraying the fact that making love to Harry had no effect on her feelings towards women.

'You are too kind. You have a good body yourself. Somewhat firmer than this old lady's!'

'You always look good to me!'

'We have a little more in common now, Ethel,' said Eugénie, looking across to her friend.

'Really? What's that?'

'Not wishing to sound crude, but neither of us is a virgin now. It was just you on our last trip!' she laughed.

Ethel wasn't sure what to say. This was typical of a remark that Eugénie would make which was meant to be amusing but didn't quite work. She tried to think of something witty to move her onto a different subject. She replied in desperation.

'I imagine you have a splendid view of the night sky from The Thistle.'

'Don't you remember from our last cruise, Ethel?'

'Actually, I don't.'

'The skies are amazing, but for one thing. Henri must keep the lights on at night. We daren't extinguish them or we could collide with another vessel. That would be the end. I've even suggested to Henri that we turn them off... just for a few minutes so we can look at the sky. But he refuses. He once said, "even if you threatened to fire me, Your Highness, I could not take the risk." So I've never given him the instruction. Help me up, Ethel, and we'll go down for something to drink.'

Ethel enjoyed Sardinia so much she told Eugénie that she would never forget that beautiful island and its friendly people. She treated Eugénie to a meal in one of the nicest restaurants in Ajaccio where they moored for the night. They then set off for Civitavecchia.

*** 

'What are you doing here, Ethel? I thought you were on a Mediterranean cruise with Eugénie, and here you are knocking at the door of my new apartment! I am a lucky man!'

'It's a delightful story, Harry. I'd planned to come to see you after our return from the cruise. I had a flash of inspiration as we boarded Eugénie's yacht. It's a wonder it hadn't occurred to me back in England. She said then that she really wanted to go to Sardinia. I just went along with the idea. But when we were on the yacht, I asked her if she'd drop me off at Civitavecchia so I could come to Rome. That would save me going all the way back to England on the yacht and setting off to see you from there. She had no objection at all… so here I am.'

Harry gave her a big hug and a kiss on the lips before ushering her in and showing her around.

'What a beautiful apartment, Harry. I bet it cost you a fortune.'

'I did well from the sale of the house in Florence and, even after giving the children some money, I had plenty left to buy this place. It is not large. Only two bedrooms, but each has its own bathroom. Naturally, I have the larger one.'

'I must think about whether I want to share yours or sleep alone!'

'Obviously, I'd be delighted if you'd sleep with me, Ethel. It would be like the beginning of a honeymoon!'

'But we aren't even married!'

'Whenever did that enter the question, my lovely Ethel?'

So sleep together they did. They spent the following month and more together. They cycled to Abruzzo and Harry showed her the sights and sounds of this strikingly beautiful part of Italy. As usual, she wore her tweeds. She looked quite odd cycling with her skirts above her knees. The local children laughed at this strange sight. They had never seen the knees of a grown-up woman before, and certainly nothing higher. She didn't care in the slightest.

'Stop, Harry! Stop by the side of the road!' said Ethel, as they were cycling on a quiet country road through a tunnel of tall trees which hid them from the sun.

Ethel's urgent injunction completely puzzled Harry, and he wondered what could be wrong. Did she suddenly feel unwell? Did she need a stop to relieve herself? Was there something wrong with her bicycle? A flat tyre possibly. They stopped within a yard of each other.

'What's the matter, Ethel? Are you all right?'

'I am fine and so excited. I've just thought of an idea for our next opera. This funnel of trees has inspired me. Trees are almost infinite, but we are not. I want to write an opera that shows the power of the forest. Its power over the human mind. I haven't thought of the characters yet or what happens but it's an idea. I had to stop to tell you. I didn't want it to vanish before I told you! What do you think?' she said, holding on to the handlebars of the bike, with her feet on the ground, as she straddled the crossbar.

'Interesting,' said Harry, not sure whether it was or not. He would see if the idea blossomed or whether it died before saying more. 'Let's discuss it further when you are ready. Shall we remount and set off again?'

'Let's go, Harry. Thank you for that!'

***

Harry had built up an interesting and varied circle of friends near his apartment in the Palazzo Antici Mattei. He willingly shared them with Ethel, whom he proudly showed off. In the course of her stay, Ethel became friends with several of his and some people she had separately become acquainted with. One of Ethel's was Donna Laura Minghetti, a tall, straight-backed lady whose spacious apartment was only a hundred yards from the Trevi Fountain.

'I'm so glad you could come to my little *soirée*,' said Donna Laura, one evening after Ethel had been staying with Harry for almost three weeks. 'Come through to the drawing-room so I can introduce you to more of my guests.'

Ethel followed Donna Laura down the hall into a room crowded with her women friends. Donna Laura clapped her hands to silence them.

'Dear ladies, please allow me to introduce you to my new friend, Ethel Smyth. Ethel is a composer from England. I shall try to persuade her to entertain you at the piano, after we've eaten.'

A round of applause greeted the announcement and Ethel clumsily bowed. Her mind vacillated between annoyance and flattery. What Donna Laura had said made her realise she had little choice. She'd have to perform from memory or improvise, as she hadn't prepared a thing.

Ethel could remember only a few of the names of the twenty or more they introduced her to. Some were interested in her career as a composer. Others turned away and carried on with the conversations they had started. Sure enough, as soon as the maids cleared away the plates from the table, Donna Laura announced that Ethel would play some music. She sang with verve and energy, playing some of her Mass, the Serenade and lastly some rousing tunes from Fantasio. An enthusiastic round of applause greeted her as she stood and bowed. Most of the audience then continued with their previous discussion. The exception was a short, round lady of about fifty who came over to Ethel.

'You probably don't recall being introduced to me. My name is Ingrid von Baumann. I enjoyed your little recital, and I especially enjoyed the last piece you played. It's unusual to hear German sung in these parts! I thought the words and the music were wonderful. Did you write it?'

'Yes, I remember you, Frau von Baumann.' She remembered the face and the shape of the lady, but not her name. 'I'm so pleased you like it. Yes, I wrote it myself. It's from a comic opera called Fantasio.'

300

'Has anyone performed it?'

'No, and I've all but given up on it. I've been to nearly every opera house in Germany, but although the one in Karlsruhe was interested, they delayed and delayed their decision so no one intends to perform it at the moment. The one I gave you all could well be its last,' said Ethel, looking quite sad.

'What about Weimar?' said the lady.

'No, I've not tried Weimar.'

'Why not?'

'I don't know. Is there a major opera house there? I have to confess my almost if not total ignorance of musical conditions in Weimar.'

'Music is thriving there, Miss Smyth. We have a very active opera house. It is a very cultured city, especially under the Grand Duke, Charles Alexander. In fact, he and I are good friends. I also have some influence over the Intendant of the opera house. If you wish, I will mention your work to them.'

'I'd be thrilled if you would, Frau von Baumann!'

'In which case, I will do all I can for you.'

Ethel couldn't conceal her joy at meeting Frau von Baumann. She almost ran back to Harry's apartment. If only they would agree on one performance, she would give it to them, free, just to hear it live. She wondered on the way whether to ask Levi about Weimar and see what he thought.

She burst in through Harry's front door. 'Super news, Harry! Fantasio. I've found someone who'll help with a performance!'

She sat on the sofa and breathlessly told him the story.

'That's truly exciting. What do we do next?'

'I'll write to Levi. He will know someone there who can help us. I didn't like to ask the Frau when we could hear from her. So if Levi says we could succeed there, I at least should go to investigate. What do you think?'

'Sit and write to Levi. Tonight!'

Harry posted the letter first thing the following morning. Levi must have dealt with it immediately because six days later his reply dropped into Harry's letterbox.

'Amazing, Harry. He's given me a letter of introduction to Bernhard Stavenhagen, apparently the principal conductor of the Weimar Court Opera. Here it is, signed by Levi, telling him all about Fantasio and how well it did in the opera competition! It recommends he should perform it before it's performed by Mottl! I could hug him. I really could.'

'So what do you do next, Ethel?'

'Write to Mottl. I'll tell him about the Weimar plan and about Stavenhagen. It might spur him into action!'

At first, Mottl's reply mortified Ethel. It said he had written to Stavenhagen saying he envied him the honour of performing the premiere of Fantasio, an honour which unforeseen circumstances had deprived him of conducting himself. She soon realised that Mottl's decision could be a blessing. He might anyway never have performed it in Karlsruhe.

Ethel spent some time back at One Oak. Despite her enjoyable time with Harry, she had missed her loveable Marco and felt obliged to be with him. They greeted each other like long-lost friends while Ford looked on and smiled. Ethel spent some time in the garden and took Marco out for some long walks. These regular interludes helped her develop her ideas for the opera on the powers of the forest. But her urgent thought was to achieve Fantasio's first performance. Weimar beckoned.

# CHAPTER 29

## Weimar

Ethel thought hard about whom to approach in the city. Should she try to meet Stavenhagen or locate Frau von Baumann? She had no idea where she lived but would surely find her. She spent days trying. All enquiries failed. Then she had a smart idea: she would try the central post office. Surely, they would know. She spoke to a clerk at the desk at which they accepted parcels.

'Yes, Madam. How can I help?'

'I wonder if you can. I need to know the address of a lady who lives in Weimar. Her name is Frau von Baumann.'

'Weimar is a big city, Madam. I don't know offhand, so I must look her up in our index. Would you mind waiting here while I check?'

'Not at all.'

The clerk seemed to have gone for his morning break. Ethel looked around at the queue building up behind her. He suddenly appeared.

'I have to ask you some questions, Madam. What exactly is your relationship with Frau von Baumann?'

'I'm a friend of hers from London. I haven't known her long. We first met about six months ago when she offered to help me convince the Weimar Opera House to perform my new opera.'

'Is this some kind of joke, Madam? A new opera?' He laughed.

'I am serious, my man. I am a composer of music. My latest work is an opera which I and Frau von Baumann are promoting. We want it performed... here in Weimar. At the opera house.'

'Right, Madam. I'm sorry. I should have taken you more seriously. Our policy on giving out addresses is that we don't. However, we ask our addressees if they wish to contact the person who has made the enquiry. So could you please write your address in London and your address in Weimar on this form? In that space…' he pointed to an area on the form… 'Say who you are and that you wish to meet her, in Weimar.'

Ethel did as asked.

'That'll be twelve Marks.'

'What? That's almost the train fare from Calais!'

'Sorry, but we do that to discourage fraudsters. So, I'll tear the form up, shall I?'

'No. Here are the twelve Marks.'

'We will post it today, Madam. Obviously, I cannot say when the lady will reply.'

Ethel went back to her hotel room and laid on the bed. She wondered if Frau von Baumann would remember her and reply. Could she have gone back to Rome for some obscure reason? Ethel never discovered why she went there. She would have to be patient. Rather than lying on her bed for any longer, she would use this time to look around Weimar and do some thinking about her new opera. She visited Liszt's house, the Theatre, various parks and the Opera House. Two weeks of walking, sightseeing and working on her opera passed without a word from Frau Bauman. She could wait no longer, so would try to speak to Stavenhagen. She discovered, at the opera house, that he was performing a Liszt piano work in Munich and would be away for a further week. In total despair, she ambled back to her hotel. The ebullient receptionist greeted her.

'Miss Smyth, this letter has just arrived for you!'

Ethel had written to Harry a week before so was half expecting a reply. She immediately realised it was not Harry's writing on the envelope. Ragingly impatient, she tore it open in front of the receptionist. It was from Frau von Baumann. She dearly wanted to meet Ethel and asked if they could meet for dinner at Ethel's hotel. She asked if Ethel would mind replying with a few dates. They met in reception on the Tuesday afternoon.

'I am so pleased you contacted me, Ethel. I hope you don't mind me calling you by you first name. Please call me Ingrid.'

'Of course, Ingrid, I am more than happy to be on first-name terms. I'm delighted that you replied to the post office's message. It all sounded very formal, but I quite understand. It was a huge mistake of mine not to have asked for your address before we left Rome. I feel so lucky to have met you!' said Ethel, almost overwhelmed to meet this charming lady again.

'Well, I have some excellent news for you. I have spoken to the Grand Duke and he is very interested in your opera. He loves to promote the works of new composers and is famous for it. At some point he'd like to meet you. I have also spoken to the Intendant of the Opera House and he sounds keen, too. The chief thing though is that we have won over the Grand Duke!' she said, with gleaming eyes, full of genuine enthusiasm for Ethel's opera.

'I can't tell you how grateful I am, Ingrid. You said you would help me as much as you could, and you have done far more than I could ever have wished for!'

'But we are not there yet, Ethel. We need a conductor. The one I have in mind is our principal conductor, Bernhard Stavenhagen. He's brilliant. The next step is to see him and show him the score. You have a complete score with you, Ethel?'

'Of course! I also have a letter of introduction to Herr Stavenhagen from Hermann Levi. He is also eager to have Fantasio performed.'

'So we are nearer than I imagined to a performance! This is so exciting!'

'The problem is that Stavenhagen is in Munich, and won't be back for nearly a week.'

Frau von Baumann looked downwards. 'How do you know?'

Ethel explained that she enquired at the opera house and that's what they told her.

'In which case, we will go to see another influential friend of mine and leave Herr Stavenhagen until he is back. She is Baroness Olga Meyendorff. You will love her and she'll love you! She is a great admirer and supporter of modern composers. Especially the ones she likes! She loves contemporary opera, comic or not. So she's sure to fall for Fantasio!'

'Will we need an appointment to see her? We can't just arrive at her front door!'

'I'm always calling on her unannounced. Let's go there now. We'll take a cabriolet!'

About ten minutes later, the two of them were outside the Baroness's beautiful house in the Steubenstrasse, near the opera house. After brief introductions, they were sitting in her sumptuous lounge, drinking Asbach brandy and eating apple strudel.

'I'm so pleased that Ingrid brought you to see me,' said the Baroness. 'I am a prominent supporter of young composers. I am a champion of Wagner and was a great friend of the late Franz Liszt whose works I have also promoted. Not least, I have considerable influence with the Grand Duke. I am regarded as a major force on what happens in Weimar. So between us, Ingrid and I are certain to achieve the performance of your debut opera. Do you have the score with you?'

Ethel didn't know what to think of the woman. She sounded pompous and self-aggrandising. Ethel needed to be careful. However conceited she found her, she dare not upset this potentially powerful ally. She might eventually like her. She reminded Ethel of what she was like before she saw the Light and before it went out again.

'I feel so privileged to have your support, Baroness. I have the score in my bag.'

'Let's go into the drawing-room. I can play some on my piano.'

Ethel and Ingrid followed the Baroness. Ethel could not work out how old she could be. She was at least twenty years older than Ethel but was comfortably large, dark featured and apparently in good health. She put the score on the music stand of her piano and started. The quality of her playing surprised Ethel. It wasn't up to concert pianist quality but was in the higher bracket of competence.

This was the first time anyone but Ethel had played a single note of the opera. Ethel sang the lines of the soloists. She enjoyed the tunes she was hearing. It was better than she expected.

'Ethel, it's brilliant. We will perform it in Weimar, won't we, Ingrid?'

'Certainly. It is a magnificent work!'

'I'm so grateful to you two for your incredible support.'

'The next person to speak to is Herr Stavenhagen,' said Ingrid.

'I agree. I'm going to leave that to you, Ingrid, because I'm far too busy at present. I am seeing Cosima Wagner tomorrow. Poor lass is still mourning the death of her beloved Richard. What twelve years ago?'

Ethel felt that the Baroness had spent enough of her valuable time with her and Ingrid von Baumann. She puzzled how they could make the first move to leave without offending her. Ingrid provided the solution.

'Olga, we are so pleased we came to see you. I detect we have interrupted your busy day, so we will leave you now to your more important ventures.'

'Equally, I am delighted you thought of coming to see me. Should you detect any resistance to performing Ethel's opera here, please let me know. We will soon neutralise it!'

Ingrid stood up first, quickly followed by Ethel. The Baroness escorted them to the door and off they went.

***

Ingrid and Ethel would attempt to meet the elusive Stavenhagen on the following Monday. In the meantime, Ethel would work on her next opera and write to Harry, Mary and Eugénie to tell them about the interest Fantasio was generating, at least among this small, apparently influential, circle of friends.

Ethel liked Stavenhagen. Uniquely, she actually felt that he respected her as a composer, not as a woman composer but simply as a composer. He was a surprisingly modest man and told her he had become principal conductor of the

Weimar Opera orchestra by a simple stroke of luck, a case of being available and living in Weimar when his predecessor retired. He also told Ethel, and presumably reminded Ingrid, that he had the privilege of conducting the first performances of the works of several modern composers, including Mahler and Wagner. Ethel believed this slim, handsome man was younger than her by at least four or five years.

'If you've brought your score with you, Miss Smyth, or may I call you Ethel? I would love to see it.'

Ethel withdrew it from her bag.

He put it on his desk and opened it. After he'd spent about twenty minutes thumbing backwards and forwards through it, he spoke.

'Yes, I will perform your opera, Ethel. Only one barrier stands in our way. My friend the Intendant.' By the way he said 'friend', she felt that it was a term of convenience or even irony.

Ethel beamed and kissed Stavenhagen. 'You are making all my efforts so worthwhile, Bernhard. I can't praise you enough.'

'Yes,' he continued. 'Our illustrious Intendant is a rather conservative individual who much prefers us to play the better known works of established composers, but there are ways around him, if we need to travel that road. Ingrid knows exactly what I mean,' he said, turning towards Ingrid, who had hardly uttered a word during this exchange. 'We now need to draw up a contract and to agree a performance fee with you, Ethel. I will deal with the Intendant. The next thing you will hear from me is the date of the performance. We will then prepare the performing versions of the score, appoint the soloists, organise the rehearsals, and so on. I expect you will want to play your part in all this?'

'Of course, Bernhard. I would love to help.'

Ethel gave Stavenhagen her addresses, both in Weimar and in Farnborough and said she would be staying in Weimar for another few weeks and could be reached at the hotel.

***

Ethel spent the next eighteen months rushing between Weimar, to see if there was any progress on the opera, Rome to see Harry, and One Oak, mainly to see Marco but also to meet up with Eugénie and Mary Ponsonby. She found it difficult to bear the uncertainty about when Fantasio would be performed in Weimar, assuming they would perform there at all. Her moods varied from the ecstatic to the depths of misery. Eventually, she heard they had set a date, then silence for months then another date. What agony Ethel was suffering.

That wasn't her only problem. It became clear to Harry that Ethel didn't enjoy the act of sexual intercourse anything like as much as he did. Her initial enjoyment declined. It became a case of endurance rather than pleasure. So Ethel reluctantly agreed that Harry could have a mistress in Rome, as long as he told Ethel nothing about her and she did not appear when Ethel was visiting him. She told him to ensure the woman was clinically safe so he couldn't pass any transmissible diseases to Ethel. While she was unhappy about this arrangement, to begin with, she eventually reconciled herself to it because she loved him and didn't want to lose him. At least he had been honest about it.

She was also struggling with her composing. She had spent many hours thinking about the new work, composing and recomposing, but was certain only of the title. She called it 'Der Wald' in homage to the forest where much of the action takes place.

Once again, Eugénie came to the rescue. She took Ethel to Cap Martin for a holiday. They stayed in Eugénie's beautiful villa and went on several day trips up the coast on The Thistle.

The excuses for not giving a performance date for the opera were obscure and unreasonable. To Ethel in Frimley, reading the occasional letter from Frau von Baumann in Weimar, they made no sense. In one of her missives, the Frau said something about the reluctance of the Intendant's wife to have Fantasio performed when in a letter about a month previously, she said his wife 'was fire and flame' for it. Ethel was completely at a loss. What had the Intendant's wife to do with what works were performed? Surely, that was a decision for the Intendant in consultation with the conductor.

Then suddenly, soon after Ethel returned from her holiday, there came an urgent injunction from Baroness Meyendorff. She demanded that Ethel come to Weimar. She had arranged an enormous party in Ethel's honour. Amazingly, the Grand Duke would be attending. The Baroness had spoken again to the Grand Duke who said that there was not the slightest doubt they would perform Fantasio that season, regardless of all other commitments. Apparently, she had told him about the views of Mottl and Levi but what had influenced him more than anything was the discovery that The Empress Eugénie was a supporter of Ethel's career.

'You won't believe this, Eugénie. Your influence even extends to deepest Weimar!' She handed her the letter so she could see for herself.

'I'm not surprised, my pet. Charles Alexander and I go back many years. I appointed him as a military observer at the Battle of Sedan, which we lost, of course, and he and I were family friends for years before then. He is a highly loveable man and a great patron of the arts. Rumour has it that as a lad, he sat on Goethe's knee.'

'I hope it wasn't too bony! Rather him than me!'

'The Baroness is the bearer of tremendous news, Ethel. You must go to Weimar. When are they holding the party?'

'Apparently, she hasn't yet fixed the date because the Grand Duke is away, but it's likely to be in January. He must attend, otherwise the entire event would lose its purpose.'

'It is January now! So you must go, Ethel, as soon as you can! Write a quick note to the Baroness and tell her you are on the way! Go to her mansion. Settle in again and make sure they see you in the city and at the opera house. See Stavenhagen again. Make a nuisance of yourself. But pack some nice clothes so you look good at the party! And it will be cold, so wear your warmest!'

Within a few days, Ethel was travelling to Weimar. She hadn't felt so happy for a long time.

***

310

'I'm so pleased to see you, Ethel,' said the Baroness as she opened the door to Ethel. 'Do come in. I have even more news for you. I'll first ask the maid to make us some coffee.'

They settled into the drawing-room. The Baroness could wait no longer to tell Ethel what was happening.

'Your opera is proving very controversial, Ethel. The problem is the Intendant's wife.'

'Yes, Frau von Baumann told me.'

'She's right. She loved the idea of your opera and of you until she made an interesting discovery.'

'Discovery, about what? Me?' Ethel feared that she had discovered Ethel's passion for women, of which she may have disapproved.

'No, me, Ethel. She hates me, I'm afraid, and as soon as she found that I was promoting your opera she decided she'd do everything she could to prevent its performance.'

'That at least solves a mystery in my mind. In one of her letters, Frau von Baumann said the Intendant's wife was being difficult about it and I wondered why she inveigled herself into the decision making. Now I know, Olga!'

'It's ridiculous, I know. The Intendant is a nice man, but his wife is a witch. I loathe her, so the feeling is entirely mutual.'

It astounded Ethel that her opera had become the subject of a pitched battle between these two apparently influential women.

'So how do you think this will end, Olga? I feel very much the centre of this dispute.'

'It is hard to know for certain, but we are holding many of the cards. For a start, the Grand Duke is on our side and will attend the party. And what will make him more committed to our cause is you playing some excerpts from the opera at the party. That is, if you will play them?'

'Of course, Olga. Just you try to stop me!'

Ethel did as Eugénie suggested. She visited Stavenhagen who, to her delight, had appointed soloists for the performance and arranged for the printer to produce the orchestral, choir and solo parts. He told Ethel that the Intendant was keen to have it performed and he was in discussion with the Intendant about a date.

She called on the Intendant at the opera house. He was, as she expected, a short, insignificant looking character, older than her, probably in his fifties. He told her the date for the performance was something he could 'under no circumstances discuss with her'. As the composer of the piece, she found his view unflattering, if not an insult. She could gain nothing from arguing with him so politely left him brooding over his papers.

# CHAPTER 30

## The Party

The Baroness took charge of the seating arrangements. The Intendant's wife tried her best to sit next to the Grand Duke, but the Baroness thwarted her efforts. She invited the Grand Duke to sit where he couldn't even see her. She sat the Intendant next to the Grand Duke with her on the other side of him.

Ethel nodded to the Baroness and started. She sprayed the room with wrong notes. Hitting the high ones and singing in tune failed her. The result was one of the worst performances she had ever given. Her disastrous efforts almost literally brought the house down. The applause was so loud and lasting.

Ethel's performance shocked the Intendant's wife. She didn't know where to look. She hadn't expected this level of adulation for a presentation so far from perfect. Her muted applause hardly made a sound.

'Congratulations, Ethel,' said the Baroness. 'Everybody loved it. Not perfect, but that doesn't matter! I loved it even more than when I played it to you! The subject is so vibrant and the music so fitting to the plot. You made it sound more interesting than my weak performance. You put so much energy into it. I thought you were going to wreck the piano!'

'I was terrible, Olga. I couldn't stop making mistakes! But I did give it my best and perhaps it was that which generated the applause!'

The Grand Duke and the Intendant joined the conversation. 'Brilliant, Miss Smyth,' said the Grand Duke, holding a glass of wine. 'That settles it then, Herr Intendant. Friday, the thirteenth of May, it shall be!'

'I agree, Your Grace,' said the Intendant, as if he had a choice but knowing that he hadn't. 'I will negotiate the terms with Miss Smyth and talk to Stavenhagen about rehearsals. I believe he has already appointed some soloists.'

'Thank you! Thank you!' said a bewildered Ethel, almost choking on a bite of apple pie but smiling all over her face. The last thing she expected was an actual date for a performance to emerge from a gathering such as this. As the two men then moved to another part of the room, the Frau Intendant came over to join Ethel and the Baroness.

'This opera may be a charming example of its genre, but there can be no question of playing it here this season,' she said.

'Oh, but they've just agreed the performance date,' said the Baroness.

'Nothing of the sort,' snapped the Frau Intendant. 'It would upset our whole repertory!'

'Nonetheless,' said the Baroness, in a firm and loud response. 'I'm afraid you are in error. Did you not hear what the Grand Duke said to Miss Smyth? They have just set a date… and with your husband's concurrence.'

Ethel looked away. The woman's face changed from vaguely normal to crimson and then to purple. Fury consumed her. Everyone there turned towards the raised voices. The Frau Intendant staggered on her feet and almost fell over. They all thought she was about to have a heart attack. She realised she had lost the battle. Her fight with the Baroness was over.

Ethel couldn't contain her joy. 'I am so grateful to you, Olga and Ingrid. I could never have succeeded without you. It was your idea, Ingrid, to have the work performed here. You have both promoted my opera with the Grand Duke and with the aid of your party, Olga, we have a definite date.' Ethel hugged and kissed them both. She was almost in tears, tears of boundless joy.

There was much to engage Ethel before the performance. She helped with the rehearsals. Stavenhagen delegated some of this work to Ethel, who formed good relationships with her singers. More than once, she conducted the choir and soloists, while she played the piano to mimic the orchestra. The conductor and the composer worked hand-in-hand for the final rehearsals.

Harry and a large contingent of the Smyth family appeared in Weimar three days before the performance date. They all stayed at Ethel's hotel, The Elefant, near the Goethe Park and an easy walk to the Opera House.

314

Ethel was more pleased to see Harry than any of her family, but delighted that so many of them came, too.

'Mary, I'm so glad you could make it. All the way from Scotland. What a journey you must have had. And it's so good to see you, Kitty and Sylvia. You look as pretty as your mother!'

'The journey was ghastly, Ethel. It was fortunate that we had a comfortable hotel in Pimlico. Otherwise, we would have turned around and gone back!'

'Oh dear!'

'Yes, Sylvia was travel sick. The sight of her being ill made me feel bad, too.'

'I am sorry,' said Ethel. 'What about you, Alice?'

'It was a very easy but a long journey for us, Ethel. But we enjoyed it, didn't we, Nina? Especially the two nights we spent in Cologne.'

'Yes, Mama. That cathedral is magnificent!'

'That is a relief, Alice!' said Ethel.

'I'm so pleased to be here, too,' said George Henschel. 'I seem to be at all your premieres, Ethel! I'm sure this will be the best! You have met my daughter, Helen, haven't you?'

'Of course, George!' Ethel leant over to kiss Helen. The other daughters looked at each other and wondered why she hadn't kissed them.

'I trust we will all be dining together tonight. What do you think, Harry?'

'Delighted. I'll book a table.'

Eventually they all arrived at the hotel restaurant. Harry and Clotilde were characteristically late. George Henschel spoke first to the excited gathering.

'I'd like to tell you all about something Ethel said to me over twenty years ago. It was that she wanted her first opera performed here in Germany before she was forty. She might have forgotten, but I remember! Ethel, you have just about

315

managed it. You signed the contract just before your fortieth, and the performance is in three days' time. Let's raise our glasses to Ethel. Congratulations, my dear friend, for achieving your ambition!'

They all did as George suggested. Ethel smiled and raised hers too. She was too overcome to speak. He continued in a different vein.

'Don't forget, all the waiters speak English and are all spies. So don't criticise the Germans or Germany, not even if you whisper. The walls have ears! If one of them reports you, the Consul will help you out of trouble but it may mean a period of house arrest, which would be tiresome and not worth the bother.'

'You sound very serious, George,' said Harry.

'I absolutely am. Free speech doesn't exist in these parts. That's the main reason I became naturalised as English!'

'Why do you insist we eat sausages? There is nothing vaguely tempting on your menu!' complained Mary.

The waiter looked astonished at her remarks. 'I don't quite know how to respond to that, Madam.'

'It's very simple. Just make sure in all our future meals there is beef and chicken available.'

'I'm not sure we have enough chickens in the whole of Weimar, Madam. I shall investigate and report back to you,' he said, smiling sarcastically.

'Then buy some in from Dresden, Berlin or wherever you like!'

The waiter had had enough of this exchange and vanished, probably thinking he'd been dealing with a madwoman.

'I hope you have brought your most revealing dresses, ladies. Not your daughters, of course!'

'What do you mean, Ethel?' said Mary.

'I've attended several formal events here and they love nudity!'

'Nudity? They don't walk around naked, do they? Surely not?'

'No, not naked, but the women's dresses expose their complete breasts. You will never see such a display of feminine pulchritude as long as you live!'

The daughters all laughed in unison.

'Well, I'm not exposing my breasts to any of your strangers,' said Mary.

'Nor me!' said Alice. 'And I'm not especially looking forward to seeing them either!'

Ethel just smiled.

\*\*\*

'I'm afraid I have bad news, Ethel,' said Bernhard Stavenhagen, as Ethel arrived early for the premiere. Surely nothing else could go wrong after what she had suffered in securing a performance.

'So what's the problem, Bernhard?'

'As you know, we had a strenuous dress rehearsal yesterday. Well, the result is that the tenor who plays Fantasio woke up this morning to discover his voice had gone.'

Ethel laughed out loud. 'So another postponement then! Just my luck. He should surely be all right in a day or two.'

'Yes, but we have a busy schedule so we are performing it on the twentieth, if that suits you,' he said, knowing they had fixed the date, whether or not Ethel agreed.

'Of course, Bernhard. The silver lining to that particular cloud is that the tribe of my relatives and friends can stay another week in Weimar. They can see the sights of this wonderful city!'

'I'm so glad you aren't angry, Ethel!'

'Not at all. I'm treating it as an amusing diversion!'

Not everyone thought it was that comical. Critics had come from all over Germany and the thought of staying another week in Weimar, a city they knew so well, was an irritation. It especially annoyed Herr Fritsch, the chief editor and owner of the 'Signale', and a friend of Ethel's in her student days. She knew him so well, she escorted him back to the station, anticipating his return.

'I'm so sorry you have come for nothing,' said Ethel, just before the train was to depart for Leipzig.

'Don't worry about that,' he said. 'I shall be back for the twentieth. I don't expect there will be much sleep for you until the following Wednesday!'

Ethel was about to ask why when she suddenly realised that the Signale came out on the Wednesday.

'Oh! The worst will be over immediately after the performance,' said Ethel. 'The porter at the Elefant will tell me exactly what he thought of it. He is one of the most musically sensitive people I know! And as for his knowledge of opera...'

Herr Fritsch looked at Ethel with a scowl. 'Well, if his opinion ranks higher than mine, it will save me coming back on the twentieth!' He spun away sharply and climbed into his carriage. Ethel just stared at him, realising how clumsy she had been.

\*\*\*

Incredible enthusiasm greeted the first night's performance. The audience burst into applause, stamped on the floor, and ended by giving it a standing ovation. They loved it. Ethel attracted many curtain calls. She was overjoyed. Tears ran down her face. All the efforts she had made to achieve its performance seemed suddenly worthwhile.

The press trampled on her joy. They slated it. They praised the orchestration and the thematic material but disliked Musset's story, which they regarded as too fanciful and light. Ethel wondered if Herr Fritsch had, by some devious means, poisoned their views. But the more she thought about it, the more she believed their thoughts on the work may be justified. By then, she was too engaged on Der

318

Wald to revise Fantasio. Harry said it needed no changes. He loved the first product of their joint efforts.

# CHAPTER 31

## Der Wald

One of Ethel's enduring abilities was to make friends, mainly among women but especially with women of influence. She could attract them to her like iron filings to a magnet, and the attraction was nearly always mutual. While staying with Harry in Rome, she became close friends with Laura Beccadelli di Bologna, a friend of Ingrid von Baumann. It took several meetings with her before she discovered that she was the mother of the German Chancellor's wife, Princess Maria von Bülow.

Ethel loved Der Wald. She regarded it as her best work. It made her feel like the mother of a newborn baby. It staggered her that she convinced Covent Garden to perform it. They accepted it but didn't say when they would enter it in their programme. By then, the Garden had just about lifted itself from the torpor of playing only accepted, familiar works in its repertory. Having experienced so many false dawns, she decided not to rely on the London opera house but to set off on yet another tour of Germany.

'I can't believe you, Ethel. The Garden has accepted it and off you want to go to Germany!'

'You can't rely on these people, Harry. In one breath they say they will accept it and in the next they turn it down… in favour of some stagnant continental offering. I simply don't trust them.'

Harry was staying at One Oak at the time, and doing yet more work in Ethel's back yard. By then, Ethel had taken up golf. She regularly rode her bike to Woking Golf Club, her bag of clubs slung over her shoulders and looking a rare sight in her tweeds and golf shoes. As much as she tried to persuade Harry to take up this king of sports, he steadfastly refused, even to swing a club. Ethel didn't object so much because it gave her an interest which, unlike all her others, she didn't have to share. She loved the game, which gave her a less gory alternative to fox hunting. She became a highly competent golfer and could beat many men of her age and ability.

Harry and Ethel spent many interesting afternoons and evenings with Eugénie, whom Harry regarded as quite superficial at first but eventually grew to like her, especially as she related her stories about her eminent position in Paris.

'Can you understand why Ethel is so enthusiastic about going to Germany, Eugénie? Especially as Covent Garden want to perform Der Wald?'

'Yes, I can. I have spent many hours listening to Ethel's stories of disappointment and disasters. Her tales of woe. The number of times performances have been delayed. Even cancelled. And often for no tangible reason. So yes, go to Germany, Ethel, but try not to do a grand tour as you have so many times in the past.'

'My intention is to go to Berlin.' She told the other two about meeting with the mother of the Chancellor's wife, Princess Maria von Bülow.

'My God, Ethel. You must go there! I can help you.'

'Actually, Eugénie, I did well financially from Fantasio so I can fund myself. Thank you so much for the offer.'

'No. That's not what I am saying, Ethel. I know the Kaiser and the Chancellor and his wife. I will write to them and give you letters of introduction.'

'Who in Europe don't you know, Eugénie?' said Harry.

'Not quite, Harry! It's a large place. I know the Kaiser because his mother is Queen Victoria's daughter, Princess Victoria. As you know, I owe so much to Her Majesty, including my continuing use of the Birkhall Estate. All three of us should have a holiday there, once you've had Der Wald performed, Ethel.' So again, Eugénie demonstrated her diplomatic skills, this time in dealing with Harry's presumptuous remark.

'I'd be so grateful,' said Ethel. 'It will be so much easier if you can ease my way.'

'Give me a couple of days and I'll get the letters in the post. And don't forget to come back for the ones I'll write for you to take.'

***

The saddest event in Ethel's life then was the passing of Marco. He had been a wonderful companion, especially when despairing at the loss of Lisl. While Ethel clearly regretted the death of Marco, essentially through tiredness brought on by old age, Ford was distraught. Ethel spent more time comforting her than dealing with her own loss. She wanted another dog so bought a sheepdog puppy she called Pan. He proved to be a delight.

*\*\**

Ethel set out for Berlin. No woman had ever traversed the continent with Ethel's confidence. If she missed a connection, as she did those years before in Cologne, she would calmly find out when the next train was due. And if it was not for a couple of days, she'd book herself into a hotel. However, other barriers were to confront her. Despite the letter from Eugénie, she almost had to fight the guards at the Chancellery building. They wanted proof of identity, the sight of a return ticket to England, and they had never heard of Empress Eugénie.

Ethel explained while a guard looked her up and down. Ethel peered into his eyes. She could almost read his thoughts. Standing there in her tweeds and smoking a cheroot, with an attaché case by her feet, he probably thought she was some sort of madwoman. And as for coming to Germany in the middle of the Boer War, whatever could she expect: the Germans' sympathies lay firmly with the Boers.

'Wait here,' he said, condescendingly. 'I shall make some enquires.' Then, leaving Ethel in the charge of a fellow guard, he disappeared into the palace. As suddenly as he went, he reappeared with the most beautiful woman, who seemed about ten years older than Ethel. She had the most intense brown eyes and wore an ankle length, dark blue dress. Ethel could see her mother in those gorgeous, smiling features.

The woman came directly up to Ethel. 'I am Maria von Bülow,' she said. 'And you are Ethel Smyth. I have heard so much about you from my mother who loves you! I am delighted that you came to see me. Do come into the Reich Chancellery. The least I can do is to offer you something to eat and drink, and we can have a talk about your work. You may even want to play me some!'

She followed the Princess through the main gates and into the courtyard of this monumental structure, built in the Gothic tradition. Apart from The Crystal Palace and some continental concert halls, it was by far the biggest building Ethel had ever entered. Enormous blocks of three-storey complexes flanked the courtyard. Surely, they could not all be residential.

'So where do you live in this massive edifice?' said Ethel, unable to contain her curiosity.

'What you see on either side of us are offices, occupied by the administrators of the state, Ministers and civil servants, as well as the military command. We live in that quite imposing building we are walking towards. I hope you like large rooms!'

This attractive woman charmed Ethel. She needed to restrain herself. A physical delight she might be, but Ethel's reason for being here was to seek tangible support for at least one performance of Der Wald in this city.

'Do you prefer coffee or tea, Ethel?' said the Princess. 'We do a fairly strong coffee or you may prefer our Chinese tea, taken without milk or sugar. Not in the English way at all!'

'I would love a coffee,' said Ethel. 'I've had so much weak coffee in Leipzig, something stronger would be much to my taste!'

They sat at each end of a gigantic sofa that could easily sit five. The room swallowed it up like a whale would swallow a herring.

'My mother absolutely loves you, Ethel. She enjoyed your company in Rome. She mentioned you in at least three of her letters. I think you even played some of your music to her and I hope you will do likewise for me. As you can see, I've deliberately brought you into the room with the grand piano!'

Ethel played the Princess excerpts from many of her works, The Serenade, some movements from the piano sonatas, Fantasio and ended with Der Wald.

'You are an amazing composer, Ethel. I enjoyed everything you played. Did you really compose it all?'

'I did and am so pleased you like it!'

'I think I'd like you to visit me regularly so you can play the whole of your repertory. Would you like to do that? I would pay you of course and we could enjoy meals together and each other's company. I am quite lonely here. Although the Chancellor has an office in this building, I hardly see him from one day to the next. And of course he travels to many parts of our country on state business.'

'I would love to play regularly to you... and we will arrange something. But let me explain my principal reason for coming to see you, Your Highness.'

'Go on... but call me Maria and I shall call you Ethel. In fact, I already am!'

'I need help in promoting my new opera, Der Wald. I have to confess that you are not my first port of call. I first saw the British Ambassador who knows one of my sisters. He explained the structure of opera in Berlin. I discovered the man with controlling power is the Director of the Opera House, an Englishman called Pierson. The Intendant, a Count Hochberg, is putty in his hands. I played the full opera to Pierson. He said he was certain he could convince Count Hochberg to stage it and sent me to the principal conductor, Karl Muck. He liked it and said he would be willing to play it. It has been over three weeks now and I haven't heard from Count Hochberg about a performance. So I am desperate for help.'

'Your timing is immaculate, Ethel. My mother knows Count Hochberg. They are good friends. She is on her way from Rome, and I'm sure she will help you with the meeting you want. She should be here in a couple of days!'

'That's incredible, Maria. What a great idea! I'll need all the support I can get. And your mother is a very influential woman.'

The Princess was right: Laura Beccadelli di Bologna arrived three days later. Ethel explained her plight. Her friend from Italy sat down the following day and wrote a letter to Count Hochberg. She read it to Ethel who was shocked at the forceful tone.

'He won't reply to that. It is so demanding. You are telling him to meet me. You can't do that, Laura.'

'I just have, Ethel. Don't worry. I know him well. He loves and hates me but will do anything within reason I ask!' She sealed the envelope and gave it to one of the Princess's servants to deliver by hand.

A few days later, Ethel was sitting at Count Hochberg's desk with her score in front of him.

'You are lucky to have such an ally in Laura Beccadelli di Bologna. We have known each other for many years. I have spoken to Karl Muck about your opera and he thinks it is brilliant and Herr Pierson has a very high opinion of it, too. So we will perform it here, Miss Smyth, at our opera house and Karl Muck will be the conductor. We are looking at the programme and hope to perform it five times, if we can programme it. There is much to do beforehand. It is September now and we will probably put it on in May '02. I have asked Herr Pierson to draw up the draft of a contract. Your fee will depend on the size of the audience, above a base payment. And we will pay your fares from London and your hotel here.'

Ethel went around the desk and kissed him.

'Really, Miss Smyth. There is no need for that,' he said, still recovering from the shock.

Ethel dashed back to the Chancellery to tell Laura and the Princess her news.

'I'm not a bit surprised,' said the Princess. 'My mother is such a powerful voice in these parts. It all sounds excellent, but we must make him stick to his word. I have an idea... but it means you staying here for a few weeks, possibly a little more.'

'Are you going to elaborate on your idea?' said Ethel.

'I'm afraid not because I wouldn't want to disappoint you if it fails. I will tell you, of course Mama, but not in Ethel's presence!'

For the following couple of weeks, Ethel acted as court entertainer to the Chancellor and his wife, but mainly to the wife. Almost every lunchtime and evening, she played music she had composed and some of other composers. She played tennis with the Princess and golf with the Chancellor. Although at first she didn't like him, she made a study of his character and eventually found him to be a charming and reliable friend. She admired the sincere love he showed for his wife. This did not surprise Ethel. She saw the look in his eye as he gazed at her reposing on the sofa. As he rarely saw her for more than two hours in a day, he made the most of these delightful interludes. He also impressed Ethel with the generous way he played golf with her. She wondered if he could help her achieve her ambitions for Der Wald.

It was about then she heard, to her surprise and sadness, that Georg Pierson, her undoubted ally, had died suddenly. She hoped his tragic death would not diminish the chances of her latest from being performed in Berlin. She wrote a long letter to Harry and another to Eugénie, telling them her news.

* * *

'We are going to have a special party here tonight, Ethel. And you are cordially invited,' said the Princess as she, Laura Beccadelli and Ethel were enjoying their breakfast in the sumptuous dining room of the private apartments in the Chancellery.

'You absolutely must attend,' said Laura Beccadelli. 'It is very important! Our principal guest will issue the invitations.'

'I'm not sure I understand, ladies. Do you mean that you are holding a party here and you are not responsible for the guest list?'

'Exactly that,' said the Princess. 'Whenever he dines here, he selects them. You should know that he has specified that you should receive an invitation!'

By then, Ethel had worked out for herself that this special guest must be Kaiser Wilhelm. What a privilege to be at a party with the supreme leader of Germany and Prussia. Not only was Ethel invited, The Kaiser insisted that she sit next to him at the table.

'So you are the distinguished English composer whose works are only ever performed in Germany,' he said, as he so skilfully managed his knife and fork with his withered arm.

'That's not quite true, Your Imperial Highness. I've had several performed in England, my Serenade for example and the Mass. But I admit, you in Germany are the only audience for my operas. I haven't had one produced in England yet, but I haven't given up!'

'I understand you were successful in Weimar, where they enjoyed your Fantasio. You should see if you can get it performed here in Berlin! Mind you, it's all very well having it performed in Weimar. That is hardly the centre of the universe for the Performing Arts. Nevertheless, you did well to have it performed there. My good friend Grand Duke Charles Alexander has for many years been a great patron of the arts, and I imagine he was to some extent influential.'

'Yes. The Grand Duke was hugely supportive. In effect, he decided on the date they would perform it. He brushed everyone else aside! It would be a great privilege to have it performed here, but the current issue is to secure a performance in Berlin of my second opera, Der Wald.'

'You must tell me about it!'

So Ethel outlined the plot. She told him about her meetings with Muck and Count Hochberg.

'So have they agreed a performance date?'

'No, not yet. But I feel fairly confident they will, probably in May… especially after what Count Hochberg told me.'

'Leave it with me. I shall come back to you within two days with a definite date.'

Ethel could have kissed him. She could not believe that this man of such immense power could even contemplate helping her. But that was what he said. All she could do was to accept he meant it.

'I am so grateful for your intervention. I hope I'm not putting you to too much trouble. And please don't let me give you the impression that I am doubtful of Count Hochberg's intentions.'

'No such thing, Miss Smyth. Now let's turn to other issues. I've said for years that the British have no idea how to organise an army. What do you think?'

327

'I'm not the best person to answer that question! My father was a general in the Royal Artillery which is an elite regiment. Without doubt!'

'It is a great regiment, but it isn't the likes of the Royal Artillery I am talking about. I refer to those silly little regiments based in the counties. They are too small and local. They need integration. And your overall army is ridiculously small! If there was a war, your attackers would overrun you in days! I ought to know. My grandmother made me colonel-in-chief of the First Royal Dragoons.'

Ethel didn't know what to say. After a pause she replied. 'So you know about our army... but to conquer our country, an aggressor would have to cross the English Channel... which the Royal Navy patrols!'

'Maybe, but they are not well armed or easily available. We all recognise the difficulty of protecting a coastline. A concerted attack at one point would be hard to defend.'

'Don't forget, our navy beat the Spanish in 1588!'

The Kaiser insisted on having the last word. 'Yes, but the design and propulsion of ships has advanced a long way since then!'

Ethel said no more on this topic. She didn't want him to change his mind about securing a date for performing Der Wald. Fortunately, he changed the subject himself and spoke to a man across the table from them. It sounded as if the man was an artist, possibly a court painter.

'It takes one man to paint a tree,' said the Kaiser. 'Good. And another to paint a human being. Even better. But it takes a true artist to combine the two on one canvas.'

What ridiculous nonsense, thought Ethel. He knows even less about art that he does about defending the British Isles.

'An amazing pronouncement,' said the painter. 'The whole of art in a nutshell!'

He's just trying to please his boss, thought Ethel. Silly man.

Then the Kaiser moved onto the Boer War and how wrong the British were to be fighting the Boers. He complained of British imperialism and the blind pursuit of empire. Ethel explained the war in terms of the English character and some English history.

'I dare say you are right.'

'I know I am,' said Ethel, daringly.

*** 

'Great news, Ethel,' said Princess Maria von Bülow, at breakfast two days later. 'The Kaiser has succeeded. There will be four performances of Der Wald, the first of which will be on 21 April 1902. I'm so pleased for you... delighted!'

'I'm delighted, too! Four performances! Utterly incredible!'

It seemed odd that Ethel hadn't received this startling news through a more direct route. She immediately kissed the Princess.

'Thank you, Ethel. It was wonderful but unnecessary of you to kiss me. I did nothing... only give you the Kaiser's wonderful message.'

They sat at the dining room table and finished their breakfast. Immediately after taking her last sip of coffee, the Princess spoke. 'I have asked my chambermaid to run a bath for me. It is a large bath, as you might expect in this place. The Chancellor and I often share it. But he is away in Prussia for a week, and I just wondered if you'd like to share it with me instead. The decision is entirely yours, Ethel. You won't offend me in the least if you would prefer not to do so.'

This amazing offer shocked and delighted Ethel. This ragingly beautiful woman, a pinnacle of European beauty, wanted to share her nakedness with her. How could she possibly refuse?

'Yes please, Maria. I'm not even sure where the bathroom is!'

'I shall show you, Ethel. It's near your room. I wouldn't want you to get lost in this immense building, especially if you were undressed or even partially so!'

Ethel followed the Princess out of the breakfast room, up a flight of stairs and along a narrow corridor. She was approaching the sound of running water. 'Here we are, Ethel,' said the Princess, as she opened the door to show Ethel in. The chambermaid, a girl in her late teens, was holding the taps and adjusting the temperature of the water. Ethel had never seen a bath this size before. It was at least nine feet long and about five feet across.

'It is a large bath, Ethel, so there is plenty of room for both of us!'

With the chambermaid still present, the Princess removed her dressing gown and slipped her nightdress over her head. Ethel followed. She tried to stop herself from gazing at the Princess' glorious nakedness. She would love to cuddle up to her.

'I'll get in first, Ethel. Then you can follow.' The Princess lifted a leg off the floor to display the totality of her womanhood as she climbed in. She gradually submerged herself in the water. Ethel tried to look away.

'Come on. What is stopping you?' she said, apparently not realising how Ethel felt about women. Or perhaps she did.

'I'll get in now!'

The two of them sat there facing each other, washing themselves. Such was their concentration, they hardly exchanged a word. Then suddenly, Ethel felt something soft, wet and warm hit her in the face. The Princess had thrown a wet sponge at her. Ethel wondered what to do. She picked it up and threw it back, hitting the Princess on the left breast.

'Now I'm going to punish you!' said the Princess, as she lobbed a bigger sponge at Ethel, laughing loudly as she did so. Ethel ducked her hands under the water and scooped some up, only to slide her bottom over towards the Princess and tip it on her head. The two of them continued enjoying these childish exchanges until water covered the floor.

'I suppose we should stop now,' said the Princess. 'That was such fun, Ethel. I'm not sure who enjoyed it most, you or me!'

'I think I did,' said Ethel. 'You have such a beautiful body and you do something to me when you move it about!'

'You are a beautiful woman, too. Ethel. Don't lose sight of that. And a composer into the bargain. I've never seen a naked composer before,' she laughed. 'I hope you've made a note of that! Even a crochet!'

They both laughed.

Princess Maria and Ethel became close friends. They spent hours together telling each other about their life experiences, their friends and loves. Ethel entertained her by playing the piano. They sang duets together, ate together and went out together. Life was bliss.

\*\*\*

The reality of all this was the forthcoming premiere of Der Wald. Ethel despaired at the quality of singing and playing at the rehearsals. It was as if there was little enthusiasm in either the orchestra or the singers to perform this, her new and treasured baby. The last rehearsal, conducted by Muck, was the worst of all.

'I'm dreading the actual performance,' Ethel said to the Princess at dinner the night before.

'Don't worry, Ethel. You know what they say: "it will be all right on the night!"'

Sadly, it wasn't. The reception of the premiere was a disappointment. The audience gave it catcalls, boos and hissed themselves out of the concert hall. Ethel couldn't understand it. With Muck conducting, according to Ethel's judgement, the orchestra and the singers performed well, if not with complete perfection. And the audience seemed to enjoy it. She suspected that this was some sort of organised demonstration. She had no idea what their thinking could be. The press slammed it.

This strange reaction mystified Ethel. She met the Kaiser again at the Bülows', a few days afterwards. He obviously hadn't heard about what happened. He asked her what she thought of the Opera House and Berlin audiences. Princess Maria went pale as she dreaded what she might say. At first she didn't know quite how to respond, but settled on praising the venue and the audience. He just laughed. Then he said he wanted to turn Berlin into a world cultural centre like Paris or London. They turned to discussing English politics, the British Empire and British humour. Whatever Ethel said, he could not stop laughing. He almost fell off his chair when she said the British sense of humour was far more advanced than theirs.

***

'So where is Herr Muck?' asked Ethel, as she rushed in ten minutes late for the rehearsal of the second performance. Members of the orchestra sat waiting on their chairs. The singers and soloists just stood there.

'We can't find him,' said the leader. 'He's not in the building. Would you conduct it for us?'

This unusual request stopped her in her tracks. Then having thought for a moment she replied. 'I don't see why not!' She'd never lifted a baton before in her life. She stepped onto the rostrum, hit the music stand with the baton, and off they went. She slipped into this role as if trying on a well-tailored dress. With her score on the stand and knowing the location of every performer, she directed like a professional. She hit the baton on the stand when she wanted them to stop and change something. If satisfied, she told them to continue and how well they were playing and singing. I'm enjoying this, she thought. I've chosen the wrong profession!

'You were brilliant,' shouted one of the bass players. 'You should take this up for a living.'

'You flatter me,' said Ethel, trying but only slightly to hide her embarrassment.

'No, seriously,' said the leader of the second violins. 'We all think your opera is simply magnificent.' They all applauded his pronouncement.

'Yes, and the public will love it, despite those stupid remarks in the press,' shouted the tuba player from his place at the back.

And love it they did. The second, third and fourth performances could not have gone better. At each, the audience packed the house and thoroughly enjoyed it. The applause and foot stamping were deafening. Ethel dared to take some curtain calls. Even the press, including some English newspapers, gave it their fulsome praise. Ethel had achieved a major triumph.

# CHAPTER 32

## Covent Garden

Ethel had never felt so satisfied with her achievements as a major, modern composer. Her success in Berlin had raised her spirits even more than the performance of her Mass at the Royal Albert Hall. She could do no wrong.

'You'll never believe this!' said Ethel, as she dashed into Eugénie's lounge.

'Go on, Ethel. You are dying to blurt something out so come on, tell me!'

'The postman has just delivered a draft contract from Covent Garden. They want to put on Der Wald within the next three months!' She leant over the sofa and kissed Eugénie's cheek.

'That's tremendous news. Let me organise you a coffee.' She rang a bell to summon a maid. 'They must have read those reviews of the performances in Berlin. I'm so glad you didn't upset them when you ignored their interest and flew off to Germany. I must admit, I encouraged you in your German exploits!'

'I'm convinced I did the right thing, Eugénie. I'm sure they would have procrastinated like fury if I'd just relied on them to get the thing performed. They aren't keen on unknown works... not in their boring repertoire. Can I ask you a direct question, Eugénie?'

'Please do, my sweet!'

'Are you or Mary Ponsonby behind this?'

'Goodness me, no, Ethel. Absolutely not. I've had several meetings with Mary while you've been toing and froing to Berlin. But I can honestly say we have never discussed helping you in this way. They've based their offer purely on the merits of your work... not on any interference by us!'

'I'm even more pleased, in that case!'

'Who will perform it? Do you know?'

'The stage director is Francis Neilson. He was the man who was so difficult over Fantasio. I remember playing my piano version of it to him in someone's house in Battersea, I think. It was obvious he detested it. What didn't impress him was I was quite nervous and had to stop periodically to light up a fresh cigarette! His friend offered me a cigar, which I put in my top pocket. I told him I didn't want to smoke it then at the risk of ruining it when it went out!'

Eugénie laughed. 'So you won't be asking him to direct it, then.'

'On the contrary, he's just the man!'

'He'll get one of his minions to put it on!'

'I'll pull out if that's what he does!'

*** 

Knowing that Neilson would be working there, Ethel turned up at Covent Garden at ten o'clock one night with the complete score tucked under her arm.

'Ah, Francis Neilson!' said Ethel, as she spotted him in the bar drinking a gin and tonic.

At first, Neilson ignored her.

'Mr Neilson, please may I have your attention for a moment?' she said, with her nose only four inches from his.

'It's my good friend Ethel Smyth,' he said to no one in particular and leaning his head back. 'Of course. I'd love to speak to you,' he lied. 'How can I help you?'

She thrust the complete score of Der Wald into his arms. 'You will know that the Royal Opera Syndicate has offered me a performance of my latest opera, Der Wald. Well, I'm here to ask you to direct it. And this is the score.'

'I can't give you a decision now, Ethel, but I'll read it over the weekend and let you know. Could you come back at say seven o'clock on Tuesday? Would you care for a drink?'

'Yes, please. A pint of bitter? I'll see you Tuesday, then. Good night.'

After this rather awkward exchange, Ethel drank her pint while quietly pushing her way around the crowded bar. She didn't see anyone she knew so drank up, placed the glass on a side table and went.

Neilson spent almost the entire weekend working on Ethel's score. He soon realised that Ethel had written a true masterpiece. Despite his misgivings over Fantasio and his uncertainty over whether he liked her, decided they would perform it at Covent Garden and that he would direct it. He would choose the conductor. It would be Otto Lohse.

'I'm absolutely delighted, Francis!' said a smiling Ethel, as Neilson told her the good news. As was her habitual reaction, she kissed him on the cheek.

'I have to tell you, Ethel, it is an interesting and beautiful thing. My opinion of you as a composer has gone up one thousand percent!'

'I'm so pleased you like it,' she said, still smiling all over her face. The stiffness in their relationship had vanished.

Neilson began designing the sets and, after an unsuccessful attempt at getting it commercially translated into English, Ethel worked day and night to translate the libretto herself. Harry checked it. She then helped Neilson select the soloists and with her boundless energy, deeply involved herself in training the soloists and choir. She slipped easily into the role. They all enjoyed her wildly enthusiastic but demanding approach.

Ethel could not believe that everything was going so smoothly. But suddenly it wasn't. After a week of rehearsals, Neilson spoke to her.

'I've some not good news. Do you know of Lady de Grey?'

'Yes, I know the name.'

'Well, she's a member of the Royal Opera Syndicate. She told me this morning they wanted to delay Der Wald to make room for two new French operas. I told her that was impossible. We were so far down the rehearsal road with yours and to fit in two new ones before the end of the season was out of the question. She told me I wouldn't get away with it and flew off to see Higgins who is the Syndicate Chairman. Within an hour, he was in my office telling me we had to perform these works and that the contracts were already in place. I'm so sorry, Ethel. I don't see what I can do. Higgins is my boss.'

'What a blasted nuisance. I could use much stronger Anglo Saxon, but I won't. Who do these damn people think they are! I shall think of a plan, Francis. Leave it to me!'

Ethel was already thinking of how she might find a way to reinstate Der Wald. Whether the Syndicate expected Ethel to thwart their plans was unclear. But to confirm their position, they announced through the national press that they had postponed the performance of her opera until the following season. When Ethel saw the article, she swore out loud. She tore off to see Neilson.

'Come with me, Francis. I have a plan. I want you to accompany me on a short cabriolet ride! Put your hat on!'

'Really? To where?'

'I'll explain in the cab.'

Ethel hailed a single horse cab and they climbed in. 'Do you know Lady Warwick?' said Ethel.

'Yes. The rumour is that she's the King's mistress. Is that right?'

'I don't want to comment on that point, but I think she may help us bring Der Wald back into this year's programme… but only if you agree?'

'I have no idea what you plan is, Ethel. But you have my total support.'

The cab pulled up in front of a delightful house in Kensington Gore. 'You stay here, Francis. I'll be back in ten minutes.'

Ethel stepped out of the cabriolet and asked the driver to stop there until she returned. Neilson kept looking at his pocket watch, wondering what was happening. She seemed to be gone forever. Twenty minutes passed… then twenty five. Then the driver looked in.

'Where's your lady friend gone? This fare is mounting up. It's over half a crown already.'

'Please be patient, my man, she'll be back shortly.'

Within a few more minutes, Ethel came dashing back, grinning and nodding madly.

'Back to Covent Garden please, driver,' she said, as she clambered into the cab. 'Everything will be fine, Francis. The Garden will receive a message tomorrow asking for the date of their first performance of Der Wald as the King will wish to send a representative!'

'You are a genuine wonder, Ethel! I could kiss you!' So he did.

A few days later, Neilson had some good news for Ethel. 'This will amuse you! I was on stage last night when Lord de Grey came rushing up to me. I was surprised the old codger could move that fast! It was obvious something was upsetting him. "Neilson," he said. "How soon can you produce Der Wald?" I said we could produce it within a week. "In a week?" he said, looking shocked. "Has it been in rehearsal?" Yes, I said, for some time! "Then I have been misinformed."'

Ethel exploded in laughter. 'Wonderful. Good for Lady Warwick! She's a gal! I wonder what she had to do to convince the King. On second thoughts, perhaps we shouldn't ask!'

· 'So next week, Ethel, on 18 July. You'd better start telling your friends and selling some tickets. I can get them printed tomorrow!'

Rehearsals resumed at a frantic pace. The last thing the choir and orchestra wanted was a delay. They loved Ethel's direction and her entire approach to rehearsals. They soon reached a high, professional standard and more than satisfied Ethel's demands.

'We need a word with you, Ethel,' said Mary Hunter with Neilson alongside of her, two nights before the performance.

'Really? What's the problem?'

'I'm not sure how to put this diplomatically,' said Mary.

'Well, you've known me long enough now, sister. Just say what you think. I won't be in the least offended. I promise!'

'Francis here and I have been talking about what you should wear.'

'What do you mean, what I should wear?'

'You are about to have a major work performed at the most famous opera venue in the country. There will be royalty and all. Goodness knows who will be in the audience. We don't want you to turn up in your tweeds, Ethel.'

'I don't see why not. They are my trade mark.'

'I agree with your sister, Ethel,' said Neilson. 'There will be curtain calls. They will expect you to bow towards the Royal Box. You really should look your best.'

'What I am proposing Ethel is that we go to an outfitters... today... and I will buy you a dress you'll look good in.'

'You win, Mary.'

***

The audience gave the Covent Garden premiere, on 18 July 1902, a rapturous reception. The choir, orchestra and soloists gave it their fiery best. They could not have performed better. Arm-in-arm with Lohse and Neilson, Ethel spent ten minutes after the performance taking curtain calls and bowing awkwardly to the audience and to the Royal Box. She was wearing the not especially attractive heliotrope dress that, between them, she and Mary had chosen.

'Who is that woman taking the bows?' said Mary Ponsonby.

'It's Ethel Smyth, the woman who wrote the opera!'

'Never! I've never seen her dressed like that before!'

The press, especially The Times, gave Der Wald generous praise, noting the close fit between the libretto and the music. Even so, the critic claimed it dragged a little in places. Ethel had never felt so satisfied with a performance of one of her works. It was a blazing triumph.

As for the dress she wore, it was a pity that neither Ethel nor Mary could have consulted one of the talented designers of the turn of the century. This was especially so because the Empress Eugénie was, at the pinnacle of the Second Republic, one of the leading fashion lights in Europe. And Mary always took great care over her own appearance. The drab heliotrope number, which she wore on several other such occasions, failed dismally to identify Ethel as one of the most vivid personalities of her era.

In the week leading up to the Covent Garden premiere, Ethel and Mary organised a sumptuous dinner party. They would hold it at Mary's London hotel. The ever generous Mary offered to foot the bill. Ethel readily accepted. They invited Dame Nellie Melba who would attend the premiere. She refused to attend unless at least three duchesses also came. The ever resourceful Ethel found just three: one lame and two stone deaf. Harry was in Rome so couldn't attend.

'Ethel, you must be delighted,' said Eugénie. 'Everybody loved that performance. And the people who were there. I saw Henry James and Mary's artist friend John Sargent, didn't you Ethel?'

'Just a minute, Eugénie. I'm not sure what I should read into you reference to me and Sargent. We are friends but just that,' shouted an angry Mary.

'Many apologies, Mary. My reference was to pure friendship and nothing more. How can I put matters right?'

'Just don't refer to him as my friend again.'

Ethel thought Mary was being oversensitive, but stayed outside of this little spat. She had thought for years that there was more to the relationship between Mary and Sargent than Mary wanted publicly known. She wondered how Eugénie knew, or if she was being a little clumsy in her phrasing.

'What is your next venture?' said Neilson.

'A second performance at Covent Garden?'

'I'm certain we will arrange that!' he said.

'And I have another project up my sleeve… a new and totally different opera! I shall say no more!'

'I hope you will give me the honour of conducting it!' said Otto Lohse, grinning broadly.

# CHAPTER 33

## New York

It wasn't long after Ethel's scintillating success at Covent Garden that she and Harry were spending a relaxed few days at One Oak. They were enjoying a drink in Ethel's garden, which was adorned with summer flowers, the fruits of Harry's prodigious efforts. Ethel and her new home assistant, Mrs Faulkner - by then Ford was retired - had trained Pan and the two of them were playing with him.

'I don't think I've mentioned this before, Harry,' said Ethel, as she stopped fooling with Pan. She took a sip of her pale ale, lit a cigarette and inhaled deeply. Harry looked straight into her eyes, wondering what secret mystery she was about to reveal.

'Don't look so serious, it's nothing but an idea I've had for another opera.'

'Really? Shouldn't we be doing more to promote Der Wald before starting on a new one?'

'Not at all. Never suppress an idea. Let it appear in full daylight and see if it blooms into a masterpiece. I remember Heinrich Herzogenberg saying something like that when I told him about a piano sonata I couldn't decide whether to write or leave in my head!'

'Go on then, Ethel. Tell me about it!'

She told him that about twenty years before, she visited the Scilly Isles with some friends who took her to some smugglers' caves. They descended into Piper's Hole which, through a narrow passage, led to a subterranean lake. The guide's stories fascinated her. He explained how the local people, by using decoy lights, lured passing ships onto the rocks and looted them. He told of rape, murder and kidnap. These people regarded it as their right to commit these outrageous acts, which to them were a reasonable way of surviving.

'I'm not sure how the idea came to me, Harry, but the opera I have in mind is a tragic love story. Two young lovers decide that this wrecking is wrong, so light

342

warning beacons to steer the ships away from the rocks. The villagers discover their deception and condemn them to drown together in a flooding cave!'

'My goodness, Ethel. That's a brilliant idea for a plot. How are you going to develop it?'

'I'm not sure yet. I haven't worked out the full story, but soon will. I'm pleased you like the idea… delighted, in fact.'

'I'd love to help you with it, Ethel. We were a great team on Fantasio and Der Wald. It's only natural that we collaborate again!'

'I'll press on with writing the plot and send it to you as soon as it's finished. You can let me know what you think, and what part you would like to play.'

'I'd be thrilled to do that, Ethel. Good luck with the plotting.'

They then turned to working out when they might visit Eugénie when Mrs Faulkner came over with a letter.

'Some post for you, Miss Smyth. Postmarked London, SW2.' She handed it to Ethel with an opener.

'Leave it on the table please, Mrs Faulkner. I'll read it later.'

'What do you think that could be about, Ethel?'

'How can I know without opening it?'

'Why wait?'

'What makes you so curious, Harry?'

'I'm not curious for myself, Ethel. But for you. It could be important. It could contain a cheque. We could dine out tonight! To celebrate your new opera!'

'All right. I'll open it.' Ethel took the envelope and slit it open. She quickly read it. 'Oh my God, Harry! You'll never believe this!'

'Believe what?'

'It's from Neilson. The Metropolitan Opera House in New York want to perform Der Wald. There's a draft contract. See! Have a look. I'm amazed and thrilled! I must go, Harry.'

'I'm not sure about you travelling to America, Ethel. Why can't Neilson go or Lohse or both of them?'

'Neilson says here that he can't go. Too many commitments at the Garden. Lohse won't be conducting it over there. The New York Opera will appoint their own conductor.'

'I still don't think you should go, Ethel. You'll find it exhausting. And there are other factors.'

'Such as?'

'They regard you as a serious composer over here. Indeed, in the whole of Europe. America is a brash place. Americans are brash. You won't fit in and it will ruin your reputation.'

'Nonsense, Harry. I fit in everywhere I go. I'm a bit brash myself and you know that as well as anyone! A few performances in America could make a fortune! And a woman venturing solo, that far from our shores, might encourage other women to be more daring. Whatever you say, I'm going!'

'Let's not fall out over it, Ethel. You've decided to go so you have my blessing!'

It took Ethel another week to complete her draft of the plot of the new opera. She liked it and enjoyed the writing. By the time she had finished, Harry was back in Rome so she bundled it into an envelope and sent Mrs Faulkner out to post it.

***

Ethel didn't know anyone as extravagant as her sister Mary Hunter, who became one of the most famous hostesses of her day. Mary favoured Hill Hall, Epping as the venue for throwing her parties. Days after hearing about the extraordinary request to perform Der Wald at the New York Metropolitan Opera, Ethel and Harry attended one of these parties. Mary had invited several of their

344

mutual friends, including Eugénie and Mary Ponsonby, as well as her friend John Sargent. Ethel barged into a conversation between Sargent and Mary.

'So when are you going, John?'

'I'm setting out from Liverpool on the eleventh of February on The Cedric's maiden voyage.'

'I'll follow you, John. Probably from Southampton.'

'So where are you two going?' interrupted Ethel.

'We are going to America,' said Mary.

Several thoughts passed through Ethel's mind. Were they lovers and having a tryst over there? And what a coincidence: Mary and John were going there at the same time as she was!

'I'm going there, too!' said Ethel.

'Are you serious?' said Mary, her eyebrows raised.

'Yes, I am. I have a contract for performing Der Wald at the Metropolitan Opera in New York. And there is a strong possibility of a performance in Boston. Why are you two going?'

'Congratulations, dear Ethel! John is doing some work in Boston on some frescoes in the City Library and I shall be going with him.'

Ethel smiled as if Mary had just confirmed that they were lovers.

'I know what you are thinking, Ethel. You are as bad as the rest of them. No. John and I are not lovers. We never have been and never will be. Charlie would kill me at the thought of it. So you can cast that one from your mind!'

'I'm sorry, Mary. Quite the contrary. I have always defended you. When I have heard that rumour, I have always spoken in your defence.' She decided not to say she did not believe the rumour. That would have been a lie.

'In that case I apologise, Ethel, for making such a bad misconstruction.'

'Please don't worry, Mary. No apology is necessary.'

'In fact, I have an idea, Ethel. What if we travel together to New York? I haven't booked a passage yet, so it would be easy to arrange. I can stay with you while your work is being played in New York and we can travel to Boston together. If they do play Der Wald there, that will be a wonderful bonus. What do you think, John?'

From the look on Sargent's face, Ethel concluded that the two could well be lovers and that the arrangement Mary was proposing disguised the fact. She had given him no real choice. 'That all sounds perfect to me. So we meet in Boston after the performances of Ethel's opera in New York?'

'That's exactly right,' said Mary.

***

Nothing in this world is straightforward for a certain type of person. Whether through lack of foresight, the minimum of planning, or just through chance not acting in their favour, such people are constantly facing some kind of problem at best and disaster at worst. To be consistent with virtually all her previous experiences in achieving the performance of her works, the inevitable problems needed confronting. On arriving in New York, she discovered that Maurice Grau, the impresario who directed the Metropolitan Opera House, and who had made her the offer to put her opera on in the spring, had become seriously ill and had resigned. His successor, a German director, wanted his girlfriend to sing the role of the seductive evil genius in the opera.

'What type of singer is she?' asked Ethel.

'Well, none in particular. But she has an attractive voice.'

'Is she a trained opera singer? Is she a mezzo soprano or a soprano, contralto or what?' said Ethel sharply.

'She's never had formal training…'

'In which case it is totally out of the question that she has any role at all. She could have a behind-the-scenes one but nothing more!'

'So how do I keep her happy if you won't allow her to sing?'

'That's your problem, not mine. You'll have to find something else for her. A theatre production, perhaps, but not in my opera!'

The timid director put every obstacle he could in the way of rehearsals, hoping that Ethel would relent, but she didn't. Eventually, the girlfriend realised she would look stupid if she sang in Ethel's opera and backed down, much to Ethel's relief.

'I'm afraid I have another issue that I should report to you,' said the director. 'Lillian Nordica is scheduled to sing in Il Trovatore, on your premiere night but before your work.'

'That is totally unacceptable!' said Ethel, screwing up her face and raising her eyebrows. 'However many more barriers are you putting in front of my New York premiere? I demand that you change her position in the programme. I haven't come all the way from London to be second fiddle to Nordica!'

'I can't possibly do that, Miss Smyth. She would slay me!'

'In which case I will ask her myself! Where is she staying?'

'As far as I know, in the Hotel Victoria in the Broadway.'

Straightaway, Ethel went there. She asked the receptionist if she could see her and, without him asking any questions, he spoke to her on the telephone, told her a Miss Smyth, a composer of music, wanted to see her and within moments she was walking serenely towards Ethel in the reception area.

'Good afternoon, Miss Smyth. It's wonderful to meet you. Your opera is being performed alongside Il Trovatore at the Metropolitan Opera. That's right, isn't it?'

'It is, Miss Nordica. I'm pleased to meet you, too!'

'I'm puzzled as to why you have come to see me, but it is good to meet a famous English composer, I am compelled to say! Let's sit in these chairs, shall we?'

'Good idea. I understand you are the lead singer in Il Trovatore and that, according to your contract, you are entitled to have Il Trovatore performed before my modest offering.'

'That is correct, Miss Smyth. That is my entitlement which I have taken up. So your opera, which sounds interesting, will take second place in the programme.'

'Is there any possibility of perhaps... just foregoing your entitlement and letting my work lead in?'

'I'm afraid not, Miss Smyth.'

'I fully accept that, Miss Nordica and I will make no further such pleas.'

'Thank you, Miss Smyth. That settles the issue then, does it not?'

'Indeed it does! The only other question I have to ask you is, well... more of an invitation really. I wondered if you would care to join me for dinner tonight. You would be my guest, of course. I understand you have an excellent restaurant here.'

'That is exceptionally kind of you, Miss Smyth. I have no current plans for dinner so I am delighted to take up your invitation. Shall we meet here at say, six thirty?'

'Perfect. I'll see you then. In the meantime, as you are the guest here, would you mind reserving a table?'

'Of course not, Miss Smyth. I looking forward to dining with you!'

***

'Where have you been, Ethel? I've been to the opera house and the concert hall but couldn't see sight or sign of you,' said Mary, as Ethel appeared in the bar of their hotel.

'I'm sorry, Mary. I should have told you. I've been to see Lillian Nordica about changing the programme. They've put Il Trovatore on before Der Wald, and I'm damned cross about it. Furious, in fact! I asked Nordica if she would allow my work to go first, but she refused. Anyway, to show there are no ill feelings between us, I've invited her to be my guest at dinner tonight at her hotel.'

'What am I supposed to do while you are treating her?'

'I have a little plan, Mary. I haven't given up and if I can loosen her up at dinner, I may just be successful.'

'So you expect me to dine alone here? I am paying for all this and that's how you treat me!'

'Please don't upset yourself, Mary. If I can achieve first place in the programme, your money will be even better spent. You may not realise how grateful I am in having you here with me, but please, just for one dinner, may we be separate?'

'I suppose so, Ethel. Not that I have much choice. I will help you chose what to wear.'

Ethel turned up at the Victoria Hotel, looking resplendent in a light green dress that Mary had chosen while they were still in London. It was not the kind of garment she usually wore, so didn't feel especially comfortable in it. She met Nordica in the reception area. She escorted Ethel to a table for two near a window.

'You've chosen an excellent spot for us, Miss Nordica!'

'Yes, I told the *maître d'hôtel* that I was being entertained by a famous English composer and wanted a good table, so he put us here!'

'Excellent, so what would you like to drink?'

'I'll start with a g and t, if you don't mind, then move to a white wine, a Chablis if that suits you?'

'Perfect. I'll forego the g and t but join you with the Chablis!'

Ethel ordered a double gin and tonic for Nordica and the wine. They each pondered the extensive menu and decided a lamb shank would suit each of them.

'I do enjoy a drink, Miss Smyth,' said Nordica, as she downed her gin and tonic in a couple of gulps.

349

'By all means, have another, if you wish,' said Ethel.

'No, thanks, the one will be fine, but let's call the wine waiter over and we can start on the wine!'

'Good idea!'

Nordica asked Ethel about her journey to America and where she was staying. Ethel told her she was with her sister, Mary.

'You should have brought her along with you!'

'She's not the musical type really and is quite happy to eat at our hotel, just on this occasion.'

'Just as well then, Ethel. Are you married? A pretty lady like you should be in the arms of a fine man, not travelling with your sister!'

Ethel told Nordica about Harry and that he couldn't be here because he was busy working on a new libretto while staying at his apartment in Rome.

'Are you in love with him?' she said.

This intimate question, so early in the conversation, surprised Ethel. 'I am in love with Harry. But we prefer our own independence, so we will never marry. We meet regularly. He stays at my house near London and I often go to Rome to be with him.'

'You are very lucky, Ethel. I have had no end of trouble with men. I am on my second marriage. My first husband was a millionaire. We never really got on. Our intimate life was a disaster. I sued him for divorce and you could never guess what happened before it came through.'

'Go on...'

'He disappeared in a balloon accident. He either died or simply assumed a different identity. The divorce took an age to come through because he failed to lodge a petition. I never received a cent!'

'I'm dreadfully sorry, Lillian. What terrible luck.'

'That's not the end of the story. I am now suing my second husband for divorce. I rushed into marrying him too soon after the split from my first! He's a tenor from Hungary. Let's say he's of minimal talent. He can barely make a living on his own account, so I've done much to support him. The biggest mistake I have made! But I shouldn't burden you with my troubles with men! What about you? Is this Harry your only love or have you had others?'

'My problems have largely been over women,' said Ethel, as she poured Nordica another glass of wine, leaving her own glass empty. 'When I was a student in Germany, I fell in love with the wife of Heinrich von Herzogenberg, the composer. We loved each other with a passion. We went everywhere together and did many things together. Then, because I started seeing Harry, and because she was told some lies about me by those who were jealous, she abandoned me. I was ravaged by her rejection. But since then I've had several other lady loves which Harry is more than happy to tolerate! Some have not reciprocated my feelings for them but others have!'

'Goodness, Ethel. You have had an interesting set of lovers.'

'One I especially loved was the singer Augusta Redeker. She was wonderful to me and good looking... and has a wonderful voice.'

'Augusta? I know her well. I've sung with her, here and in Europe. She may have loved women then, but she is married now!'

'Yes, I know,' said Ethel. 'What a waste!'

The two of them moved to discussing their career interests, their favourite concert venues, their respective musical educations and their childhoods, Nordica's there in Boston. By then, the two of them were on their second bottle of wine. Nordica was drinking avidly while Ethel watched.

'This is quite an interesting hotel,' said Nordica, slurring her words. 'It's a suite hotel... an enormous building, but there are only eighteen suites. Would you like to see mine?'

'I'd love to,' said Ethel. 'Just let me foot the bill and you lead the way.'

'I'll just finish this glass of wine,' said Nordica.

Nordica, her face lit up in a smile, looked at Ethel as she unlocked the door to her suite. She put out her arm to invite Ethel in. 'Well, here is the entrance hall,' she said. 'In there is the kitchen. Through that door is a dining room and my bedroom through that one. And here is my drawing-room.' She opened the door and Ethel walked in.

'What a comfortable place to stay,' said Ethel, as she gazed at the beautifully furnished room, replete with a large sofa, two armchairs, a bureau and a small polished table surrounded by four closely placed chairs.

'I know,' said Nordica as she almost fell into a sitting position on the sofa. 'Come and sit next to me.'

Ethel did as instructed.

'Ethel, you have been so good to me,' said Nordica, her speech breaking up even more. 'With sympathy and patience, you have listened to my rantings on the men in my life. Despite the trouble one, in particular, has caused, you have told me intimate detail about your loves. And you have been so generous over the meal, especially over the drinks. I feel quite tipsy now! But not too drunk to come up with a new idea!'

'And what is that?' said Ethel, almost certainly knowing she had achieved her aim.

'I relent on what I was so mean about this afternoon. I will tell the director tomorrow, first thing, that we can change the programme and that he must put Der Wald on first! He'll just have time to print the programmes and the flyers!'

'That is so generous of you, Lillian. I just don't know how to show you my appreciation.'

'Just lead me into the bedroom and help me onto the bed.'

Ethel helped her up from the settee and put Nordica's arm over her shoulder to help her stay upright, and slowly manoeuvred her into the bedroom and onto the bed.

'You are still wearing your dress. Are you going to sleep like that?'

'Yes. I'm not going to undress. So I'll stay here as I am. Thanks, again, Ethel,' she said, just about putting sentences together. 'Would you mind seeing yourself out?'

'Not at all. Good night, Lillian. I'm sure you will be better in the morning.'

***

Advertising for the performance proved to be a great success. The audience packed the Metropolitan. They had come from all over New York State, not just the city. The women wore their most extravagant dresses, almost to compete with each other for attention. They had bedecked themselves with their finest gems and their elegant hair styles fitted the occasion. Even Ethel wore a special dress, chosen with the help of Mary. Its black diaphanous material showed off Ethel's figure to a degree unseen before. Mary pinned a bunch of red roses to the shoulder. She looked beautiful.

The audience loved Der Wald. The applause lasted a full ten minutes, during which Ethel took endless curtain calls. She couldn't believe their reaction, especially as she thought the performance was poor. The majority of the press approved it. The sheer number of their reports amazed her. She wrote to Harry telling him she could have papered a room with them.

The second performance at the Metropolitan was equally mediocre, but not according to the audience who enjoyed that one, too.

# CHAPTER 34

## Boston

After Mary's lavish party, which celebrated the success of the New York performances, the two sisters travelled by train to Boston.

'So what exactly is Mr Sargent doing in Boston that warrants your being there with him?' asked Ethel, while they sat in a first class carriage, not knowing quite what to expect for a reply.

'I'm not sure what you are expecting as a response to that one, Ethel. It sounds prying to me. As you know, because I have said so, John and I are good friends. We have been for many years. He asked me if I'd like to accompany him on this visit and I agreed. It is as simple as that. I told you before we left England, he is working on a commission to fresco the Boston Library. He's been there on and off for about ten years.'

'But what about Charlie? What does he think?'

'I have his full blessing,' she said, in a way which didn't convince Ethel.

She was tempted to ask a more intimate question about the relationship but, partly because Mary was paying her expenses, decided not to do so. She would probably work it out for herself when she saw how they interacted with each other in Boston.

Just over four hours later, the train pulled into South Station, in Downtown Boston.

'There's John! He said he'd meet us off the train!' said Mary, standing by the window and sounding overjoyed to see him. 'He said he'd book all three of us into the same hotel. Is that all right with you, Ethel?'

'Of course,' she said, again realising that Mary would be footing the bill and feeling she should accept. She was certain it would be an expensive, comfortable one and it would save Ethel the trouble of finding one for herself.

Mary led the way out of the carriage, rushed towards Sargent and gave him a hug and a kiss. Ethel decided a handshake would be a sufficient greeting so offered her hand. He lifted it towards his lips and kissed it.

'You're welcome!' said Ethel, smiling but surprised. She was puzzled that he was so formally dressed in a grey suit, a white-collared shirt and a bow tie. She didn't remember his extravagant growth of beard, only his large, cumbersome moustache.

'We have a pleasant hotel at Long Wharf on Boston Harbour. You'll both love it!' said Sargent.

Ethel wondered whether he and Mary would have separate rooms. She imagined they would, even if they might be quite adjacent. All three, along with Mary and Ethel's luggage, piled into a two horse cabriolet which soon arrived outside the hotel. Surprisingly, it was nothing like as grand as she expected. It looked distinctly shabby and in need of a coat of paint.

'I have booked nothing extravagant,' said Sargent. 'This is where I'm staying while working at the library, which is an easy walk from here.'

'I see,' said Mary, with a straight face. This wasn't the quality of hotel she expected. Ethel looked on, quite amused at her sister's reaction.

The bell boy showed them to their rooms, which were on the third floor. All three were in a row, with Mary in the centre. The rooms reflected the state of the exterior. Ethel wondered what Mary thought.

'I can't say I'm impressed by this hotel, John,' she said, as all three met in the lobby. 'It's hardly fit for a tramp, let alone your visitors from England. There's a pervading, odd smell in my room which I can't identify and one of the taps is constantly dripping.'

'Maybe, we'll find something a little more to your taste, Mary. It's still only four o'clock in the afternoon.'

Within a couple of hours, they were booking into the Parker House Hotel, near the Waterfront and much more to Mary's liking. Although Sargent also booked a room there, he retained his room in the hotel on the Long Wharf, which the Boston Library was paying for anyway.

'This is much more of the quality of hotel, I am used to,' said Mary, as all three of them were sitting at a dining table, selecting from the menu. 'What do you think, Ethel?'

'I'm absolutely delighted with my room,' said Ethel. 'It truly is beautiful. I've seen nothing as sumptuous since I stayed at Le Grande Hotel in Paris.' She didn't say it was Eugénie's suite, and that she stayed in more modest accommodation.

Ethel found dinner with the two of them awkward, as if Sargent and her sister wanted to say things they didn't want Ethel to hear. So after the main course, she said she felt tired and went off to her room.

*** 

Because of her feelings in the presence of the other two, Ethel decided on an early breakfast. She'd just finished when Mary and Sargent arrived. Interesting that they are together, thought Ethel.

'Good morning, my lovely sister,' said Mary, as she leant over to give Ethel a kiss. 'What are your plans for today?'

'I'm going to the opera house. I've promised to meet the director, and he wants me to attend a rehearsal.'

'Are they still planning to perform it on the Saturday?' said Mary.

'As far as I know.'

'You won't have seen the Grand Opera House,' said Sargent. 'It's not an opera house at all. It's a theatre!' he laughed, as if to minimise the significance of the venue and that Ethel's opera was to be performed there.

'That doesn't worry me one iota,' said Ethel, in sharp response. 'They can perform any opera in a theatre, and an opera house is anyway little more than a glorified theatre.'

Ethel wished them a good day together, recovered her copy of the score from her room and set off for the Grand Opera House, in Washington Street.

'Ah, we are expecting you, Miss Smyth,' said the lady at the ticket office. What a relief thought, Ethel. For once, I don't need to fight to enter the place.

Moments later, Ethel introduced herself to Wilhelm Geriche, who would take the rostrum.

'I'm delighted to meet you, Miss Smyth. I'm so pleased to be conducting your wonderful opera!'

'Oh,' said a surprised Ethel. 'I'm so pleased you like it!'

'It's one of the most original operas I've heard since Parsifal. It is truly brilliant and your music meshes so well with the libretto.'

Ethel could have kissed him but restrained herself. 'I'm absolutely delighted!'

'I am so pleased the cast of the Met performances are playing here, too. That makes it so much easier for me as the conductor! Miss Gadski, the lead soloist, has been so helpful, I'm sure the performance here will be unforgettable!'

This lovely man impressed Ethel. He reminded her of Tchaikovsky, not only because he was so sympathetic and gentle but he also looked similar to the great composer. She could only hope that the Boston performance under Geriche would be better than those in New York. It couldn't be much worse.

'Is there anything particular you would like to contribute to the rehearsal, Miss Smyth?'

'I don't think so, but I would like to attend,' she said. 'But if I can see something that needs changing, do you mind me interrupting?'

'No, Miss Smyth. Let's go through to the auditorium. The entire company is ready to start!'

The rehearsal went well. Ethel made a few interjections but only when she thought the orchestra were overpowering the soloist or a section of the choir. She returned to the hotel satisfied and expected a high-quality performance, especially as a good number of the orchestra were members of the Boston Symphony, including the conductor.

***

The performance of Der Wald in Boston was one of the worst performances Ethel had heard of her works, or anyone else's. It was as if the orchestra and the soloists and choir had never met before the night, let alone having spent two days in full rehearsal. Geriche had totally ignored Ethel's pleas for a greater balance between the orchestra and the singers. At one point, the choir were silent when they should have accompanied the soloist. At another a soloist failed completely to sing her lines. It was worse than either of the New York performances, and they were bad enough. Ethel was therefore utterly staggered at the amazingly enthusiastic reception the audience gave it. She and Herr Geriche took bows for an age. Again, apart from the Daily Telegraph, the press were unimpressed.

To celebrate the event, Mary invited all the singers, Geriche and the mayor and mayoress of Boston, to a party she had organised at the Parker House Hotel.

'Congratulations, Ethel. That was a brilliant success. You won't be forgotten in Boston for a very long time,' said Sargent, as he uncorked a bottle of champagne.

'I totally agree, Ethel,' said Mary. 'It was a privilege to attend. And what an incredible reception!'

'I don't understand,' said Ethel. 'The performance was an utter disaster. What happened, Herr Geriche? What went wrong?'

Geriche stuttered and stumbled. 'I'm not sure what you mean, Miss Smyth. Would you care to elaborate? It was a success. The audience loved it!'

'It was a disaster,' shouted Ethel. 'I was ashamed to be there. It was the most unmusical event of the century... so far. If Saint Cecilia had been there, she'd have run out and jumped off the Washington Street Bridge!' Ethel couldn't help displaying her fury.

A soloist overheard her. 'I agree with Miss Smyth. Your orchestra almost drowned us out,' he said, speaking directly to Geriche.

'I don't agree,' said the conductor. 'Your singing was always clear. How could you know? You weren't on the rostrum.'

'Our singing absolutely could not be heard!' said one of the other soloists. 'It was one of the worst pieces of conducting I've had the misfortune to experience. You even put off the soloists! It was a miracle that the audience reacted so well. I'm pleased for Miss Smyth that they did. Had I been in the audience, I'd have walked out!'

'Hear, hear,' said one of the male soloists. Turning to Geriche he said, 'If I was your boss I'd sack you on the spot and run you out of the concert hall!'

'I'm going now!' said Geriche. 'I've had enough of these unjustified insults. This is becoming nasty and I don't intend to be on the receiving end of a punch.' He promptly left. No farewells. Not even an acknowledgement of the hostess.

'That was all a bit strained,' said Sargent.

'Served him right!' said Mary. 'Although I must admit, I couldn't see much wrong with the performance. Speaking solely for myself, I quite enjoyed it.'

'That's because you are not familiar with the score,' said Ethel. 'But let's not prolong this line of argument. We are here to celebrate!'

'I agree,' said Mary. 'That's why I've invited all these people. I'll have paid good money for this and I don't want it to degenerate into a series of recriminations over what some regard as an unsatisfactory performance!'

'Now that the prime culprit has left, I'm certain that order will be restored,' said Miss Gadski.

'I truly hope so,' said Sargent. He banged a spoon on a table to silence those present. 'We are here as guests of the Honourable Mrs Mary Hunter to celebrate the performance of her sister Ethel Smyth's opera, Der Wald, in this famous city. Could you please raise your glasses to honour Miss Smyth?'

An enthusiastic round of applause filled the capacious room. Ethel looked at Mary. She wondered if Mary had asked Sargent to make this announcement but by the scowl on her face and her raised eyebrows thought not.

'Tell me, John, would it be possible to see your work in the library before Mary and I return to England? How long have you been working on them?'

'Over ten years now and there is still much to do. It will take at least another ten years! Yes, Mary has seen a lot of the work, but you must see what I have done so far!'

*** 

On seeing John Singer Sargent's work in the Boston Central Library in Copley Square, Ethel realised, if she hadn't before, that he was a giant of an artist, a master in his own field. She felt overawed by these touching, profoundly religious works, full of symbolism and emotion.

Ethel was beginning to feel homesick for One Oak and Pan. She regarded her sojourn to America as only a partial success. While the performances of Der Wald made good money for the opera houses and a modest amount for her, she thought her work was wasted on the Americans and vowed never to return.

# CHAPTER 35

## Winnaretta


Ethel and Mary spent more time apart on the return journey than they did together. While they were close in some ways, as they were when causing havoc at school, over the years they had grown some way apart. And Mary made it clear, if not by direct reference, she regarded herself as the superior of the two, because she was the wealthier. That Ethel was the more talented didn't feature in her landscape. Ethel made sure, mainly not to upset Mary, that they ate together, but between meals Ethel would usually find something separate to do such as to play deck quoits or practice her golf shots in an improvised driving net. She also spent time working on her new opera. Various ideas for the title entered her mind. Finally, she decided on 'The Wreckers', the name the Cornish locals used to describe themselves and their ship destroying activities. Harry would surely approve.

***

'I'm so glad to see you,' said Mrs Faulkner, as Ethel walked through into the hall of One Oak. 'Everyone has missed you, especially the Empress Eugénie, who has been here several times to ask when you would be back. Pan has missed you, too. Anyway, you look well after your trip. How did it go?' Before Ethel could utter a word, Pan bounded up to her and licked her face.

A tired Ethel patted Pan on the back and told Faulkner in outline, not wanting to spend too much time talking. She was more interested in her correspondence. 'Have we received many letters while I've been away?'

'Looks like a lot of bills, but one big one from Rome, presumably from Mr Brewster. I'll fetch them.'

Ethel was soon opening the thick envelope from Rome. It quite surprised her. He'd enclosed the draft libretto for the opera. She put it to one side to study after a good night's sleep. She read it at breakfast. As they had agreed, he had written it in French, the language he felt more at home with than English. The more of it she read, the more she enjoyed it. It bowled her over. Harry's monumental work inspired her to press on with the score.

'You look very excited, Miss Smyth,' said Faulkner, as she brought Ethel a cup of tea and a rack of toast.

'Mr Brewster has written a libretto for my new opera. You remember you posted the story to him before I went to America. I am delighted with it. Thrilled! It is a masterpiece. I will do for the music what this wonderful man has done for my life!'

'I'm pleased for you, Miss Smyth. Would you like another cup of tea?'

'Yes, please, and could you bring my cigarettes?'

***

'It's you, my dearest!' said Eugénie, as she put down The Times. 'I wondered when you'd be back. I've been over to yours twice to see whether you'd returned. And Mary Ponsonby has also been trying to contact you. She joined me for the afternoon only yesterday. So how did it go? Did you like the Americans?'

Ethel launched into her report, explaining the various problems she'd encountered and how she'd overcome the ones she solved and the ones she didn't.

'You're not telling me you got Nordica drunk and seduced her into changing her mind.'

'Definitely not. Yes, I plied her with drink and ended up helping her onto her bed! But nothing else happened, honestly.'

'I believe you, Ethel. Why shouldn't I? Anyway, well done! So the performances were that bad then?'

'On the whole, I was disappointed. Ironically, the audiences loved Der Wald. I had curtain calls, standing ovations and everything I could expect. The New York press went crazy over it. I've brought back enough notices to paper my lounge! But the quality of the playing and singing was abysmal.'

'The main thing is the reception, Ethel. It's not what you think of it. No one cares about that, only you! It's what the paying public thinks! You must take something from the fact that you are the first woman to have their work performed at the New York Metropolitan Opera!'

'You are probably right, Eugénie. But I've never subscribed to the idea of being a woman composer. I'm a composer and my gender doesn't come into it. It is a record all the same!'

'You still haven't taken up my idea of a holiday at Birkhall… with Harry, if you wish. He'd love it there. We could laze in the gardens, visit Balmoral and even go to Edinburgh if you wanted to.'

'You are good, Eugénie. We'll definitely take you up on that. But I don't remember telling you about our latest project.'

'No. Our latest?' said Eugénie, stressing the 'our'.

'Yes. We're writing another opera.' Ethel explained the idea and how it had occurred to her. She told her about Harry's brilliant libretto and how delighted she was with it.

They spent the rest of the morning chatting until Ethel returned home to work on the new project. She started by having a closer look at Harry's libretto. She began to have second thoughts, not about the whole thing but about various aspects of it. So rather than resume work on the music, she wrote to him about what in the libretto she didn't like. His reply didn't please her. He told her that her understanding of the nuances in French was wanting. He rejected most of the changes she suggested. She responded with further ideas for change and dismissed several of the changes he wanted in his reply. A stream of correspondence followed. There were arguments about whether the lovers' past should feature in the opera and several exchanges about the number of syllables in a particular word. Eventually they agreed on the full text.

In the meantime, she pressed on with the score. She made rapid progress. She wrote to Harry to tell him she had never felt more confident about her skills as a composer, especially at orchestration.

'Mrs Faulkner! Mrs Faulkner! I have to tell you! I've completed the score for The Wreckers! I've finished it!'

Mrs Faulkner didn't know quite what to say. 'That sounds good news to me, Miss Smyth. I have enjoyed listening to some of the tunes when you played them on the piano!'

'Only some of them, Mrs Faulkner?'

'I liked the softer ones, but some were a bit too noisy for me,' she said, sounding apologetic.

Sensing she had made Mrs Faulkner feel embarrassed, Ethel replied. 'The fact that you like some of them is quite sufficient for me!' Mrs Faulkner smiled.

***

Eighteen months after she returned from America, Ethel started touting The Wreckers around the great opera venues of Europe. One of her greatest skills was playing her works to prospective customers. Raging enthusiasm greeted her committed renderings. Ethel failed to gain a contract out of one of them. Arthur Nikisch, then director at Leipzig, was ready to sign, but the board fired him for unnecessary extravagance before he could take his pen from his pocket. Ethel was bitterly disappointed. She thought that to achieve a performance at the opera house there would be one of the crowning glories of her career. Neumann, the opera director in Prague, thought The Wreckers was an utter masterpiece but claimed he had insufficient funds to perform it. Eugénie felt awful about Ethel's failed efforts. She attempted to help by contacting her close friend, the Prince of Monaco, for a performance in Monte Carlo. That looked promising until the resident director left in a huff and his successor abandoned the idea.

***

Ethel loved Paris. She went there for a short break but also to engage in the cultural activities of this great city… and to promote The Wreckers. She met a wide spectrum of artists, musicians and writers. John Sargent arranged for her to be invited to a salon where she could meet a number of people of similar interests to hers. The hostess greeted her at the door.

364

'Good evening. May I ask who you are?'

'Of course. I am Ethel Smyth. I compose music and live near London. I am on good terms with John Sargent, the American artist. He is a good friend of my sister Mary.'

'Ethel, I am so pleased to meet you! I know him well. He's even painted a portrait of me! He's told me so much about you and I feel we may be like-minded people! Do come in. There are several composers here and I'll introduce you to them. Oh... I am Princesse Winnaretta de Polignac. I'm sure we will speak to each other later and I will tell you more about me and you can tell me more about yourself. In the meantime, I will do some introductions.'

Ethel thought she was in a dream. She could not believe the range of people she was meeting. Claude Debussy, Maurice Ravel and the young Eric Satie. Ravel said he loved the Princesse who had sponsored a number of his works. He had dedicated Pavane pour une Infante Défunte to her, such was the level of his admiration. Debussy said he'd love to hear some of Ethel's work, so they promised to arrange a meeting later, either in London or there in Paris. Princesse de Polignac interrupted Ethel while she was talking to these fascinating composers.

'My dear Ethel, I apologise for abandoning you for so long. Leaving you with these noisy people. You must tell me more about yourself and we can exchange our life's experiences.' They sat at a table away from the general bustle of the party.

Ethel told her about her music and her loves. She told her about her relationships with Lisl, Pauline Trevelyan, Mary Benson, Mary Ponsonby, Harry and Empress Eugénie.

'My God! You love women in the same way as I do. I've fucked more of them than you, I guarantee! I just hate sex with men! On the wedding night, with my first husband, I was terrified. Just to escape his cock, I ended up on top of the wardrobe. I couldn't stand the thought of it. There and then, I threatened to kill him! It wasn't long before I divorced him! My second aristocrat of a husband was much older and compliant. He was Prince Edmond de Polignac. We had a wonderful life together until he passed on, just five years ago. Since then, I've never looked back, and am achieving my ambitions in promoting these young composers, writers and artists. They love me! They know I won't cause them any problems. Quite the opposite. I've spent thousands on them. Thousands.'

'You've led an amazing life, Winnaretta. It definitely has parallels with mine!'

'Ethel, we must meet in more relaxed circumstances. I'd love to know you better. We should become friends. Would you like that?'

How could Ethel resist? This amazing woman philanthropist may even be willing to help her. 'Of course. When should we meet?'

'Tomorrow for lunch. I am staying at the Le Grande Hotel. Would you be free then?'

'Yes. In fact, I've stayed there twice before. It is an excellent hotel!'

***

Ethel met Winnaretta in the hotel reception. A waiter escorted them to a table overlooking the Boulevard des Capucines.

'Well, here we are, Ethel. We started talking to each other at the salon, but I'm sorry we could go no further. Unfortunately or otherwise, I was the hostess, so I had to circulate!'

'I was so amused by what you said about your first wedding night and climbing onto the wardrobe!'

'It's true, Ethel. He knew all about my love of women and agreed he wouldn't fuck me. So as he got his cock out and wanted to try it on, I jumped on the *armoire*. It wasn't a high one! I took out a knife and threatened to kill him. I managed to keep him at bay. We never consummated the marriage, not once in the five years. He ended up hating me and moving out. Mind you, I hated him just as much!'

While surprised at her brutal coarseness of language, this slim, attractive woman fascinated Ethel. She would have been about ten years younger than her and looked modern, dressed in a floral print dress with her hair cut short. She wondered if Winnaretta would find her as attractive as the many women she said she had made love to. Ethel had never met a woman before who was so open about her Sapphism.

'So tell me more about the women you've had relationships with, Ethel. It quite excites me to talk about such things!'

Ethel told her more about her relationship with Lisl and how it all ended. She talked about her fondness for Pauline Trevelyan and how strongly they felt about each other. Then she told her about her encounter with Princess Maria von Bülow and their bathing together. The story ended with making Lillian Nordica drunk and leaving her on her bed.

'Don't tell me Ethel, you made love to her before you left her!'

'I did no such thing,' said Ethel, raising her voice. 'But I left a note on her dressing table, reminding her that she'd agreed to put my opera first on the programme at the Metropolitan Opera!'

'I'll tell you what, Ethel. We'll go to my room and you can play me some of your music. I am quite good on the piano and I'll play for you, too!'

They finished their lunch and made their way to Winnaretta's room. Ethel wondered what would happen next and what this woman really wanted of her. Winnaretta opened the unlocked door and they stepped in. The scene that confronted them shocked Ethel into silence. Two young women were lying naked on the bed. They appeared to be asleep.

'Oh, I'm sorry, Ethel. These are two young friends of mine. We had a threesome this morning and I thought they'd have gone by now! Come on you two. Time you fucked off.' She went up to the bed and shook them awake. Hoping Ethel hadn't seen it, she then picked up a dildo from the bed and slipped it into a dressing-table drawer.

Ethel looked on as they draped some bedclothes around themselves and disappeared into the bathroom. Winnaretta and Ethel stood silently in the middle of the room. Moments later, the two girls appeared fully dressed.

'Goodbye,' said Winnaretta as they left, looking more than slightly embarrassed.

An upright piano stood by the wall opposite the window. 'Let me play you something, Ethel. Sit on the bed and I will play you a piece by Chopin. I can see you are shocked by what you've seen and this will calm you down.'

She played several of the Etudes from Opus 10. The exquisite quality of her playing amazed Ethel. 'You are a brilliant pianist, Winnaretta. That was simply a delight! You really know those pieces and play them with incredible sensitivity.'

'What praise, Ethel. Now it's your turn to play something!'

Ethel played the overture to Act 1 of The Wreckers. She hammered it out in her usual style.

'Whatever piece is that, Ethel? I've never heard it before. It's a work of true genius.'

'I wrote it myself. It's the overture to my latest opera, The Wreckers.'

'An opera, Ethel? So what is the story?'

Ethel explained the background and the origin of the title. 'It's really a tragic love story, Winnaretta. Thirza is married to the local priest. Mark falls for her and abandons Avis, his love until then. Mark and Thirza can see that the activities of the locals in stealing the ships' cargoes is wrong. So they divert them back to their proper course using beacons on the cliffs. What they do disgusts the locals, who sentence them to death by drowning in a cave as it fills when the tide comes in. They die in each other's arms. So quite a tragedy.'

'My God, Ethel. What a bloody fantastic plot! Is it original? It sounds very English!'

'Yes, I invented the plot some years after going to where these people actually wrecked the ships and looted them.'

'Has anyone performed it?'

368

'No. I've touted it all around the opera houses in Europe, but no one wants to play it. The nearest I've got is a promise in Leipzig, but they dismissed the director for overspending his budget! His replacement sounded quite interested but I haven't heard a word from them since I was there, just a few months ago. I've all but given up hope.'

'Ethel, I can help you. Have you tried the opera house in Brussels? Only I have some excellent contacts there.'

Ethel's face lit up. 'No. To be honest, I've never tried Brussels. It would be wonderful if you could succeed where I have failed!'

'Leave it to me, my new friend. I'll write to my contact at the Royal Theatre of Monnaie. I can't guarantee you a result, but at least I can try.'

'Dear Winnaretta, that's a wonderful thing to do.'

At that point they were both sitting on the bed. Winnaretta moved closer to Ethel and hugged her. She then leant over and kissed her firmly on the lips. Her hand touched Ethel's thigh and began to stroke her. Ethel wasn't sure how to respond or whether to respond at all. She had to admit that she found this younger woman attractive.

Then suddenly Winnaretta broke the silence. 'I'm sorry, Ethel. I can't go through with this!'

'Please don't worry,' said Ethel, quite relieved. She felt strangely awkward about this encounter. She didn't want to feel obliged to engage physically with the woman in return of her promise of help with The Wreckers. That would have been wrong.

'It must be because I did it with the other two this morning. I'm so sorry!'

'No, please, Winnaretta. I'm grateful to you for what you are doing for me. So it's not a problem.'

Ethel believed the younger woman didn't find her especially attractive, and that is why she stopped. That wouldn't worry Ethel in the least.

Ethel spent a week and more in Paris. She felt welcomed in Winnaretta's circle of friends and acquaintances. Winnaretta introduced her to Hélène de Caraman-Chimay, a Romanian by birth who a few years before had married Prince Alexandre de Caraman-Chimay, a minor member of the Belgium royal family. Hélène and Ethel became good friends. A musician in her own right, Hélène looked up to Ethel for her achievements. She introduced Ethel to her mother, a charming lady, a few years older than Ethel, who also lived in Paris.

Ethel played her chamber works and sang her songs in Winnaretta's salon to a startling range of famous people, Sickert, Diaghilev, Stravinsky, Verlaine, Cocteau, Fauré and Chabrier among them. Although she did not meet all of them, in any direct sense, they all applauded her playing and singing. She dined on the adulation. Influenced by homesickness and the need to see Pan, she decided she'd had enough of this socialising and returned to England.

# CHAPTER 36

## The Wreckers performed?

Ethel was becoming more and more depressed about her failure to secure a performance of The Wreckers. Harry worried about her health. She became so introverted and nervous, she wouldn't even go to the local shops to buy a packet of hairpins. Even her relationship with Pan cooled off. The poor dog seemed as worried as Harry, who thought of taking her to Rome for a few weeks. That would give her a chance to recover in relaxed surroundings, away from the pressures of running One Oak and the persistent memories of her failures abroad.

They were sitting out on the balcony of his apartment there having a summer evening drink when Harry suggested an idea to promote the opera.

'You said the director in Prague liked The Wreckers.'

'Yes, that's right.'

'And they couldn't afford to stage it?'

'Right.'

'I have a thought. I would like to invest £1,000 in persuading them to perform it there.'

'My God! You can't do that, Harry! It's simply not fair for you to back it with your own money. I won't have it. It's simply not right.'

'It's my money, Ethel, and I can do what I like with it. If I choose to spend it on your opera... or rather our opera... that's my prerogative. So that's what I'm going to do! It might even turn out to be a profitable investment!'

'Harry, you are too generous. I graciously accept your proposal. Not that you are giving me much choice in the matter. One thing is clear, though. I love you so much!'

'I'm not sure whether the opera house will regard it as bribery and corruption. I don't really care. But I'll send the director a cheque. What did you say his name is? Do you have the address?'

'Just a minute, Harry. I'll fetch my diary. It's in there... Here it is. Oh yes, I remember now, his first name is Angelo... Angelo Neumann.'

Between them, Harry and Ethel composed a covering letter and posted it that day, then settled back into their relaxing break in Rome. In Harry's company, his way of cooking Italian food and with a generous share of Italian wine, Ethel was soon feeling much better so, after a fortnight's recuperation, returned to England.

No sooner than she had been at home, she received a letter from her new friend, Winnaretta.

'Guess what, Mrs Faulkner! The director of opera in Brussels wants me to go there and play a piano version of The Wreckers to him!' Ethel was overjoyed. Up to then, no one had shown sufficient interest in the opera to invite her to play it to them.

'That sounds great, Miss Smyth! When shall I pack you a bag?' asked the cheery housekeeper.

'Not just yet. I must sort out a date to go there and make the bookings. My first task is to write to my friend in Paris.'

***

Within three weeks, Ethel was sitting at a grand piano on the stage of the Royal Theatre of Monnaie singing her condensed version of the opera to an audience of three, the opera director, the potential conductor and the choirmaster. They absolutely loved it. A round of applause greeted the sad ending.

'It is a stunning opera,' said the director. 'The plot is so original. The audiences in Brussels will love it!'

'Your two overtures are tremendous,' said the conductor.

'The words are so sensitive and powerful,' said the choirmaster.

372

Their comments enthralled her. There was something magical about the way she performed these recitals. She had mastered the art of playing her works with an enthusiasm that affected the toughest and most critical of listeners.

Within a few days of returning to England, she received a letter postmarked Brussels. She tore it open. Disappointment. The director said how impressive the work was but couldn't see how it would fit into their programme. Ethel could have sworn out loud.

Undeterred by this setback, she thought again how and where she might succeed. She convinced herself that these obstacles were artificial, synthetic excuses for not performing what she regarded as her best work to date. It became obvious what she should do next: go to Vienna and persuade Gustav Mahler to direct The Wreckers there!

She wondered how she might play this interesting card. Should she write to him with the score? He doubtless received many requests to perform operas and other works, mainly from Austrian or German composers. Did she want The Wreckers to be one of dozens of works in his in-tray? No. She would go there unannounced to see him in person.

She could hardly sleep that night, she was so consumed by this new idea. And what an accolade to have the thing produced in Vienna by no less than one of the most famous conductors and composers of the twentieth century. She had heard none of his work performed, but had read some startling reviews of his songs and symphonies.

'It looks like Mr Brewster has sent you a letter, Miss Smyth,' said Mrs Faulkner, as she brought Ethel a second cup of tea at breakfast. She was expecting a letter from him and its content delighted her.

'Mrs Faulkner, you'll love to hear this. The opera director in Prague is definitely going to perform The Wreckers. He wants me to go there to hear the singers he's chosen, presumably to help select them for the roles they'll be playing. He's already conducting rehearsals! They will play it in the 06 to 07 season, probably in November, so only a couple of months away.'

'That is wonderful news, Miss Smyth. I'm so pleased for you, after all those visits you've made to Germany and France.'

'It is good news, Mrs Faulkner! I cannot tell you how delighted I am. He wants me to go over as soon as possible and he'll pay my expenses.'

***

Just over a week later, Ethel was sitting in Angelo Neumann's palatial office in the State Opera House in Prague. She remembered his bright brown eyes and his enormous moustache, which protruded several inches beyond the width of his head.

'I'm pleased you could return here so quickly, Ethel. As you will know from my letter to Mr Brewster, I thought you should be able to listen to whom we had selected to sing the vocal parts in your opera.'

'It is an honour for me, Angelo. I have struggled so much to push this opera towards a performance. I believe it's my best composition. Mr Brewster wrote the libretto so I'm much indebted to him.'

'I said when you were here before that it's an utter masterpiece and I mean it now as I meant it then.'

'You are too kind, Angelo!'

'I have scheduled a rehearsal for tomorrow at ten o'clock, so would you be available to attend? We'll concentrate on the solo parts, which is why I have asked you over. I hope you will be comfortable in your hotel. Have whatever you like for dinner and don't forget a drink. I would join you, but I have another engagement tonight.'

'That's not a problem, Angelo. I'll see you at ten o'clock.'

Ethel made her way to her hotel and went to her room, where she promptly fell asleep. She must have slept for hours because it was dark when she awoke. She made her way to the restaurant, ate on her own, enjoyed a cigar with coffee afterwards and then went straight to bed.

The following morning, as soon as soon as Ethel arrived at Neumann's office, he placed a document in her hand. 'This is addressed to you. It's a telegram. I hope it's not bad news.' She opened it carefully, wondering what it could be about. Could something have happened to Mary Ponsonby or Eugénie? Or even to her sister Mary? Had there been a fire at One Oak? She scanned it.

'I'm amazed, Angelo. It's from Richard Hagel, in Leipzig. My friend Harry in Rome forwarded it to you. He is performing the Wreckers there on 11 November. I'm ecstatic. Isn't that wonderful news!' I huge smile formed across her face.

'Ethel, I'm thrilled for you! That could be its first performance. I have scheduled it for the second week in December. So I'm pleased for you and disappointed at the same time. I'd loved to have been the first to perform it. But no matter. Let's take you through to the auditorium!'

After the amazing news from Leipzig, the rehearsals seemed an anti-climax. Ethel listened intently. The soloists Neumann had chosen seemed good. None was known to her, but each could clearly sing their role. Ethel wondered what her part could be in this rehearsal. He had selected them and it would have been difficult if not impossible for Ethel to suggest he replace anyone.

'Congratulations, Angelo. You have chosen a superb group of soloists and I'm certain they will do a brilliant job in the actual performance!'

'I'm glad we have your approval, Ethel. I'll write to let you know the exact date. You must come!'

'I will be there, of course! And now I must catch a train to Leipzig to discuss the opera with Richard Hagel.'

'Good luck, Ethel. We'll see you in December, then!'

***

Ethel felt exhausted by the time she arrived in Leipzig. On the train, she wondered what Hagel's attitude would be. Surely, he would be less than enthusiastic about an opera championed by Arthur Nikisch, his predecessor. She'd heard that he was a temperamental individual who could explode like a Chinese firecracker. She met him in the foyer of the New Theatre.

'I'm delighted to meet you, Miss Smyth,' he said. He stood a full six feet six tall. His facial skin was blotchy and powdery, so he appeared to suffer from some form of dermal complaint.

'Likewise, I'm pleased to meet you, Herr Hagel.'

He was so kind to her. He took great trouble in showing her around the New Theatre. She had been to several performances there when a student but had never seen the theatre in such detail before with its maze of corridors which seemed to lead nowhere and its vast number of rooms. He took her into one of them, which turned out to be his office.

'I am so pleased to take over the production of your opera where Arthur Nikisch left off. As you will remember, he showed you a draft contract the director had drawn up and, essentially, we would like to offer you the same terms. I'm not sure if you are aware, but there will be two performances, the premiere and the second, two nights later.'

Ethel was too tired to tease out the meaning of 'essentially' so accepted what he was proposing.

'And we are using the same singers and chorus which Arthur chose. Is there anything you would wish to stipulate, as the composer?'

'I'm delighted with what you have told me and your incredible kindness. I'm thrilled that you will play it twice. That is absolutely wonderful! There is only one thing that I ask. It is that you should make no changes to the score without my expressed approval.'

'Miss Smyth, we wouldn't dream of doing otherwise. You can rely on the company here not to touch it without your written agreement. If we want to change something, we will write to you at your home address. Is that all right?'

'Of course. I would expect no less.'

'In which case we look forward to seeing you at the rehearsals!'

They shook hands and said goodbye to each other. Ethel felt delighted. She had secured the deal which Nikisch had agreed, or all but, and could make her way home knowing that this gentleman would write if there were any issues relating to the performance. She felt happier and less tired on the journey back to London.

***

On her first night at home, lying in her bed and unable to sleep, Ethel wondered what role she should play in the performance in Leipzig. She'd discuss this with Eugénie.

'Tell me, my dear friend. The New Theatre in Leipzig are playing The Wreckers on the eleventh of November. I shall go there, naturally. I usually go well in advance and become quite involved in the rehearsals from several points of view. To be honest, I feel tired. I don't want to go there beforehand. I'm thinking of going just for the performance. Leaving all the details to the director and the conductor. What do you think, Eugénie?'

'The answer is simple, Ethel. Leave them to it. You become too involved in these performances. You react badly when the director doesn't stick exactly to your score. Frankly, it doesn't matter. I've told you before, the key is what the audience thinks. How they react. It's not what you think. So, have a few weeks at home and arrive a few days before the performance. Honestly, Ethel. That's my view… for what it's worth!'

'You are too modest, Eugénie. But do you know what? I'm going to take your advice.'

Ethel wrote to Richard Hagel to tell him she would trust him and his company to take responsibility for the early rehearsals and that she would play no part. She said she would attend the performances.

***

Ethel turned up in Leipzig the day before the final dress rehearsal.

'Please, Herr Hagel, could you let me see your preforming version of my score?' Ethel skimmed through it. The first two acts were exactly as she had written it. But the third was almost unrecognisable.

'So you lied, Herr Hagel. I'm bitterly disappointed with you! You've desecrated my score without even telling me. That was not what we agreed. Act three is a total mess.'

'We made a few changes because it was too long and confusing.'

'You are talking utter rubbish. I shall not be attending your dress rehearsal or the performance. I shall be visiting some friends of mine here, instead.'

'Please, Miss Smyth, you can't do that. We've arranged a gigantic party in your honour.'

Ethel relented and, when the time came for the performance, hid herself in the audience. She was amazed how well it went. The orchestra was especially good. An enormous round of applause erupted after the second act. A blast of clapping and foot stamping greeted the end of Act 3. The audience were delirious in their reception of it. The director and Hagel were ecstatic. Ethel revealed herself and made her way onto the stage. She, Hagel and the director took thirteen curtain calls.

Ethel basked in the adulation heaped upon her at the director's party. Each of the principals in the orchestra attended, along with the soloists, the lead singers in the chorus and critics from the press. Even her old teacher, Carl Reinecke, was there. All of them congratulated her, even Reinecke.

'There is something I would like to suggest to you, director. I've been thinking.'

'Please, tell me, Miss Smyth.'

'I would like you to reinstate the parts you have cut from the opera. If you agree, we will meet at half past ten in the morning, with the cast and orchestra and simply put the parts back. It won't take long. You would then perform it as I wanted.'

'What do you think, Richard,' said the director?

'I'm sure we can all agree to that reasonable suggestion,' said Hagel.

So the night ended in smiles and a joyful air of happiness.

The following morning, just as Ethel arrived at the New Theatre, Hagel's assistant presented her with two notes, one each from Hagel and the director. Hagel said he would not re-insert the cut parts. He would either play it as he had the night before or not at all. The director simply said he was sorry that he could not persuade Hagel to do what they agreed at the party. Ethel asked the assistant for some notepaper and scribbled a reply to each of them, saying unless they agreed to make the changes by that evening, she would withdraw it and there would be no second performance. Neither of them replied.

Ethel drafted a letter setting out her proposed actions and sent it to the local daily newspaper, the Leipziger Tageblatt. On the third day, she went to the empty orchestra platform and retrieved every piece of Wreckers script, the full score and all the stage directions, piled them into a case and took the midday train to Prague. She had possibly made an enemy of every opera director in Germany, but perhaps she had not.

# CHAPTER 37

## Mahler

Ethel went straight from the railway station to the Opera House. There were people milling around in the foyer, some talking urgently to others as if something important had happened. She spoke to the lady at the ticket office. She knew no Czech, so spoke in German.

'My name is Ethel Smyth. On 12 December, the Opera House will perform my opera, The Wreckers. Herr Neumann will conduct it. Is Herr Neumann available? I'd like to speak to him, if possible.'

'I'm afraid I have bad news for you. Herr Neumann has suffered a stroke and is very ill. Have you seen the newspaper reports?'

'No. I've just arrived from Leipzig.'

'I see. He is in bed, paralysed. He's unconscious and unable to speak. It's chaos here. No one knows what is being performed and what we will cancel.'

'Is there anyone in authority I can speak to?'

'I don't know who's in authority now. All I can suggest is that you go into the main auditorium and speak to someone there. There are some members of the orchestra, several of the principals, and you may even find a conductor. They may be about to do a rehearsal. I'm not sure.'

'I'm grateful. You have been so helpful.' Ethel was shocked, upset and disappointed. It reminded her of the situation in Berlin when Pierson died. Although the opera house was unfamiliar to her, she soon found her way into the auditorium where scattered groups of musicians were talking to each other. She approached a group carrying violins and explained who she was and why she was there.

'Do you know if you are going to perform my opera? It's due on 12 December,' she said, speaking to the entire group.

'I've not heard of it,' said a young girl. 'Do any of you know?'

'No. I'm not aware of it,' said a bearded man who looked quite a lot older.

'I know of it,' said a young musician who admitted he was a student. 'It's on the programme, but I've heard nothing about rehearsals.'

'If you want to find out more, I suggest you come back one night, after a performance,' said the young girl. 'That way you might speak to a conductor. But we don't have a director for now.'

Ethel spent the following weeks trying to inject some order into chaos. She visited the opera house every day, but some days there was not a soul there. She could not detect a rehearsal because, apparently, there was none. No one seemed to know anything about The Wreckers, except that it was in the programme for 12 December. She discovered that several other works under Neumann's control had been removed. It took her little effort worked out why hers was there: Harry's cheque. Had the opera house or Neumann taken the money? She hoped it was the Opera House, despite the cheque being written out to Neumann. Then she thought again. Surely, if Neumann had pocketed the cash, the opera house would not know about it and Ethel's opera would be treated like any other. No. Neumann had given the money to the Opera House, and that's why it was being performed. She smiled to herself. Angelo Neumann had proved himself an honest man.

The performance was a disgrace, even worse than the one of Der Wald in Boston. There had been no rehearsals at all. Every member of the orchestra was reading from sight, as were the soloists and chorus. Ethel could have cried to hear her creation so badly mutilated. The press demolished the orchestral playing. They had never heard this pre-eminent ensemble play so badly. One of the German papers attributed it to the scoring, but Ethel knew otherwise.

This was the second major disappointment she had suffered over The Wreckers. So she felt even stronger about seeing Gustav Mahler, whom she regarded as a strong, proud individual who would ensure a brilliant performance. Few had a better name in Europe for conducting opera.

***

After she arrived back at One Oak, she went to see Harry at his daughter's house. It wasn't far away, so she walked there with Pan on his lead. She explained to him what had happened in Leipzig and Prague.

'Are you sure you won't regret taking all the music and leaving poor old Hagel with nothing to perform? You could have antagonised many people, Ethel. After all, the audience enjoyed the performance he gave. And from what you say, the press were quite receptive, too.'

'I have no regrets. Not for one second, Harry. They reneged on the agreement they made the night before. I gave them the chance to change their minds. They refused. So I was within my rights to take back the music.'

'I'm not so sure, Ethel. The proof will be when you want anything else performed in Leipzig or anywhere else in Germany. You did something that no one else will have done... ever before... and many will know about it soon if they don't already!'

'Are you castigating me, Harry?'

'Not at all, Ethel. I'm just making observations! I'm on your side. What you did was highly courageous! So they didn't perform it well in Prague either?'

'Harry, it was a total disaster. The orchestra hadn't rehearsed a note between them. I felt sorry for you. I'm afraid we wasted that £1,000 you sent them.'

'I did it for you, Ethel! At least they performed it, however badly. So what are you planning next?'

'I'm going to try Vienna. Gustav Mahler will make a wonderful job of it.'

'Mahler?'

'Yes, the opera director at the Vienna Opera House. He's well known as a composer, too. He writes songs and symphonies.'

'Hmm... long way to go, Ethel. Haven't you had enough of begging the opera directors of Europe... and all that tiresome travel?'

'I'm having one more shot before I try Covent Garden. I'm going to turn up at Mahler's office with the score and play it to him. He won't know how to refuse.'

'That's not the best idea you've had, Ethel. He'll just turn you away. Write to him. Send him a copy of the score.'

'What makes you think that?'

'Turning up looks amateurish. And you are a well-known professional, Ethel. You can write a wonderful letter. I suggest you write a fairly relaxed request, asking him if he might wish to perform it in Vienna. The tone should be that you don't really care if he performs it or not. You can tell him you've had it played in Leipzig and Prague. In referring to yourself, you could tell him about New York and...'

'All right. All Right, Harry. Are you writing it or am I?'

'Excellent. You agree then!'

***

Ethel wrote a superb letter to Mahler. She decided not to send the score. The almost inevitable result was he invited her to Vienna. She couldn't wait to show Mahler's letter to Harry.

'You were right, Harry. Your idea of a letter worked beautifully. Here's Mahler's reply. Written in his own hand!'

Harry cast his eye over it. 'Brilliant, Ethel. I'm so pleased for you. I'll go, too, if you agree!'

'Yes. I'd love that. At worst, we'll have a wonderful time in Vienna.'

Within a few weeks, Ethel and Harry arrived there, full of anticipation. They had given themselves two days in the city before Ethel left Harry in the hotel to take up the appointment with Mahler. A young lady greeted her in the foyer and took her upstairs, along a corridor to an office. The lady opened the door and put out an arm to usher her in. A well-dressed, clean-shaven gentleman stood up from behind a desk and introduced himself.

'Good morning, Miss Smyth. Thank you so much for coming to see us. I trust you had a pleasant journey. My name is Bruno Walter. I'm Herr Mahler's deputy. He asked me to invite you to play the piano version of your score to me. I will then report back to him. But first we would like to know more about you as a composer.'

Ethel's smile evaporated. She wondered whether to complain to the man but thought the chances of their performing it would be much reduced if she did. She shrugged her shoulders. 'I'll start in Leipzig, if I may. I studied first at the Conservatory. Then with Heinrich von Herzogenberg. Brahms loved my chamber music. He was very complimentary when I played him some. My opera Fantasio was premiered in Weimar in '98 and my second, Der Wald, in Berlin in '02. The audience and press reacted well to each.'

She noticed Walter's eyes glaze over. He was not paying attention. He'd obviously heard variations on this script before.

She continued. 'I achieved two performances of Der Wald at the Metropolitan Opera in New York in March '03, as well as one in Boston a week later.'

His face lit up. 'That is simply amazing. Well done!'

'I'm glad you're interested.'

'Interested? I'm staggered by what you've accomplished in your career, Miss Smyth.' Ethel was puzzled because she'd said all this in the letter to Mahler. She wondered if Walter had seen it. 'I shall now take you into one of our rehearsal rooms, which has an excellent piano.'

Despite his apparent lack of knowledge about her past, Ethel could not help but like this man who had an obvious warmth of character. With her usual verve, Ethel played the first page and then the second.

'Marvellous!' said Herr Walter. 'I love it. It's a delight to behold! I shall now ask Herr Mahler if he can afford a little time to listen to it.'

He left Ethel sitting on the piano stool and returned in about five minutes. 'I'm dreadfully sorry, Miss Smyth. He cannot spare the time. I shall give Herr Mahler the most favourable report.'

'When are you likely to decide, Herr Walter?'

'I must ask you, Miss Smyth, not to press us for a decision at this moment. I'm afraid I'm not at liberty to divulge the reasons. But please believe me. We will invite you back in due course, which I hope will be sooner rather than later.'

Ethel's instinct was to trust this unassuming and charming man. She left on good terms and went back to One Oak as Harry returned to Rome.

***

It wasn't long after returning that Ethel jolted herself into writing some songs, feeling she deserved a rest from thinking of subjects for operas and the effort of writing them. Since reading some of his writings in Eugénie's library, she had longed to put some of Henri de Régnier's poems to music and one of Leconte de Lisle's. She was pleased with the four she had written and one afternoon, on the day after finishing them, cycled to Eugénie's with the music in her saddlebag. She let herself in and went into Eugénie's favourite drawing room.

'She's out in the garden,' said the maid, as Ethel came back out into the hall. 'Should I tell her you are here?'

'Oh yes, please do!'

Moments later, Eugénie arrived in gardening gloves, carrying some secateurs. 'Ethel, I'm so pleased to see you. You've kept yourself to yourself since you told me about not seeing Mahler!'

'I didn't know you were a gardener.'

'I wasn't until Mary Ponsonby converted me! Would you like a coffee or tea?'

'Yes, a tea, please.' Eugénie nodded to the maid. 'I can't wait any longer to tell you why I'm here!'

'Go on! Not just to see me then?'

'Don't be silly, Eugénie. I constantly want to see you! You know I love you!'

'I only jest! So?'

'I've written four songs, three based on some poems of Henri de Régnier and one by Leconte de Lisle. And I'd love to play them to you. And give you a break from gardening!'

'Why those two?'

'I read some of Régnier in a book I found in your library. And I've liked the poem by Leconte de Lisle for many years.'

'Harry is always saying I know everyone in Europe. But I don't, of course. However, I knew Leconte de Lisle moderately well. My husband knew him better. He was an influential supporter of the Second Republic. In a moment of madness Charles granted him a pension for life. The Third Republic would have killed him if they could! He died about ten years ago, if my memory is correct. Enough of the history! What are the songs about, Ethel? Give me the programme of what you are going to sing!'

'I've scored each for a single voice, flute, violin, viola, cello, harp and percussion. The first is a sad love refrain about a person who falls in love for a lifetime but the one he falls in love with never recognises it until too late. The second is a song about a dancer. She performs a waltz to the tune of a flute played by the one who watches her. Trees in the wood look on. The flautist envies her beauty and energy. Another sad one follows. It's about the failure of love at the point of death when eyelids close.'

'There is quite some variety in these songs, Ethel. Presumably, you will sing and play the lead melody on my piano?'

'Let me tell you about the fourth one, just to complete your programme.'

'All right. Go on then!'

'It's about a couple of ancient Greeks who drink too much wine. It's a vigorous and energy filled song which is good to finish with.'

'Come, Ethel, let's go through to the piano.' Ethel followed Eugénie into another drawing-room. Eugénie sat on a sofa while Ethel took her position on the stool. She sang the songs beautifully and played the piano with unusual sensitivity. Eugénie applauded.

'My God, Ethel, they are brilliant. The best songs you've written. And you performed them well. The second one reminds me of Der Wald with those trees looking on! They deserve a much wider audience. You should arrange with your sister Mary to play them at one of her venues. And we could organise a recital here, if you wish.'

*** 

No sooner had Ethel returned to One Oak than she sat at her desk, pulled out a sheet of writing paper and wrote to Mary Hunter to ask if she would like to host a recital of the songs at Hill Hall in Epping. Ethel proposed a short programme, supplemented by tea and cakes.

'Could you please post this letter, Mrs Faulkner?' she said, as she appeared in the kitchen while Mrs Faulkner was preparing dinner.

'Yes, Miss Smyth. I'll drop it in the post tomorrow morning, all right.'

'Of course.'

'By the way, have you seen the letter from Austria that came while you were at the Empress's this morning?'

'No. Is it on the hall stand?'

'Yes. I'll find it!'

'No. I will. You are too busy here.'

She opened it in her study. It was from Bruno Walter, saying that Mahler agreed to meet her and to listen to her playing The Wreckers. She couldn't believe her eyes. She exploded in laughter and rushed back into the kitchen.

'Mrs Faulkner, I shall shortly travel back to Vienna to play The Wreckers to the opera director! I'm so excited!'

387

'That sounds like good news. Does that mean they will perform it there?'

'Aha. We'll see. If he likes it, maybe! If he doesn't, then no!'

Ethel received a reply from Mary almost by return of post. She didn't want to use Hill Hall for the recital but the London home of an outrageously rich American woman called Mary Dodge who was a friend of Ethel's sister Violet. Dodge lived in Warwick House, St James, the location of which would attract more to the recital. According to Mary's letter, Violet discussed the idea with Mary Dodge who supported it and invited Ethel to her house to discuss the detailed arrangements. She had suggested the following Friday morning at 10 o'clock.

At exactly on the hour, Ethel knocked on the front door of the palatial mansion. A woman in a white dress and pinafore opened it and took Ethel through the house to a modestly furnished room that overlooked a tightly mown lawn with an array of delightful blooms surrounding it. A woman whom Ethel thought was about the same age as her, possibly slightly younger, was sitting near the window in an upright chair. She wore a mauve dress and matching bonnet.

'This is Miss Smyth, Miss Dodge.' Ethel was mildly surprised that this wealthy woman was unmarried.

'I'm pleased to meet you, Miss Smyth. I won't stand up if you don't mind. My arthritis is causing me much trouble today.' As she spoke, she looked out to the garden. She seemed not to want to look Ethel in the eye.

'I'm pleased to meet you, too, Miss Dodge.' Ethel walked over to her and shook her gloved hand while she continued looking at her garden. A hungry robin pecked at a bird-feeder. Ethel had never experienced a welcome quite like it. She wondered how she could come to know this woman who couldn't even look up at her. She took an immediate dislike to her but daren't show it.

'I'm delighted that you have agreed to host my little song recital, Miss Dodge. I cannot tell you how grateful I am, especially as your beautiful house is so central in London.'

'My pleasure,' she replied, showing not the trace of a smile. It was as if it was her duty, in order to satisfy the demands of Violet or Mary Hunter.

'Basically, and as you know, I've come here to discuss the detailed arrangements.'

'All I want to know is that you will have a proper programme drawn up. I don't want it to last more than an hour and a half, two hours at the most, including intermissions. One of my assistants will see to the printing and distribution and ensure there is an announcement in The Times. Marion here will help you with all the other items. Between you, you can choose what food and beverages you would like served. Is that acceptable, Miss Smyth?'

'Yes, of course.' Ethel was disappointed but not surprised that Miss Dodge didn't want to become involved in the detail.

'I am feeling tired now, so I'm going to my bed. Marion will take up a cup of tea. You may join me in my bedroom if you wish. Would you like a cup?'

This entirely unexpected development took her aback. 'Yes, I would be delighted. Would you like me to come up with you or sit here until you are in bed?'

'You can come up with me, if you wish. We are both women of that certain age. Marion, could you please prepare enough tea for the two of us?'

'Of course, madam. I'll do it now.'

'I wonder, while we are up there, if I could ask you to help me into bed, Miss Smyth. As I said, my legs are quite bad today.'

'I am so grateful to you for helping me, that is the very least I can do.'

'I would normally ask my house-mate, but she has gone to Nottingham to be with her family and won't be back until late next week.'

Ethel wondered why Miss Dodge hadn't asked her maid to 'help her into bed'. She wondered whether it was something to do with women of a one class seeing others of a different class in a state of undress. The reference to a 'women of a certain age' puzzled her.

Moments later, the servant girl reappeared. 'I've put a large pot of tea on your bedside table, Miss Dodge, with two cups and saucers. Oh… and a plate of biscuits.'

'I'll lead the way to my bedroom,' said Miss Dodge. She slowly stood up from her chair and shuffled into the hall. She pressed a button on the far wall next to a door. 'Mine was one of the first houses in London to have a lift. My bedroom is on the second floor,' she said. This was the first time she looked Ethel in the eye, and the first time Ethel saw her smile.

'I have been in a lift before,' said Ethel. 'But only in America!'

Miss Dodge's room was exactly opposite. She opened the door to invite Ethel in. Bright pink completely dominated it, from the curtains to the carpet and bed covering.

'Could you please help me out of my dress?'

Ethel undid the buttons on the back of the mauve dress while Miss Dodge put her hands up to take off her bonnet. Ethel was struck by the quality of the fabric and how it felt. It must have been expensive. Ethel let the dress drop to the floor. Miss Dodge stood there wearing a corset, purple stockings with bright red tops, and suspenders.

Ethel commented. 'You are a beautiful woman, Miss Dodge. Quite petite and very pretty.'

'That's nice of you, Ethel. You can call me Mary, if you wish. I don't want to seem impertinent or prying, but do you mind if I ask you a question?'

'No, please go ahead, Mary,' she said, unsure of what to expect.

'I believe you have a certain passion for women. Is that so?'

Ethel hesitated for a few seconds before answering. How did she know? Who told her? Not Violet, surely? 'Well… yes, as it happens.'

'As a matter of fact, I do, too. I'd be so grateful if you'd cuddle up to me on the bed, if only for a few minutes.'

This was a situation similar to the one she had experienced with Winnaretta de Polignac. She didn't feel she could engage with this woman, except possibly for a hug or a kiss or two on the cheek. This was all so rushed. She had met her less than an hour before. They sat on the side of the bed to drink their tea. 'Can I just sit on the bed?'

'All right. That will be fine.'

A little kissing and hugging followed, against Ethel's wishes but with her reluctant compliance.

'I'm grateful for that, Ethel. It makes me feel valued, if not loved. I really feel like a sleep now, so could you please speak to Marion and tell her what refreshments we should serve. It has been a great pleasure to meet you and I look forward to seeing you at the recital.'

'It has been pleasant to meet you, too, Mary. I hope we can become good friends... over time. Again, thank you for letting me use your beautiful house for the event!'

Ethel, still in shock, took the stairs down to speak to Marion. She didn't want to risk using the lift.

***

A few days before Ethel was to return to Vienna, she heard from a Times correspondent friend of Harry in Vienna that, because the Opera House had seriously upset him over their budget, Mahler was on the verge of resigning from his role as director and ready to dedicate himself entirely to composing. Apparently, the rumours had caused an uproar in Viennese opera circles. He had established the city as the leading centre for opera in Europe, and no one wanted him to give it up. She went anyway, hoping that if he finished there, he would persuade his successor to accept The Wreckers for performance.

Bruno Walter met Ethel at the station in Vienna. It was November and freezing cold. He and Ethel were in overcoats and scarves.

'Gustav Mahler wants to see you this afternoon, if that suits you, Ethel. He is so busy. There is a lot going on here. I'll elaborate in the carriage. Let me take your bags.'

He explained to Ethel what she already knew, except that Mahler had made his decision to resign. He would leave it to Mahler to name his successor.

'Allow me to introduce you to Herr Gustav Mahler, our director,' said Walter, as he walked into Mahler's office and held out his arm towards him.

Mahler immediately stood and came over towards Ethel. He was smiling broadly and looking over his circular rimmed spectacles. 'I'm longing to hear you play some of your opera for me, Miss Smyth. Bruno here said he loved it. I'm so grateful to you for coming here to see me. I hope the journey wasn't too tiring.'

'I appreciate you inviting me. I hope I haven't come in vain because I understand you have resigned as director,' said Ethel.

'You have not come in vain, I can totally assure you. I will listen to what you played for Bruno. My successor has promised he will honour all my commitments so, if I agree to a Wreckers performance, he will definitely play it.'

'May I ask who your successor will be?' ventured Ethel.

'Of course. It's my friend and fellow composer Felix Weingartner. You'll like him. He's a nice man. Let's go into the rehearsal room, the one you used with Bruno, and you can play The Wreckers to me, if you will. Are you coming, Bruno?'

'Of course, I'd love to hear it again!'

Ethel played while Mahler and Walter stood by and listened, Mahler with his hand on his chin and Walter slightly behind him. After Ethel had played the overture to Act 1 and about four pages of the main score, Mahler tapped her on the shoulder to stop her.

'My God, Bruno. You didn't tell me it was this good. You said it was good, but this is a work of genius. I wish I could have written it! Could you play some more please, Miss Smyth?'

Ethel continued playing until the end of the first act. Mahler greeted it with applause. 'It is truly a wonderful opera. I can guarantee that Felix will play it!'

At that point, Mahler rushed off, leaving her and Walter in the rehearsal room.

'I've never seen him so enthusiastic about a new opera,' said Walter.

'But can I trust him to commit to playing it here?' said Ethel, the smile having vanished from her face.

'Of course. He says he'll tell Weingartner, so he has made a commitment to you, which he will keep. And Weingartner is the sort of man who will honour it. I'm certain. You did well. I cannot remember Mahler referring to another contemporary composer's work as a work of genius. You impressed him, undoubtedly. Now, Ethel, I'd like to invite you to dinner tonight with me and my wife. I shall pick you up at your hotel at six o'clock. Is that all right?'

'Wonderful, Bruno! I accept your kind invitation and look forward to meeting your wife!'

Ethel had a wonderful evening with the Walters. She found his wife as pleasant and as charming as Walter himself, and she was an excellent cook. Walter promised to play The Wreckers himself when an opportunity showed itself. All three vowed to remain friends.

The following day, Walter took her back to the station to start her journey home.

# CHAPTER 38

## Harry

By the time Ethel arrived back, Mary Dodge's assistant and Marion had all but completed the preparations for the song recital at the house. Excited by this progress and her visit to Vienna, she wrote to Harry in Rome to bring him up-to-date. With pen in hand, she told him what a reasonable woman Mary had turned out to be and how helpful she had been about the recital. Saying she seemed a shy person, she wondered how she would cope with hosting the event. On the new director at the Vienna State Opera, she said that she could not possibly rely on him, now that Mahler had resigned. So she would approach Covent Garden as insurance against the failure of the Vienna idea.

Harry's reply worried Ethel. He said he had experienced some strange effects in his health. He suffered several episodes of deafness, pains in the jaw bones and stomach pains. Ethel wrote back, instructing him to see his doctor.

The assistant advertised Ethel's recital all over London and in some continental newspapers. She had even had some poster advertisements printed, which by some means or other appeared on street hoardings and at railway stations. The result was that over a hundred people came on the day. Ethel appeared at Warwick House about an hour before to make sure Mary Dodge and her staff had everything in place for a successful concert.

'Before we start, Ethel, I need to tell you something important,' said Mary Dodge.

Ethel's face dropped. She wondered what shade of catastrophe Mary was about to reveal. 'Go on,' said Ethel.

'I shall attend and yet I won't. As you have gathered, I am a very shy person... but not with you, Ethel... and could not cope with being in the same room as all those people. So I will sit alone in the room next door. I will listen through the wall which is not especially thick.'

'But you are the host, Mary. It's your house! You can't do that!'

394

'I've decided, Ethel, and whatever you say, that's what I'm going to do. You and Marion will host the recital. It's your recital, after all.'

'You've shocked me, Mary. I've never hosted my own recital before, but if you don't do it, I suppose I must. You haven't given me much notice.'

People began appearing at Mary's front door a good half hour before the recital was due to begin. Mary wanted nothing to do with them. So Ethel instructed Marion to let them in and escort them to their numbered seats in the recital room. In the meantime, Ethel jotted down some notes on a piece of music paper for introducing herself. She then welcomed incoming members of the audience.

'I wasn't expecting to see you here, Arthur!' she said, as she greeted Nikisch, who had brought a woman colleague with him. 'What are you doing in London?'

'I'm conducting the London Symphony Orchestra for a number of concerts over the next three months. I'm on a contract. You should come along to them! It's a very young orchestra, as you're aware.'

'You know The Wreckers so well, you could play one of the overtures at one of them! Or even Act One!'

'Interesting thought, Ethel. I feel I let you down badly in Leipzig so I'll see what I can do!' Marion then took them to their seats.

Winnaretta de Polignac appeared with two young women. Ethel was sure they were the two Winnaretta threw out of her bed.

'Hello, my darling Ethel!' she said, as she entered the recital room. 'We thought we'd give you a surprise. We saw your recital advertised in Paris and thought we'd come and spend a week in London.'

'Let's meet for a meal while you are here,' said Ethel.

'Damn good idea, Ethel. We'll fix up something after your do.'

Ethel introduced herself, the songs and the individual instrumentalists. She used what she'd rehearsed with Eugénie as the substance of what she said, except that she introduced each song individually. She sang with great sensitivity, capturing the exact sentiments of the poems. Gone was the brash exaggeration she often used to introduce her works to prospective opera houses or conductors. The difference was that she was actually giving a performance, not promoting her work or herself.

Presumably, because they held the recital in a private house, the audience gave it a muted but enthusiastic reception. They did not shout or stamp their feet, but everyone applauded. Ethel returned their reaction with a beaming smile and a bow, then invited the individual players to take a bow. They had performed well, too.

Marion had set up some tables with the tea and cakes in a separate room into which most of the audience gradually drifted. A distinguished-looking gentleman Ethel had not met before came up to her.

'I enjoyed your recital, Miss Smyth. Those songs are an absolute delight and you sang so well.'

'I'm pleased you enjoyed them, Sir. Do I know you?'

'Probably not. But you may have heard of me. I am a composer and I've just taken up the post of director at the Vienna State Opera House. My name is Weingartner, Felix Weingartner.'

'Oh, you will know Gustav Mahler, whom I met in Vienna not two months ago!'

'Of course he and I are good friends, even though we compete to have our works performed!'

Ethel smiled and explained the reasons she was in Vienna. She told him what Mahler had said about Weingartner taking on his commitment to play The Wreckers.

'He never mentioned you or your opera to me, Miss Smyth. I'm sorry to say.'

Ethel felt embarrassed, disappointed and angry at the same time. Was Weingartner lying? But why would he? It would be easier to say Mahler had said nothing than to have to explain why he wouldn't play it. It wouldn't surprise her if

Mahler hadn't mentioned her opera. He clearly hadn't shown Bruno Walter the letter she had written to him. She didn't know what to conclude, except they would not be playing The Wreckers in Vienna.

As she was collecting her things together, Mary Dodge appeared. 'That was a tremendous success, Ethel. Well done. I heard it all. I'm so pleased for you and the other musicians. We will have to arrange some other recitals here. Perhaps we could have some private concerts at which we invite only people we know. They would be easier for me and I could probably take part.'

'We'll do just that, Mary. What an excellent idea!'

*** 

Ethel spent the following weeks organising further performances of her works at Mary Dodge's house and at other venues, including the Queen's Hall in Langham Place. Louis Fleury, the French flautist who played the flute solo at Warwick House, came up with an interesting idea when Ethel met him for lunch in London.

'You must come back to Paris and sing in a Smyth Chamber Concert. We could plan it to include your songs and some of your chamber works.'

'Honestly, Louis, I am so busy here that I couldn't possibly spare the time to organise a concert in Paris. I am discussing a performance of The Wreckers at Covent Garden and hoping for a London Symphony Orchestra performance. I am also trying to convince my friend Harry, who is not especially well at the moment, to have a break in Greece.'

'I must tell you this, Ethel. I've discussed the idea with Gabriel Fauré, Hélène de Caraman-Chimay and her mother. We would do all the organising and publicity.'

'Fauré would help?'

'That's what he says. He loved you when you met him at one of Winnaretta's events.'

397

'Well, you could knock me over with a robin's tail,' said Ethel, with an unshed tear in her eye. She stood up and went around the table and dropped a kiss on Louis' cheek, just avoiding the waxed tip of his moustache. 'I am so grateful to all four of you!'

They spent the next half hour putting together a programme.

'All we want you to do, Ethel, is to appear for the final rehearsal and obviously sing some songs.'

'We'll do it, Louis. I do love you! So I'll see you in Paris then, on the date you will announce!'

\*\*\*

Ethel visited Warwick House to help with setting up the private recitals which Mary Dodge had suggested to her.

'Oh, good morning, Ethel. I'm so pleased to see you,' said Mary, as Marion escorted her into her lounge. She was sitting on a settee, holding a cup of Chinese tea. 'I had a letter delivered this morning, addressed to you. Here it is.'

'It's postmarked London!' Ethel couldn't understand why anyone wouldn't send a letter directly to One Oak. She sat next to Mary and opened it. 'This will surprise you, Mary. It's from Arthur Nikisch. He has persuaded the London Symphony Orchestra to play one of the overtures from The Wreckers.'

'Congratulations, Ethel!'

'I'm pleased and disappointed at the same time! He said at the recital that he would ask the London Symphony Orchestra to play some parts of The Wreckers. This was because he couldn't complete a deal in Leipzig. My regret is that he is only playing an overture. You would think they'd play at least one act out of the three.'

'You must be satisfied with what they are doing. Playing the overture might generate sufficient interest for another orchestra or opera house to perform the whole opera. So just be grateful and accept and enjoy it. It will be the first performance of any of it in England. Right?'

'Yes, Mary. Of course. I will take your wise counsel! But I may push for more!' She shuffled along the sofa and kissed Mary on the cheek. 'I will love you for the rest of my life.'

'I shall love you for ever, too, Ethel. We must do some cuddling up before you go!'

'All right, we will. As I remember, we quite enjoyed it last time,' said Ethel, thinking she wasn't really sure. 'So how are the arrangements progressing for our first private recital?'

'My assistant is doing well. She's invited all of your friends, including the Empress Eugénie, Mary Ponsonby, George Henschel, John Sargent, whom I also know, Arthur Nikisch and several others. She's invited some of your contacts at the palace. All those on your list, as well as someone from Covent Garden and the manager at Queen's Hall. We should have about twenty five altogether.'

'That's brilliant, Mary. Maybe we could invite a few from the press, The Times and the Daily Mail?'

'We'll do that. I'll tell her.'

'I'm concerned about the costs. I cannot afford to take a loss, and we have to play the musicians. Not just for the day as we'll need a couple of rehearsals.'

'Don't worry, Ethel. I'll foot the bill. You are being so good to me, it's the least I can do.'

'Bless you, Mary. You are so kind.'

'Let's go up to my room and have that cuddle! You kiss me so nicely!'

\*\*\*

On her way to see Nikisch at Queen's Hall, Ethel reflected on a letter she had received that morning from Harry in Rome. He claimed his health had improved somewhat. He said he was suffering from a group of kittens hiding under his waistcoat, which called themselves Rheumatism. Luckily, he said, they had retreated to the zoo, and he was now feeling better. She decided he was covering up the reality of his problems and would write to him, insisting he saw a specialist physician.

Nikisch greeted Ethel like an old friend. He had met her several times before, from her student days in Leipzig, through the meeting there only months ago about performing The Wreckers, to seeing her again at the recital in Mary Dodge's house.

'It's a pleasure to see you, too, Arthur. I thought it would be worth meeting to discuss your idea of playing a Wreckers' overture with the LSO. But first, may we take a coffee or something together?'

'Yes, there is a little coffee shop just around the corner. Let's go there.'

They took a table near the window where a pretty waitress brought them their refreshment.

'First, may I say I'm thrilled that you are to play a Wreckers' overture? Which will it be?'

'The prelude to the Second Act, On the Cliffs of Cornwall. I like it a lot. The audience will love it, too!'

'I agree! I just wondered, not to rock any boats - if you'll excuse the pun - whether the LSO would perform, say, Act One or Two, following the overture?'

'I thought you might ask, Ethel. I've tried it with the director, but he was quite adamant that he'd agree only to an overture. So that's it, I'm afraid. It's all I can do for you!'

'I have another idea, Arthur. I'm determined to have a performance of at least two Acts of The Wreckers in London this season… that is, before October 1908. So I plan to hire an orchestra, choir and soloists to play them at the Queen's Hall. I'd love you to conduct the LSO in this startling venture. What do you think?'

'Ethel, that sounds brilliant to me. I'd love to do it. And as I've only secured the prelude up to now, I'd conduct the orchestra for you at a very modest fee! And I know the work so well, it will make the rehearsals that much easier.'

After another couple of rounds of coffee, the two of them had concocted a plan. Arthur was content with a basic fee. He would easily persuade the orchestra's director to cooperate. After all, it meant money in the bank. And he would convince his friend, the singer Blanche Marchesi, to play the role of Thirza.

'You are a genius, Arthur, and a brilliant impresario into the bargain.'

Within a matter of days, Nikisch, along with a little help from Ethel, had made all the arrangements. The LSO would perform the prelude to Act 2 of the Wreckers on 2 May. Ethel's concert performance of Acts 1 and 2 would take place on 28 May at the Queen's Hall. Blanche Marchesi had jumped at the chance to be Thirza. It appealed to her sense of drama and musicality. She even refused a fee and suggested that the chorus comprise her students and a few old professional friends. Ethel could not have been more pleased.

*** 

Ethel wrote a strongly worded letter to Harry, insisting he saw a proper physician. It showed her irritation at him using zoological metaphors to describe his problems. In the same letter, she told him about the arrangement with Nikisch for performing the first two acts of The Wreckers at Queen's Hall. She hoped he would be well enough to attend. His reply wrung with contrition. He said he meant it as a kind of reassuring joke and promised her he would ask a highly reputable Italian physician to examine him. She implored him to do so immediately.

The first question Mary Dodge asked when Ethel called again at Warwick House was, 'How is Harry? I know you are anxious about him.'

'Yes, I am worried, Mary. He's been playing me along with daft letters to fool me into believing he is all right… when I know full well he isn't.'

'You've got enough to worry about with these concerts and recitals. And didn't you say the lease was soon to expire on One Oak?'

'Yes, but I've got at least six months left on that, so it's not at the front of my mind at the moment!'

401

'Well, Ethel. I've been thinking. Over recent months we have developed a wonderful relationship with each other. It is a true meeting of minds. The incredible thing is that we are so different in many ways, but despite that we are truly fond of each other. We enjoy a kiss and a hug, but there is much more to it than that.'

Ethel couldn't help but wonder where this was leading. Mary said some odd things but sounded sincere, and the relationship had certainly benefitted them both, even if Mary took more from the mildly physical side of it than Ethel.

'So what I'm going to do is to buy you a house near One Oak. You can then live the rest of your life there with no worries about where to go next. I will also give you an annual allowance of £100 for as long as I live.'

Ethel immediately pressed a kiss onto Mary's lips. Then burst into tears. It took her a couple of minutes to regain her composure.

'Mary, you are so kind. I cannot believe how generous you are. No one has ever been so generous to me. Never. Not in the whole of my life.' She started to cry again.

'Here is a handkerchief, Ethel. Wipe your eyes.'

She still couldn't believe what was happening to her or what she had heard. She had only known the woman for a few months. Was this a dream? No, it was a wonderful reality. Ethel vowed inwardly to preserve her relationship with Mary for as long as they both lived. What an amazing woman and so generous. And to realise she disliked her at first.

'Changing the subject, Marion has completed the arrangements for the private recital for a week on Wednesday. They were all rehearsing yesterday.'

'I'll attend the final rehearsal on the Tuesday, Mary. Usual time, ten thirty? Presumably, they've printed the programmes?'

'At the printers now.'

Ethel leant over to kiss Mary before she left. 'I can't express my gratitude to you, Mary. I shall love you forever. I really will.'

She then headed home constantly thinking how incredibly generous Mary had been. It gave her a wonderful sense of security, not having to worry about her future after One Oak.

# CHAPTER 39

## Departure

The letter which greeted Ethel at One Oak frightened her. It was from Christopher, Harry's son. He said that the doctor Harry knew was out of Rome then, but that he would arrange for him to see his father as soon as possible. Although his father says he is all right, Christopher added, he had never seen him so bad and in such pain. He suggested Ethel prepare for the worst.

Although she attended the concert on 2 May, she was so worried, she may as well not have been there. She could think only of Harry and could not contemplate life without him. She wondered what Nikisch was doing when he called out her name. It was, she suddenly realised, to invite her to the stage to take a bow. When she faced the audience, she seemed to be in a dream. She barely raised a smile. The one thing she gained from the concert was that Nikisch and the LSO had made a brilliant job of playing her overture. She marvelled at Nikisch's committed style of conducting. She again felt comfortable as an English composer of substance.

She wrote to Harry to tell him about Nikisch and the LSO's outstanding performance and how happy she was about it. She said she would willingly postpone the concert on 28 May until he was better, perhaps nearer the autumn. His reply only cheered her slightly. He said the doctor had diagnosed a liver problem and there was nothing wrong except his liver was 'congested and there were some angry spots.' He told her not to delay the concert at Queen's Hall, saying it was only a matter of being a little patient and he would be well enough to come.

Christopher's letter which arrived in the same post was not so optimistic. He said the postponement would be a death warrant and that his father insisted on coming. Christopher would come too.

She rode to see Eugénie, to bring her up to date with what was going on in her life and, in particular, to tell her about Harry.

'Ethel, you might have told me about him before. You have been carrying the weight of this all alone.'

'I've mentioned it to May Dodge but honestly, Eugénie, I've been so occupied arranging concerts at her house, at the Queen's Hall and in Paris, I've hardly had a moment to tell you. And I know you love him, too.' Ethel's tears began to flow.

'Now, now my pet, my lovely friend. He'll probably pull through. Congestion of the liver, you say?'

'That's what he says, and he insists on coming to my concert in the Queen's Hall.'

'I'll definitely come to that, unmusical as I am. I can help pay for it. I can understand your worrying about him… but there is nothing you can do to help from here. I'm glad you told me, and I hope that makes you feel better. A problem shared, as they say…'

'You are such a great friend, Eugénie. I can't say how much I love you! I'm so glad you are coming to the recital on Wednesday.'

\*\*\*

Mary Dodge surprised her by being such a brilliant host. She and Ethel welcomed all the guests as they came through Mary's front door. Ethel put Harry to the back of her mind while she sang and conducted the little ensemble. Everybody enjoyed it and, with tea and cakes afterwards, it was like a grand reunion.

'Let me be the first to congratulate you,' said George Henschel. 'You have come so far since those heady days in the forest in Thuringia. Do you remember playing your piano sonata to us and jumping over the table?'

'I don't remember jumping tables, George. I remember swimming in the buff!'

'I missed that. It must have been before I arrived!'

One of the most satisfying aspects of the post-concert gathering was the conversation Ethel witnessed between Mary Dodge and The Empress. Ethel wondered if Eugénie might be a little jealous of Ethel's relationship with her. To her relief, they spoke as if they were old friends.

Ethel and Mary Dodge agreed that this would not be the last of these delightful recitals.

***

Ethel met Harry and Christopher off the train at Victoria. She ran along the platform with her arms outstretched to greet them.

'I am thrilled to see you, Harry, my love! You look amazingly well and you are walking well, too.'

'So you agree, Ethel! I was right to come!'

'Of course. It wouldn't be the same without you!'

'I'm going to the theatre tonight. Do you want to come?'

'We'll see, Harry. It's wonderful you could come, too, Christopher!' She kissed his cheek. She'd never done that before, not even in the Florence days. 'I've booked both of you into the Hotel Cecil, in the Strand. You'll love it there. Your rooms overlook the river... Oh! And I've also arranged for a top London physician to see you, Harry. I hope you don't mind. It simply reflects my concern.'

'Well, if he has a cure for cancer of the liver, I'll buy him a barrel of whisky!'

'Cancer of the liver?' said Ethel. Her eyes filled with tears. She didn't expect to hear that, not while walking along a platform at Victoria Station.

'That's what they say. It's inoperable. So I'm finished. My doctor has given me strychnine to keep my strength up. The good news is I've finished my new play, Buondelmonte!'

They stopped and she hugged him. 'I'm speechless, Harry.' She let her tears flow. She held his hand as the three of them made their way silently to the cab rank.

'You couldn't have chosen a better room for me, Ethel,' Harry said, as the hall porter put his bag and a case by the bed. He turned to give the lad a tip. 'The view is magnificent. Better than from the room I had at the Savoy. That was a few years ago!'

Ethel admired his apparent carefree attitude, but his face looked white. She lived hoping he would improve. 'I've got us some good tickets for the concert. A balcony in my favourite position, on the right, facing across to the violins! And I've booked myself into this hotel... a room just along from here... so if you want me, I'm not far away.'

Harry was too tired to go to the theatre and wanted an early night. So Ethel and Christopher decided they would meet for dinner together. Apart from the early days when she met him and his sister, Clotilde, in Florence, she had spent hardly any time with this charming young man.

'I cannot tell you how much I'm worried about your father, Christopher. He is being so brave, but I'm afraid of what could happen to him. He is the love of my life,' she said, on the verge of tears and holding a glass of Chablis.

'I fully understand, Ethel. I am equally concerned. All the way here, I have watched him, spoken to him and listened to him. I have reconciled myself to his passing. There is no known cure for his illness, I'm afraid.' He shied away from using the word 'cancer'.

'I'm coming, reluctantly, to the same conclusion,' she said, with tears running down her cheeks. 'We must try to make his final days as comfortable as possible. Has he told you, I have a concert in Paris on the fourth of June?'

'Yes, and he'd like to go to that.'

'Is he strong enough?'

'He'll decide for himself, but let's not press him.'

407

***

The reception the audience gave Nikisch and the LSO's performance enthralled Harry, who sat next to Ethel in the box. He looked pale and hardly moved throughout the whole concert. Nikisch invited Ethel to take a bow from up there and Harry stood beside her, also taking a bow.

'Not a bad job of translating my text into English,' he said, through a muted laugh. 'I'd have been hard pressed to do a better job myself!' He then sat straight down again, unable to stand for longer.

Mary Hunter, with her customary generosity, laid on a spectacular meal for Ethel and Harry's fiends, the artists and, of course, Nikisch himself. Harry was delighted, not only with this *soirée* but also with the reception the press gave the concert. For once, they were uniform in their praise.

'We must find an opera house to perform it all,' said Nikisch. 'It's so good, someone should perform it as a proper opera and not just as a concert piece.'

'I agree,' said Mary Dodge. 'I loved it and am more than willing to help fund a full performance, in England or elsewhere!'

'You are always so generous, Mary,' said Ethel. 'We must promote it some more.' She spoke as if she had other things on her mind.

Despite Harry's dangerous condition, she had no choice but to honour her commitment to the Paris concert. She simply could not let down Fauré, Louis Fleury, Hélène or Hélène's mother. She felt an immense burden of guilt when she kissed him goodbye and left him at the Cecil Hotel. He tried to make it easier for her by saying he and Christopher were thinking of going to the West Country for a few days, whether or not they were.

Ethel tried to persuade Eugénie to go to Paris with her, but she decided against it. 'You know I'm not that musically inclined, and I have to say, I'm a little afraid of being seen at a public event in France. It was different when you and I went.'

'I think I understand that, Eugénie.'

***

Ethel could not conceal her concern for Harry from her friends in Paris.

'Please don't cry, Ethel!' said Louis, as they welcomed her to the café where they agreed to meet. 'You never know. He could well pull through. The universities are always looking for cures for this dreaded disease. And they may just find something in time.'

'Louis is right,' said Gabriel. 'Where there's life, there's a way. Don't give up.'

'I agree,' said Hélène. 'Our hospitals here are working at it all the time.'

'Harry is being so philosophical about it,' said Ethel. 'He seems more worried about me worrying than what's happening to him. That is typical of the man, of course.'

Even though it was difficult to keep Harry's illness to the back of her mind, Ethel performed well. Her role was to introduce her chamber works and to sing her songs. Hélène and Louis had selected some highly accomplished musicians. Ethel was overjoyed at the way they all played. So was the audience. She got out of bed early the following morning and went to a newsstand where she bought a copy of every French newspaper. She rushed back to her hotel room and quickly turned to the review pages. Every paper praised the concert. They complimented the players, Ethel's singing and her composing. She took in a breath of pride. I'm an accepted composer on the continent now, she thought, as if there could be any doubt. Her Parisian friends wished her well and Harry a speedy recovery before she caught the train to Calais.

***

Harry took on a new life as Ethel read him the reviews. It was as if they had performed some kind of miracle.

'My dearest Ethel, I have never before seen such universal praise of your work. The English press are also complimentary, and so are the Germans. I'm utterly thrilled!' he said, smiling all over his face. Ethel thought she might even have seen a few shades of colour in his cheeks.

409

Sadly, the reviews had not performed a miracle. A few hours after, Harry's condition worsened. Ethel and Christopher discussed it.

'Father, Ethel and I have been talking and are going to take you to Clotilde's house. I hope you agree. You shouldn't be in this hotel.'

'Actually, Christopher, I agree. What will you do? A cabriolet to Waterloo?'

'Just that,' said Ethel. 'Christopher, you do you father's packing. I'll sort out a cab.'

The three of them met Mrs Faulkner at Farnborough station. Thinking ahead, Mrs Faulkner had hired a Pickfords fly and brought Pan and Ethel's bike. Harry loved Pan, and it would surely cheer him to see this delightful creature. Pan went up to him with his tail wagging, but Harry ignored him. This lack of interest in Pan shocked Ethel and Mrs Faulkner. She was so stunned she could hardly speak. One Oak was only three miles from Clotilde's so Ethel cycled there every day, not only to give Harry's children some respite but also to be of some comfort to Harry. She felt compelled to be there.

She was impressed by the way Christopher and Clotilde attended to him, massaging him and feeding him with a spoon. The way Christopher gently rubbed his back to relieve his constant pain was something she could never emulate. She felt she could never be that gentle.

Every day, Ethel sat by his bed. The doctor came often, and after a week gave him something that made him virtually unconscious. A day later, she said his name. He squeezed her hand, opened his eyes and smiled at her, as if he had reached a goal. He finally closed his eyes and departed.

*** 

Nine years later, Ethel was on a mountaineering holiday in the Pyrenees. She was serving in the Great War as a radiographer at the Vichy military hospital. At that moment, she was thinking of the recovery of the French Army, following its disastrous setback under General Nivelle. She was climbing the Puy de Sancy, the highest peak in the Massif Central. As she reached the summit, she saw Harry, walking beside her, smiling mischievously. He was wearing a suit she recognised.

He twice said the name of the town of Vendôme. This quoted a nursery rhyme about the Hundred Years War, a verse he told Ethel he would remember until his dying day. She responded that she hoped he now realised that she admired France enough to satisfy him. As he was about to reply, he vanished.

The End